Wha

"Ms. Morgen pens a superb romantic tale with a little danger and mystery thrown into the mix. Her well-developed characters [and] their passion for finding the truth makes REDEMPTION a hard book to put down. The sex scenes and the language in this book are graphic and may not be suitable for some readers. But if you enjoy spicy, hot sex scenes, and a great story to boot, then REDEMPTION is definitely for you." - *Michelle Gann, The Word on Romance*

"This story starts out with a bang and keeps you spellbound to the very last page. It is the type of story you will pick up to read over and over again. I know I will. Shelby Morgen's REDEMPTION definitely belongs on everyone's keeper shelf. I wish I could rate it more than Five Stars because it definitely deserves a ten. I highly recommend REDEMPTION for your reading pleasure!" - *Charlene Smith, Sime~Gen*

"The sex was great, but this is definitely more than a simple erotic story. The mystery unfolds slowly and gently, but is totally enthralling." - *Ann Leveille, Sensual Romance Reviews*

Discover for yourself why readers can't get enough of the multiple-award-winning publisher Ellora's Cave. Whether you prefer e-books or paperbacks, be sure to visit EC on the web at www.ellorascave.com for an erotic reading experience that will leave you breathless.

www.ellorascave.com

Ellora's Cave Publishing, Inc.
PO Box 787
Hudson, OH 44236-0787

ISBN # 1-84360-620-8

Redemption edited by Martha Punches & Cris Brashear.
Cover art by Darrell King.

Warning: The following material contains strong sexual content meant for mature readers. *REDEMPTION* has been rated Hard R, erotic, by a minimum of three independent reviewers. We strongly suggest storing this book in a place where young readers not meant to view it are unlikely to happen upon it. That said, enjoy...

REDEMPTION

Written by

SHELBY MORGEN

Disclaimer

The city of Martinsburg does exist and is, in fact, the county seat. All other places, characters and events depicted in Berkeley County, West Virginia, are fictional. No reference to any actual person or event, in whole or in part, is in any way implied by any scene or character representation in this novel. The county sheriff is still an elected official in the State of West Virginia.

Acknowledgments

My thanks to the Berkeley County Prosecutor's Office, the West Virginia State Police, Martinsburg Barracks, the Berkeley County Sheriff's Department, and the Martinsburg city police for answering endless questions with unfailingly good humor.

Dedication

For my mother, who loved Drew with all her heart.

Prologue

SATURDAY, March 13th, 1993

Charlie never knew who called the police. It wasn't Allen. He crawled into the closet to hide, naked as the day he was born, and stayed there until Charlie was led away in handcuffs. It wasn't the little blonde, either. She ran screaming from the house, wearing nothing but her coat. The police found her sitting in a booth at the corner bar, drinking a Scotch-on-the-rocks she was too young to buy and couldn't pay for anyway, as she'd left her purse beside Charlie's bed. Nevertheless, the police came. When they got there, Charlie was huddled on the top step outside, ignoring the rain streaming down her face, the empty .25 at her feet.

It was the longest weekend of her life. Her brother Jamie was on retreat in Ireland. Mother had the ringer on the phone turned off. Charlie's sister, Frances, the attorney, had an unlisted number, and Charlie couldn't remember it. Charlie paced and watched the minutes tick by on the huge wall clock at the end of the hall.

It wasn't until Monday morning when Frances came into her D.C. office that she found Charlie's message on her machine. Frances was the one who went to find her little sister at the county jail a little after noon on Monday. It was Frances who stood beside Charlie in front of the judge at 1:30 that same afternoon.

Allen didn't show up to testify, and neither did his young friend. Since no one had actually gotten hurt, the judge let Charlie off with a thousand-dollar fine for disturbing the peace and unlawful use of a firearm. Unfortunately, there wasn't a thousand dollars left in Charlie's checking account. There wasn't anything at all left in her checking account.

Even the furniture was gone. The only things left were Charlie's suitcases, shattered vanity and the mattress full of bullet holes leaning against the wall. Frances studied the mattress. "You're an excellent shot. How could you possibly miss at this range?"

Charlie snorted. "I'm not stupid enough to try to kill him. The bastard wasn't worth going to prison for."

Frances peered at the bullet holes again—six shots arranged in a ten-inch radius. "I thought you were going for the heart. What on earth were you aiming at?"

"It was a small, moving target. The mattress is standing upside down. I was trying to shoot his damn balls off."

"And the vanity?"

Charlie shrugged. "He left his wedding ring sitting on it."

Chapter One

TUESDAY, May 3rd, 1994

It was disconcerting, getting off the bus at a fast-food joint. Better, though, he supposed, than the old downtown bus stop, where you'd wonder if you might have to fight your way out, and you'd never dare to go to sleep on the bench. The bus stop wasn't actually in the restaurant, anyway. There was a little building behind it that you couldn't see from the road, not much bigger than one of the buses.

A great many things had changed around here in the last twelve years.

He rubbed a hand self-consciously over the stubble darkening his jaw, wishing he was already home. He stood there on the little platform beside the ticket office, waiting, while all the other passengers collected their baggage and began to disperse. He searched the parking lot with his eyes, barely turning his head, giving nothing away, should anyone be watching. But there was no one there.

He ran his fingers through his tangled hair uneasily. He was on time. Even without a watch, he knew that. The bus driver had been in no particular hurry coming over the mountains. They definitely hadn't arrived early. There just wasn't anyone here to pick him up.

A pang of jealousy and desire swept over him as, one by one, the car doors open and closed, swallowing families. There were children returning home to their mothers, brothers or sisters or best friends greeting each other, wives welcoming husbands with open arms and open hearts. One way or the other, they were all gathered up. They all had a place to go, somewhere they belonged.

Everyone but him.

He tried not to stare out the corner of his eyes like some sick voyeur, but as the other passengers disappeared, he was left where he'd always been. Alone. It hit him this time, harder than ever before.

Not that he'd been exactly looking forward to his welcoming party. But he knew better than to head out on his own. They were supposed to pick him up, here, today, at four. He'd seen the paperwork, had copies of it in his wallet. He didn't bother to take it out and read it again. He knew what it said.

He took a seat on the bench outside the bus station, surveying the parking lot uneasily. This was a bad start to things. He hunched his shoulders defensively and drew his feet up under the bench, wishing he were smaller, less noticeable, less likely to attract unwanted attention.

He would wait. He knew how to wait.

A cop car pulled into the parking lot. Maryland State Police. He shrunk back into the shadows. *Get a hold of yourself,* he ordered, pushing down the fear. *Even Robert Waite has to obey jurisdictions.* A bitter taste rose in his mouth, and his upper lip wrinkled into a feral snarl. *Not this time, Waite. Not this time.*

The patrol car circled the parking lot again, then drove off. It was another twenty minutes before he relaxed enough to settle back onto the bench.

About an hour later the man from the ticket counter stuck his head out as if to say something, then thought better of it, and went back inside. A biker on a Harley rolled through the parking lot, then came back around for a second look before he, too, drove off.

The biker made him nervous, although the man wore no visible colors. Still, better safe than dead. He rose slowly, stretching his tall, lean frame, scanning the parking lot one more time before he moved inside. He'd wait there until the office closed.

His presence in the little building seemed to unnerve the ticket agent. The little man sorted the same paperwork three times, straightened all his pens, and took out the trash, all without ever making eye contact with the big man who lounged on his single bench.

He closed his eyes and drifted off to the private place he'd built in his mind. He could see it so clearly. *He walked toward the back door of the farmhouse he'd grown up in, and as he laid his hand on the doorknob, it opened from within. A little girl's voice called to him. "Daddy! Daddy!" as she launched herself into his arms. "Momma, Daddy's home!"*

Laughter as sweet as a singer's voice floated out to him, and he hefted the child to one hip as the door opened again, and the woman moved toward him, more slowly than the child had, but just as eager, the smile on her face matching the laughter in her voice. "Welcome home," she whispered as she stretched her arms out to him.

"It's six o'clock."

The ticket agent's voice pulled him back to the present. A bleak, unwelcoming present.

"We close at six. You'll have to leave now. You can't stick around here all night. The cops'll be by again soon. They don't like no one loitering around here after hours."

The irony of that statement hit him hard enough to pry loose a hint of a smile. With an economy of movement, he rose from the wooden bench, straightening to use his full 6'7" height to overshadow the smaller man, secretly enjoying the agent's discomfort. He spared the agent a brief nod and shouldered his bag.

Outside, the big man surveyed the sky. It was getting late, and it was going to rain. It was more than obvious by now that no one was coming. They'd have been here long ago. This was, indeed, a very bad start to things. There was a pay phone, but he didn't have change for a long distance call, and he wasn't about to ask the ticket agent for anything. Besides, he couldn't think of anyone he could call who might actually come to get him.

He wasn't really surprised. Somehow or other, he knew Robert Waite was behind this. Waite had political pull. The man would know he was out. Waite hated him. The man would do anything he could to get him sent back.

He had to get home. Had to get back across the state line into West Virginia. He didn't bother to stick out his thumb. No one would give him a ride. He didn't have to do anything to scare people off. He just looked like trouble. His size alone frightened most people. And if that didn't do it, the old army duffel bag would. It labeled him a drifter, or worse.

It was going to be a long walk home. He put his head down and let his long legs settle into a determined stride as he headed down old Route 65 towards Sharpsburg. It would have been shorter to head out along the Interstate, but it was only fourteen miles to the state line going this way, and it was all back roads, where he had a better chance of staying out of sight. With any luck, the Maryland cops wouldn't hassle him before he got to the West Virginia border. A little more luck, and Robert Waite wouldn't have the Shepherdstown PD watching for him to cross the river.

* * * * *

"You look exhausted."

Charlie nearly dropped the tray of coffee cups. "Jesus Christ, Janelle, I never even heard you come in. What happened to the damn door bell?"

"Jumpy tonight, aren't you? I came in through the back door. I do have a key. I work here, remember?"

The girl's laughter reminded Charlie of children playing. She wondered if she'd ever been that light hearted. "Oh, yeah. So that's why I keep running into you. I thought you were a stalker."

"You're too sweet to notice, but I'm actually ten minutes late again. Don't tell Harry, okay? Not that he'd find anyone to replace me. I just don't want to listen to him bitch."

"No problem. You didn't miss anything exciting." Charlie ran the back of her arm over her forehead, wiping the unruly curls off her damp skin.

"Like I said, you look exhausted. Rough night or no sleep?"

"No sleep. The guy who rents my hay field left four hundred bales of hay dumped at the barn doors. I couldn't even get them shut. It's actually been kind of dead here tonight. I've just been setting things out for the morning rush just to stay awake. One man wandered in a few minutes ago. He's the first person I've seen in half an hour. The rain's kept the traffic down."

Laughter tugged at Janelle's mouth again. "You finally found yourself a man? Where is he? You got him tucked away somewhere so you can have him all to yourself?"

Charlie laughed at the thought. "Not that one. I may be lonely, but I'm not that desperate. He's just some cowboy who wandered in a few minutes ago, waiting to get a ride from a trucker, I imagine."

Janelle looked around curiously. "Where'd you hide him? I don't see anyone."

Charlie pointed with her chin toward the left-hand side of the L-shaped dining room. "He's all the way around back, in the last booth, near the back door to the kitchen."

Janelle's eye flitted toward the left wing, even though she couldn't possibly see the last booth from the front counter. "Well, from what I've seen around here, you can't afford to be too picky. What's he look like? Is he handsome?"

"Jesus, Janelle. He looks like a drifter. Long and lean and drenched from the rain. Probably hungry, too. Why don't you fix him something? I didn't want to go in the back while I was here alone, but I imagine he could use a decent meal. Looks like it's been a while."

Janelle licked her lips. "Doesn't it make you a little nervous, having some drifter lurking in the corners when you're here alone?"

Charlie shrugged absently. "He looks harmless enough. Just wet and tired and hungry. You know the type." And if there was something about him, something beyond the rain and the night, she wasn't going to try to explain it to a girl barely out of college.

Janelle cocked one hip and rested a hand on it, appraising Charlie with a parental frown. "You going to feed every homeless cowboy who comes through here?"

Charlie didn't bother to answer. Instead she turned and walked back into the kitchen. Hell. She couldn't have explained it if she'd tried. There was just something about the man. It wasn't just his looks, though he was handsome enough in a tough, bad-boy sort of way, with that long dark hair and bronze skin and just a trace of a beard shadowing a hard, strong jaw.

No, it wasn't his looks. Maybe it was his stance, feet spread wide, standing so still as the door closed softly behind him, rain puddling around his feet. Maybe it was the way his eyes swept the room, coming to rest on hers for just for a moment as he paused there at the door. He'd nodded his head, once, as he raised his hand to touch the hat he hadn't been wearing. Like a cowboy.

He was just a drifter, down on his luck and headed from nowhere to somewhere else. Maybe she'd just been alone too long. He hadn't even spoken to her. But there was something about this particular drifter that slipped below her guard. What was this stupid urge she had to rescue the ones who needed her the least?

Still, she crossed the kitchen to the row of coat hooks by the back door. It was there, right where she remembered seeing it – an old jean jacket some former cook had used to work the walk-in freezer. The denim was worn, but relatively clean and dry. A whole lot dryer than the sodden flannel shirt the man back in the corner had on.

Janelle followed Charlie into the kitchen, then brushed on by as she headed for the big grills. "I thought you took this job because you needed money. How are you going to make any money if you feed every tramp who comes through here?"

Charlie just laughed, but as she picked up the coffeepot and dropped a handful of creamers into her apron pocket, she heard something start to sizzle. No matter what the kid said, Janelle could no more stand to see a man go hungry than Charlie could.

She took another look at the man as she crossed the room. No, not at all bad looking, if you didn't mind the wariness about him. The man was tall and broad-shouldered, though he sat scrunched way down, as if trying to look smaller – a difficult feat for a man of his size. He wouldn't have had to struggle for seven hours trying to stack all that damn hay the way she had on Wednesday.

No. Charlie shook the thought from her mind. She might be lonely, but the last thing she needed was some homeless drifter to be responsible for. Besides, the man hadn't asked for her help. He barely looked up when Charlie turned over his cup to pour the strong, bitter smelling sludge the truckers liked to call coffee into his mug. Charlie divested the contents of her apron pocket onto the tabletop. She'd grabbed up half-a-dozen creamers. There was probably a little protein or something useful in them somewhere. The only way she could drink this stuff was to cut it with cream and try to drown the taste.

Her hand accidentally brushed against the man's arm as she laid the jacket on the bench next to him. His head jerked at that. He glanced up just enough for Charlie to meet his eyes for a fleeting moment, up close this time. She got a glimpse of flat, wary eyes that no longer expected anything from anyone.

He wouldn't ask for her help. He wouldn't *ask* for anything.

Charlie deliberately laid her hand back on the cold, wet fabric of his shirt at the shoulder, pleased that he didn't pull away or try to avoid her touch. "Someone left this jacket here, some cook, long before my time. It ought to fit you. You need to get out of this damp shirt, or you'll get pneumonia."

She didn't wait for an answer. Didn't expect one. When she came back a few minutes later with "The Trucker's Special," a plate of Janelle's meatloaf and mashed potatoes and green beans, all smothered in gravy, Charlie was pleased to see that he'd changed out of the wet shirt. The man's eyes flicked up to her face, the wariness she'd seen before replaced with something strangely soft and vulnerable for a moment. He looked down just as quickly, the emotions strangled, a trace of a dark red stain showing against the deep tan of his skin.

She hadn't imagined that look. For just a moment, she'd seen something there – a need that frightened her with its intensity.

She didn't need anyone, and no one needed her. Charlie turned away quickly. "I'll get you more coffee," she offered, ducking back in the kitchen door.

Janelle looked up at the sound of the kitchen door banging. "What's wrong?"

Charlie shook her head. "Nothing. It's – nothing. Just that man – the cowboy. He has the most amazing eyes. One minute they were gray, and then, I swear, they turned green. Deep, emerald green. Spooked the hell out of me."

Janelle stared at her. "You got a good enough look at his eyes to notice they changed color? What were you doing, asking him out on a date?"

"He just looked up. It was like something out of a sci-fi movie. Spooked me a little, that's all." It was the best she could do on the spur of the moment.

Janelle didn't ask any more questions. She scuttled to the kitchen's side door and ducked her head out long enough to take a good look for herself. She was back less than a minute later. "Well, I couldn't see his eyes, but he looks like he's got a strong back, and he's not too hard to look at. Why don't you hire the man? You wouldn't have to pay a drifter like that too much. A roof over his head and a dry bed ought to keep him happy.

Let him sleep in your barn. If you don't hire someone soon, you're gonna work yourself right into the ground."

No. She shoved the idea out of her mind. "Good Lord! That's all I need. Some drifter hanging around my barn." Charlie grabbed the coffeepot and headed back to the dining room. "If I need help, I'll hire some of the local kids. Keep 'em out of trouble."

But a quick look in the mirror told Charlie Janelle was right. She was a mess. No wonder no one ever asked her out. She looked worn and frazzled and her damn hair looked like a rat's nest. She hadn't had time to do anything with it. She's stuck it up in a parody of a French twist with an ink-pen again. Make-up was a thing of the past. There just weren't enough hours in a day. She'd been working double shifts for a month now. Worse yet, she'd lost two more pounds. Charlie thought back to last fall. It hadn't seemed like the farm would be so much work in the beginning.

Some of the farms she'd looked at had been in such bad condition that she couldn't afford to even think about them. She'd have had nothing left once she paid for the land and the remodeling. The places Charlie could afford had no style. No history. She was beginning to feel like giving up when her real estate agent insisted Charlie had to go check out just one more listing. The farm was farther away than Charlie had originally planned to move, but the agent promised it would be worth the drive.

It was late afternoon on a Friday in mid-October when Charlie crossed the Potomac River just south of Hagerstown, Maryland. Three miles past the West Virginia line she left the Interstate to enter a rabbit's warren of old country roads. Charlie followed the directions carefully, but still, it took three tries to find the farm. Charlie couldn't see anything but trees from the road. She finally spotted the real estate agency's sign lying in the weeds. With some trepidation, she headed the old Jeep down the rutted farm lane.

There, at the end of a quarter mile of rocky, washed-out drive, stood a rambling stone and brick house on top of a rocky hill surrounded by maple trees. Wisteria had so taken over the back porch that the door was completely hidden from view. Behind the house, leading to the space where the vegetable garden had once stood, an arbor covered with climbing roses had fallen over, allowing the roses to become a bramble hedge.

A stone's throw away from the main house across a badly deteriorated gravel parking area stood an old two-story barn with a stone foundation. It, too, was covered with clinging vines. The agent had warned her that the old man who'd owned the farm hadn't kept it up over the last few years. It looked more like decades. But Charlie saw past the water-damaged plaster to the once beautiful hand hewn cedar plank flooring. The old wood-fired cook stove was filthy, but it could be cleaned, and it was a classic.

Underneath years of disrepair, the central staircase was early Victorian. Once the wood was stripped and refinished and a few of the stair treads replaced, it would be the showplace of the house. The chandelier in the dining room could be restored to the elegance it must have presented before the Civil War. The master bedroom upstairs was the size of the whole ground floor in Charlie's Alexandria townhouse, and there was a walk-in fireplace in the great room at the bottom of the stairs big enough to hold whole tree trunks.

The house needed a new roof. After that she'd have the whole thing gutted, rewired, and insulated, and all the plumbing and the furnace replaced. The remodeling would be expensive, and there would be months of dealing with contractors, even if she did a lot of the inside work herself, but she could do it. She'd even have enough money left to remodel the barn and buy the mares, and still live for a while without any help from Frances. If she was careful, very careful.

Charlie made her offer as soon as the broker who'd listed the property showed up. Twenty-five days later, just three days after closing, the demolition crew went to work. Charlie moved in the day the new kitchen door was installed. Spring was officially here and hundreds of flowering plants were in full bloom across the yard. Forsythias waved their bright yellow arms over lush carpets of phlox and oceans of crocuses and tulips. Virginia Blue Bells dotted the lawn. The yard was a veritable artist's palette of color.

It was the first of April. The first day of Charlie's new life. She thought it the best April Fool's joke ever. She, Charlotte Giles, was going into the horse business.

Momma, of course, took it all very badly. "What are you thinking?" she scolded. "I didn't send you to college just so you could spend the rest of your life shoveling manure for some rich people's playthings! They don't even race these horses!"

Grandma merely gave mother *the look*. "I paid for her college. Leave the child alone. Let her do what she wants to. She will anyway."

Just back from Ireland and feeling very serene and sure of himself, Jamie took everything in stride. "Join the local parish. Then get a job." He held up his hand like a traffic cop when she would have argued. "Don't take anything you can't afford to quit. Just a part time job. Anything. Not for the money. You need to be around people, Charlotte. Horses are great, but you need friends, too, somebody close who'll notice if you don't show up for work and come looking for you. I don't care if you wait tables over at that truck stop. I don't want you alone all the time."

Charlie swallowed her arguments. Jamie rarely insisted on anything. "I will, I promise," Charlie agreed.

Maybe, just maybe, he had a point.

The sound of the bell on the front door yanked Charlie back to the present. It was after 7:00 AM. The sun should have been up, but the sky was so dull and sodden that dawn was little more than a lightening of the murky paste. Irene and Maryam, the morning shift crew, were here.

The cowboy still sat in the back corner. Charlie took him one last cup of coffee before she left. He still didn't speak, but he looked up this time, his eyes actually meeting hers for more than just a second or two as she crossed the room, and he offered a tentative smile. It did wonders for his face. He looked younger and less tired and a lot more amiable than he had when he first walked in the door.

Lord. She'd been alone too long. The things that smile did to her...

Charlie offered a quiet "Good night," before she hurried out the door. She needed to make sure she was out of sight before Harry appeared, or she'd get sucked into staying until the morning rush was over. That was why she left in such a hurry that morning. She needed to sleep.

It was a lie she could live with.

Charlie had to pull herself up into the truck cab. She was tired – so tired she didn't even want to think about the work ahead of her. Maybe she wouldn't go get grain this morning. If she lay down for just a little while...

The cowboy with the stormy green eyes and broad shoulders haunted her.

The road home paralleled the backside of Charlie's farm. She looked out across the ragged hay field that would someday be her back pasture – if she ever had the time and energy to get it fenced in.

Charlie sighed. At this rate she'd never get to the back pasture, or anything else. She needed help. She should have listened to Janelle. The cowboy might not stay around long, but even a few days work from a set of shoulders like that would help.

It wasn't like she was planning to sleep with him. She just needed help with the hay...

Charlie pulled off the side of the road into the ruts the hay trucks had left behind. She nearly got the truck bogged down in the mud as she turned around.

The back corner booth was empty when Charlie walked back into to the truck stop again. Just as well, Charlie consoled herself. She didn't really need some drifter hanging around, no matter how tired she was. No matter how good looking he was, or how much work he might save her from. He wouldn't have stayed anyway. Men never hung around very long in her life. Besides, she didn't really need anyone. She was just a sucker for a sad set of eyes. She always seemed to pick the needy ones. The ones who would take and take and never have anything to give back. Well, this one had wandered off on his own, saving her from another huge mistake.

Yet, long after the mares were fed and the curtains drawn against the cold of the gray drizzle, those stormy green eyes haunted her sleep.

Chapter Two

The radio was what finally drove her over the edge. The stations kept changing overnight. The first time it happened Charlie just stood staring at the little black box, almost afraid to touch it. Finally she yanked the plug out of the wall. She wasn't hallucinating. There was no way she'd ever have left the radio tuned to a country music station.

Back in her bedroom, Charlie opened the little wall safe and stood staring at her .25 semi-automatic, then put it away again. There was no reason for this paranoia. She had worked for the Agency too long. Still, the hair on the back of her neck stood up when she looked out the window at the barn.

Her nerves were getting to her. Even Janelle noticed. "Don't you ever sleep? You look about half dead. Is everything okay?"

They hadn't had a customer in over an hour. Charlie was just too tired to think up a good lie. "I guess I am working too many hours. I seem to be forgetting things."

Janelle straightened her long, lean frame. "Like what?"

She'd been out of circulation too long. She was losing her edge. Besides, the girl was going to think she was nuts. "Maybe nothing. I'm not sure. Some nights when I get home from this place, I just check on the horses and go to bed. I don't always finish things – pick up things and put them away like I should. At least I think I don't. But they're done when I go to tidy up the next morning. It's like the brownies come while I'm asleep and finish things for me."

Janelle gave Charlie one of her looks. "Brownies steal things. Anything missing?"

There was no easy way out of this now. "No, not really."

"Which is it? No or not really?" Those green eyes drilled into Charlie's.

Charlie shifted her attention away uneasily. "Well, I thought I left a full jar of peanut butter in the tack room. I use it to bait the rattraps. When I went back, the jar was empty. But that's not really stealing."

"So, you have a ghost who eats peanut butter."

There was a story about the eccentric old man who'd died there on the farm. It had made Charlie a little nervous when the real estate agent mentioned it. "I don't have a ghost!"

"Right." Janelle's voice had that edge Charlie had come to expect. "Weird things happen when you're not around, but you never see anything. But you don't have a ghost. So since you're mostly Irish, maybe it's a leprechaun."

For the rest of a very long night, Charlie had to listen to tales of the little people, stories Janelle claimed to have learned from her Irish Grandmother. One way or the other, it beat the ideas Charlie had come up with. She didn't need to be worrying about an Agency plant spying on her. She wasn't doing anything worth spying on, damn it.

"How's your ghost?" It was Thursday night, and Charlie had just walked in the door. For once Janelle had made it in on time. Tonight Charlie was late.

"Fine," Charlie assured her, hoping Janelle would get the hint that she didn't want to discuss it again. The truth was, the more she thought about it, the more uneasy she became. Not that she believed in ghosts. She'd seen too much in life to be superstitious. There were enough real threats out there to deal with without making up imaginary ones.

Janelle cocked her head to one side. "Yeah?" Her expression was curious. Interested. A little too interested. "Did he introduce himself yet?"

"Sure. His name is George, and he hates classical music." Charlie let her sarcasm leak through, hoping Janelle would get the hint and change the subject.

"George Washington, maybe? I heard he slept around here." Janelle's tone was equally sarcastic now. She started slamming things around the kitchen.

Charlie circled the pick-up island to enter Janelle's domain. "I do not have a ghost, Janelle. The Peanut Butter Thief stacked four hundred bales of hay for me Saturday night, after the damn truck driver dumped it everywhere again. I got maybe thirty bales moved before I came to work, and I thought I was doing really well to manage that. When I got home it was all stacked nearly to the roof beams."

Janelle would never let this go, now. But in reality, Charlie was more than a little intimidated by this "ghost," and there wasn't anyone else to tell. Frances would call the cops, and Jamie would call an exorcist.

"What are you saying?"

"I'm saying," Charlie admitted slowly, "That I'm scared. I think there is someone living in my barn." And if the Agency hadn't put him there, where had he come from?

Janelle looked thoughtfully at the load of bacon she was grilling up for the breakfast special. "Stacking hay's a lot of work."

"Yes, it is," Charlie agreed. "I guess I should be glad I didn't have to do it all myself instead of getting all worked up about a little help."

Janelle sighed softly, the pretense of play gone from her face. "Sounds like some drifter's living in your barn. A big, strong male drifter from the sound of things. But if he was going to hurt you, I think he would have done it by now. And I'll tell you something else. A man who can work like that needs more to eat than peanut butter. You want to catch him, you start putting out food. He'll show up, soon enough. When he does, you tell him to get lost, before you call the law. And then you can go back to stacking your own hay." The girl looked up from her bacon, punctuating her speech with the spatula. "Or you could get smart, and hire the man. Seems like you need the help."

A man. Just some drifter who had moved into her barn. Someone like the green-eyed cowboy with the broad shoulders. No boogie monster. No shades from her past come back to haunt her. Just an ordinary man. "I'm not feeding some homeless man or asking him to stick around." Charlie shivered at the thought. "Can we just go back to ghosts, please?"

Janelle cocked an eyebrow at Charlie and went on with her cooking. But a few minutes later she was back. "You were ready to hire that cowboy who passed through here two weeks ago. I saw you come back looking for him. What's the difference? This one's already helping you out. Any man who'll work that hard for a jar of peanut butter ought to be worth keeping around."

Charlie didn't have a ready comeback for that one. The truth was, although she didn't like to admit it, she did need the help. Lord, how she'd dreaded stacking the rest of that hay.

Two hours later Charlie entered her barn through the first floor doors, stopping long enough to leave a white Styrofoam carryout box containing Janelle's handiwork on the last row of hay bales. Three eggs, over easy, with home fried potatoes, two big slices of country ham, sausage, and biscuits with butter and jelly, along with a 24 oz. cup of coffee. She said a little prayer to St. Jude, the Patron Saint of lost causes.

He balanced there, plastered against the barn's huge main upright, heart hammering against his ribs, looking down at the top of the woman's fiery head. Lord. He'd been trying to think of ways to get close to her, but not like this. She'd nearly caught him. Quick thinking had propelled him up into the familiar old beams that made up the barn's rafters. He was safely out of sight as long as the woman didn't look up. He could move among the beams more easily than most people walked along the ground, but he just barely made it up here in time. He'd gotten overconfident. He couldn't let that happen again.

The woman set a package on the hay. He watched her cross to the stairs, an odd mixture of tired and sexy that sent his emotions spinning. She stopped at the top of the stairs, searching the open areas of the barn briefly. He nearly lost his balance as the smell of hot food assaulted his nose. Ham, unless he missed his guess. His stomach rumbled so loudly that he was sure the woman would hear.

"I brought you breakfast." She didn't speak loudly, but her voice carried. "I'm tired. I'm going to bed as soon as I feed the ladies downstairs." She turned away, but her voice still reached him. "Janelle's a magician. Don't let her food get cold."

Hell. He knew she was tired. Could see it written all over her. Frustration shot through him. He was doing all he could, damn it. The urge to drop out of the rafters, to go to her, to take her in his arms and hold her until the lines of worry eased from her face was so strong he nearly gave himself away. He wanted. He needed…

No. The thought was insane. He didn't need anyone, and no one needed him. As soon as he moved, as soon as he gave away his position, he'd be caught, and that would be the end of this little game. Then he heard her, from the feed room below, give the same speech again. If she was downstairs, how was she going to catch him upstairs?

The cats began to move in, circling his breakfast, tantalized by the smells. Soon all six of them were circling the food container, trying to figure out how to get it open. Then the big tom took a more aggressive approach, and started chewing on the Styrofoam.

Caution had its place, but he was so hungry the smell of the food made his head spin as he balanced there in the rafters, and he was about to lose that breakfast to a fat old tomcat.

His heart raced as if he'd just run laps. She knew he was here. Maybe even knew who he was. Any other woman would have called the law. This one brought him food. He wasn't going to let the cats have his breakfast. He swung down off the beam like a gymnast, scattering the cats like so many scraps of paper in the wind. Years of practice made his landing in the soft, loose hay almost inaudible. His hand trembled as he opened the Styrofoam. The cats had been right. It was too good to ignore. He ripped and tore like a wild animal, burning his mouth on the coffee. By the time the food was gone, he decided he would gladly lay down his life for the woman, should she but ask.

His stomach full for the first time in weeks, he slipped quietly down the stairs and changed the radio to the local country music station. How could a woman with such obvious taste pick such a boring radio station? They didn't even offer local news…

Saturday morning the woman brought him steak and eggs with a huge pile of hash browns. Sunday morning it was hot cakes. Six of them, the size of a small skillet each, with butter and raspberry jam and syrup, a double order of bacon on the side. And still, the woman made no move to catch him. He ate crouched in the hay, eyes constantly darting to the doorways, ready to bolt at the first sign of trouble, but she never came back. There was never any other sign of her. It was as if she didn't really want to catch him – as if she, too, understood that this was a fragile dream that might disappear if either of them opened their eyes.

* * * * *

Charlie didn't hang around to see if the man came out. If she didn't see the man, he didn't really exist. Charlie told herself she was a fool. She shouldn't encourage this stranger to hang around her barn. There was no way to rationalize what she was doing.

Maybe he really was someone the Agency had put here. No. That made no sense. She didn't have any information anyone would want. Not anymore.

Maybe the man really was just a drifter. He could be a little crazy. Normal people didn't hide in the shadows. Of course, normal people didn't feed some homeless drifter who was hiding out in their barn, doing his best to stay out of sight. It had been easier when she thought of him as a ghost, haunting the place. He hadn't frightened her then. A big man, strong enough to move bales of hay for hours, that ought to frighten her. Encouraging him to hang around just didn't make sense. Did it?

Hell. Maybe she was the crazy one. That scenario seemed more likely.

Monday morning Charlie took a trip to the dog pound. She knew as soon as the adoption lady opened the door to the dog runs that the big mutt who watched her so intently, with what looked for all the world like a grin on his face, was going home with her. She signed the papers and promised to obey all the rules, and handed over her fifty-five dollars.

Charlie named her new friend Ghost.

* * * * *

He was just finishing the latest addition to the haystack when the woman pulled up. She was late. He was sure of her routine by now. Every Monday morning she went grocery shopping. She usually came home at about seven, slept until about ten-thirty, then fed the horses before she went shopping. She got home from the store around noon. He watched her carry groceries into the house every Monday, then unload the feed for the horses. It was hard, watching her lift things that were too heavy for her without showing himself, without offering to help. If she would just have the sense to leave the feed in the truck, he'd gladly unload it once she was out of sight.

Today, it was well after 1:00 PM when she got home.

She hadn't brought him breakfast.

She was laughing. He risked a quick look through a missing barn board. A dog. A huge dog. It looked something like a Saint

Bernard, but with a spotted coat, like a bird dog. When it jumped up on the woman playfully, the dog's head was taller than hers.

Hiding from the woman was easy, but he could never hide from the dog. He should have known when she started feeding him. As soon as he ate one of her breakfasts, she would have to quit pretending he didn't really exist. But he'd been hungry. He was hungry now, and things would only get worse from here on out. Once the dog gave him away, he'd be back on the highway. He went to pack his duffel bag. He would fill a t-shirt with oats and bran from the feed bins downstairs if he got a chance before the dog found him. It didn't taste very good, but it would keep him alive for a little while longer. Unless Robert Waite caught up with him.

He laid in the top of the haystack the rest of that first day after the new dog arrived, hidden in the hay bales, his duffel bag at his fingertips. He was out of sight but still had a quick escape route available. He dozed off from time to time, waking up at the smallest sound, expecting the dog to find him at any moment. Instead, the dog spent most of the day trailing the woman around, getting used to the horses. The woman took mare after mare into the small paddock she'd built, out where the calf pens used to stand. The spot was easily visible through the upper hay doors that opened out on the barnyard.

If it hadn't been for the gnawing fear, he'd have enjoyed the day. She was at her best working with the mares, the lines of worry gone from her face, the cares no longer bowing her shoulders. He would have been content just to watch her for hours.

He was an idiot. What the hell was he doing here? He was damn lucky she hadn't called the law on him. If only he could get over this desperate need to be near her, to fix what was wrong in her world. Right. Try telling that to the cops. *I only wanted to help her…*

He couldn't leave just yet, at any rate. Once he was out in the open the dog would spot him for sure. He would wait. He was good at waiting...

"Daddy! Daddy! Momma, Daddy's home!"

Laughter floated out to him, and he hefted the child to one hip as he pushed through the door. The kitchen smelled like pies baking and coffee, and there were crayons scattered across the table. The woman ran down the stairs as he entered the kitchen, the smile on her face matching the laughter in her voice. Sunlight poured in the window, lighting her long auburn tresses on fire. "Welcome home," she whispered as she stretched her arms out to him. His eyes closed as she pulled him down into a kiss helped to heal the empty places inside.

"I missed you both so much."

"I missed you too, Daddy."

She ran her fingers through his long sable hair, her touch sending shivers down his spine. "What do you say we have some pie, and some milk, and then we take a nap? I bet Daddy's tired after his trip."

He turned his head to kiss the palm of her hand. "Daddy's glad to be home."

He woke up in the dim light of evening, roused by an unknown sound. He tried to roll over, but couldn't. A crushing weight had him pinned down. It took all his strength to remain calm and think rationally. He was hot. Much too hot for this time of year. The noise came again, and he kicked frantically, freeing himself of the weight.

He twisted out from under the inert mass, desperate to see what had pinned him down. It was the dog. That damned big dog had climbed up into the haystack and laid down almost on top of him, and now the dog was using him for a pillow.

And despite being shoved aside rather rudely, the dog was still snoring.

* * * * *

There was something about Ghost that made Charlie feel better about coming home from work. No matter what the time of day, Ghost would hear the old Jeep and come bounding in from the fields to meet Charlie. Invariably, Ghost would launch himself at her from about ten feet away, usually knocking her flat. But Ghost did nothing about identifying her invisible man.

Charlie thought of the man as George, now. It helped a little. George was a good, solid name. Not too ambitious. Friendly enough. There weren't any horror movie villains named George.

Charlie tried to figure out where George was sleeping, but never could find any trace of him. It wasn't hard to tell where George had been, though. The water buckets were always full, and the hayracks were kept stuffed. If Charlie worked double shifts, the stalls would be cleaned when she got up in the afternoon.

Her heart beat just a little faster whenever she entered a dark passageway. Ghost learned to pad along beside her without being called, following her everywhere she went, but, if there was anyone else in the barn, Ghost never gave Charlie any sign.

Maybe she didn't really want to catch him, she told herself. Any man capable of stacking hundreds of bales of hay in an evening could probably break her in two, despite her training. And Ghost seemed like he'd lick an intruder to death before he'd do any real damage. Besides, Ghost had to be spending all the time Charlie was at work keeping George company. Just because the man helped out with the horses and the barn repairs didn't make him a model citizen. He was probably a loony, or running from the law.

He was sure as hell no romantic hero from one of her books, here to save her from…from what? Herself? Loneliness? Not bloody likely. Not when he wouldn't even show himself to her. Still, it was hard to be afraid of a man who seemed to want nothing more than to make her life easier.

And what had she done for him? Take out food from a truck stop five days a week seemed little enough.

With a touch of inspiration, Charlie added an electric coffeepot and a grinder and stocked the tiny little freezer in the tack room with coffee beans. After that, there was always fresh coffee on, no matter when she came down to the barn. She added more real food to her grocery list, so there would always be something for him to eat, even when she wasn't working with Janelle.

It was impossible to tell what the man liked and didn't like. Whatever she left, it disappeared. She started leaving little sticky pad notes on things. "Good morning!" or a smiley face. Charlie dropped a tool catalog from the Feed and Supply in the barn one day. When she found it again, it was on the table in the tack room with her notes attached to several pages. George must have been saving them. There were three smiley faces on page nine framing a circular saw and another on page twelve below a 24-oz. roofer's hammer. Charlie laughed out loud as she found the last one, attached to the order page, right below the line with her name printed on it. It was a simple little note she'd left one morning after another load of hay had come in. All it said was "Thank you."

"Not fair!" she laughed to the barn walls. "Now you know my name, but I still don't know yours!"

From his hiding place he could hear her clearly, but he knew better. Once the woman knew his name, she'd figure out the rest, and then the gig was up. He should be leaving anyway. Summer was moving on. He should have been long gone that first night, but instead he listened to her through the walls, and allowed himself to live this daydream. He whispered her name. Charlotte. Charlotte Giles. In his fantasy world, she was close enough to touch. Close enough to smell. She turned her face toward him now, and the sunlight set her hair on fire. She usually wore it in a tight, thick braid down her back, but today it was loose, wild and unruly in the breeze, begging to be touched.

He ached to sink his fingers into its silken masses. The color fascinated him – warm mahogany streaked with frost on a tin roof, all on fire like the last rays of the sunset. He could almost feel it in his hands.

He should have been gone long ago, he thought again. But there was the woman in the way. He told himself Charlotte needed him, because the truth was even more painful. She'd worn a flannel shirt over her t-shirt one morning, then discarded it when the sun rose higher. He held it to his face now, breathing deeply. The shirt still held a lingering trace of a subtle perfume and another, headier smell that was uniquely her own. It frightened him, this need for her. He wasn't a man who needed anything or anyone – not anymore. He'd learned the hard way how expensive that could be – how easily a woman could claim your soul. How she could rip your heart out and stomp it into the dirt.

No. He refused to believe that. It wouldn't be like that with *this* woman. Not this time. Charlotte was different. She was...Charlotte touched people. She cared. Maybe not about him, but about people, in general. She wouldn't hurt him.

Not intentionally.

He hugged the soft shirt tightly against his chest, trying to ease the ache inside. He'd had the dream again last night – the dream was so much better than reality could ever be. In the dream she tucked the baby in for her nap while he watched from the doorway, then she turned and led him down the hall by the hand. She closed their door, she stripped slowly out of her old jeans and pulled her t-shirt over her head, and then she came to him, naked, wanting, touching, demanding.

When he touched her, she responded to him, pulling him close...closer. When he carried her to the bed, sliding his aching cock into her tight, wet sheath, she was ready for him, wanting him, and he watched her shatter over and over again as he drove her to the edge of her endurance. In the dream he was enough for her. In the dream he was all she had ever wanted or needed.

In the dream he satisfied her.

You're a fool, he told himself. *She'll never even know your name.*

Chapter Three

The rough-hewn boards Charlie had ordered began to disappear, taking their places in the upper walls of the battered old barn. Charlie hadn't been able to find a contractor who would even consider scaling those walls to replace the old, rotted lumber near the roofline. The work was too dangerous, requiring manhandling the huge pieces of barn-board at a height equivalent to three stories on a house. Charlie couldn't figure out how George managed to make the repairs all by himself. He never even made enough noise to wake her up. But one thing she did know. She owed the man a debt that simply feeding him would never repay.

Charlie started leaving cash on the table in the tack room, whenever she had a little extra, $10.00 one day, $20.00 another. It lay there undisturbed for a few days, until she paper-clipped a note over the bills. Just "You've been a great help. Thank you, Charlie G." It wasn't much, but evidently it was enough. The next day she pocketed the empty paper clip with a little smile.

Charlie added men's things to her grocery list again, like shaving cream and disposable razors and an aftershave she imagined she caught a whiff of one morning when she came home from work a few minutes earlier than usual. She stood in the tack room, searching for his scent on the air, as if trailing a lover, her eyes sliding closed as she imagined him stepping out of the shadows to put his arms around her.

With a small shake, Charlie snapped herself back to reality. This was foolish. She didn't even know what the man looked like.

But she could still dream.

"Mommy, Mommy, Daddy's home!"

She hadn't even heard the truck. Charlie ran down the stairs, her heart in her mouth.

He stood in the kitchen, their little girl cradled in the crook of his arm, his eyes smiling at her as she ran to him. He swept her up easily with his free arm, pulling her into a tight embrace as he whirled around with both of them. Sara laughed as her head bent back, her bright red hair streaming out behind her.

He smelled like soap, and aftershave, and something else, something indefinable that was uniquely his own. Charlie breathed in deeply, capturing the essence of him and holding it tightly. She laughed as she slid slowly back to the floor, still holding him close enough to feel how much he'd missed her. "Welcome home," she whispered against his lips. "We missed you."

* * * * *

Janelle interrupted Charlie's early morning reveries over a Horseman magazine with a sharp poke from a bony elbow. Charlie looked up just as the front door swung open and caught her breath in surprise.

The green-eyed cowboy was back.

He nodded once by way of a greeting and swung his lanky frame onto a barstool. He looked freshly showered and shaved, and his long, unruly sable hair was pulled back into a ponytail that hung halfway down his back. He was still wearing the jean jacket she'd given him, though it looked to have been washed since she'd seen him last.

As Charlie approached, her customer-friendly smile at the ready, the cowboy turned a coffee mug right side up and pushed it toward her. Charlie filled it and laid out a handful of creamers from her apron pocket. He used them all, and still grimaced as the shock of the first taste hit his tongue.

Charlie laughed softly. "It's pretty bad, I'll admit, but the truckers seem to like it like that. Can I get you anything else?"

The man just shook his head, his eyes on his coffee.

Charlie smiled again. "Looks like you're not much of a morning person. I don't do mornings too well myself. I'll leave you alone. Just holler if you need anything." She refilled his coffee cup twice more before the 6:00 AM masses started showing up. Soon the place was filling up. Somewhere in the crowd the green-eyed man drifted off again. When she went to clear his place, she found he'd left a ten-dollar tip.

Charlie waved the tip under Janelle's nose. "What do you make of this?"

Janelle laughed. "I think he likes you."

Charlie rolled her eyes. "He was here for over an hour and he never even spoke to me. That's a lot of money for a bad cup of coffee. Where does a drifter get the money to tip like that?"

Janelle shrugged. "Doesn't look so much like a drifter anymore. Must have gotten a job. Who knows. Maybe he was paying you back for the meal last month."

"Yeah," Charlie agreed, chewing on her bottom lip thoughtfully. "Maybe. And maybe he had a good reason to be here. Like he was waiting for a ride to work or something."

Janelle shook her head as she bused the counter. "He could start a new trend. Maybe word will get around and some of these truckers will get the hint. He could teach them a thing or two about tipping. Anyway, he cleans up nice, and he tips well. Why don't you try asking him out?"

"Ask him out? Are you insane? I don't even know the man's name!"

"Well at least try talking to him next time he comes in. You could do worse."

Charlie stared at the ten-dollar bill in her hand. Just talking to him couldn't be too dangerous. Charlie nodded noncommittally. Maybe she would. If he came back. She could talk, even if he didn't. Indeed, the man had cleaned up very nicely. She'd tried hard not to stare as she studied the way his shoulders filled out that jacket, but her eyes kept drifting back to him. There was just something about the man…

Don't even start thinking thoughts like that, she chided herself. *He's just a drifter. Even if you could get him to talk, what difference would it make? He's just a big tipper. He's not interested in you. He'll move along soon enough. Men never stick around, do they? It's just a matter of time...what would you do with him, anyway? Hell. You can't even get George to trust you enough to show his face.*

* * * * *

She awoke beside him as the early morning light began to filter through the windows, feeling warm and contented. He held her in his sleep, his arm resting possessively around her side so that the fingers lay tantalizingly near her breast. She snuggled against him, pulling him closer. The skin against her rippled with a light play of tendons as its owner felt her stir.

Warm fingers brushed gently across the curve of her breast, until the nipple he searched for budded to a peak through the sheer nightshirt. She shifted slightly, letting her weight rest more firmly against the body behind her. She could feel the outline of him, hard and lean and well muscled, all of those considerable muscles beginning to stir more fully awake.

Indeed, everything about him was coming awake.

Charlie stretched, enjoying the warmth of his body against her, taking the liberty of sliding her toes along the curve of his calf, smiling self-confidently as her thigh brushed across his awakening cock. He twitched at her touch, then leaned into her, letting the outline of his erection burn itself into her flesh.

"You're not a morning person, remember?"

"Mmm." He raised his leg to wrap around her bent knee and used the leverage to roll her towards him as he shifted slightly. His head bent so that his mouth could cover the nipple he'd been courting, while his fingers stroked over her belly, then lower, pausing to stroke through the dampness of the curls between her thighs before exploring deeper, two fingers teasing her to match his morning arousal.

She thought about telling him how ready she was, how she'd woken up ready, but his fingers would find out soon enough, and she didn't need to be in a hurry. They had time. They had all the time in the world…

* * * * *

Except for the dreams, life at the farm settled into a kind of a routine. Charlie gave George a shadowy face in her mind, made him look like the cowboy from the truck stop – big, but not too scary – calm and quiet and not asking for much. She began to think that if she ran into George one morning, they might just exchange greetings and go on as if nothing had really changed.

Except for the dreams. She wondered what that green-eyed cowboy would think if he knew the sort of dreams she'd been having about him. She needed to get out more. She needed to date. The hell with dating. She needed to get laid, damn it. Not that there was any chance of that happening any time soon. She hadn't even been out on a date since the divorce. It was her own fault, really. She'd come to the conclusion that talking to men was generally a waste of time. They never seemed to listen.

Except George. Charlie didn't talk to George, not really, though she sometimes babbled to the barn walls as if he might be close enough to hear her. Whether he could hear her or not, George always seemed to be paying attention to her. He was always one step ahead of her, as if he were trying to anticipate her needs.

Allen had never done that. Never even tried to figure out what Charlie needed, even though Allen lived with her for ten long, exhausting years. Charlie had lived with her invisible man for less than two months, and sometimes she thought he already knew her better than Allen ever had. Maybe it was just the feeling that George was paying attention to her that softened her heart toward him. But there was something reassuring in having things done for her without having to ask, let alone beg, plead, and argue.

George had a way of taking over her hardest jobs, the ones that really wore her down, just when Charlie felt like breaking – the way he had with the hay. The way he did with the grain.

The grain was her least favorite job, therefore she tackled it on Monday, to have it out of the way. The Monday after the 4th of July she left seven 100-pound bags of grain in the back of the old pick-up, rather than lug them down the steps to the feed room as soon as she got home. After all, she told herself, the feed bins were nowhere near empty. Since last Monday had been a holiday, she'd gone to the feed store on Tuesday. The bins wouldn't run empty before she fixed the ladies their dinner.

She'd just finished up her third double shift in a row. She just didn't feel like lifting all those bags. Besides, if she was going to get any sleep, it would have to be early. The air was already stifling hot, and there wasn't any sign of rain on the way any time soon. She should have added central air when she remodeled the house, and screw what the ductwork would do to the Victorian architecture. She needed to sleep. Well, it was too late now to regret winter's decisions. She'd sleep in the morning, while she could, and tackle the grain later.

She never got the chance. By the time she got out of bed, the grain had all been unloaded and poured into the feed bins. The dust had long since settled. She called out a grateful "Thank you!" to the walls, nearly sobbing in relief.

The firewood went much the same way.

She didn't need the fireplaces for heat – she'd had the furnace replaced when the house was remodeled – but there was just something so romantic about the huge walk in fireplace. However the romance died quickly once she noticed the draft the chimney let in. It would have been cheaper to just wall up the fireplaces, but instead Charlie had wood stove inserts added throughout the house. The huge cast iron fireplace insert with its glass front doors managed to preserve the romance of the period setting without allowing dust storms to cloud up the living room. And the fires would provide a nice relief to her oil-heating budget.

Except for the fact that when the wood arrived, it had to be split and stacked. She supposed she should have known that, but she was a city girl, after all.

Charlie quickly discovered there was an art to quartering the big logs that took practice to master – practice and a strength she didn't have. She couldn't seem to get the hang of it. The ax blistered her hands until they were raw and bleeding. Still determined, she worked at it every day for a week, until she came home one morning, and the ax was simply gone. She looked in the tool shed, and inside the back porch, but it just wasn't there.

Split wood lay stacked in neat, orderly rows against the wall of the tool shed, stacked as high as a man's waist and two rows deep, and George had hidden the ax from her.

She sulked for a while, and thought about buying another ax, but then the humor of the situation caught up with her. Somehow, somewhere along the line, Charlie had forgotten to be frightened of this man who lived in the shadows of her barn. She'd grown to count on George being there, even if she never saw him.

Perhaps that was for the best. If she never saw him, if she never had to deal with him in person, maybe they could avoid the inevitable disillusionment that followed when romance and reality met. No man could ever live up to her dreams, any more than she could ever live up to any man's expectations.

But George himself seemed determined to foster Charlie's romantic illusions. She found little things he'd left around the barn for her. One morning she found a four-leaf clover when she came home from work, its stem tucked under her coffee mug, which was full and still hot, and had just the right combination of cream and sugar. Charlie sat staring at it in wonder for a long while before she pressed it in one of the record books to dry. Another day she found a bouquet of freshly cut flowers from the back yard in a jar on the counter – a peanut butter jar, at that.

"Thank you!" Charlie called out to the walls. "The flowers are lovely! And the gardens look wonderful!"

After that, there were fresh flowers in the old peanut butter jar almost every morning.

Later, when the last of the garden's flowers had faded in the summer heat, Charlie found a single rosebud in the now empty peanut butter jar, carved out of wood and painted barn red. It looked so real she almost expected it to smell like a rose. She lifted it to her face with a little cry of joy. The gift seemed personal, intimate, somehow. A dozen long stemmed red roses from a florist's shop could never have touched her the way this one little wooden flower pierced her heart.

Perfect. A pretend rose from a man who didn't exist.

* * * * *

Harry, owner of the truck stop, proved to be the catalyst who intervened to twist fate in Charlie's favor.

There'd always been a pool table at the truck stop, which drew the locals in on Friday and Saturday nights. Harry got it in his head that he wanted a liquor license to go with the pool table. They could serve beer with dinner, maybe draw in the locals for more than just weekends. Charlie told him it would only lead to trouble. It was a truck stop, after all, not the local bar. Beer meant drunks, and drunks would keep the truckers away. The truckers were there for the food and maybe a shower and a phone call or two, a few hours shuteye in the cab, then some breakfast, and back on the road. There was no room in that scenario for locals and beer.

But Harry didn't listen. Less that two weeks after Harry got his beer permit, on a rare Monday night off, Ghost woke Charlie up with his barking. This wasn't anything like the friendly noises he made when she got home. This was a deep, menacing rumble coming from way down in his chest. Charlie yanked a pair of jeans on over her t-shirt and jumped into her moccasins, practically falling down the stairs in her haste to get to the kitchen door before Ghost tore it down. As soon as she turned the doorknob Ghost bolted toward the back pasture.

By the time Charlie turned around to grab her keys and the shotgun, Ghost was out of sight. She didn't have any trouble following him, though. She could hear Ghost clearly even over the Jeep's protesting coughs. The big dog was headed across the back pasture, the one the hay man had just mown again, down toward the road. The old Jeep bounced over ruts that would have broken the axle on a cheap little import. Charlie swore as her head hit the roof. "This better not be a midnight groundhog raid," she warned Ghost. Though somehow, she knew it wasn't.

What she saw as she topped the rise and the headlights flooded the slope down by the road made her blood boil. There was a fight going on. Actually, more like a beating. Five, no six, men were swinging their fists at a man they'd surrounded. The man in the middle stood a head taller then the rest. He swayed, then finally went down, and booted feet attacked him like so many snakes just waiting to strike.

The big man was struggling to make it back to his feet when Ghost joined the fray. The huge dog launched himself at the nearest attacker from a distance of about fifteen feet at a full run. The result was like dominoes. Those who didn't fall in the initial impact found themselves facing a hundred-and-fifty pounds of gnashing fury. Then Charlie was there, firing a warning shot over the men's heads as the beam of the pick-up's huge headlights outlined the little party.

The night was suddenly quiet except for the breath of panting men and the dog's deadly growl. "Ghost," Charlie ordered, "Hold." She wasn't sure he would listen, but Ghost stayed where he was, fangs bared and haunches quivering.

Charlie looked around the men slowly picked themselves up and closed ranks. They were just boys, really – boys she knew – most of them no more than sixteen. Ghost stood guard over the object of their attention, who had failed in his attempt to regain his footing, and now lay face down in the dirt. *Have the sense to stay there*, Charlie thought. *If you stand up you'll be directly in my line of fire.* She eased herself slowly around to the big man's right.

"Tommy," Charlie commanded, addressing herself to the older of the two Robinson brothers, "This is my land. You're looking at trespassing charges, as well as assault and battery. You've got some fast talking to do."

"It ain't nothing, Miss Giles. We was just chasin' off this dirt bag. It's our duty to protect the women folk around here. Can't have trash like this hangin' 'round." The young man swayed when he gestured with his hands, and his speech was slightly slurred.

Charlie considered the situation and the amount of beer the boys had probably consumed. Damn Harry anyway. She moved closer to the fallen man's side, her shotgun still raised. "Who appointed you this man's judge and jury? Aren't you supposed to have white robes with hoods for this sort of thing?"

Charlie had only the one shell left in the second barrel. She hadn't thought to grab the box of ammo. Not that she'd want to have to shoot any of these boys, anyway. She was sure they'd regret this once they were sober.

"We weren't planning no lynching here, Ma'am!" Tommy protested. "We was just doin' our civic duty, tryin' to run this bum off." Tommy seemed to gain courage as he embraced his theme. "Why, it's womens like you we was trying to protect. Livin' all alone like you do out here, you don't want no vagrants overrunning your farm."

Charlie shot the boys a look of contempt. Movement from the ground distracted her momentarily. Surprisingly enough, the man on the ground was attempting to push himself up again. Shotgun still pointed in the boys' direction, she dropped to her haunches, offering the man her hand. "I didn't ask for your help and I don't need it, boys. Not every stranger who crosses the county line is a vagrant, and it's not your right to deal out vigilante justice."

Charlie stopped there, distracted by the man on the ground. She went hot and cold as she recognized the battered face that slowly rose out of the dirt. She wasn't hallucinating. This wasn't a dream. There was too much blood for that. She had to give herself a mental shake to continue.

"I don't live out here alone at all. I have a hired man who helps me out. At least I had a hired man, until you boys decided to rearrange his face. If he leaves me after this, you boys are all going to be out here mucking stalls at 6:30 AM every single day of the week. Count on it. If it was up to me I'd see that every one of you gets to spend the night in jail."

She looked down into dark, wounded green eyes that held no trust. "I think we should follow these boys right down the road to the State Police barracks," she announced calmly, as if she had conversations with this man every day. "Are you willing to press charges?"

The cowboy shunned the hand Charlie offered. He buried a hand in Ghost's thick coat, instead, and pulled himself to his knees, then unfolded like a gangly new colt, trying to get his legs for the first time. Charlie followed him up with her eyes until her head bent back awkwardly on her neck. My God, the man was tall.

He glared at each of the boys in turn, apparently memorizing their faces. Cold, naked fury burned in those eyes, and Charlie was afraid for a moment that the fight wasn't really over, but after a long, silent deliberation, the big man slowly shook his head. Not much more than a quarter turn to the right.

"You should know, Ma'am," Tommy announced, "Anything this man's told you is a lie. You can't trust him, and it ain't safe..."

Charlie took a step forward, shotgun pointing directly at Tommy's rib cage. She kept her voice calm, low, but she couldn't keep the anger out of it. She didn't even try. "What isn't safe, Tommy, is you boys spending one more minute on my property. I suggest you all go on home and try to think up some real good story to tell your mothers, because each of them is going to get a call from me tonight just as soon as I get back to the farm. I assure you, your mothers are not going to like what I have to tell them. Most of you boys aren't even old enough to drink.

"Tomorrow, Harry and I are going to have a long talk about him selling beer to minors – right before I talk to the Alcohol Control People. None of you will be welcome in the truck stop at any time for any reason for the rest of the summer. Now get on home before I have any more time to think about what you've done here tonight, and I decide to let loose with the other barrel of this shotgun just to improve the gene pool."

Dismissed, the boys knocked into each other trying to shove their way back into Tommy's pick up truck. Charlie stood where she was, beside her green-eyed drifter, close enough to feel the heat radiating off his skin, close enough to smell his blood oozing from a dozen minor wounds, but farther away than she'd felt all summer. They stood, side by side, avoiding each other's gaze, watching Tommy's pick-up pull away.

Charlie cursed herself for a romantic fool. She didn't need some damn idiot kids to tell her to be careful. She didn't have to look again to know the man beside her was dangerous. Anger radiated off of him like the heat from a cookstone in a campfire. She was stalling, putting off the moment of truth. She had to order him to move on, before any of that anger let loose at her.

It was the only sensible thing to do.

Beneath the blood and the dirt, the man's face was like a mask now, revealing nothing. But the eyes hadn't changed. They flashed with anger, and the bitterness still etched lines around them, visible despite the rapid swelling on the left side. There was nothing in those eyes that suggested trust, or any feelings for Charlie at all.

Charlie turned to face the man who'd been living in her barn all summer. She knew what he was. She'd labeled him that night she'd first seen him, months ago, cold and wet after a hard spring rain. What she remembered most about him was his eyes. Angry, bitter green eyes. He was a drifter. He was the sort who'd end up on the wrong end of the law before he outran that anger.

Yet he was the same man who'd whittled a rosebud for her. The pieces just didn't fit. It didn't make any sense. He didn't make any sense. What Charlie was about to do didn't make any sense.

The cowboy swayed drunkenly, his hand still buried in Ghost's coat. Charlie took a deep breath and reached out to lay her hand over his arm. He flinched as if Charlie had struck him, but he didn't pull away. Charlie tried to keep her voice soft and non-threatening. "We can't stand out here all night just staring at each other. Let's go home."

He blinked slowly, frowning as if trying to understand something complicated, but still said nothing. Charlie moved closer, her heart hammering, and slid an arm around the big man's waist to steady him. He made no attempt to resist as she propelled him toward the truck. Charlie's head barely reached the man's shoulder, and he must outweigh her by close to a hundred pounds. Just what she needed. A huge, angry, uncommunicative man to contend with.

But then, the mares outweighed her closer to ten fold, Charlie reminded herself, and they didn't talk much either. Somehow, she managed them just fine.

Charlie buckled up her courage and opened the truck door with her free hand. "Get in," she ordered in the same tone she used with a balky mare. To her surprise, the big man obeyed without any sign of protest.

Charlie's mind filtered through half-remembered first aid courses from years ago. "Don't you pass out on me, George," she warned in the same no nonsense tone. "You're too big. I'll never be able to move you." His eyes were slipping out of focus as she reached in and buckled the seat belt around him. "George!" she barked. "Stay with me, George." He shook his head and took several long, deep breath. As soon as Charlie opened the driver's side door, Ghost crowded in between them on the front seat, making it difficult to shift gears.

Charlie headed for home, though by way of the roads and the driveway this time. She craned her neck occasionally to see around the huge mound of fur that had taken over the better part of the seat. The man's eyes drifted shut a couple of times, but he was still conscious when she got him to the house. Although he leaned rather heavily against her this time, no longer remembering to pull away defiantly, he managed to walk the length of the sidewalk to the kitchen door primarily under his own power.

He seemed to rouse himself there, studying the new door for a brief moment before his gaze dropped to Charlie's once again. His eyes were stormy gray now, the angry glitter replaced with uncertainty.

"Come on," she encouraged gently, keeping her voice soothing, the way she'd coax a young colt to trust her. "Let's get you to bed."

It seemed the longest time he just stood there, staring at Charlie as if mesmerized, before she could get him to move again.

Charlie led the man to the back bedroom and turned down the covers. He moved slowly, taking it all in, as if reading something in the very walls. She noted the way he winced when he moved his right arm. Someone had stomped on it at the wrist, maybe ground a boot heel into it. She had to help him out of his shirt. When she'd fantasized about that chest, it had never looked quite like this. Still, she wanted to touch. He was all hard angles and bronze skin and sinew and muscles, and scars. A long jagged white line, pale against that bronze skin, ran from his collarbone across his chest on the right side, and there were two more scars that looked like knife wounds below his breastbone. There was a bruise rising fast on his right side, just above the waistband of his Levi's. She wondered absently whether the incredible bronze of his skin ended at the waist of his jeans. She reached for the stud at the waistband, but he twitched and stared up at her, his eyes wild.

She jerked her eyes away from that fine line of hair that disappeared into his waistband. "I'm going to go get some disinfectant." Charlie decided to ignore the bruise for now. "I'm going to wash these clothes, too. I'll pick up your jeans when I get back."

The man was safely stripped of his filthy clothing and under the covers, looking like he'd fallen asleep, by the time Charlie returned with a bowl of hot water, the washcloths, and the disinfectant. She turned the covers back, taking a moment to study his chest.

He was thin, too thin, but still incredibly well built, with the hard muscled body of an athlete. The top of one naked hip revealed no tan line. Either he was in the habit of sunbathing nude, or his skin really was that dark a bronze by nature. And there was that line of dark fur, disappearing below the edge of the sheet. The sheet was thin, allowing a hint of an outline to show though. He looked big, and thick, and touchable, even at rest. There was enough there to make her want to fold the covers back a bit further, just to look.

Not one of her better ideas. The timing was wrong. But damn it his very nearness made her long to touch. She felt the urge to kiss each bruise, as if that would help, but no. It really wasn't a good idea. Still, she could touch…Charlie wrung out the cloth and moved her hand to his chest, just to disinfect the cuts and scrapes.

His uninjured hand shot out to grab Charlie's wrist in a surprisingly strong grip. There was something frightening about the intensity of those wild, angry eyes. Whatever he'd been through, trust was not something he parted with easily. "It's all right, George. It's only me. Charlie, remember? I'm not going to hurt you. I just wanted to clean your face up a little."

Face. Yeah. Right.

Well, his face needed attention, too, she thought defensively. Dirt and blood crusted along one long, high cheekbone, promising a shiner by morning. The hand that gripped her looked big enough to squeeze a grapefruit down to the pulp in one move, though he merely held her immobilized. All her instincts, all her years of Agency training, told her a hand like that was dangerous. She could have broken his grip, probably should have, but she didn't. She studied the hand, instead.

His hand was undamaged – not a single split knuckle, or even a rising bruise. It wasn't the first time Charlie had cleaned up a man after a fight. But Jamie's knuckles always looked worse than his face. She studied the hand that gripped her thoughtfully. George wasn't hurting her, but he could have. With just a little more pressure in that huge hand and a quick flick of that powerful wrist, he could break her arm. Yet she hadn't actually seen him swing at any of the boys. Charlie didn't remember any of the boys looking hurt, either, except bruised prides and posteriors, where Ghost had knocked them down.

She met the big man's eyes again, letting him study her, watching the anger and defiance slowly fade. "George?" he asked, in an amazingly deep voice that sounded rusty from disuse.

Charlie graced the man with her best smile. "George Washington Carver. He invented peanut butter."

A flicker of a smile pulled at the undamaged corner of his mouth for just a moment. His hand moved, hers still captured within it, and for a moment she thought he'd seen where her eyes had wandered, and was guiding her to – but no. His fingers loosened and fell back to his side.

Charlie took a deep breath, trying to regain her composure. She bathed his face carefully, soaking off the matted dirt and blood, trying not to make the cuts hurt any more than they already did, but if the disinfectant stung, George didn't let it show. His eyes rested on her as she carefully cleaned the cuts on his chest, but he made no move to fold the sheet back any farther. Her hand itched, but she quit at the bruise on his hip. There was no sense in pushing her luck.

"Get some sleep," she offered. "You'll most likely feel even worse in the morning, but I think you'll live."

A trace of a smile lingered around his eyes as they drifted shut.

Chapter Four

"Good morning."

The big man blinked slowly, letting his eyes travel around the room without moving his head.

"How do you feel?"

Green eyes came to rest on her. "You been there all night?"

"On and off. I slept out on the couch for a while once I figured out you weren't going to wake up any time soon."

"You call those boys' mothers?"

"Of course."

"Then you know who I am."

"I know your name," Charlie confirmed. She'd thought about it most of the night. How important this conversation would be to both of them. Charlie put her heart into persuading him to believe her, into persuading him to believe in her. "Your name isn't who you are. You're the man who's made me coffee every morning for the last six weeks. The man who stacked eight hundred bales of straw for me, and over a thousand bales of hay. You're the man who split six cords of firewood for me, without once asking me for anything." She smiled at the memory. "You're the man who carved the rose."

Charlie held those green eyes captive. The firewood weighed heavily against the prison record. The rose weighed more heavily. "I'll tell you the same thing I told Mrs. Robinson. I don't know anything about who you were thirteen years ago. I don't much care. If you feel like you need to talk about it, I'll listen, when you're ready. I've got a little start on who you are now, and I haven't seen anything I don't like."

The big man let his eyes slide closed, and Charlie thought for a moment he'd drifted back to sleep. But then he swallowed hard, and those amazing emerald eyes met hers again. "You're a rare woman, Miss Charlie G. I hope you don't live to regret standing up for me like that last night."

Charlie had a feeling Andrew knew what those phone calls had been like, and referred to them as much as the shotgun out in the back pasture. "I'd like you to stay here," Charlie told him, "But we've got to have a few rules."

The man's eyes closed down again, like a curtain pulled across his soul, and his expression went flat. "It's your home, Ma'am. You make the rules."

"Call me Charlie."

He seemed to be studying a spot on the wall, just behind her head. "Yes, Ma'am."

"No more hiding from me. No more sleeping in the barn. You use this room, and I get to see you from time to time, like across the table at breakfast. Maybe even a passing conversation every now and then. You think you can handle that?"

His expression changed again, like clouds passing in front of the sun. "Lord knows why you're willing to take a chance on me, Ma'am. I'll try not to let you down."

"Mr. Bailey, you've already proven your worth to me. The work you've done on the barn alone has saved me hundreds of dollars, as well as countless hours of arguing with contractors. I only wish I could pay you what you're worth."

"I can't take your money, Ma'am. I won't have you working in that place just so you can hand me your paychecks."

"That may be the single nicest thing anyone's ever said to me," Charlie confessed. Memories of Allen hit her hard, and Charlie turned her back on Andrew, trying not to cry. She couldn't cry. Not now. She hadn't cried once. Not once since that night sitting on the steps in the rain. Now was not the time to start.

A strong arm slid around her waist, and Charlie let herself be drawn back against a warm chest. She didn't feel trapped, no matter how strong that arm was. The warmth of his touch overrode Charlie's better judgment. She leaned back into his embrace, laying the back of her head against his chest. After what seemed like a score of years, his arm moved, his hand rose to her face, his finger, just one finger, tilted her head back, giving him access to her throat. Bending his neck around, over her, he kissed his way slowly up to her mouth.

The lips on hers were lush and soft, so soft, so gentle. God, what a kiss. It ignited a fire in Charlie she'd thought long dead. Her mouth opened to his, questing, demanding, until the kiss was not enough. His fingers grazed softly across her breasts, two liquid mounds of fire. She turned in his arms, needing to touch, to stroke, to devour his naked body.

Hard muscles jumped at her touch, and his arms pulled her tighter, until she could feel his erection pressing against her through the fabric of her jeans. His cock was hard and hot and thick and pulsing with need. His hands were touching, stroking, lighting a fire in her wherever they went. She ground her hips against him, wanting, demanding. She stroked the long, hard length of cock, loving the feel of him, satiny skin over smoldering heat.

He groaned as she circled his cock with her fingers, stroking slowly. "I've been watching you all summer. Wanting you."

Her voice sounded thick and alien. "I haven't been able to sleep for thinking about you."

"I've dreamed about you." His teeth closed over her nipple, greedy and demanding.

"I've dreamed about you," she admitted with a gasp of delight as his fingers combed through her damp curls. He parted her swollen lips to slip a finger inside her, drawing her breast into his mouth as he lifted her off of her feet, pushing her back against the edge of the bed. She came for him almost immediately, so wet and eager that she nearly passed out with the intensity of it. Then he was pulling her t-shirt over her head, sliding into her, hot and thick with need as he filled her, her legs wrapping around his waist, pulling at him as he stood between her knees at the edge of the bed, driving into her as she came again and again...

Charlie woke up reaching, desperately clinging to the dream, trying to pull it back, wanting more, so much more, before the euphoria wore off, and the embarrassment took over. Her body still aching with need, she could feel the path the dream man's lips had traced across her breasts. Charlie jumped out of bed, struggling to deal with reality and yesterday's jeans. Only she wasn't in her bed. She'd fallen asleep downstairs on the couch in her t-shirt.

Charlie knew everything she felt would show all over her. It always did. Daddy had warned her years ago never to play poker. She washed her face in the kitchen sink, hoping the cold water would help. It didn't. She reminded herself that the man in the back bedroom looked and acted nothing like the one in her dream.

The real Andrew Bailey was but a battered, bruised substitute who might someday look almost as good as that dream man, but not for quite a while. Charlie had a man in her house, all right. A dangerous man with a prison record, a bad reputation, and, as far as she could see, a bad attitude. The last thing she needed was to get involved with anyone, let alone a man who could snap her wrist with a flick of his hand.

A man who'd carved her a rose.

Charlie struggled to fit reality into her consciousness, but it was hard to shake the dream off her traitorous body. She brushed her teeth and poured a cup of yesterday's coffee, then dumped it down the sink when she realized it was too bad to even bother trying to drink. Squaring her shoulders, she knocked lightly on the door to the back bedroom.

There was no answer. Not that she'd really expected one. Communication didn't seem to be one of the man's strong points. Charlie turned the knob and pushed the door open slowly, to give him time to grab something if he wasn't decent. Not that it mattered. The bedroom was empty.

The bed was made up perfectly, almost as if he had never slept there, which was impossible. Charlie had tucked him in herself at a little after one o'clock this morning. Besides, the clothes she'd washed were gone.

Certainly a man who'd been in prison would know how to make a bed up neatly. Perhaps he wasn't hurt as bad as he'd looked last night. Charlie tried not to panic as she made her way back to the kitchen and pulled on her boots. She wasn't running as she crossed the gravel parking area on her way to the barn. She was just in a hurry.

Charlie knew what she'd find even before she got there. She felt it, like a fist closing around her heart. A hollow, empty, panicky sort of feeling. Still, she had to look. Charlie checked the tack room first. No coffee waiting on the counter. A quick survey of the stalls confirmed her suspicions. No hay. No water. Son-of-a-bitch. No man.

"So what else is new?" Charlie screamed at the empty barn walls. "Why would I think you'd stick around, anyway?"

Even Ghost had deserted her, apparently happily chasing ground hogs in the back pasture. The horses could take care of themselves this morning. One morning out wouldn't hurt them any. There was plenty of grass in the fields and three fresh water springs. Charlie didn't feel like dealing with the barn work by herself this morning. Not this morning.

Charlie kicked at the dirt floor and slammed the barn doors shut, cursing herself for a fool. While she'd been busy dreaming about some romantic fantasy hero, the man had been hauling his ass out of town. Probably listening to her snore and laughing at her stupid t-shirt. Frances had given it to her. It said, of all things, "Follow your dreams."

Charlie realized belatedly that she hadn't even thought to check her purse. The cash would be long gone. She would have to cancel all her credit cards. Again. Son-of-a-bitch. This was just too goddamn familiar a feeling.

At least this man hadn't had access to her checking accounts. He couldn't have gotten much more than a hundred and fifty dollars. She didn't usually keep even that much cash in her purse, but she hadn't been to the bank since last Friday morning. Every penny of that money had been earned with the sweat of her body. She had the ache in her back to prove it. Somehow, that hundred and fifty dollars meant more than the thousands Allen had made off with.

Charlie didn't even bother to run on her way back to the house. It was much too late for that.

Her purse was sitting on the top of the buffet, right where she'd left it. Charlie dumped it out on the table. A quick inventory seemed to show everything as it should be. She'd been wrong about the money. There was $265 in cash, a Platinum Visa, and her American Express card. Charlie's driver's license and Social Security card were in their right places. As far as she could see, he'd taken absolutely nothing. To make matters worse, Charlie suddenly realized why the man had been coming by the truck stop so often lately.

He would come in, pick up a newspaper, sit down at the bar, drink two or three cups of coffee, and eventually, after he'd read the paper and put it neatly back on the rack, disappear again. He always left at least a ten on the bar under his cup. Sometimes a twenty.

He had given her the money back – the money she'd left for him in the tack room – in tips. Not all of it, but enough that Charlie should have figured it out weeks ago. He'd put at least a hundred dollars back in her purse this morning.

Charlie said a few choice words as she kicked over the kitchen chairs.

While she was bruising her toes, the phone rang.

"Morning," Janelle's cheerful voice announced. "Did you lose something?"

"Like what?"

Janelle pitched her voice low, like she was trying to make sure no one could hear her. Harry must have been somewhere close by. He didn't like personal phone calls. "Tall, green eyes, long wavy brown hair, a face somebody used for a punching bag?"

How did the girl know? How had she figured it out? And when? Had she known all summer?

"Son-of-a-bitch," Charlie hissed, kicking another chair. "George is there? Andrew Bailey?"

"Not for long," Janelle warned. "Some trucker just agreed to give him a ride to Denver."

"Denver? Why the hell would anyone want to go to Denver?" Not that it mattered. She'd known he would take off the first chance he got. "Son-of-a-bitch. When will I ever learn? Tell him I said thanks. No. Screw him. Who needs men, anyway?"

"Come tell him yourself. Better yet, just come get him, whatever his name is, and take him back home with you. I'm sure you'll think of something to do with him." Janelle laughed as she hung up.

Take him home? Like hell she would. No man would ever get the chance to walk out on her again. But Janelle was right about one thing. The man was damn sure going to get a piece of her mind.

Charlie drove across the field rather than take the long way around by the roads. She thought of a dozen things she wanted to say to the man. This time, by God, this man was going to know how she felt – and just how angry she was.

This man was just lucky she keep her .25 locked in the safe.

He was slouched down in the back booth, the same booth he'd sat in that first night, trying to make himself invisible as he nursed his coffee through the good side of his mouth. By this morning, the other side had swollen badly. He was still wearing the denim jacket she'd given him – the one she'd washed and stayed up to dry until 3:00 AM this morning. He was huddled in it, one arm cradled against his chest in an awkward position. He glanced up as Charlie stalked up, then looked away, gray eyes distant, defeated.

Charlie wasn't sure what she'd expected, but it wasn't this. The man looked smaller today, hardly the romantic lover from her dreams, more like the drifter she'd taken him for that first night last spring, a lost soul washed up on one of life's beaches. She could feel her temper losing its edge.

Charlie hesitated for a moment before she slid into the booth, across the table from him. She took a deep breath, trying to keep her tone reasonable, give him a chance to explain. "If you needed a ride somewhere, you could have asked me."

He wouldn't even meet her eyes. Not that that surprised Charlie much. She reached out to examine his injured arm, but he turned slightly, keeping it out of her reach. "I'm sorry. I should have taken you to the emergency room last night. Is your arm broken?"

He gave his head a slight shake, still avoiding her gaze.

So he was back to not talking again. Charlie felt her frustration rising. "Where are you headed?"

A shrug, though the move must have cost him.

This was getting her nowhere. "I wouldn't have tried to keep you from leaving if that's what you want to do. That's your choice. I just wish you'd thought enough of me to at least bother to say good bye." She tossed the money he'd shoved into her wallet back at him. "Here. You earned this. You'll need it in Denver." He made no move to pick up the cash. Not that Charlie stayed around to watch. She was out of her seat and half way to the door before he responded, his voice so low that she barely heard him.

"Didn't figure anything I had to say would matter much after you made those phone calls."

A tired, bitter voice. A voice that felt sorry for itself.

Charlie stopped, the anger boiling like floodwaters behind a dam. She turned and stalked back to the table. He was staring at his hands, not even looking in her direction. Charlie rested her palms flat on the table, leaning as far into his field of vision as she could get. "Didn't think at all, did you? Did you even consider how I'd feel when I woke up and you were gone, not knowing if you'd crawled off in some hole somewhere to die or just decided to run? I guess I should be glad it's the second. At least I won't stumble over your decomposed body someday."

"You men are all alike. You stay around just long enough to let me get used to you, then just when I think I can trust you, off you go. I ought to be used to it by now. You're not the first man to disappear on me. But you'll damn sure be the last."

Charlie didn't care who heard her by then. Her anger carried her out the door and into the Jeep before she started to cry. She peeled out of the parking lot fast enough to ping gravel against the side of the building. Harry jumped out the kitchen door to shake a fist at her, but Charlie was past caring. The worst Harry could do was to fire her.

Charlie pulled off into the back pasture, not far from where she'd parked last night. All the tears came now, the ones she hadn't cried over Daddy or Allen. She pounded her fists into the steering wheel. "Why do I always have to end up alone?"

God, in his infinite wisdom, said nothing.

It was a stupid thing to do. He knew it even as he swung the duffel bag over his good shoulder and threw a dollar bill on the counter next to the cash register. He was going to lose his ride. Rides weren't all that easy to come by for a 6'7" ex-con. He was a fool to follow her. Charlie obviously hadn't made those phone calls like she'd said she would, or she'd have come after him with that shotgun instead of being angry that he'd left.

Nobody had ever been angry with him for leaving.

He was an idiot. What kind of an idiot chased after a woman who screamed at him in front of a room full of witnesses, anyway?

Nobody'd cared enough about what he did or didn't do to scream at him for a very long time. How was he supposed to just walk away from that?

Besides, Charlie's hair had fallen down, and the sunlight had caught it as she flew out the door. She'd spun around to jump into that truck, and it had tossed wildly, spreading out like a halo around her, giving her face an aura of fire, like a spectacular sunset in an artist's picture book. He could no more have walked away from Charlie than he could have kept himself from breathing. No matter what the consequences, he had to try.

He didn't have to walk far. She'd pulled off the road where she'd found him last night. He stood beside the truck for a moment, hesitant, but she didn't look up, even though his body blocked the sunlight out of the truck's cab. She had her head on the steering wheel, and, impossible as it seemed, it looked like she was sobbing, almost hysterically.

He set his bag in the bed of the pick-up and opened the door, slowly, giving her time to react. She didn't. Not even when he eased his weight down onto the creaky old seat. She really was crying. Bawling her eyes out. He'd never seen a woman cry so hard. He had the urge to take her in his arms and hold her, but he knew how far that would get him. So he sat. And he waited.

He didn't have to wait long. "Leave me alone," she hissed through her tears. "I don't want anyone around who's going to run at the first sign of trouble."

He didn't have any notion of how to answer that, so he just sat next to her and let her cry. At last she blew her nose on a handful of truck-stop napkins and ran the sleeve of her t-shirt across her cheeks.

"Never had anybody mad at me for leaving before. Folks generally seem pretty glad to see me go." His voice was low, barely audible.

"You're going to miss your ride."

He had to swallow hard to make the words come out at all. "I thought maybe I could catch a ride with you." He tried to catch her eyes, to judge what she was thinking, but she was studying the pattern molded into the vinyl of the steering wheel. "I was thinking – " He lost his nerve, leaving the sentence dangle there. But it was no good like that, so he tried again. "I was thinking maybe I'd stay here. If you still want me to."

Red-rimmed eyes glaring up into his. "How long? How long are you going to be around this time? A week? Another month?"

He took a deep breath. It would have been easier to look away, to avoid her angry, demanding eyes, but this time he held his ground. "As long as you want me to. I'll stay here until you tell me to leave." Which would be tomorrow. Or as soon as she picked up that phone.

Charlie swiped at her eyes again. "Nobody stays."

His voice sounded thick. He knew he was giving away too much. But he couldn't back down now. "I will. If you want me to."

"Why?"

He couldn't say what he felt. She'd have him arrested on the spot. He was the one to look away this time, before she read the truth in his eyes. "I don't have anywhere else to go."

"I'm sorry I made a scene back there at Harry's," she offered at last. "I'm not usually that...vocal."

She seemed to be making an effort at peace. He sensed she hated losing control like this. Well, he hated leaving himself this vulnerable, too, but he had to know. "Did you call those boys' mommas?"

"Of course. Every one of them. Did you think I'd let those boys get away with what they did to you?"

He shrugged again, then winced as his ribs felt the impact. "You didn't have to. It wasn't your responsibility." *I'm not your responsibility*, he thought.

"It happened on my land."

"This was my grandfather's land." *It should be my land now*, he could have added. But he didn't.

"So you come with the place? Sort of a package deal?"

He met her eyes at last, stared at her, waiting for the fear to hit. "I didn't have any idea my grandfather had died. I just got out of Moundsville."

"I know."

When she didn't react, it hit him. Charlie wasn't from West Virginia. She didn't know about Moundsville. "The West Virginia State Penitentiary at Moundsville," he explained carefully. "It's the State's maximum security prison."

"I know what Moundsville is," Charlie assured him.

She knew? No. She couldn't know everything, not and say it so calmly. "I did twelve years for manslaughter."

"You want to tell me what happened?"

He let his eyes shifted to a point on the horizon. "I beat a man to death in a barroom brawl."

"Would you do it again?"

That caught him by surprise. A sardonic smile tipped one side of his battered mouth, though it hurt. "No, Ma'am. I don't think so. Not even that particular man."

"Then I guess you learned something in the last twelve years."

Hope hit him like a fist between the shoulder blades. He beat it down, knocked it back with a cold dose of reality. He knew better. It was being so close to Charlie that was upsetting his equilibrium. He wanted to reach out and wrap his fingers in that Irish red hair, take her in his arms, hold her, kiss her eyelids until the heat in them subsided, run his hands up under her shirt...

Instead he looked down at his arm again and flexed his fingers tentatively. "I'm not going to be much use to you for a while."

Charlie reached out to lay her hand over his uninjured one. He flinched when she touched him, he couldn't help it, but he didn't let his arm jerk away. Something in his defenses crumbled when she touched him. He couldn't meet her eyes again. She'd see too much.

"You've always paid your own way, haven't you?"

He didn't have a clue how to answer her – or what to do with her hand, laid across his, offering so much more than she knew. No one ever touched him. When Charlie pulled her hand away, another piece of his heart went with it. He closed his eyes and rested his head against the back of the seat. If there was a wrong thing to say or a wrong way to say it, he would find it. Better to just keep his mouth shut. Though that was probably wrong, too.

Charlie switched on the ignition. The old Jeep started up with a chatter and a cough. She noted the way his jaw muscles knotted, but he said nothing – a habit she could see he'd long cultivated. "You need help with your seat belt?"

He glanced at Charlie, his eyes distant again, then pulled the belt around awkwardly, buckling it one-handed. For a moment, there, there'd been something else in those green eyes. A flicker from the soul within. It was gone now, but the fact that Charlie had seen it, just for that moment, made this all seem just a little more reasonable. Charlie let the clutch out and turned the truck around.

He didn't say another word until Charlie turned into the hospital's large circular drive and headed for the emergency room doors. "I can't go in there," he stated flatly.

He decided that now, after they got here? "Just where the hell did you think I was taking you?"

"Out to the highway, or something." He was staring at the horizon again.

"Yeah, I can see that. I'd just dump you off at the Interstate. 'Bye now, it's been real.' I'm like that."

"Would if you had any sense."

"I don't have a lick of sense, or we wouldn't be here, now would we? But we are here, and you are going in. We're going in, together. You're going to get that arm x-rayed and make sure it's not broken."

"No." His voice conveyed cold, terse, uncompromising – fear?

"Look, Mr. Bailey, if you don't want me to drive right up to those doors and drag you in there, you damn well better talk to me. Don't think I can't do it. You weigh a hell of a lot less than one of my mares."

His jaw clenched again. "They'll send me back to prison."

Charlie tried to keep the shock out of her voice. "Back? Why?"

"Computers. Everything's hooked up to computers now."

"So what? Why should the computers worry you?" Charlie wondered uneasily if his mind had slipped a gear.

He spat the words out. "Parole violation."

Charlie nodded slowly, as if it all made sense. "That's why you wouldn't press charges against those boys."

He snorted derisively. "One reason."

Don't volunteer anything. "Any of the others worth hearing?"

"Bob Waite."

"Robert Waite Junior, the county sheriff?"

"Heard he is now. Wasn't when I knew him."

Charlie still hadn't dismissed the insanity notion. "I suppose that would make a difference. If the county sheriff is looking for you, he'd be sure to notify the local hospital."

"Waite gets his hands on me, I'll get shot, trying to escape."

Charlie chewed on her upper lip pensively – a habit she was going to have to break. "What kind of trouble are you in?"

He glanced at her sideways, then went back to staring off toward the horizon. "Never checked in with my parole officer."

Charlie sighed. It was going to be a long morning. "You mind telling me why? Do you want to go back to prison?"

"Probation officer was supposed to pick me up at the bus terminal when I got out. I waited. He never showed."

His voice was flat. Emotionless. She tried not to imagine him sitting there, waiting…perhaps for hours. It didn't work. She could almost taste the way the worry would have gnawed at him. *Welcome home.*

"Did you do anything at all once you were here? Go check in with your probation officer or anything?"

"Long walk," was all the answer he had for that one.

"I see." Charlie drummed her fingers on the steering wheel. Paranoid or not, he was probably right about the computers. If Waite had an APB out on him, the computer system at the hospital would catch it as soon as his name was entered into the database.

If she couldn't take him to the hospital, where could they go? Any doctor would do, if Charlie could trust him. All she needed was an x-ray and a cast. But most doctors sent you to the hospital for x-rays. They would need a doctor who could do an x-ray at his office, like a clinic or something. Or…

Harrison Keeler had a fluoroscope. Keeler said he owed Charlie a really big favor. This was pretty big.

"What is it going to take to get you right with your parole people?" Charlie questioned.

He glanced over at her again, then shifted his gaze back out the window. "A miracle."

Charlie pursed her lips thoughtfully. "My cousin used to be a Priest. I'll give him a call when we get home."

Redemption

"Yeah. You do that."

"Look. If you promise me you'll call somebody when we get home and at least try to get this straightened out, I'll do everything I can to help you. I doubt the state really wants you back. Keeping a man in prison is expensive, you know. More than thirty grand a year. I'll go see the parole officer if you want. The fact that you have a job and a place to live ought to help."

Brilliant green eyes searched hers, questioning. "Do I?"

For just a moment, something soft and vulnerable showed in those deep green eyes. Charlie felt the beginnings of a smile pulling at her lips. "You do, if you want it."

His voice was tinged with shock and confusion. "Why would you go to so much trouble to help me?"

Charlie chose her words carefully. "Why did you start doing all the things you've done to help me?"

He shrugged, wincing a little as his arm shifted. "Seemed like you needed the help."

"And you don't need my help?"

He closed his eyes for a moment. When he opened them again, that little flicker of humanity was gone. "What I need is some pain killers."

Charlie put the truck back in gear and headed for Doc Keeler's. It was going to be a long, long afternoon.

Chapter Five

"You took him to the vet?" Janelle exclaimed in horror. "I know he's big, but he's not a goddamned horse!"

"Doc Keeler owed me a favor, and I didn't want Andrew disappearing on me again," Charlie explained, trying to keep her voice patient. She didn't feel very patient. The last thirty-six hours had taken their toll on her.

"You're missing my point here. Doc Keeler is a Veterinarian. An animal doctor."

"I know that." Charlie pressed her fingertips against her eyes. "You think human bones look all that different from animal bones? Keeler's got a fluoroscope big enough for a horse, and he'll keep his mouth shut."

Janelle slammed around the kitchen for a few minutes before poking her head out the order window. "So just what did the fluoroscope thing show?"

"Fractured bone in his right arm at the wrist," Charlie responded with a sigh. "Couple of cracked ribs. Nothing displaced. He should heal quickly enough. Doc taped up the ribs and put the arm in a soft cast for four weeks."

Janelle's tight lips relaxed slightly. "So how did Mr. Bailey take to being hauled in to the vet's?"

"It's hard to tell. The man barely speaks. Apparently he hates answering questions, especially from me. But he did go in. That's better than we did at the hospital."

"It was still a vet's office."

"Well it was better than no doctor at all," Charlie fired back. She had to watch herself. Her temper was definitely getting out of control.

It was some time before Janelle stuck her head out again. By then Charlie was drinking her third cup of coffee, trying to stay awake.

"So is this Bailey man going to stick around now?"

"Damned if I know," Charlie admitted with a sigh. "I could count the number of complete sentences I've heard him say on one hand and have fingers left over."

"At least he won't talk your ear off."

A timer went off and Janelle turned away to do something with one of her big kettles. Charlie had long ago come to the conclusion that cooks were the original magicians, and that's why people were terrified of them. Whatever Janelle was doing, it smelled great. But that wasn't any guarantee. After all, who would take the chance if the food smelled awful? Except, of course, for cheese.

Charlie watched the clock anxiously. She'd gotten used to George – Andrew, she corrected herself – getting chores done that she was now going to have to work back into her schedule. She couldn't expect too much from him for the next few weeks. The man was going to be more of a liability than an asset for a while. But then, that was something she was used to. At least he wasn't writing the world's next great novel. She wouldn't have to tiptoe around him and try her best not to disturb him. She hoped.

Charlie half-expected Andrew to be gone again when she got home, no matter what he'd promised. They hadn't spoken six words to each other after they got back from Doc Keeler's yesterday. Charlie had fixed dinner, something completely uninspirational out of a box. They'd eaten together in silence, then she'd fed and watered the horses while Andrew did his best to stay out of her way. Doc's painkillers had pretty well knocked him out for the rest of the evening. He slept right through the loud squawking of Charlie's alarm clock. She'd managed to get four hours sleep before she left for work at quarter till midnight.

No time for any more erotic dreams.

Charlie wanted nothing more now than to go home and crash, but that wasn't available. She had responsibilities. There was too much work to be done. She was definitely going to miss the old George.

Andrew presented a whole new set of problems. She would have to find a way to reach the man. He had so many defensive shields in place that he might as well have still been hiding from her. She'd felt closer to him when he was just an invisible entity in the shadows of the barn. Charlie slid out of the truck with a heavy heart and headed for the kitchen door. Even Ghost couldn't cheer her up this morning.

The last thing Charlie expected when she slipped quietly into the kitchen was breakfast cooking. She could smell coffee – coffee and bacon, and that was just the beginning. How did a one armed man flip flapjacks? Charlie had never been able to manage it with both hands.

"Merlin," she whispered, overwhelmed. She'd have hugged him if she thought she could get away with it.

Andrew laughed at that – actually laughed. A friendly sound from a friendly, if battered, face. Brilliant green sought hers, questioning. "Then you don't mind me taking over your kitchen, M'Lady?"

"Mind?" Charlie wondered absently if the painkillers had affected the man. If so, she'd ask Keeler for more.

"It is your kitchen."

Charlie slumped gratefully into the chair he pulled out for her and accepted the cup of coffee he set down at her place. "My dear Merlin, I would never dare to voice such a petty objection to a magician who could conjure such smells from the contents of these poor cupboards."

He offered a graceful, sweeping bow. "You are too kind, Lady Guinevere."

So. He could cook, he was well-read, and he had a sense of humor. The future suddenly looked a little less gloomy. Charlie smiled up at her giant magician. "I feel more like Morgan LeFay."

He laughed, his eyes meeting hers. "You have just enough time to get out of that uniform before breakfast, Morgan."

Right. Charlie dragged herself back to her feet. Wait. How would he know... Charlie thought of the times she'd come through the door, losing pieces of the uniform as she went, never once thinking about the windows. He'd been watching her. She grinned back at him, her fingers pausing on her shirt buttons. Maybe she'd wait till she was upstairs to strip today.

"Ma'am?"

She paused on the stairs, bending back over the banister so that she could see his face. His eyes flicked to her breasts, just about to spill out of the half open uniform shirt, and he blushed. That was kind of cute.

"I just wanted to tell you – this house – I heard Granddad really let the place go after Gram died. But even before that, it was never like this. Not in my lifetime. I thought it would be...different. Too fancy to live in. But it's not. You did a real nice job on the place. Gram would have loved it."

Charlie smiled down at him, feeling a little less tired. "Thanks. I wanted it to feel like home." She didn't wait for a reply – was pretty sure he wouldn't have one – so she left him to think on it. This time she waited until she was in her own room with the door closed to finish undressing. He was handsome enough, but there was no sense in pushing things.

Yet.

By the time Charlie came back down the stairs he was setting her plate on the table. Two poached eggs stared up at her like yellow eyes from atop a bed of flapjacks smothered in blueberries. What's more, the man was humming a song she'd heard on that country station he liked.

"You always wake up in such a good mood?" Charlie teased.

His eyes glittered with laughter. "I can't claim I woke up in a good mood, but it's had time for improvement. I've been up since five."

The man got up at five? When he could have slept in? "What on earth for?" Charlie demanded incredulously.

"Always work to be done around a farm. Besides, I had a phone call to make."

Charlie's fork stopped in mid-attack. "A phone call? To your parole officer?"

"Yes, Ma'am."

"Well, what did he say?"

"He is a she. She said, 'Who are you?'"

"Who are you?" Charlie stared at him as the meaning sunk in. "She didn't even know your name? You mean she wasn't looking for you?"

"Nope." He poured himself a cup of coffee, refilled hers, and sat down across the table from her. "Didn't even know I existed."

Charlie blinked twice, feeling off balance. "How did that happen?"

He laughed out loud. "Computers. The state lost my paperwork."

That really shouldn't have surprised her. Charlie had been in enough government offices to know how good they could be at losing things. The miracle was that they ever found anything. "So what happens now?"

"After my parole lady gets whatever forms she needs from Moundsville, I have to go in for an interview." His eyes met Charlie's questioningly. "Figured I might ask you for a ride?"

He was going to stay. Charlie flashed him a brilliant smile. "I think I can manage that."

The man could speak in full sentences, he had a smile that threatened to be blinding once his battered mouth healed, and he could cook. Charlie breathed in the pungent aroma of fresh brewed coffee. "Andrew Bailey, you are a joy to come home to."

Green eyes met hers and held for the length of two long heartbeats – eyes that had forgotten to be wary, at least for now. "Call me Drew, Ma'am," he replied, his voice dropping even deeper. "I thank you, Ma'am. I think that's just about the nicest compliment anyone's ever paid me."

Drew. It suited him. "I'm Charlie," she told him again. "I spent ten years eating Chinese take-out with a man who couldn't boil water. Macaroni and cheese is my personal specialty. I can barely keep myself from starving. I thought maybe that was why you were taking off. Couldn't take any more of my cooking."

"Charlie," he paused, then tried again, his voice raw with emotion. "I wasn't running out on you, Charlie. It just never occurred to me that you'd want me to stay."

* * * * *

If life were even the least little bit like one of Allen's love stories, Charlie reflected, Drew would somehow have managed to get all the barn work done, despite the broken arm, the boys who beat him up would have come over to apologize and make it up to him by helping out, and Mrs. Robinson and the other mothers would have all become her best friends. And, most important of all, Drew would have fallen desperately, hopelessly in love with her, culminating in the most fantastic sex she'd ever had.

So much for cheap paperbacks.

In reality, Charlie heard nothing more from the boys or their mothers. She'd never had more than a passing acquaintance with any of them, but she always tried to be polite, at least saying hello to anyone whose name she could remember. Now they seemed to disappear before Charlie got a chance. None of them bothered to speak to her.

Drew did get a lot of the barn work done in the weeks after the fight, probably more than he should have, although definitely not all of it. He still managed to carry the feed in, but she had to help once it was in the barn, to Drew's obvious annoyance.

The kitchen was the one place Drew seemed totally at ease. He took over the cooking completely after that first day. Charlie didn't offer a single argument there. She quickly acquired a bad case of hero worship over his culinary skills, but as far as she could tell, that was the end of the romance, at least on his part.

Drew kept a careful distance between them at all times. He never laid a hand on her arm when he talked, or let himself brush against her when he walked behind her, and he made sure he moved out of her way when she wanted something in the kitchen. He set her coffee down rather than hand it to her, where their fingers might brush.

Charlie deliberately brushed her fingers across his arm when she reached for the ketchup one evening. He jumped back as if she'd burnt him. Their eyes met, surprise in both of them. "Sorry," Drew murmured as he turned away. "Must have been a static shock."

She wasn't buying it. Not at all.

It hardly helped matters that she'd had that dream again. The one where she lay naked next to him while he ran strong, callused hands over every inch of her body. It didn't help, either, that as the bruises faded, the man proved to be even more handsome than she'd remembered from those early morning visits to the truck stop.

Drew had filled out some physically now that he was eating better, but there was more than that. Mostly the change was in his expressions. Sometimes, if she turned around too quickly, there was something else – something he squashed as soon as Charlie caught him watching her – something that made him appealing enough for the reality to disturb her sleep as badly as the fantasy man had. He stood taller, straighter, shoulders back, moved with longer strides, and he met her eyes when he talked.

There was a confidence in his body language that caught the eye.

Drew Bailey was, as Janelle put it, "A definite hunk."

* * * * *

July slipped into August. Drew had just dropped into the truck stop for a cup of coffee. Janelle came to the conclusion that he was keeping an eye on them, just making sure everything was all right. There were a couple of cops who did that, too – state troopers working the highway on the graveyard shift. For them, it was an excuse for a cup of coffee and some conversation.

However, none of the troopers had a mile walk to get to the truck stop. The third time it happened, Charlie just had to ask. "Do you like to walk, or were you just checking up on us?" she queried with a laugh when she got home that morning.

Drew treated her to one of those brilliant smiles. Smiles seemed to come more easily to him these days, especially where Charlie was concerned, but still, a smile like that was a rare thing. It made her a little weak in the knees.

And she'd always thought that such a silly expression – the kind of thing Allen would have written in one of his old paperbacks.

Drew's smile reached all the way to his eyes when he answered her. "Just because I can."

She cocked her head to one side, studying the man thoughtfully. "What do you mean?"

Drew's eyes focused on the counter behind her, the way they did when he was afraid he'd revealed too much of himself. "In prison, if I couldn't sleep, I didn't have any choices. I had to just lie there, waiting. Now if I wake up early I can take a little walk and watch a beautiful woman's face light up just because I came through the door."

Charlie knew he meant Janelle, of course. Charlie wasn't surprised Drew thought Janelle beautiful. Any man with a pulse would notice Janelle. She was a beauty, sure enough. She was also half Charlie's age. Saint Jude wasn't doing his job too well these days. Charlie swallowed the jealousy that bubbled up. "She thinks you're quite a hunk, too."

Drew looked confused. "Who does?"

"Her name is Janelle."

Drew looked like he was trying not to laugh. "The cook? She's young enough to be my daughter."

Charlie blinked twice, like a befuddled puppy. Drew meant her. It was the closest Drew had come to anything even approaching flirtation, and Charlie couldn't think of a single response. The man was daft, of course. She was plain, at best. But every woman needed to be told she was beautiful, at least once in her life, and it felt good.

She wondered absently what would happen if she walked around the counter and wrapped her arms around Drew, but she remembered the way he'd jumped the last time she touched him, and she decided not to find out.

There was something else, too. Something going on Drew wasn't talking about. She wasn't sure just what, but she meant to find out. She became convinced that there was a bigger problem the day she took Drew to see his parole officer. It was the first day they'd been off the farm together since the trip to Doc Keeler's. The probation office was in Martinsburg. Coincidentally, so was almost everything else in the county.

It seemed like the perfect opportunity to take Drew shopping. He had, to the best of Charlie's accounting, two pair of Levi's, two t-shirts, both athletic gray with pockets, and one old flannel shirt. Drew's underwear situation was even worse. He seemed to own nothing but two pair of socks, both with extra holes.

As soon as she mentioned shopping, however, Drew's armor went up. Charlie felt like she was back to that first day, trying to take him to the hospital.

"I don't need anything," was all he would say.

"I've seen your entire wardrobe," Charlie reminded him. "You need clothes."

"I have everything I need," Drew insisted again. His face had that blank, washed of all expression look.

"Okay," Charlie prompted with a heavy sigh. "Let's hear it."

Drew didn't even turn to face her. He just stared out the truck window at the big old block building. They were in the parking lot of the Feed and Supply. "Could we please just go home?" he insisted, his tone none too friendly.

"Not until you talk to me."

Drew didn't bother to answer. He just wrenched open the door and jumped down out of the truck. He was half a block away before Charlie recovered enough to move. "Where the hell do you think you're going?" she demanded as she pulled up next to him.

"Home," Drew barked tersely.

"Get back in this truck," Charlie ordered.

Drew ignored her, his long legs eating up the concrete sidewalk.

She pulled over half a block ahead of him and got out, standing in the middle of the sidewalk, facing him, feet wide and planted. "In case you're wondering, we're still within shouting distance of the Feed and Supply, so unless you want whoever you didn't want to deal with down there to hear me, you better get back in the goddamn truck."

Drew just stared at Charlie, as if she were some alien life form. Finally, he circled the truck and got back in, slamming the door for good measure. Charlie approached her door with caution, fighting down the urge to scream in frustration. They made the entire ten-mile trip back to the farm without another syllable between them. When she parked, Drew jumped out and headed for the barn. Charlie had to run to catch up with him. She planted herself in his path again, but he just skirted around her.

"Drew!" Charlie shouted at his retreating back. "We have to talk about this!"

"Yes, Sir, Boss, Sir," he answered, and kept walking.

Charlie took a big gulp of warm, dusty air and marched after him toward the barn. She found him in the tack room, slumped on a chair staring at his hands, looking like the world had just grown too heavy to bear. He didn't look up when she sat down across the table from him.

Charlie said nothing, this time. She just waited.

He waited, too. The silence became oppressive.

Finally, she walked around the table and laid a hand on Drew's arm, slowly, so he knew what she was going to do. Charlie wasn't sure what she expected. That Drew would pull away, perhaps. Almost anything except what he did. In one of those faster than the eye could follow moves of his, Drew wrapped his arms around her, yanking her down onto his chair, her breasts smashed flat against his chest as his mouth covered hers in a kiss that was both angry and passionate at the same time.

She kept pushing him. Trying to get inside his head. It was as if she didn't understand how hard he was working to keep himself under control. As if she didn't see what it cost him. She didn't seem to understand how dangerous he was. How vulnerable she was.

Charlie laid her hand on Drew's arm, and that carefully maintained control snapped. What had happened and why, none of that mattered afterward. Nothing else mattered, because Drew wasn't holding Charlie against her will. She wasn't even trying to get away. Her arms struggled free of his, but only to pull him even closer, her hands stroking upward until they tangled in his hair.

Drew tried to regroup, to get his thoughts straight, but Charlie had other ideas. She pulled him back and met him with a kiss that was just as hot and hungry and demanding as his own had been – a kiss that shattered him and rebuilt him on the spot. His hands found their way under her t-shirt, cupping her breasts as his thumbs circled the outline of her nipples. He wasn't sure which one of them was more demanding as he lowered his mouth, her back arching as she pulled his head down toward her chest. His eyes slid shut as his lips closed over one hard, pointed nipple.

He wanted – he needed – more. His right hand slipped lower, cupping her through her jeans, stroking as his breathing became labored.

No. He was moving too fast. It was just the anger, the tension that had been bubbling there between them, it was…

Her fingers laced through his hair, stroking, pushing her hard, greedy nipple against his lips. "God that feels good."

His cock jumped in painful awareness, trying to escape the confinement of his jeans. His hands slid around her waist, pulling her hips against him until he could feel her heat pressed against his throbbing cock.

You must be insane. This is a good way to end up homeless. Even if she doesn't object now, she will afterwards…you know how this will end.

Time to end this insanity, before it was too late. If it wasn't already too late. Drew pulled back a little, letting his hands fall still, just to look at her.

She didn't look angry. Lord, how he wanted to believe it would be all right to follow his body's demands. But he knew better. He couldn't push this. Not now, not ever. If things were going to go any farther, she'd have to take them there…

Charlie just sat there, her knees on either side of Drew's hips, their bodies so close that she could feel the hard, thick length of his rigid cock pressed against her. Her hands stilled in his hair, her eyes searching the depths of his ocean green ones. They weren't angry eyes now. She could see clean through to his soul. There was wonder there, and vulnerability, though he fought to keep it out of sight, but, more importantly, there was need. The need for the touch of a human heart, a human hand. Her heart. Her hand.

"Wow," Charlie managed, her voice little more than a whisper. "I don't know where that came from, but it sure beats the hell out of fighting with you." She leaned forward and kissed him again, slowly, thoroughly, just to be sure. "Oh, yeah," she managed, a little breathless. "Much better than fighting." She ran the tip of her tongue across his lips. "You taste like that wonderful cinnamon stuff you made for breakfast."

If she let her hand slide lower, if she followed her instincts…No. She'd pushed things far enough. His body had responded, but a man didn't have that much to say about that, not at this distance. She'd pushed herself inside his wall of reserve. She wouldn't push any farther. If this was going to go anywhere, he'd have to want it to enough to say so.

"You're the most confusing woman," Drew commented at last, his voice gentle, now. "Don't you know you're supposed to be afraid of me?"

"I'm terrified," Charlie agreed. "Can't you tell?"

"You should be."

"I'm afraid for you," Charlie compromised, "because I know you're afraid, and I don't know why or what of, and you won't let me help you."

"I can't let you help me," Drew corrected. "Do you really think it was an accident, me running into your 'boys' out there in the field, Charlie? I don't tramp around in the pastures at night making myself a target for drunks with a score to settle. I went to meet someone. You brought me the message in a bag of grain. All it said was 'I have information for you about what really happened that night. Meet me in the pasture near the truck stop at midnight.' I knew better, but I went anyway. Sure enough, it was a set-up. Someone wants me dead, or at least out of the way. Someone who has access to that the Feed and Supply. I used to work there. They all know me. They all know where I've been for the last twelve years and why."

"So? If they sent you a note, they already know where you are."

"If I'd gone in there with you today, they'd have all assumed we were together, like a couple. It's hard enough watching my own back. I don't want to put you in danger, too. Right now, you're just the woman I work for. People get the idea we're more than that, you become a target too."

Charlie took her time, digesting his story. It reminded her a little of his paranoia over the computers, which bothered her, because Drew had a valid reason to be paranoid about the computers. She had a feeling that, no matter how far-fetched this sounded, Drew had a reason for the way he was feeling now. "Maybe you better start at the beginning," she suggested.

Drew pulled back, slowly untangling their limbs, and set Charlie on her feet. She leaned against the table as he paced the room, running his hand through his hair as his story unfolded.

"I was married," he explained. "I had a little girl. Her name was Savannah. Darby left me when Savannah was four, took my baby with her. I never really accepted the fact that they were gone, that they weren't coming back. Three and a half years later, Darby was murdered. When Darby died, I went on a drunk. Stayed drunk around the clock for almost two weeks. One night, this local thug came into the bar where I was trying to drink myself to death. Wendell Macey. We all called him Weasel. Weasel came right up to me like he was looking for me. He was laughing. Told me what a..."

Drew stopped, his back to Charlie, staring at the wall for a moment, as if trying to regain control. "Weasel said he'd had sex with my ex-wife, just before he killed her. Said he'd been paid to kill her, but the rape was just his bonus. I grabbed Weasel by the throat and hit him with a right to his temple so hard I felt my hand explode. You know the rest. Twelve years in Moundsville."

"What kind of a God-damned idiot would walk up to a man your size and say 'Hi! Here I am. Hit me!'" Charlie asked in amazement.

Drew turned back to face her now, twelve years of anger glowing behind those expressive green eyes. "Weasel was a thug for hire – the kind of scumbag who would gladly have taken a beating for a few bucks and then testified against me in court for assault and battery. Weasel was an idiot, but he didn't expect to die. He wouldn't have killed Darby unless someone paid him to. Whoever hired Weasel in the first place wanted me out of the way. Weasel's death was just a bonus. Another loose end wrapped up."

Charlie shook her head, not quite following his scenario. "And then what? Simple assault, a barroom brawl, you would have been out in a year or two. Your moneyman had to know you'd come hunt him down. Why take that chance? Why not just kill you?"

"I was kind of popular around here, before. People would have started asking questions. I was supposed to die in prison. I survived five knife attacks and four riots. I heard the price on my head was ten thousand dollars. Men in prison will kill you for a fucking pack of cigarettes."

Those scars, Charlie thought. She'd thought they looked like knife wounds. "Did you hear who was supposed to pay this reward?" she asked.

"No. There was never any name. Just the rumor. Then one day they called me before the parole board. I wasn't even supposed to be eligible for another two years. Six weeks later I was on a bus headed for Hagerstown, but when I got there, there was no one waiting to pick me up. I figured it was a setup. I expected to be arrested before I crossed the state line, so I waited until dark to start walking, and I went the long way around, through Shepherdstown. Figured that was the last place they'd look. I thought I would be safe once I made it here. Then I found that note in the feed bag."

Charlie chewed her bottom lip thoughtfully, trying to absorb it all. "You have any theories as to who was behind all this?"

"Oh, yeah," Drew assured her.

"You want to share them with me?"

"You'll think I'm crazy -if you don't all ready."

"Try me," Charlie encouraged dryly.

"Bob Waite, the county sheriff." Drew spat the name out with distaste, as if the mere feel of the man's name on his tongue soured his mouth.

To Serve and Protect. Right. Charlie stared at Drew, wondering if he really was crazy. "Why would the Sheriff want to kill you?"

"Bob Waite has hated me since we were kids, and I've never known why. I'm just trying to stay out of his way. I don't want to violate my parole, and I don't want to end up dead. And I sure as hell don't want you hurt."

Charlie stared up at him, trying to read his eyes. "So you're just going to wait around until he tries to kill you again?"

"You got any better ideas?"

"Yeah," she echoed. "Oh, yeah."

Chapter Six

"You still haven't slept with him?"

Charlie slammed the dishes into the racks. "What on earth makes you think I'm even considering a relationship with Andrew Bailey?" It was early Friday morning and they were the only ones left on duty.

"Who said anything about a relationship?" Janelle demanded. "I'm talking about sex. What's wrong with you? I've seen the way Drew looks at you. You're both single. He's gorgeous. You know damn good and well he hasn't been with a woman for at least twelve years. You said he's a great kisser. Who needs more reason than that? You keep bitching about wanting to get laid. You got any better offers you're not telling me about?"

"Why not?" Silverware clattered into the drainer. "Andrew Bailey is an ex-con with a bad attitude. He was in prison for manslaughter, Janelle. Not grand theft auto, you know? He could break me in half if he wanted to. I have to be insane letting him stay around. And you want me to have sex with him? Just because he's handy? I'm not that desperate!"

"Yeah, right." Janelle shook her head, laughing as she disappeared back into the kitchen. "You just keep telling yourself that. Maybe after a while you'll even believe it."

Charlie repeated it like a litany. She couldn't afford another relationship like the last one. She didn't need to get involved with this man.

But the feel of his hands was branded into her skin. The heat of his thick, rigid cock so close to where she wanted him lingered into her dreams, haunting her, teasing her, until she could barely manage to get any sleep. As for the other point Janelle had made, although Charlie certainly didn't say so out loud, she hadn't had any other offers at all, except for a few overly flirtatious customers, which she certainly didn't take seriously.

If it hadn't been for Drew, and the way he kept popping into the truck stop, even after the episode in the barn, Charlie might have spent a few more disquieting moments in front of the mirror, worrying that she was beginning to show her age.

Age was another subject Charlie surely wasn't going to discuss with a twenty-one-year-old girl. Janelle would have laughed at her anyway, the way she did whenever Charlie insisted she wasn't interested in Drew.

Now that he wasn't hiding from her, Drew had taken to working shirtless in the heat of the noonday sun as he dangled from a rope harness, hauling boards for the barn repairs up with a pulley system. She would watch him from her bedroom window when she was supposed to be asleep, admiring the bulge of his muscles as he attacked the ancient barn. The sight did nothing to improve her sleep.

If she could see him out the window, he could see her. She thought about it, remembered the times she'd undressed without pulling the curtains, thought about doing it again, deliberately this time. But what if she did, what if he watched, and still nothing happened? Maybe he hadn't come to her because he didn't want to. Any man would respond, when you were in his arms and he was angry. But that didn't mean he found her attractive.

That didn't mean he wanted anything more than what they had.

She couldn't even flirt with Drew, let alone seduce him. She held too much power over him – his home and his job and even his freedom. She couldn't push this any farther than *he* wanted it to go. He had to make the first move. And there was still all that anger, just under the surface. Drew hid it better now, but it was still there, and so far her attempts to solve the mysteries of his past had raised more questions than answers. Charlie knew he hadn't told her everything yet. He'd tell her when he was ready to trust her.

But it made her edgy, having him so near, so close, and yet farther away than he'd been before. It was as if, after the tack room, he'd retreated even farther into his shell. As for Charlie, what went on in her mind was her own business. Even a divorced woman over forty had the right to her dreams.

The mysteries of Drew's past became Charlie's obsession. She didn't want to involve any of her contacts from the Agency unless she had to. She sent discrete e-mails to friends she trusted, including her brother Jamie. Jamie had friends – friends he wasn't supposed to have, perhaps, but useful friends. He had the kind of friends who had done their best to help keep the publicity down about Charlie's little shooting incident.

Charlie sent out a list of names – Bob Waite, Wendell "Weasel" Macey, Darby Anne Bailey, and, though she hesitated, Andrew Bailey, himself. She had the feeling that whatever Drew wasn't telling her might be very important.

Drew never brought his suspicions about the fight in the back pasture up again, but Charlie knew it was never far from his mind. She'd catch him, staring out the window, miles away. They talked, but never about his fears, and never about the fight in the barn, or the things they'd done or hadn't done.

But she thought about it. Thought about that fight often, and wondered what would have happened if she'd let her hands drop just a little lower, touching him where she'd wanted to touch…run her hands over the soft, worn denim until she held him cupped in her hands, feeling the heat of his cock spreading through her, igniting her until she nearly burst into flames, until she slid off his knees to unbutton the stud on his jeans…

She thought about it, and she felt herself getting more and more frustrated. It hadn't been like this with Allen. Even when they'd been together, she hadn't wanted him. Not like this. Not with this kind of desperate urgency that threatened to drive her over the edge of sanity.

It was working on Drew as well. She was sure it was. She could see the temper in his body language, in the way his eyes snapped to her when she spoke, in the way he watched her when he thought she wasn't looking. He was becoming bolder, as well, letting her know that he thought she should turn down the double shifts at Harry's, but she'd never been good at saying no. Harry had a hard time keeping help. Besides, the overnight truckers tipped well. They were tired and grumpy, but they tipped well.

She couldn't sleep without dreaming of him, but the dreams didn't relax her. They served only to heighten the tension that ripped though her. Charlie tried to avoid the mirrors, but she knew there were little lines around her eyes, now, and dark circles under them most of the time. She fell asleep at the table less than two weeks after their 'fight.' She came awake with a start just as Drew plucked her favorite coffee cup out of her hand. It had been about to slip from her fingers. Charlie jumped to her feet as she snatched the cup back up, gulping at the coffee, burning her mouth.

Drew's eyes flashed like sun off a mirror. Charlie paced the kitchen warily, knowing what was coming.

"Why are you working at the truck stop?"

"It's my job."

"You didn't buy this place and work your butt off to make it what it is so you could spend every waking moment working at that damn truck stop for an asshole like Harry Schlotz. You're working two waitresses' shifts."

Charlie felt the fires of rage growing like living things within her. "This isn't about Harry, is it?"

Drew tossed a towel at the sink with a frustrated sigh. "Doc Keeler came by this morning."

Keeler. Damn him. Charlie should have noticed, the last of the bandages were gone, and Drew's arm showed white and scrubbed where they had been. "I'm glad he came by," Charlie offered cautiously. "How's your arm?"

"Fine. I'm fine. Doc said I've used the arm enough to keep the muscle tone good. I can do anything that doesn't hurt. He gave me a clean bill of health."

"And you're pissed off about that?"

"I'm not pissed off about anything."

"Right. So what else happened?"

"I told Doc I owed him."

Drew's eyes reminded Charlie of sparklers at summer picnics with her nephews. Pretty, but you had to be careful or you could get burned. Well, if he wasn't careful, he'd be the one getting burned.

"I told him I expected him to hand me a bill, just like he would any of his other customers. It might take me a while to pay it, but I would. Somehow, Keeler seemed to think you'd already paid that debt, and several others. So I asked him what you'd done for him."

An angry flush climbed Charlie's face. She really hated to have to justify herself. "Your average ninth grader could have designed a computer system to do what Doc wanted it to do."

"Maybe so," Drew agreed. "But you don't work like a ninth grader. You work like a professional. You impressed Doc, and his description impressed me. So I logged on the Internet and did a little snooping. Thought maybe there were a few things I ought to know about you."

Charlie didn't even know Drew knew how to turn a computer on, much less how to figure out her password. She set her cup down carefully on the table, ramming her hands into her pockets. "Find anything interesting?"

Drew's voice was an accusation. "I found a copy of your resume."

Resume? Great. Just great. Nice piece of work, guys.

Drew's voice gentled. "Why are you working at Harry's, Charlie?"

Charlie stopped her pacing, her eyes hot enough to have proved a warning to anyone who knew her well. "You want to know what my life was like? I worked sixteen-hour days then, too, more, when the situation called for it. I couldn't talk about my work to anyone. I still can't. I traveled a great deal. Sometimes I'd be out of the country for months at a time. I went wherever the Agency sent me, for as long as they wanted me. My last assignment was in San Diego. I was there for seven months. I came home on every three day holiday weekend."

And she'd dreaded even those three days, toward the end. They'd spent more time fighting than making up. Well, it looked like she was heading for the same place again.

"I'm not asking you go back to work for this *Agency*, whatever the hell that is, Charlie. I'm not asking you to do anything. I'm just saying, you don't have to work for Harry. You know computers. You could work anywhere, freelance. You wouldn't need to take any job you didn't want to. City Hospital's called you four times. I figured you must owe them money. But you don't, do you?"

Drew's eyes tried to meet with hers, but it was too late. She ignored him, staring off into the dust motes near the window, her shoulders rigid.

"There are a dozen offers in the e-mail that you've been ignoring. People pleading for your help, desperate to pay you to solve their problems. Some of them are even relatively local. Any one of those offers will pay more in a few months than you'll make at Harry's in a year."

Charlie felt her last line of defense eroding as the anger surged up past her control. "You read my e-mail?"

"Yes, I did. I see you getting more worn out by the day, and I feel responsible. Something's got to change, Charlie. You're killing yourself."

"You're sure as hell right. My password."

Drew stepped in closer, his sheer size overshadowing her, his knuckles white where he gripped his coffee cup. "I'm an ex-con, Charlie. I just got out of prison. Prison, remember? It's amazing the kind of people you meet there, and the things you can learn."

He had her boxed in, a chair blocking her way back around the table. "I didn't think you were a choir boy," Charlie countered, "But I didn't expect you to read my fucking e-mail, either."

Drew's jaws clenched, and Charlie thought he was going to crawl off and sulk, but he didn't back down. "You're thirty-seven years old and waitressing in a run down dive of a truck stop for $2.05 an hour plus tips. What's wrong with this picture?"

"It's none of your goddamned business!" Charlie kicked the chair out of the way as she backed away from him. "Stay out of my personal life!"

He'd be leaving in another few minutes anyway. Drew would throw his things in that old duffel bag and hit the road again. No man had ever stuck around once she lost her temper.

Instead, he moved to block her path again, quicker than she'd thought such a big man could possibly move. Drew's voice was soft and low, gentle despite Charlie's anger. He touched her. His hands on her shoulders were not forceful, yet he radiated raw masculine power, and frustration, perhaps, but not the anger Charlie expected. "This is my business. You made it my business out there in that field. I owe you my life, Charlie. I won't see you kill yourself trying to support me." His calm, reasonable tone infuriated Charlie even more. The man couldn't even fight the way she expected him to.

"You think that earned you the right to tell me what to do?" Charlie tried to push him away, but it was like pushing against a stone wall. "You arrogant bastard. Get out!" she screeched. "Get the fuck out of my life!"

Drew held her, staring into her eyes. "You don't mean that."

Charlie stamped down hard on his instep, twisting free of his grip as he stepped back in surprise. "Get out. Now!"

Drew let his hands drop slowly back to his sides, but his eyes never left Charlie's. He waited, for what seemed an eternity, before his eyes went dead, and he turned and walked away.

Charlie spun to face the wall. *I'll be here until you tell me to leave.* Behind her, Charlie heard the kitchen door bang shut. She wanted to run after him, call him back, but it was too late. It had been too late since that first time she'd reached out to touch him and he'd pulled away. She needed a good, stiff drink. Then perhaps she would sleep.

There was a decanter of brandy in the living room.

But her knees wouldn't carry her that far. She sank to the floor beside the stairs, sobbing uncontrollably. For once, she'd gotten exactly what she asked for from a man. This time it would destroy her. Because she couldn't hurt like this unless she was falling in love.

She was a fool.

Anyone that stupid deserved whatever she got.

* * * * *

Drew made it out the kitchen door before the pain hit him, way down low, like a shiv to the gut. This was no way to end things. No way at all. He'd known all along there was no room in Charlie's life for a man like him. He just hadn't been able to convince his heart.

Ghost appeared, bounding up out of nowhere as he usually did, and jumped up to lick Drew's face. "You love me, don't you, old boy." Drew gently removed the muddy paws from his chest. A dog would always love you, no matter what you did. A dog would always forgive you.

Drew gave the big dog a final pat, letting his eyes survey the rolling hills around him. Not so long ago, Drew had been furious to learn he'd lost this place. Now he knew the place meant nothing without the woman.

Things had been going so well. For the first time in years, he'd felt like he was part of something, like he mattered. But he'd pushed her too far.

He'd blown it the moment he touched her.

Idiot. Thinking with your dick instead of your brain. Got you just as far as it did last time, didn't it?

He had invaded her privacy. He'd stepped over the line. He'd read too much into that kiss back in the barn. Maybe, if he apologized...if he could just make her understand...

Drew turned resolutely, determined to face her wrath and see it through.

He found Charlie beside the stairs, curled on the floor now like a child, bawling her eyes out. The little speech he'd planned got lost as he reached out to lay a hand on her shoulder. "Charlie? I'm sorry, Charlie. Don't cry. Please don't cry."

Charlie sprang to her feet as she jerked away from him. "Don't touch me! If you ever put your hands on me again, I swear I will fucking kill you."

There was something so wild in her eyes he was almost afraid of her. Of what she might do, if not to him, then to herself. Drew held out his hands, shoulder high and palms up. "Okay, Charlie. I'm sorry. I didn't mean to frighten you. I swear I'd never hurt you. You know that. Think about it Charlie. I'm not a violent man. You know that much about me. I'm not going to hurt you."

"I thought I told you to leave!"

"You did." Drew did his best to sound agreeable. "I tried, Charlie. I really tried, but I didn't get very far. I don't want to leave, Charlie. I don't want to leave you."

"I don't care what you want. Get out! Just go away!"

"You don't mean that. Not really. You're just scared, Charlie. We can make it through this."

"I'm not scared," Charlie spat at him. "You don't know anything. You couldn't possibly understand."

He managed to stay out of her way as she tried to stomp on his foot again, but as fast as he was he couldn't dodge both of her fists. He caught the right, pinning her hand within his, but she managed to land a hard left to the chest, nearly knocking the wind out of him, before he captured her other hand.

"Okay. You're going to have to listen to me before I let you go." But he reckoned without her feet kicking him hard in the shins as he lifted her clear of the floor, or her angry mouth lunging at him, teeth bared.

That was too much. He dropped to the floor, rolling with her till he held her pinned, his weight laying over the length of her hard, muscular body, immobilizing as much of her as possible.

He met her angry, wicked mouth with his own, capturing her lip between his teeth, then holding it while her eyes calmed, cleared, focused on his.

Oh, shit.

This was a really, really stupid thing to do.

His lips trembled as he kissed her, fear warring with anger and need. He drew his knee up, slowly, caressing her bare thigh as the uniform skirt slid out of the way, teasing her legs apart, until he could feel the warm, moist heat of her, already wanting.

No.

No, whatever he felt or thought he felt, she'd been ready to kill him moments before. She didn't want – couldn't...

"Bastard." Her voice was soft, and a little breathless.

"I'm sorry, Charlie. God as my witness, I'd never hurt you. Never. I—"

She kicked him, hard, and he released her hands to guard his balls as she brought her knee up, trying to block her blow. With a strength that surprised him she shoved him back, rolling until she was on top, her skirt riding high on her hips, her heat pressed against his aching cock, her breasts smashed against his chest, her hands tangled in his hair, yanking his mouth back to hers.

She bit him, hard, on the lip as she ground against him, riding the bulge his jeans did so little to contain, then she claimed his mouth, licking and biting and plundering like a wild animal until he could barely think.

Her uniform shirt shredded under his hands, and her bra lost a hook as he freed her, groaning as she spilled into his hands, full and round, with stiff, hard nipples growing tighter at his touch. She arched back over him, allowing him full access to her heavy, needy breasts. "Charlie," he breathed. "Do you have any idea what you're doing to me?" He swallowed hard. "You're trying to drive me insane, aren't you? Is this your revenge? Break my mind, and then toss me out again?"

Her hands reached for the waistband of his jeans, fighting with the old metal stud, then jerking the waistband over the stud when it didn't obey her quickly enough. He groaned as she yanked at his jeans, pushing away from the floor enough to allow her room to pull them down over his hips. "What I do to you?" She stroked the hot, hard, wanting length of him, her touch nearly unmanning him. "What I do to you? You drive me insane, then you go out of your way not to even *touch* me, and you want to know if I'm trying to kill you?"

She wrapped both hands around his cock, pushing the tip against the already soaked crotch of her panties. He surged up off the floor, rolling her nipples hard between his fingers, kneading her breasts in rhythm to her hands.

He wanted to close his eyes and take her, right then and there, to just fuck her until she had no thought of anything but him, branding her with his seed until words like "get out" were permanently lost to her vocabulary.

Too much. It was too much. He wrestled with her, rolling until he was over her again. Drew held her hands pinned next to her head, his breathing ragged, like a horse after a wild run. "Not like this, Charlie. I want to be able to look you in the eyes tomorrow and know you don't hate me. We have to slow down and think."

"The hell with thinking. You've had months to do that."

"Don't you understand, Charlie? I spent twelve years learning not to take anything for granted. I wanted to earn the right to be here. The right to touch you like this. I have to know I didn't push you somewhere you didn't want to go."

"I have to tell you it's all right to *touch* me? You're here, Drew. I'm here. What are you afraid of?"

Get off me! You're hurting me! Drew struggled to push the voice from his mind. "You're so tiny," he whispered. "I'll hurt you."

"I'm not tiny!" she insisted, her damp eyes flashing. "You can't hurt me, Drew."

She strained to reach his lips, but he stayed just out of reach, trying to find his equilibrium.

"Drew, I'm not going to break. And I'm not going to change my mind. I want you. I want to feel. I want you inside me." She fought to reach any part of his body she could bite or lick. "Fuck me, you idiot."

He was an idiot. He'd thought she wanted romance. This was just about sex. He wasn't anything special to her. He was just handy. She—

And then he forgot what he was objecting to as her fingers locked with his and she thrust up against him, only one piece of thin, sheer fabric between his cock and what he wanted, what he needed, what his body demanded.

Hell. He'd never been anything special to anyone. Why should this be any different? She was willing enough. To hell with romance. He'd lived without that all of his life. The sheer fabric of her panties parted under his impatient hands. She cried out in greedy pleasure as he pushed into her.

She was right. They fit together just fine. He kept his eyes on hers as he thrust into her again and again, anger and need and desperation setting a pace that was hot and furious.

Charlie pulled at him, her nails raking his hips as she rose up to meet him, her pace as hard and raw and demanding as his own. He slowed, deliberately, watching her eyes darken and her face flush as she tried to push him faster, finding redemption in her moans of desperation as she wrapped her legs around his waist. She clung to him, seeking to pull him deeper into her, jerking against him with a need that was impossible to deny.

He nearly broke as he felt her tighten around him, nearly lost what little control he still possessed, and then she was over him, on top again as she rode him hard, a race horse toward the finish line, her hands stroking his chest as her tongue licked and sucked, her breasts flattened between them.

"Still mad at me?" he managed.

She laughed as she shattered around him. "Yeah," she assured him breathlessly. "You can apologize again – later."

"Later," he groaned as he emptied himself into her.

It seemed like hours before he could move again. When he had the strength to raise his hand, Drew gently pushed the hair away from Charlie's face, struggling to think of the right words to say.

Women expected that. Needed to hear the words.

But this one wasn't listening.

Charlie was asleep. She lay curled on his chest like a sleeping kitten, a contented smile resting on her lips.

The hallway light was still on. It lit her hair a warm summer sunset red. Drew brought a handful to his face, breathing in the scent of it like an exotic flower. Sweet. Spicy. Clean.

All the things he'd been afraid of seemed pointless. It might be just sex, but this was still Charlie. She wanted him. At least for the moment. If, somewhere in his heart, he still dared to hope for more, he kept his thoughts to himself.

* * * * *

"Hey."

Drew kissed the top of her head. "Hi there. Welcome back."

"Put me down. I can walk. This has got to be bad for your back."

He kissed her nose as he turned to keep her feet from hitting the banister on the landing. "You don't weigh any more than a bag of grain."

"Do so. One-twelve." She pressed her face against his chest, hoping he couldn't see through the lie.

"Yeah, right."

"Damn, let a man have sex with you once and he starts getting pushy."

"You're damn right." He pushed the fear into the background, trying to sound as self-confident as if he'd done things like this every day. "We're gonna work on this, Charlie. Together. More sleep. Less coffee. More food."

She reached out with the arm that wasn't wrapped around his neck to open her bedroom door. "More sex?"

"Any time," he murmured against her neck.

He carried her to the edge of the bed. Charlie slid down his body without actually letting go of him. "Drew?"

The ache claimed him again, filling him with the need to touch her. It was just sex, he reminded himself. She didn't need him. Not the way he needed her. He held her tightly against the length of him, as if he could somehow keep the cold hard reality out. "Charlie?"

"I'm really sorry I punched you."

He wanted to laugh with relief, but he wasn't sure it was time just yet. "You pack a hell of a left."

"I don't lose my temper often. I'm not a violent person. Really."

"I know that, Charlie. And I'm sorry I stuck my nose where it had no business being. What you do with your life is your business."

"No. You're right. I did make it your business. I asked you to stay, and I wanted you to be more than just hired help, but I never bothered to try to talk to you. Not about the things that matter."

"You don't have to talk about it, Charlie. I understand." One hand rested on her shoulder. The other one brushed back the hair from her face, caressing lightly, reassuring her. "It doesn't matter what you do. I'm not going to leave you, Charlie."

"How can you promise me that?" Charlie demanded, mesmerized by his soft, throaty voice. She wanted to believe him. How she wanted to believe him.

"Where would I go, Charlie? When you're homeless, people walk by you on the street, and they don't see you. If you die, they don't even bury you. Did you know that? If nobody claims your body, you get sold to some medical school. That's where I was headed. A cadaver on a steel table at West Virginia University. My own daughter could have taken a knife to me, and never known. The only reason I'm not there is because of you. Because you refused to look through me. Because you gave me a dry jacket and a hot meal, and when I followed you home, you didn't call the cops. I prayed that maybe, just maybe, if I worked real hard, you might let me stay. I never even dared to dream you'd find out and still want me here."

Drew's hands framed her face, tilting her head up to meet his eyes. "How could I walk away from you, Charlie? Why would I want to? I'm here, Charlie. I'm not going to run out on you. Trust me. I'll be here."

Charlie took her time answering. "I was married."

"I know, Charlie. I know about Allen. You don't have to talk about it if you don't want to."

How could he...He'd found the article that had run in the Post. Of course. She'd scanned it and saved it to the hard drive. Charlie swallowed hard. "You don't know. Not everything. It was all about money. That's all I was to him. Allen – Allen was a writer. She was his research assistant. I paid her salary. She was seventeen. Not even out of high school."

Drew's hands stroked her back, in small, comforting circles. "I'd never do that to you, Charlie."

"Everyone leaves me eventually," Charlie reasoned.

"I'm not going anywhere," Drew promised again.

"I have a nasty temper."

"And a .25 semi-automatic. But you don't need to use a pistol on me, Charlie," Drew promised. "All you have to do is tell me what you want. But don't ask me to walk away from you again, because I don't think I can do that."

Charlie's hands found their way to the back of Drew's head, pulling him within reach of her hungry mouth. Drew held back a little, his eyes hesitant. She answered his hesitancy with her lips, hot against his, her tongue demanding entrance, plundering when his lips parted, tasting, savoring, while her hands raked through his hair, and her breasts crushed against his chest, stirred by the friction of their embrace to hard, needy peeks. She watched his carefully maintained control collapse at last, until they were wolves at a kill, no longer tasting, devouring now, feasting with wanton abandon. "I want you."

He stepped back, holding her at arm's length. "Charlie, listen a minute. We need to slow down. I'm sorry. I wasn't thinking too straight earlier. We didn't – I didn't use anything. For protection. It's not the sixties anymore. I should have thought to buy something over at the truck stop, but I wasn't planning on this. I'm not prepared..."

Charlie licked her suddenly dry lips, staring up at him as understanding crept into her brain. Oh God. She'd heard about what happened to men in prison...and Drew knew Allen had cheated on her. "I never cheated on Allen, not once, even after I suspected he had other women. And I had myself tested, after I...after we separated. I was scared. I knew too much about Allen's tastes. I'd never asked before. Nobody talked about AIDS when we got married. I'm safe."

Drew met her gaze steadily. "There's been no one. No woman. No man. Not since I was twenty-one. Even before that, there was only Darby. I was tested in prison, when I got stabbed, to protect the health care workers. I'm clean."

Only one woman, a long time ago. Drew didn't have much to compare her to. Maybe, just maybe, she would be enough to satisfy him, at least for while.

Drew didn't let her go. "What about..." She watched him swallow, watched his eyes waver, then return to hers. "What about babies? You might get pregnant."

Yeah. That would bother him. He'd been there already. Charlie took a deep breath. "I wish I could. I always wanted a little girl. But it's too late."

Drew blinked slowly, like an owl. "Too late?"

Charlie was the one to look away this time. "I'm forty-four, Drew."

"You lied on your resume."

"I didn't write that resume. I've never even seen it." Charlie met his eyes, wondering how to make him understand. "Forty-four, Drew. I'm the older woman, seducing the handsome younger man. What will people say?"

"It isn't anyone's business, is it, Charlie?"

"What I'm trying to say is, this morning was great, but you don't have to...I mean, you don't owe me anything. We don't have to do this, if you don't want to."

"I've wanted you since the first time you touched me." He leaned in to claim her mouth again. Charlie surrendered to the taste of him, the power of the arms that held her. He was strong, yes, but his physical strength was nothing compared to the power of desire that held her there. Still, he held back.

Her hands moved to cover his, caressing his fingers. "Make love to me, Drew. I want you to make love to me."

"Well. That's different, isn't it?" Drew let his fingers slide down her arms, caressing her skin along the way. His eyes never left hers as he freed her hair from the band that held the braid in place, letting the heavy mass escape its restraint. His breath caught as it tumbled free. "That takes a little more time than just 'Fuck me.'"

"That was fun, Drew, and just what I needed, but I want more from you. I want everything."

Hands buried in her hair, Drew leaned in to take her lip between his teeth, sucking, probing gently with his tongue as her mouth opened under his. "I've wanted to do this since the first time I saw you. You are so beautiful. I'm going to wake up any minute now and find out you're just a dream."

Charlie ran her fingers through his hair, and he shivered at her touch. "I'm far from beautiful, but I'm real, Drew. I'm real, and I want you."

Drew released her so that he could strip out of his Levi's, but Charlie stopped him. She lifted his hands away from the metal stud at his waist.

"Let me do this."

Drew looked up quickly, surprise easy to read in his eyes, but he didn't object. Charlie pushed him back against the edge of the bed, remembering a scene in one of Allen's books. She'd been curious ever since she'd read that passage. Allen's character had undressed the hero using just her teeth. Charlie wanted to know if it could really be done.

It was time consuming. And the longer it took, the more she thought she might burst into flames from the wanting of him. The shirt buttons weren't too difficult, though the thread broke on one of them. She pulled the shirt open, dragging it free of the waistband of his jeans, sliding it back off his shoulders.

Her tongue paused to trace the outline of one small, hard nipple, enjoying the way his breathing shuddered to a halt, then pulled in with a gasp as she sucked hard on the tender bud. So much skin to savor. She kissed her way down his chest, brushing her lips along the angry scar that ran through his breastbone, enjoying the way he shivered at her touch. So far, everything was working just the way it was supposed to. His jeans, however, were another matter. Drew's breath hissed in sharply as Charlie lowered her mouth to the metal stud at the waistband.

The stud took forever. Every time Charlie got one side through the buttonhole, it would spin around and slip back before she could get the other side undone. Drew's hands clutched at her shoulders.

"You're still pissed at me, aren't you. You really are trying to kill me."

"This won't kill you. Be patient."

"I am being patient," Drew informed her. "But I don't know how much more I can take. There is an easier way to do that."

"How?" Charlie muttered around her teeth, ready to consider all options.

"With your fingers."

Charlie snorted with irritation. "I'm on a mission," she pointed out, returning to her task. With a growl of frustration, Charlie changed her hold to the end of the waistband and yanked. The old rivet broke, and the stud flew across the bedroom.

The zipper pull was just too much. Long before she had it even half way down, Drew was groaning, straining for control, his hands tangled in her hair. He thrust against her as she struggled to keep her hold on the tiny metal tab.

"Hold still!" Charlie admonished through clenched teeth.

"I'm trying," he hissed.

At last, she managed to get the zipper undone, freeing his cock with one swift tug on the waistband of the jeans. He spilled out, eager for her touch. She'd been in too much of a hurry to really look earlier. She took the time now, her breath catching as she admired him. His cock was as long and thick as she'd imagined, fulfilling the promise of that outline below the sheet so long ago to perfection. She could tell from the way he watched her that he was worried, still thinking she'd run at the sight of him naked before her, so she stopped long enough to let him see the truth in her eyes. She smiled as she looked up at him. "You're beautiful. I could just look at you for a very long time."

"You're daft, woman. I'm big and scary looking, remember? You're supposed to be afraid of me."

"Right," Charlie agreed. "I'll try to remember." She ran her hands around his waist, then over the hard, tightly clenched muscles of his hips, shoving the jeans out of her way as she pulled him towards her. Slowly, with more wonder than practiced skill, Charlie kissed the hot, hard length of his cock, marveling at the way he jumped when she ran her tongue over the sensitive tip, tasting the first drops of release that leaked into her mouth. His hands buried in her hair, fisting before he forced them to relax. Relentless, she licked and sucked until Drew's legs would no longer support him.

"Good God, woman, you really are trying to break me."

Charlie laughed as she pushed him back onto the bed. She stood before Drew, naked, her hair a wild mass tumbled around her face, afire from the morning light leaking in around the curtains.

She climbed up onto the huge four-poster bed, straddling his hips, looking down into emerald eyes that glittered with passion now. "I want you," she told him again as she linked her fingers through his. She brushed against his cock, her eyes dancing with laughter. "Right here, right now."

Drew held his breath as she slid over him slowly, very slowly, easing carefully onto his rigid length. The pleasure was so intense that it was almost painful. Charlie stayed there, unmoving, long enough for Drew to relax just a little.

Drew grasped her hips in a hold of fierce possession. His voice sounded alien, hoarse, ragged. "I'll be here for you, Charlie. I'm not going anywhere. You can do whatever you want with me. Whenever you want. I'm yours."

I love you, he wanted to say. But she hadn't asked for that, and he knew it would dangle there in the air between them, harsh, unexpected, unwelcome. Drew swallowed the words and pulled Charlie down to kiss her instead. She tasted like some exotic spice from the orient. Sweet. Subtle. Addictive.

Slick, wet heat clenched around him, promising, demanding. Charlie rocked up on her knees, leaving him feeling naked and exposed, then enveloped him again, riding him hard and fast, like she was breaking a young horse to saddle. Drew couldn't get enough of her – the taste of her – the smell of her – he thrust up to meet her, stroke for stroke, driving into her with a need that was as primitive as any ancient mating ritual. His hands stroked over her skin, pulling her down harder against his aching cock, reaching desperately for release.

The feel of her soft skin against his hands teased him, multiplying the aching need. Never, not even in his wildest fantasies, had it been like this. This was nothing like the first time. That had been wild and angry and greedy. This was slow and delicious and building with every thrust until she threatened to consume him, and he knew that no matter what he did, it wouldn't be enough. Now that he'd touched her, he would never be satisfied with less than everything. Her pace increased to a wild frenzy as she crashed down into him, demanding, taking. Long before Drew was sated he felt Charlie convulse around him, watched her stiffen, arching backwards with a triumphant cry.

Drew tried to mask his disappointment as he let his hands trail down her hips until they rested on her knees. He tried to content himself with the feel of her muscles, still convulsing around him, the taste of her skin, the closeness of her body, so lithe and fit, like a dancer.

When Charlie could catch her breath again, she rocked back forward, laughing softly as she bent down to kiss him, grinding her breasts in hypnotic circles against the damp skin of his chest. He surged up hard within her as her nipples raked over him. She dug her fingers into his shoulders as she began the dance again, more slowly this time.

Charlie guided Drew's hands to her breasts, and he felt her little moan of pleasure when his thumb brushed lightly over one nipple. He reached for her, straining until he captured the other dusky pink tip in a kiss of rapt devotion.

The feel of his teeth nipping gently on her breast tore a cry of pure pleasure from Charlie's throat. When she soared over the peak this time, Drew wasn't far behind.

Chapter Seven

Charlie stretched a languid cat stretch, reluctant to wake up, too comfortable and contented to give up her dream world. In that world, she shared her bed with a man who worshipped her with his hands, who taught her how to make love all over again, as if she were exploring her body as well as his for the very first time.

It was just another dream.

With a sigh, Charlie rolled over to look at the clock. It was quarter after six. She swore as she threw back the sheet and rolled to her feet. Reality was waking up alone and late for work. The combination didn't put her in the best of moods. Charlie hated being late for work. She was never late for work. Never.

Charlie made it halfway down the hall headed for the shower before she woke up enough to realize she was naked. She always slept in an oversized t-shirt. Had since she went away to college. But this evening she was naked.

She was also stiff and sore and feeling a little bruised in a few places. She searched her memory for things she could be certain of. She'd gotten off work at 8:00 AM. She'd come home exhausted. Charlie remembered sitting down at the kitchen table, too tired to even change out of her uniform.

She'd fallen asleep at the table. They'd had a fight. Charlie went hot and then cold as she remembered the sound of the doors banging shut behind Drew. First the back door, then the screen door, like two shotgun blasts to her heart.

But Drew had come back. Charlie turned the shower on and let the hot water melt the stiffness from her joints. Memories of the morning came flooding in now. Charlie supposed she should have been embarrassed by some of the things she'd done, but instead she felt alive, whole for the first time in years.

A little smirk of a smile chased across Charlie's face. Allen could have gained enough inspiration for a whole book from this morning's little adventure.

This morning had been worth being late for work.

She must have forgotten to set the alarm. She'd been a little distracted by the time they finally made it up the stairs. One thing she was sure of. Drew certainly hadn't found her uninspirational. Drew seemed fascinated with all the colors in her hair, even the silver streaks. Apparently Drew didn't think her breasts were too small or her hips too flat.

Charlie ran her fingers over the places Drew had touched, smiling again as she remembered the feel of his hands on her skin. If she'd known sex could be so much fun, she'd certainly never have lived so much of her life without it.

Her heart rate jumped when she caught a shadow of movement at the open bathroom door. She dashed the soap from her eyes and peered though the translucent shower curtain to see Drew settle into the doorway, nursing a cup of coffee as he rested his lean frame against one shoulder, apparently content just to watch her.

"Funny thing," Charlie commented over the splash of the water. "My alarm never went off."

"Guilty," Drew replied without moving. His voice sounded hesitant, unsure of himself. "I turned it off." He took another sip of coffee. Charlie wondered whether he wanted it, or just needed something to do with his hands. Drew was definitely nervous – nervous as a virgin, the morning after. Charlie almost laughed. A silly grin pulled at her face. There was a power in this – a delicious triumph in owning a man's soul.

The current between them seemed to energize her on contact. She stood there under the water for a few minutes longer, running the soap over her breasts in a deliberate fashion before turned toward him fully and opening the shower curtain.

Drew took a good, long look, his breath hissing in sharply. "I woke up alone and I'm late for work." Charlie crossed the room without regard to the trail of water and shampoo she left behind. "There better be a good reason."

"You're off tonight." Drew swallowed hard. Twice. "I told Harry you weren't feeling well."

"Funny. I can't remember ever feeling better." Charlie took the coffee cup from his hands and set it on the vanity. Stormy gray eyes met hers, searching. Charlie slid her hands under the worn flannel of his shirt to run her damp palms across his chest. She could feel Drew's heart hammering against his ribs. "You okay?"

Drew snorted. "I've been pacing like a cat for the last two hours, waiting for you to wake up. If you hadn't gotten out of bed soon, I might have had to wake you up, just to keep from going crazy."

Charlie rather liked that idea. "Why were you so nervous?" she teased as she bent her head to lick the water off where it fell on his chest.

His breath drew in hard and held a moment as her tongue circled his nipple. "I was afraid you might change your mind when you woke up."

"Yeah, I'm like that." Charlie teased her way around the nipple, circling, then darting her tongue across the tip. "I'd screw you in the morning then tell you to pack your bags when I woke up again."

"You were so tired, Charlie. I took advantage of that. Caught you with your guard down." His hands slid down over her wet, naked skin, pulling her tightly against his chest.

"Right. So I think you should take advantage of me again." She slid her hands inside his Levi's at the back, pulling his hips tighter against her. She could have sworn he'd forgotten to breathe. Sliding her hands back around to the front, she unzipped his jeans and let them drop off his hips. "Do you actually own any underwear?"

His laughter sounded shaky. "No. And this is my last pair of jeans, so be gentle."

"You're going to go shopping with me."

"Charlie, I –"

"Fine. Then go naked. I'll enjoy the scenery, but you won't get much work done." Her hands stroked up his thighs, then over the fine silken skin that covered the hot molten steel of his erection. "When you figure out how to get out of these clothes, you can come help me wash my hair if you want to," Charlie invited. "If this morning didn't wear you out."

"I have a lot of years to make up for," Drew promised. "It's going to take you a lot more than one morning to catch up, let alone wear me out."

"Good," Charlie replied as she pulled the curtain shut. "Because I'm not into one night stands. Even if they are in the morning."

It didn't take Drew very long to figure out how to free himself, even with his jeans down around the tops of his old cowboy boots. Her breath caught as he slipped into the shower behind her, his hands sliding around her to take the washcloth from her. Water coursed over them as he ran the cloth over her stomach and down between her legs. She laid her head back against him as lips closed over her earlobe, sending an electrical current racing through her blood.

Charlie reached up to run her fingers through his hair, enjoying the way his skin shivered as she traced her nails over his scalp. His free arm circled her to kneed her breast until the nipple budded to a deliciously straining nub under his touch. She slipped her other hand between them to rub the head of his penis against her skin. The fingers that played with her wet curls stopped their stroking as he shuddered against her, nipping harder on her earlobe.

"You frighten me," he whispered against the skin of her neck. "I knew it would be like this. A fist, or a knife, I can fight those. You touch me and I forget everything I ever learned about self preservation."

Charlie turned to wrap her arms around his neck, trapping his erection between their slick, wet bodies as she swayed her hips against him. "Good. Because I've never wanted a man the way I want you, and it scares the crap out of me."

"So what are we going to do about this?"

Charlie pondered the problem as she licked the water from the hollow about his breastbone. "There's only one thing to do. We'll have to have sex, constantly, until we get each other out of our systems."

He closed his hand around his penis, using the head to rub against her clit as she tried to climb up his slippery body. "That could take a while."

"Years," she agreed. "Maybe even decades."

It was hard to tell whether it was the promise in her words or the shock of her teeth on his nipple that had him lifting her over his straining erection, slamming her down hard against the hot length of him until she was sobbing out his name, her fingers digging into him as wave after wave of release washed over her. And then he was pumping into her in long, shuddering strokes, his eyes losing focus as he called out her name, his final frenzy a desperate search for the absolution he found within her.

They never quite got back to the shampoo. When the water went cold, there were towels and tongues and the warm air of Drew's breath drying the moisture from her breasts, and this time it was slow and easy and delicious.

When at last they lay quietly together, limbs still entwined, Drew kissed her eyelids possessively. "You are so beautiful," he murmured, his voice a low rumble.

"I'm forty-four and not very tall and rather plain looking and ten pounds underweight," Charlie replied practically. "But when you look at me I feel beautiful for the first time in my life."

"You are beautiful to me," Drew assured her. "You're more than I ever dared to hope for."

Charlie snuggled closer against him. "It was never like this for me before," she confessed. "I never thought I was very good at making love. I always felt a little...inadequate."

Drew grinned at her. "If you were any more adequate I'd be begging for mercy," he assured her. His eyes turned serious, contemplative. "It was never like this for me, either. Never anything like this." He thought of Darby, and dared to trust Charlie with a piece of his soul. "I always felt like I was too big. I felt clumsy and awkward."

Charlie rolled to her elbows so that she could see his face. "There's nothing wrong with being tall," she assured Drew. "It doesn't seem to affect how we fit together." She picked up his hand and kissed it, admiring the long, sure fingers that had worked their magic on her. "And there's definitely nothing clumsy or awkward about you." She laid her head on his chest. She liked the way his arm encircled her, almost automatically. "I used to feel awkward, too," she revealed. "I never knew where to put my hands. Sex was always a little disappointing. Like a Christmas present that wasn't what you wanted."

"I never had that problem," Drew assured her with a tight little smile. "We never exchanged Christmas presents in my grandfather's house. He said it was Jesus' birthday, not mine. We went to church. We prayed. That was Christmas."

Charlie hugged him tighter. "This Christmas will be better," she promised. "Tell Santa what you want for Christmas," she prompted.

"You," Drew replied without hesitation.

Charlie laughed as she kissed him again, but in the back of her mind she was wondering how to make up for a dozen Christmases spent behind bars.

About the time Drew came to the conclusion that she'd fallen back asleep, Charlie spoke again.

"Drew?"

"Charlie?" He willed her to tell him that she loved him, knowing all the while that it wasn't going to happen. Sex. It was

111

just sex. Great sex, but nothing more. At least it didn't mean more than that to her.

"I'm hungry."

Drew laughed, and if there was any disappointment in his heart, he disguised it well. "You're always hungry."

"Yes," Charlie agreed. "But this time I want food."

They made it to the kitchen to raid the refrigerator without getting distracted. Charlie tried to make her voice sound casual. "Tell me something about yourself," she suggested.

The knife paused in the mayonnaise jar. "Like what?"

Drew's eyes had that wary look again. Careful, Charlie warned herself. But she never took her own advice. "Growing up. Anything."

Drew turned toward the window, resting his hands on the kitchen sink as he focused out across the fields somewhere. "I was born at King's Daughters Hospital in Martinsburg. It's gone, now. My mother wasn't married, and she ran off and left me for my grandparents to raise. They didn't do too badly, for being handed a surprise like that, I guess. Grandpa wanted me to go to college. I was supposed to study engineering. He was pretty disappointed when I got married right out of high school instead, turned down a football scholarship to work in the Feed and Supply. But Darby was pregnant. I couldn't do what my parents had done.

"We had a little girl. Savannah. She was...She made it all work for me. I didn't care about college or anything else. Then Darby divorced me four years later and married the local banker's son. You know the rest." His hands had gone still. It was all delivered in that distant, deliberate voice Drew might use with a stranger.

"What did you want to do?" Charlie asked.

Drew turned slowly and looked down into her eyes again. Daddy always said the eyes were the windows to a man's soul. "What do you mean?"

112

"You said you were *supposed* to go to college and study engineering. You didn't say that's what you wanted to do."

Drew blinked twice, still staring at her. "You're the first person who ever asked me that."

"Why?" Charlie demanded. "People just planned your life for you without asking?"

"Look at me, Charlie. I'm six inches taller than most of the guys I grew up with. I have a 25-inch shoulder span. Nobody had to ask me whether I wanted to play football. They just looked at me. I look like a football player, and I just happened to be good at running over people. And I liked the game. I really did. Nobody ever expected me to want anything else."

"And you always do what people expect you to," Charlie added thoughtfully.

"I used to," Drew amended, crossing the room to gather her into his arms. "I used to, Charlie. Not any more. I'm here now because I want to be here. I'm here because I need you and I want you and I don't think I could possibly let you go now that I've touched you. You're like a part of me that's been missing all my life."

Charlie pulled his head down to plant a quick kiss on his too serious mouth. "So, if you had a choice, big guy, what would you have done? After high school."

"I'd have gone to culinary school and become a chef."

Charlie nodded slowly. "You could have been a world-class chef. Still could be, for that matter. You could go now. Your life's not half over."

"I'm on probation, Charlie, remember? I can't leave the state, let alone the country."

"I know you're on probation, but that can't last for ever."

"I have another seven years before I could even think about doing anything like that. And where would I get the money? Tuition was over fifty grand when I graduated from high school. I'm sure it's gone up by now."

"Seven years? Seven more years? They gave you nineteen years for killing a man who raped and murdered your wife?"

"Twenty-five years. I got time off for good behavior. And nobody ever asked me why I killed Weasel."

"Nobody?" Charlie repeated incredulously. "What about your attorney?"

"Nobody," Drew confirmed.

Charlie kicked a chair furiously. "The man should be disbarred!" She could just see Frances's face when she told her this one.

A puzzled frown crossed Drew's face as he watched Charlie's display of temper. "What difference would it have made? I killed a man, Charlie. With my bare hands. His blood was still all over me when I came to. Nothing can change that."

Charlie shook her head. "Nothing can change what happened. I know that. You'd probably still have gone to prison. But you sure as hell wouldn't have received a twenty-five-year sentence. That attorney owes you several years of your life!"

Charlie watched the range of emotions cross his face as he studied her. "Are you always going to do this?"

"Do what?"

"Take my word for everything," Drew offered up in wonder. "Defend me, even from myself. Believe in me."

Charlie threw her arms around Drew, her anger defused, fitting her head under his chin. "Yeah. It's a package deal."

It took a moment for his arms to return the hug. When he did, it was fierce and possessive. He claimed her mouth with his hungry lips. "A man quits believing in miracles in prison, Charlie. Learns to quit dreaming. If you don't, you go crazy. But if I'd dared to dream, I would have imagined a home, a family, a woman like you who'd believe in me, no matter what."

Charlie chewed on her bottom lip. A family. He was still young enough to want a family. "I wish I could give you that."

Drew leaned back, his hands going to her shoulders. "I didn't mean it like that, Charlie," he insisted. "I don't care how old you are. I wasn't thinking of starting over. I already have a daughter." Drew kissed her on the forehead. "I'm not going to judge you, and find you don't measure up somehow, Charlie. Six months ago I didn't even expect to be breathing free air for another thirteen years. Now I'm here, with you. What more could any man ask for?"

A family, Charlie thought, but she didn't say it. Drew kissed her until the difference in their ages seemed as inconsequential as the knife left in the mayonnaise.

"What happened to Savannah?" Charlie asked over turkey and provolone.

"I don't know."

"Savannah didn't stay in touch with you all those years?"

Drew's voice was so low Charlie could barely understand him. "I don't think Savannah even knows that I exist."

"What do you mean?" Charlie couldn't imagine a child not knowing her father.

"I didn't get to see Savannah after Darby remarried."

"You didn't have joint custody?"

"No." There was something more. Something he was afraid to say.

"There's nothing you can tell me that will make me change my mind, Drew," Charlie assured him. Nothing she was willing to consider.

Drew looked away, his eyes distant and shut off again. "You're going to find out anyway. You might as well hear it from me." Still, there was a significant pause before he continued. "Darby left me for another man. You know that. When I found out she was having an affair, we had one hell of a fight. I was chasing her down the hallway, and she tripped. Fell down the back stairs here." Drew gestured toward the steep, narrow stairway that led from the kitchen to the servants' quarters. "Darby was pregnant again, and she miscarried. In court, when we divorced, Darby claimed I pushed her. She said I tried to kill her."

He focused back on Charlie, his voice desperate. "I didn't push her, Charlie. Never. I never even touched Darby that night, except to try and catch her. I loved her. I wasn't raised like that. I'd never hit a woman."

Drew lost his wife and an unborn child in one day. Charlie wrapped her arms around him again, wishing she could absorb the hurt, trying not to cry. "It must have been terrible for you."

The pain of it all was desperately near the surface now. "The court wouldn't give me visitation. They took my daughter away from me."

"We'll find her." It wasn't enough. It was too little, too late, but it was all Charlie had to offer.

Drew buried his face in her hair for a while, and when he spoke again, his voice was raw with unshed tears. "I kind of hope she doesn't know about me. It wouldn't have been easy for Savannah, growing up with a convicted murderer as a father."

"When I was little, my father was my hero. We were always very close. I was heartbroken when he died three years ago. I don't think I ever really got over it. I can't imagine not having that. Savannah must miss you very much."

"She'd be twenty one by now. Probably just out of college. I thought about trying to find her, but what do you say? Hi, I'm your father the murderer?"

"You're her father, first," Charlie chided gently. "Savannah at least deserves the opportunity to get to know you again. She needs to know that you've loved her all these years, even if you couldn't be there with her."

Drew's answer was a long time coming. "I don't even know where to start looking."

"Start with the last place you know she was," Charlie reasoned. "I'd say that would be her stepfather's."

Drew's gaze focused out the window again. "I'm not sure that would be such a good idea."

Charlie puzzled through his shifting moods. "You think he had Darby murdered."

Drew ran a hand through his hair. "If anyone could have gotten away with it, he could have. Weasel would do anything for a buck, but he wouldn't have gone to that much work for free."

"What kind of a man would hire a thug like that to kill his wife?" Charlie demanded.

"The sheriff," Drew pronounced with a sardonic smile. "Robert Waite."

* * * * *

Charlie paced the room, her sandwich laying uneaten on her plate. "The sheriff is an elected position here. I remember reading in that paper that Waite is just coming to the end of his second four-year term. So he couldn't have been sheriff when you knew him. What was he doing then?"

Drew closed his eyes, willing the past away. "Why are we talking about Bob Waite, anyway?"

"Because he stole twelve years of your life," Charlie insisted.

"You can't get that back for me." Drew tried kissing her as a distraction her, but it didn't work.

"No," Charlie agreed, as if there'd been no pause in the conversation. "I can't get it back. There's no way to change the past. But we can try to find out what really happened. We can try to clear your name. We can find Savannah."

Drew's gaze shifted out the window, watching the mares play in the field. "You aren't going to leave this alone, are you?"

"Do you really want me to?"

"I'm not sure what I want. Nobody's asked me that for a real long time. Maybe never. Even before I went to prison, I never felt like I was in control of my life. I was always caught up in somebody else's plan. Football. College. Marriage. Savannah was the one solid thing I had. When I lost her, everything went bad for me."

"I'd like to help you find Savannah," Charlie offered.

"You may be opening Pandora's box," Drew warned.

Charlie smiled up at him. "What have you got to lose?"

Drew's arms tightened around her possessively. "You."

Charlie treated him to a wide grin. "You'd play hell trying to get rid of me," she assured him.

Did that mean she loved him? She'd come so close. Skirted the edges from all the angles. Drew wanted to believe that was enough, but it wasn't. Lord, how he wanted to hear those words. It haunted him, like a hollow ache that had been there most of his life.

He could ask her. Come right out and ask her. But he might not get the answer he wanted to hear. Safer to wait. To deal with her questions, and to wait. He knew how to wait. He had twelve years practice.

"Waite was doing what every good little banker's son does," Drew told her with a sigh. "He was working in his Daddy's bank. He was always there. For as long as I can remember."

"Working in a bank?" Charlie echoed in disbelief. "Robert Waite was a banker? How the hell do you go from writing loans to being the county sheriff?"

Drew's fingers twined in her hair, turning it this way and that in the sunlight streaming in the window. "You said it. It's an elected position. There aren't any required qualifications. You just have to convince the voters that you can do the job, I guess. The sheriff's department handles mostly taxes. Property taxes. Maybe the voters thought taking care of other people's money was something Bob Waite would be good at. Lord knows he had enough experience at that."

Charlie smiled at the way his fingers kept finding their way back to her hair. It was as if he couldn't get enough of touching her. Even when he was light years away, some part of his body was still in contact with hers. "Okay. So this banker stole your wife. Then he had her murdered. Why?"

"I spent twelve years wishing I'd made Weasel talk before I killed him. But I didn't. I can't see how I'll ever find out now."

"Speculate," Charlie prodded.

"I have," Drew admitted. "Didn't have that much else to do. Waite hated me. Bob is five years older than I am. We shouldn't have ever really been in the same circles. But he kept ending up in my way. Sometimes I think he took Darby from me just because she was mine. Maybe because taking her took Savannah. He knew that would cut me to the bone."

"That wouldn't give Waite a reason to kill Darby."

"I know," Drew agreed, his tone morose. "I should have gotten Savannah back when Darby died. That would have really pissed Waite off. From that standpoint, having her killed doesn't make any sense. I lost her myself, that time. My own stupidity for letting myself go that far down the bottle. Savannah should have been the first thing I thought of when her mother died. She was only seven. It must have been so hard on her, losing her mother like that. Just when she needed me most, I was off in some bar getting in a fight with a man I had no business taking a swing at. I'd never have done it if I'd been sober. I'm not that stupid."

Charlie chewed her bottom lip speculatively. "There has to be another motive for Waite to have killed Darby. Did she have any money?"

Drew shook his head. "That's the thing. She didn't have a dime that I know of. She didn't get much from divorcing me, that's for sure. I didn't own anything. The farm was Granddad's. I had my truck, and that was about it. The court awarded her $25.00 a week child support." Drew had given up trying to seduce Charlie by now. But his fingers were still twined in her hair. "I don't suggest you just walk up to Waite and ask him."

"I need access to a computer. A main frame."

"You can hack into his financial records?"

"You're the hacker. I'm just a programmer."

Drew looked genuinely startled at that. "I'm no hacker, Charlie. I never even touched a computer before yesterday. I just got a few tips from this guy who transferred in right before I left. He liked to talk about computers. He'd sit and talk for hours to anyone who would listen."

"You learned how to use a computer without even seeing one?" There were people who couldn't manage that with a screen in front of them and an instructor at their side.

"I could close my eyes and see it all. Jerry talked about everything. He spent a whole week on passwords and how to break them. He had this whole list in his head of things people choose for passwords."

"Like the last 4 digits of their social security number," Charlie suggested, blushing furiously.

Drew made a noise like a buzzer. "Number one answer."

"Oh, that's bad," Charlie exclaimed. "What's number two?"

"Birthdays. Their own, then spouses', then their children's birthdays. After that, the year they graduated from high school. Most people have the same number for their passwords on everything. Credit card accounts. ATM cards. Which, by the way, I have never actually seen, either. Except on TV. Most people even have the same combinations to their luggage."

"Guilty." She changed the subject. "I'm going to call City Hospital. City's main frames are probably tied into a national database. It won't be like what I worked with at the Agency, but it will have to do."

"Just what is the Agency? I know you said you can't talk about what you did, but you keep saying the Agency, so everything can't be all that secret."

"GSA – the Government Services Agency." The lie rolled off her tongue with the ease that came from years of practice. Besides, it wasn't completely untrue. They'd issued her paychecks. "They gave me my assignments. All government computers are tied into the national database. City Hospital wouldn't have access to that, but I might get lucky and find something on Waite through the civilian databases. In the mean time, we need to start asking questions very discretely. We don't want Waite to get suspicious and come after you directly again. The longer he thinks you're running scared of him, the better."

Drew flushed slightly. "I am not afraid of Bob Waite."

"I didn't mean that you are," Charlie soothed. "But he'll probably think you are as long as you keep hiding out here and staying out of sight. What else would he think? What we don't want is for him to get the idea that Weasel told you anything. If Waite decides you know something you shouldn't, he could be very dangerous. He's already killed one person and done his best to screw up your life. We don't want him to feel threatened. Yet."

"Yet?" Drew repeated suspiciously. "What are you thinking, Charlie?"

"I'm not sure," Charlie confessed. "I don't know enough to have a plan yet. But I do know this. If Waite bought one murder, he's fully capable of buying another. He'll go after you next time. Who else would have put the contract out on you while you were in prison? Especially if you're right and that was why he seduced Darby in the first place."

"Well, if he seduced her, it must have been with money, rather than sex," Drew concluded, a trace of bitterness in his voice. "I don't think she really ever liked sex much, but she sure did like to spend money."

"Maybe that's why he killed her. Maybe he couldn't afford to keep her happy, either."

"How could you ever prove any of that?" Drew demanded.

"We need copies of his financial records from that time period. The problem is, most reporting agencies only go back seven years. However, if he applied for anything back then, like a bank loan somewhere, the bank would have put a copy of his credit report in their files. But that would be stabbing around in the dark.

"Hospitals, on the other hand, keep everything. They almost never dump their data banks. Which is why everything gets overloaded and they end up calling someone like me. Then I have to go in and straighten out their systems when they start crashing. While I'm doing things like that, I might have reason to check their hard copies on some records to make sure they matched the records in the computer. So if, for instance, Waite was ever billed by the hospital and went past thirty days paying the bill, I might well find a copy of his credit report in their files."

"And I thought programmers just sat at a keyboard," Drew teased, impressed with her reasoning despite himself.

"Actually, I did, most of the time. I had an assistant who did things like tracking down files for me and printing out reams of garbage that got thrown in boxes in the records department." Charlie chewed her lip, hesitant to make the suggestion. But she had to ask. She had to know. "If I go independent, I'll have to hire an assistant. Would you be interested in the job?"

Drew blinked twice, slowly, in that funny way he had that reminded her of a hoot owl. "Me?"

"Why not?" Charlie asked, trying not to make it sound too important. "Keep the money in the family."

"I've never even seen a main frame," he responded noncommittally. "But I could file boxes of old records without any problem."

Charlie let out her breath. He was at least willing to consider the possibility. "A keyboard's a keyboard, no matter what it's attached to. Can you type?"

Drew smiled at that. "I'll have you know I was the best typist at Moundsville State Business school," he assured her.

Charlie treated herself to a bear hug, barely stifling a victory cry.

"I'm not complaining, you understand," Drew offered, his arms molding her against his chest possessively. "You can hug me any time you want. But would you mind telling me what that was for?"

Charlie laughed and kissed Drew again, feeling no desire to let him loose. "For being the most agreeable man I've ever met."

Drew laughed so hard he nearly choked. "I wish Grandpa could have heard you say that," he managed finally. "He swore I was the most pig-headed boy he'd ever raised."

Charlie frowned, puzzled. "Pig-headed? You? The man must have been senile."

Drew laughed even harder.

"Did your grandfather raise many boys?" Did he have uncles somewhere? Someone who'd find him eventually and take him away from her?

"Nope," Drew answered with a hint of a drawl. "Just me."

Belatedly Charlie understood the old man's joke. They laughed together for a while, easy and comfortable with one another, Charlie's head tucked under Drew's chin, their bodies so close it was hard to tell where one stopped and the other began. "You must miss your grandfather," she ventured.

"He was a hard old man, tough as nails, but he did the best he could by me. He mortgaged this place to buy me a lawyer. Reckon that's how he lost it."

"Nobody ever lost this place," Charlie assured him. "He lived here till he died, or so the real estate agent told me. A young man he'd hired to help with the cows found him asleep in the rocker on the front porch one morning, and couldn't wake him up. I left the rocking chair there, in case his ghost was wandering around looking for a place to sit down."

Drew brushed his fingers across her cheek. "Thank you. Granddad used to sit out there on the front porch every night, rain or shine, and watch the animals." He was quiet for a while, stroking her hair absently.

They wandered out to the front porch, arm in arm, to sit on the porch swing. On the other side of the porch the rocker swayed slightly in the breeze. It had bothered her at first, the notion of the old man's ghost hanging around. Now she found it rather comforting. "He'd be happy to know you're back here."

Drew ran his fingers through her hair, holding it out to the sunlight. "He'd be happy to know you're here with me." And if her questions produced answers he wasn't ready for, well, they'd deal with that when the time came. That and Robert Waite.

Chapter Eight

"Your turn. Tell me something about Allen."

Charlie sighed, remembering it all as if it were a little unreal, someone else's life she was talking about. "I met him at a book signing in the mall. I was thirty-three, I'd just broken up with a guy I'd dated off and on since college, and I was lonely. Allen kind of swept me off my feet. He took me to Broadway, to the opening of a play based on one of his novels. I felt like I was dating one of his characters. I think maybe I was. Six weeks later we were married. We spent our honeymoon in Paris, so Allen could do research for his next novel."

Drew snorted. "We spent ours here on the farm, and Darby had morning sickness. What happened to the happily ever after part for you?"

"Have you ever been around a writer? They're like artists. Moody. Temperamental. The emotional stability of a four-year-old. I could never say the right things at the right times. I never quite looked like his current heroine should look. I was too thin. Too short. My hair went gray too early. I tried dying it, but the color came out wrong. I wanted him to pay attention to me when he had to stay focused on his work. He said I was the least inspiring woman he'd ever known."

Drew kissed Charlie possessively. "If he was such a great writer, how come I've never heard of him?"

"Do you read love stories?"

"Not unless the book cart ran out of everything else," Drew admitted.

"After we got married he quit writing paperbacks. He tried to move into mainstream hard-back novels, but nobody was buying."

"So he went back to paperbacks?" Drew offered.

"So he wrote another mainstream," Charlie filled in. "A mystery, this time. And another one after that. About one a year for ten years."

"Why didn't he just go back to something that would sell?"

"That was against his artistic ethics," Charlie explained. "He couldn't compromise his art for money. That's when he told me I was uninspiring. I was too bogged down with the mundane, everyday things in life. Like balancing the checkbook and investing money. At first he still had royalties coming in from his earlier books. That money ran out after the first couple of years." Charlie remembered watching the checking account dwindle with growing concern. "I was making good money, but it never seemed to be quite enough to suit Allen. So I accepted the assignments no one else wanted because they paid more. I spent one summer in Florida and another in Texas. Then there was that last job out in California. I always got bonuses for finishing up early. There wasn't much to distract me when I was that far from home."

"Why did you stay with him?"

Charlie focused on the treetops down by the stream. "I was raised Catholic. Till death do us part. I really believed in that."

Drew hugged her harder. "So Allen wrote books that no one bought and stuck you with the bill. And you stayed with him because you made a promise. He had it made. I don't understand why he'd have risked his relationship with you for a fling with some snot-nosed kid."

Charlie thought back to that afternoon almost a year ago now. She'd taken some time off from the Agency after the divorce was final.

"I didn't understand either, at first. Allen had always needed me, at least financially. Whenever we'd had a fight before, he'd always been the first to try to patch things up. This time he just disappeared. I thought it was because I shot at him. But then I took a vacation to the beach. There it was, in the window of the gift shop in the hotel's lobby. On a display of best sellers, under the number eight. *After Sunset*, by Allen McGregor. I'd read the rough draft at least four years ago. I finally understood why he hadn't called – why he didn't want me back. He didn't need me anymore."

Drew pulled back a little. "Charlie, I understand the man was a fool, but do you really think he was stupid enough to risk getting shot over the royalties from one book? How much could that be worth?"

"Allen moved out while I was spending the night at the local precinct house. I came home to an empty town house and empty bank accounts. He got about fifteen hundred dollars. His advance on *After Sunset* was probably worth another five grand or better. That would have been enough to last him until the book landed on the bookstores' front tables and royalties started coming in, and then there are the tours and signings and radio and TV appearances and a movie contract. It takes about a year to get a book to market, which means he sold it at least eight months before…our argument. I was surprised he didn't press charges against me, but then I realized he didn't want the negative publicity."

"So you did divorce him," Drew prodded. "This is your ex-husband we're talking about?"

"Oh, yes," Charlie confirmed. "I had to counter sue. His lawyer threatened to ask for alimony."

"What a worm!" Drew exploded.

That set her over the edge. Charlie started laughing, and once she started she just couldn't quit. "Thank you," she managed at last. "He was a worm. I guess I confused hero worship with love for too long. I was just a financial crutch to lean on for a while. It's easier to see that now. But at the time, I honestly believed it was somehow my fault. That if I could just be who Allen wanted me to be, everything would work out."

"Charlie, I want you to know something." His tone worried her with its seriousness. "I'm an ex-con. I don't have much education. I took some college courses in prison. Other men got degrees, but I didn't work that hard at it. I can't imagine what you see in me. It must seem like I'm not much better than Allen. Just another man for you to support. But I wouldn't take any of your money if I didn't need to eat. Don't go back into the computer stuff if you don't want to. The driver from the Feed and Supply said they're looking for help. He thought they'd hire me back again. Somehow, we'll make it work."

She traced his mouth with her fingertip. "Drew Bailey, you're a good man. You've done more for me that I ever could have hoped for. You're made my dream here a reality. I couldn't have done all this without you. I'm not worried about money, honest, I'm not. I don't want you to take a job with the Feed and Supply. That place could be dangerous for you. Whoever put that note in the feed is still out there. I don't care if you never earn a dime outside this farm. I've come to count on you being here. I don't know how I'd manage without you."

"You won't have to find out," Drew promised. "I'm not going anywhere. You'd play hell trying to get rid of me."

"I need to hear the words," she whispered, hardly daring to believe her ears.

"I'm not going anywhere."

"The other part."

His smile dimmed. She heard guilt in his voice. "There's something you should know, Charlie. It wasn't an accident, me meeting you. That first night, at the truck stop."

"You came there looking for me? Why?"

Drew watched Charlie's eyes, expecting them to be wary. Frightened, maybe. Maybe it just hadn't occurred to her yet that what he'd done was wrong. His own fear was a bitter taste in his throat, now.

"When my parole officer didn't show up, I had to walk home from the bus station in Hagerstown. It was a real letdown, having no one there to pick me up. A guy who'd known me from high school gave me a ride. He figured I should know all about this woman who'd bought my farm and brought in all the expensive horses. He said everybody figured you were in way over your head, so you had to take the job at Harry's. Made it sound like you were about to lose the place. At first I thought that sounded great. If I couldn't have it, why should you? I needed someone to blame it all on.

"I spent two weeks at the Rescue Mission in Martinsburg. Couldn't find a steady job. No one wanted to hire an ex-con. Too many people here know me. I decided to hit the road. But I had to see you before I left. I just wanted to get a look at you. So I hitchhiked out here, to the farm. But when I got here, you were at work. So I walked over to the truck stop. It was raining so hard, I was soaked to the skin by the time I got there. But I just had to see you. It was sort of an obsession by then.

"I had this picture in my head of what you'd be like. You were so different. You were kind to me. I couldn't hate you. I wasn't going anywhere in particular. Just leaving town, you know? I'd already checked out of the Rescue Mission. I didn't have much of a plan. I was just going to hit the road. So I followed you home."

Charlie smiled at Drew and laid her hand over his. "I don't believe you could have hurt me, no matter what I'd been like. I wished afterwards, that first night when you came into the truck stop, that I'd offered you a job. I even drove back to the truck stop to see if you were still there, but you were gone."

Drew met her gaze levelly. "I was in the back of your truck. Under the tarp."

Charlie laughed. "That must have been some ride." She reached up to kiss his cheek. "I'm glad you followed me home."

Drew frowned in bewilderment. "How come you didn't call the cops?"

It was Charlie's turn to look confused. "Why would I?"

She really didn't see it. "I could have gone back to prison for what I did, Charlie. There are laws about those things. They call it stalking."

Charlie laughed at that. "Half this town has stopped into the truck stop just to get a look at me. I didn't call the cops on any of them, either. At first, I thought you were a ghost. The real estate agent told me your grandfather died here on the farm, and I thought maybe he was haunting the place. Then when you moved the hay bales, I decided that I liked having the help. It was Janelle's idea to feed you."

"Please thank her for me. I was so hungry that morning I'd given serious thought to breaking into the house."

Charlie blinked at him in confusion again. "Breaking in? Why? The door was unlocked."

He stared down at her, remembering the long hours he'd spent trying to justify entering her house. "You left the door unlocked? You knew there was someone living in your barn, and you left the door unlocked? Are you out of your mind?"

"I've never locked the door here. You can't keep a ghost out with a lock, anyway, and the only time anyone's ever stolen anything from me, he had the keys."

* * * * *

"Where could the money have come from?" It was Saturday morning and they were in the barn, supposedly feeding the horses. They kept getting distracted. It wasn't just the sex, Charlie mused. It was so much more than that. They were like two high school kids, in love for the first time. Everything was fresh and new when they did it together. She felt young and alive and vital.

"The money?" Drew responded blankly. "What money?"

"Bob Waite," she reminded him. "If the motivation was money, where did it come from?"

Drew shrugged and went on about pitching hay, enjoying the fresh, clean smell of summer it brought back. "I have no idea."

"Waite almost had to have an insurance policy on her."

Drew snorted. "That sounds like a bad old movie."

Charlie had to laugh. "Does, doesn't it?"

"Anyway, it would have taken a pretty big settlement to make it worth killing Darby. She wasn't worth risking prison over."

Charlie was chewing her lip again. "Besides, Waite already had money, didn't he?"

Drew shrugged apathetically. "I guess so. There was his Daddy's bank."

"Yeah, but that was his Daddy's bank, not his. And small banks were having a hard time back then. Is the bank still in business?"

The last of the mares was fed, and Drew turned his full attention to Charlie, his eyes laughing. "I really haven't had much opportunity to look around town since I got out."

They would have to work on that. "Which bank did his family own?"

"Rosemont. Out on the West End of town."

"There's a Farmers and Mechanics out there now. That's about it. My guess is Rosemont has been gone since before Waite was elected." Charlie ran her hands down Timura's legs while she speculated. "If the bank was in trouble, though, it would have taken more than what any normal insurance policy would have paid to bail it out. When banks go down, they generally run into the multiple millions. Even figuring that this was a small bank, I can't see where a few hundred thousand would have helped any."

Drew leaned his chin on the pitchfork, watching the sure way her hands moved over the mare. "Maybe he wasn't bailing out the bank. Maybe he was bailing out himself."

Charlie straightened, her eyes meeting his. "What are you thinking?"

"Maybe he gambled. Or maybe he'd stolen money from the bank and needed to put it back. Maybe that Vette of his sucked it up."

"Maybe." They could guess all night long and not know if they were any closer to the truth. "Is there anyone you trust who would know more about Waite?"

"No."

Short. Abrupt. Clearly not open for discussion. "Okay. Let's try another angle. Weasel said Waite hired him. If he told you that, he would have told someone else. A friend. Someone he trusted. Who did he hang out with? Who were his buddies?"

Drew shook his head. "I don't remember Weasel ever having any friends."

This was getting her nowhere fast. "Who else was in the bar with him that night?"

Drew's eyes went opaque. His jaw clenched. "I don't remember."

Charlie felt her frustration rising. She felt like they'd just regressed weeks in their relationship. She was back to playing twenty questions again. "You don't remember? Not one person?"

Drew set the pitchfork aside and went to stand at the half-door, looking out into the barnyard. "I don't remember, Charlie. I don't remember anything but Weasel laughing about killing Darby. I told you, I'd been on a ten-day drunk. I blacked out. I don't remember much of anything from that whole day."

He'd blacked out? Before and after the fight? That didn't make any sense at all. One or the other. Not both. Charlie was getting a really bad feeling about this. "How many times did you hit Weasel?"

She could see the rising tension in his shoulders. "I don't know!"

She tried to keep her voice calm and reasonable, though she felt like shouting. "So what you're telling me is that you don't remember actually killing Weasel?"

She could see his knuckles on the edge of the door turning white. "I don't remember a damn thing."

"Then how do you know you even killed this man?"

Drew spun around as if she'd struck him. For a long moment he just stared her. His mouth opened and closed a few times, but no words came out. "I hit him. I know I hit him. I remember hitting him. He died."

"He died," Charlie repeated. "You saw him die? Right there in front of you in that bar. You remember that?"

Drew looked stunned. Confused. "I...No. It wasn't like that. He died at the hospital. During the night."

Charlie practiced breathing deeply for several seconds. "A man who had just been bragging in a bar in front of witnesses about committing a 'Murder for Hire' gets in a bar fight. Off he goes to the hospital. He dies later that night. Surprise, surprise."

All the color emptied from Drew's face. He sat down heavily on a bale of hay, his hands dangling across his knees. "I hit him."

"Did he hit you back? What did you look like after the fight?"

His eyes avoided hers. "I looked like hell. Like I'd been worked over with a two-by-four."

"Why didn't the cops take you to the hospital, too?"

He didn't have an answer for that. Didn't even try.

Charlie changed her focus. "Who testified against you in court?"

"I..." Drew fixed his gaze on the old oak beams that held up the barn. "No one testified against me. I pled guilty."

It was Charlie's turn to be stunned. "You pled guilty? To a murder you didn't remember committing?" She dropped to her heels before him, trying to meet his eyes. "For God's sake, why?"

Drew's face was a pasty gray color. "Because I did it! I grabbed Weasel by the throat and watched him choking as I slammed my fist into the side of his skull! Look at these hands, Charlie! Do you think a man could live through that? There was blood all over me! I killed a man, Charlie! I killed him!"

Charlie captured his outstretched fists, understanding at last his Achilles heel. "That night. Out in the back pasture. You never raised a hand to defend yourself against those boys, did you?" Her voice was soft, like a mother talking to a frightened child. "I remember thinking that it was odd that your hands weren't hurt. Just your wrist, where someone stomped on it. You didn't fight back. You just let them beat you."

Drew couldn't meet her eyes. "I'd have hurt them. Maybe killed one of them, too."

"You know you hit Weasel," Charlie agreed. "But Weasel was a full grown man, and I'll bet he was a lot closer to sober than you were. A wound to the temple wouldn't have bled like that, Drew. If that blow had killed him, it would have been from internal bleeding, inside his skull, putting too much pressure on his brain. You said you broke your right hand when you hit Weasel the first time. You were holding him. That had to be with your left hand."

She reached up is if capturing her victim by the throat. "Just think about this. I don't believe you could have managed a hard enough second blow to cause a wound that would cover you with blood. Not even you could have done that. Not with a broken hand. Not when you were so drunk you could hardly stand up. You would have had to let go of him, then hit him with a left. A pretty good trick for a drunk, don't you think?"

Charlie could see the doubt in Drew's eyes, the turmoil brewing there as he followed her line of thinking. "Why were you still wearing that shirt the next morning? If it was Weasel's blood, if the cops even thought it might be Weasel's blood, why didn't they keep the shirt for evidence? There should have been blood tests run on the stains on the shirt to prove it belonged to Weasel. Unless the cops knew all along it wasn't his blood. What if Weasel hit you back, and it was your blood? What if you blacked out after he hit you?" She still held his fists, captured between her own small hands. She could feel him starting to shake. "How did you find out that Weasel was dead? Who told you? What was the very first thing you do remember?"

Drew's eyes turned inward, measuring the past, replaying that terrible morning in his mind's eye. "I came to in the county jail. I smelled like hell. I'd puked all over myself. My right hand hurt so bad I could barely use it. It was covered in dried blood. I got cleaned up as best as I could. My shirt was ripped. There was blood all over it. A deputy came in after a while. Asked me if I remembered anything about last night. I said no. I wasn't even sure what day it was. He told me I'd killed Weasel. Beaten him to death. That's when I remembered Weasel telling me about killing Darby. I kept seeing his face turning gray as I grabbed him by the throat. I remembered my fist exploding against his skull. I knew I'd been in a fight. Everything hurt."

A picture was coming together. A picture that brought glints of steel to Charlie's eyes. "There's been a six pack of Coors in the tack room fridge for at least three months. You've never touched any of them. Why?"

Drew looked annoyed, as if she'd sidetracked the conversation. "I hate beer."

"You haven't had so much as a shot out of that fifth of Jack Daniel's under the sink, either," Charlie pointed out. "And I know you know it's there. It's right next to the spray cleaner you use on the counters."

"I don't drink, Charlie. I hate the stuff." Drew sounded impatient. Charlie was sure he wanted to move away from her. To pace the runway. Yet he stayed. All that raw power, and he would let himself be restrained by her two small hands.

"Always have, haven't you?" she speculated. "Even after your wife left you. You said you went on a ten day drunk because it was just that. Your first real bender."

"Yeah," Drew conceded. "I was never much of a drinker."

"So, follow this story with me. A young man who doesn't drink finds out his ex-wife, the woman who betrayed him, the woman he's still in love with, the mother of his child, has been murdered. He goes on a drunk, for the first time in his life. Drinks till he passes out everyday for the better part of two weeks. One morning our young man wakes up in jail. A man is dead. A man he didn't like. Somebody, a police officer, says 'You killed this man.' After a while, another somebody, say the young man's lawyer, says, 'You better accept the prosecution's offer of manslaughter, or you're going to jail for the rest of your life.'

"Now this young man is big, and very strong. He could easily have beaten someone to death and he knows it. He's fought all his life to hold back his temper, because he didn't want to hurt anyone. He remembers the dead man taunting him, throwing something in his face. The cops say he killed the man. What does he do? Does he even try to find someone else who was in the bar that night? Find someone he trusts who can tell him what really happened? I don't think our young man asks any questions, because he doesn't want to know any more about what happened. He doesn't want to hear anyone else call him a murderer. He just wants it to all go away. So he does what he's told. He accepts the prosecutor's plea bargain. No trial. No witnesses. No evidence hashed over. And who do you think benefits the most from his decision?"

Drew was shaking, his breath coming in short little gasps, like he'd been running up a steep hill. "No," he whispered. "I killed him. I know...I remember my fist hitting his head..."

"Who benefits?" Charlie insisted.

"No..." It was a wail of grief.

She said it again, softer this time. "Who benefits, Drew?"

His voice went hard. Hard and cold. "Bob Waite."

"Because?" she prodded.

His mind was working again. She could see it in his eyes. Angry eyes, once again. "Because the only person who would have cared enough to ask any questions about Darby's death was behind bars."

"And the only person who could have connected Waite to Darby's murder was Weasel," she added, "And Weasel was conveniently out of the way."

Everything Drew thought showed in his eyes, but Charlie stood her ground. She still held his fists captive.

"I was so sure. I remember hitting him..."

"You remember hitting him," she agreed. "But you said you broke your hand. Your right hand. You wouldn't have been able to throw another right. Not hard enough to have killed him. Not with a broken hand. Why didn't you just crush his larynx if you really wanted to kill him? That's what I'd have done. Where did all the blood come from? If it was his blood, you have to have hit him again. Broken his nose, or something. If you hit him again, you had to let go of him. Your next shot would have to have been a left. I've seen my brother Jamie's hands after a fight. The knuckles on your left hand would have been split, at the very least. Both your hands would have been messed up the next morning."

His shoulders jerked reflexively. The right, and then the left. "I...I just don't know," he managed at last. "My left hand didn't hurt. But I didn't have any cuts deep enough to have bled like that, and I was covered in blood. If I didn't hit him again, where could all that blood have come from?"

"Someone knows," Charlie assured him. "There were other people in that bar room. The bartender, at the very least. Someone knows what really happened."

His eyes met hers at last. Bewildered. Clouded with pain. "What then, Charlie? What do you do when you have the proof in front of you? When two or three men point at me and say 'There! That's the man. He did it!' What do you do when you realize that twelve years wasn't nearly enough time to pay for what I did?"

"Weasel's death has been paid for, whether you killed him or not," Charlie assured him. "Even if you only hit him once, and that killed him, you don't owe anyone anything else. You paid with your daughter's entire childhood. That's more than a man like Weasel was ever worth to anyone."

Charlie squeezed his hands, like a hug. "I'll tell you what we do next. We find out who was with Weasel that night and we try to prove that Waite really did hire Weasel to kill Darby. And you."

"And me?" Drew repeated in surprise.

"You already told me you thought Waite hired Weasel to start that fight with you," Charlie reasoned. "I suspect Waite wanted you dead. Your death would have wrapped things up so neatly. No one left to ask questions about Darby's death. Having Weasel dead was almost as good. No witnesses."

"How do you know?" Drew demanded. "How can you possibly know it happened like that?"

"I don't know," Charlie agreed. "Not for sure. But I'm going to try to find out."

Drew looked away, out the open barn door. "You must think I'm an idiot. I did just what Waite wanted me to do. Walked right into his trap."

"I think you're a good man, who had to deal with too much grief, too quickly," Charlie told him. "A man who lost too much, and had no one to help him find his way back." She brought his fists to her lips and kissed them gently. "I do not think you're an idiot. I think you're the strongest, bravest man I've ever known. You believed you killed that man, and you did what you thought was right. You gave twelve years of your life to repay that debt.

"Now I'm going to do what I think is right. I'm going to bring Bob Waite down. I may never be able to prove what he did, but I will find a way to make him pay." She knew how to do it. She hadn't worked for the Agency all those years without learning anything. She would tear Waite's whole life out from under him, if it would keep him from doing any more harm to Drew. Bob Waite had no idea who he was dealing with. But he was going to find out. "I love you, Drew Bailey."

Drew stared at the auburn-haired beauty who'd bewitched him. She loved him. He'd waited so many years to hear those words, and now that they lay there, in front of him, they frightened him. She had this image of him that was going to be so hard to live up to. Poking and prodding into his life couldn't reveal much of anything pleasant. He felt like a drowning man, his past closing over his head, and there was only one lifeline in sight. She'd offered him the only hope he'd ever have.

She loved him.

It could be his salvation or his undoing.

Chapter Nine

There was a subtle difference in Drew after that. A glint of hard, cold steel she'd catch in his eye. The anger was back. It wasn't directed at her. Never at her. But it was there, just the same. Maybe it had never really left. Just been pushed back under the surface for those few nearly perfect weeks.

Charlie supposed she'd changed, too. There was an anger in her she couldn't let go of. And she was dangerous when she was angry. Even Allen had eventually figured that out.

Still, Waite required a little more finesse than few shots from a .25. Charlie hadn't had even the first glimmering of a plan when she threatened to bring Bob Waite down. She simply knew he had to pay. The threat had been rash, she supposed, if for no other reason than that she'd spoken it out loud. Yet in the days that followed, although her anger mellowed a little, it merely tempered, like a fine blade cooling from the forge. It didn't fade. It was always there, just below the surface, ready to re-ignite.

Charlie attacked the problem from all logical angles. She'd kept pretty much to herself since she'd moved here. She saw that now as a mistake. She didn't have the contacts she would need locally. Still, she put off calling up old favors from the Agency. That was her back up plan. One she hoped she'd never have to use.

Charlie e-mailed Jamie again, adding Savannah Bailey to her earlier list of names, with a high priority for locating her current whereabouts. She sent out feelers to a few old friends in the financial market place, as well. She was still convinced that money had something to do with Darby Anne Bailey Waite's death.

Charlie's next major move, as she'd promised Drew, was to contact City Hospital. The job would provide both access to a mainframe and inside information on local law enforcement. Cops and hospitals just naturally seemed to go together.

The money wasn't bad, either. Drew was right about that. She set her own price, set it high, and could have gone higher. She didn't have any real competition. Old language programmers were too scarce. Almost no one under the age of forty had any hope of figuring out what was wrong with the old mainframe computers. Even if they'd studied Fortran and Cobol 68 in college, the problems had evolved with the systems and the programmers. On top of that, everyone was beginning to freak out over the whole Year 2000 thing. government agencies and large corporations were just beginning to realize that they would be facing serious problems.

Charlie knew programmers who had retired years ago and were coming back to work now in the private sector. She figured they'd all be in demand until about 2010. It would take at least that long to get all the bugs worked out of all the systems. After that she'd retire. Again.

Charlie recruited Janelle to help keep an ear to the local gossip, so that Charlie would know when she had the heat turned up high enough. Besides, it meant that Janelle had to spend time at the farm occasionally. Their unlikely friendship was one that Charlie wasn't about to let go of.

Now, for the frontal assault. It was time to attract Waite's attention. It was time to get Drew off the farm. Strangely enough, he didn't object when Charlie suggested it was time to re-do his wardrobe. Didn't give her any trouble at all. Which made her just a little suspicious.

Charlie held her breath when she pulled into the parking lot of the Feed and Supply, prepared to counter all his objections with well thought out rebuttals. She didn't need them. Drew got out of the truck without comment and approached the place like he was on a mission, shoulders squared, back straight, gait loose, only his eyes betraying his inner turmoil.

Charlie had to stretch her legs to avoid being left behind as he crossed the gravel parking area. He looked down as she caught up and smiled apologetically, slowing his stride to match hers. He held the door for her as they walked in, his fingers brushing her back at the waist.

The place was crowded. Heads raised when they came through the door together. There were a few hard looks, but most were just curious, and some were even friendly. Two men separated themselves from the line at the checkout counter for a cautious approach. Men Drew's age. Drew waited, standing absolutely still, feet slightly apart, the stance of a fighter. To a stranger, he might have looked formidable, a big man tensed for a fight, but to Charlie he looked a glass statue, and she prayed he wouldn't shatter. She stood at his right side, close enough to feel the warmth of his body heat.

Time seemed to ripple for a moment, making the aisle way seem the breadth of the cold war. Then there were extended hands, and "I heard you were back," and "Welcome home," and "Where the hell have you been the last six months," and the world began to turn again.

Charlie smiled to herself. The whole town would know Drew Bailey was back by tomorrow afternoon. More importantly, Drew was back with the flair and style of a politician moving among his constituents, gaining confidence by the moment. He had an easy grace about him, and a smile that radiated genuine warmth.

If there was anything that bothered Charlie at all, it was the way Drew introduced her. Almost off-handedly, he turned away from his newly rediscovered friends to acknowledge her, as if he'd just remembered she stood not more than three inches off his starboard side. "You guys know my boss, Miss Giles? She bought Granddad's farm."

His boss. Was that the way Drew really thought of her? Was she just his boss? Charlie knew better, remembered what Drew said about putting her at risk, but she felt the little pull at her heart, anyway. Charlie smiled politely and turned away, leaving the men to talk among themselves. She developed a sudden interest in work gloves.

Charlie might have sulked for a while longer, if she hadn't overheard the taller one, Moss, make a comment about her as she walked away. "Fine looking woman," he observed. "I hear she's single. Divorced."

"Boys," Drew replied, his voice dropping half an octave lower than it's normal bass tones, "She may be divorced, but she's not available. That territory's been claimed."

Charlie didn't stay close enough to hear anything else. That was enough. Besides, she didn't want anyone to catch her with that foolish grin on her face. It seemed absurd that such a blatantly sexist comment could send her heart soaring like that. But there it was. She'd been *claimed*. She belonged to someone. Drew wasn't embarrassed to tell his friends about their relationship. She wasn't just a joke. The older woman.

When Charlie recovered enough to wander back their way, the talk had turned to football. To her own surprise, Charlie heard herself utter words in a foreign language. "We have a huge TV room, and Drew's got the satellite up and running. Why don't you guys come over for a first game of the season party?"

Moss beamed at her enthusiastically. Duane just stared, slightly open-mouthed. "My wife Ellie's been bugging me to go look Drew up, just so she can see what you've done to that house," he confessed at last.

"So why didn't you?" Drew demanded, his eyes turning hard again.

Duane shifted his feet, looking a little guilty. "Seemed like maybe you wanted to be left alone."

There was a long pause before Drew answered. "Maybe I did," he acknowledged at last. "I'm over it now."

"It's good to have you back," Moss offered. "We'll see you next Sunday."

"Bring your wives, and I'll give them the grand tour," Charlie offered.

Drew found her hand without looking and squeezed it. His skin was warmer than normal. A little damp. "Nervous?" she asked in surprise.

"As a virgin on a blind date," he agreed.

When they left the Feed and Supply, Drew was freshly outfitted in a new copy of his uniform of choice, a flannel shirt and a pair of Levi's.

Charlie's next stop was the Martinsburg Mall. Drew just sat and stared at it as she circled the parking lot. "When did they build this?" he demanded at last.

Charlie shrugged. "I just moved here, remember? I take it the mall wasn't here when you...before."

Drew looked away from the sprawling architectural monument long enough to let his eyes rest on her face for a moment. "Before I went to prison? You won't hurt my feelings if you say it, Charlie. It's not like you're reminding me of some unpleasant detail I might have forgotten."

Charlie blushed brightly at that. "I didn't mean...."

"I know what you meant," Drew interrupted. "I know you'd rather do almost anything than hurt my feelings, because you're like that. If someone had asked any of your old friends a year ago, they'd have sworn you'd never go near a truck stop, let alone associate with an ex-con, or try to solve a twelve year old murder. There's going to be some rough spots along the way, Charlie. Some new territory to explore. But as long as you're not embarrassed by my past, you don't have to worry about hurting my feelings."

Charlie slid across the seat to wrap her arms around him. "I'm not embarrassed by your past," she assured him. "You are many things to me, but never an embarrassment. You're good and kind and strong and handsome, and you have a great sense of humor and you're good to my cats. What more could I ask for?"

Drew laughed at that. "An eye exam, to start with. I'm about as handsome as a flat tire. I'm moody and considerably lacking in the self-confidence department, and if it weren't for you, I'd join an army of ex-cons who get so disillusioned with life on the outside that they look for ways to get sent back to prison."

"On purpose?" Charlie gasped in disbelief. "Men get sent back there on purpose?"

"Every day," Drew assured her. "It's the depression, mostly. It hits the day you get off the bus and there's no one there to meet you. You go home, and your family doesn't want you back. You're an embarrassment to them. The ex-con they have to make excuses for.

"Your friends have all moved on with their lives without you. You don't fit in. You can't get a job, because if you lie about where you've been, you're going back, and if you tell people where you've been, they won't hire you. Guys who got college degrees in prison end up washing dishes in some restaurant for an asshole who treats them like they should be glad to shovel other people's garbage into trash cans all day. One day, you look around, and you realize you were better off back in prison. You knew what to expect. You didn't have to worry about where the next meal was coming from. You had friends who weren't embarrassed to be seen with you. You fit in."

Charlie searched his face with her eyes. "Do you feel like that?"

"I did," Drew admitted. "I wouldn't have dared to ask you for a job when I got back to the farm. The worst was sitting at that bus stop for hours waiting for someone to come get me. I was pretty sure as soon as I got there that no one was going to show up, but I knew the moment I started walking I'd be violating parole. Then I found out my grandfather was dead. I had less than fifty bucks to my name, no change for the pay phone, and no one to call anyway. I felt like there was a sign on my forehead flashing ex-con warnings at everybody. Two weeks on the outside didn't do anything to make those feelings go away, either. Then you smiled at me, and treated me like I didn't have to justify taking up so much oxygen, and for the first time I felt like maybe I might make it after all."

"You're going to make it, Drew," Charlie assured him. "You're going to make it. I promise. You may have lost your grandfather, but you've got a home, and a job, and a woman who loves you very much, and more friends than you know. Moss and Duane won't be alone at that party, I'll just bet you. You'll never be an embarrassment to me, I promise you that. I'm proud to be seen with you. I still think you're very handsome. What would you know about handsome, anyway? You've got a good, strong chin, the most wonderful hair, and gorgeous eyes, and a very kissable mouth..."

Drew stopped her tirade by placing that very kissable mouth over hers for the kind of kiss that left her breathless and a little disoriented, rather losing her train of thought. "You're still nuts," he assured her. "Let's go get this done. I don't know why what we got at the Feed and Supply wasn't good enough, but I do know by now there's no changing your mind, so let's get it over with."

"Couldn't we get back to that kissable mouth part again instead?" Charlie teased.

"No," Drew argued. "No more kisses for you until you give up this shopping craze and take me home. Then you can have all the kisses you want." With that he freed himself from her arms and jumped down out of the truck.

Charlie laughed and chased him across the parking lot. They spent the next five minutes dodging through the cars and chasing each other with shopping carts like they were two kids, enjoying a break from school. Charlie laughed until she had to sit down on the curb at the edge of the road. "Thank you," she managed at last. "I've been a good little girl for so long I'd forgotten how much fun being bad can be."

Drew relented and let her explore that kissable mouth theory a little further before they braved the depths of the mall.

By the time they made it back to the Jeep, they had a regular party arranged for the following Sunday, and Charlie had a totally different picture of Drew's youth. He'd been a bit of a local hero, it seemed. Very popular with the girls, as well. More than one woman bounced over to throw her arms around him with little or no warning.

"I'm sorry about that," Drew offered, more than a little embarrassed by the attention he was receiving.

"At least they don't want your autograph," Charlie philosophized with a sigh as two more women wandered away.

"And I won't be taking anyone home but you," Drew promised as he slid an arm around her waist.

The Mall was good for a couple of sports coats, a few casual shirts, and a haircut. The haircut was Drew's idea. Charlie liked it long, but she had to admit, Drew cleaned up nice. Real nice. Though the hairdresser spent a little more time running her hands through Drew's hair than Charlie thought was absolutely necessary.

Drew didn't even seem to mind trying on clothes, though he absolutely refused to even look at Charlie's idea of decent shoes. She headed for Italian Leather while he concentrated on the work boots. They eventually compromised on a new pair of Western Boots from the Tack Shop downtown, where she'd stopped to pick up a few supplies for the mares after they left the mall. The boots were Justin's, made from black mule hide with pointy toes and tall, slanted heels. They would make a funny footprint. Charlie tried to leave his old broken down boots in the garbage can when they left, but Drew hung on to them stubbornly.

Charlie's last stop was downtown, across the street from Waite's old bank. When she pulled up to park in front of the Big and Tall Men's store, Drew began to look uncomfortable. He rolled his eyes at the price tags and tried to direct her attention away from the suits. Charlie didn't argue. She just picked out what she wanted and pointed toward the dressing room.

An hour later, as they were leaving, well laden with more packages bound for the Jeep, Drew spotted a sheriff's department car parked in front of the cafe two doors down from the bank. "Looks like somebody took your bait," Drew observed.

"Bait?" Charlie repeated in surprise. His abrupt change of moods threw her into a tailspin.

"Wasn't that what this little shopping spree was all about?" Drew observed sardonically. "Show me off in public, attract attention? See who crawls out of the woodwork?"

So that's why he'd been so cooperative. "Mostly, it was to put together a wardrobe for you. But it won't break my heart if Waite finds out you're back in town. Let him wonder what you're up to. It'll do him good."

"Then take me to lunch at Peccadillo's," Drew suggested. "Let's let Bob get a good look at me." There was that coldness back in his eyes that she didn't like, but she couldn't argue with his logic. Besides, he was wearing the last suit she'd had him try on, and the new boots, and he looked like she needed to take him somewhere.

"Drew?" she said, trying to keep the worry out of her voice.

His eyes softened as he looked down at her. "Don't worry, Angel. I'm not going to do anything stupid. Not with witnesses."

"I know you won't. And neither will I."

Drew smiled as he offered her his arm to cross the street.

Allen had never done things like that. Opened doors for her, held her hand when they walked together, looped her arm through his when he stood beside her. Never slowed his steps just a little so she wouldn't have to run to keep up. Never knew what she was thinking without having to be told. Never made her so conscious of her body, and of all the places she wanted to be touched. With Drew, she felt alive, on fire all the time. Charlie had always prided herself on being a liberated woman, but she realized suddenly that, at the moment, there wasn't anything she wanted to be liberated from. Except Drew's past.

A deputy Drew didn't recognize was eating in the little cafe, not Waite himself, so a few of Charlie's butterflies settled down. It was enough. She had no doubt that Waite would have a full report before their lunch was over.

It was what Waite might do about it that worried her. But she couldn't change her mind now. It was too late. Maybe Drew was right, and he was the bait. A cold shiver ran down her back as she nodded her head at the deputy on their way out. He'd been done his meal a long time ago, and was still sitting there drinking coffee. She noted his nametag. Flannery. Kit Flannery. He had the kind of eyes that read like a closed book.

* * * * *

It wasn't until Sunday morning, when Drew headed out to the barn after breakfast and didn't come back, that Charlie finally decided to panic. She'd suspected that there was something wrong when they got home from shopping on Saturday, but, whatever it was, Drew didn't seem to want to talk about it, and she hadn't pressed the point. But he'd slept in his own room last night. That made her feel like he was only visiting the rest of the time.

Drew was sitting on the end of the haystack when Charlie tracked him down. He was wearing his last old flannel shirt, his old jeans with a button sewn on at the waist, and his scuffed, broken down boots. He was chewing on a long stalk of straw, staring out the open double-doors across the front pasture.

Charlie crossed the barn floor quietly, making just enough noise to let him know she was there without spooking him. He didn't look up. She eased down beside him on the next bale of hay, close enough for him to reach her if he wanted to, but far enough away to give him his space. She sat, and waited.

"You spent over a grand yesterday," Drew observed at last.

"You should see me in New York," she offered, trying to sound casual.

"Exactly." There was no humor in his voice.

For the first time, Charlie got a good look at his eyes. They were storm cloud gray. "Exactly what?" She had to work to keep her voice calm.

"That's not the kind of money a waitress makes." Drew's voice had a bitter edge to it.

"What are you getting at?" This wasn't the way things were supposed to go. Charlie was more than just a little frightened, now, and perhaps just a little irritated.

No.

She couldn't afford to lose her temper with him again.

Drew jabbed the stalk of hay against his upturned boot. "You spend money like you're used to having it there whenever you need it."

"I never said I didn't have any money."

"We've never talked about money at all," Drew pointed out, his voice chilly.

"Nobody told me we needed to." She could be cold, too, if that's the way he wanted it. She'd had this argument before, with Allen, more than once, but it was always the other way around. She hadn't ever spent enough, according to Allen.

"I don't even know you, Charlie. I have no idea who you really are." His back to her spoke volumes, more than his words ever could. "I fell for a waitress in a run down dive of a truck stop who looked like she needed help. Someone with a mortgage and a future that was at risk. Someone who might just be desperate enough to make use of an ex-con with a strong back and willing hands. Someone who just might need me."

Charlie felt her temper rising, felt the fear taking hold. "I can't need you without being broke? What do you want from me? Do you want me to cut up my Gold Card, sell all my Coca-Cola stocks, and donate the money to charity? Shall I give the

Andalusians all away, and take in Thoroughbred Racetrack rejects? There's a sure way to lose money. Will that make you happy?" She was on her feet now, voice climbing dangerously, inches from Drew's broad back. "I signed a contract last week that's worth over $30,000 in the next four months. That was your idea! If I want to spend some of that money on you, why shouldn't I?"

Drew turned to face Charlie, his eyes stormy gray and troubled. "It's not what you spent, Charlie, or what you do for a living. I don't really even know what you do for a living. I don't know who you are. Coca-Cola stocks, for God's sake? Do you think I'm ever going to own stock in anything? Where am I going to wear three-hundred-dollar suits? Down to the Feed and Supply to pick up grain?"

"Suits? This is about the suits? They're business suits," Charlie spit angrily. "You said you'd work with me. Do you think you can work in an office in broken down shit-kickers and Levi's with the knees blown out?"

"Business suits," Drew repeated, dumbfounded. "Three-hundred-dollar business suits?"

"I don't buy suits from Sears."

"I've never owned any suit, Charlie. Not one. Not from anywhere. I borrowed the suit I got married in from my best friend, Terry Masters." Drew's voice sounded desolate. "How can I be part of a world with three-hundred-dollar suits and Coca-Cola stocks?"

The hurt threatened to overwhelm her. "I'm no different than you are. My father worked for the federal government. The Park Service. We moved every few years. I went to six different schools. My mother moved out when I was ten. She liked to spend money, a lot more than Daddy made. She liked pretty clothes and places to wear them. I guess she got tired of moving. Got tired of never having enough money. Got bored living off in the sticks.

"I stayed with my father. I was the last one left at home. My brother Jamie was already gone. He's the oldest. Frances was away at college. It was just me and Dad till I went off to college. After I graduated, I lived in a tiny apartment in Arlington until I bought the townhouse in Alexandria. That was eight years before I married Allen. The townhouse wasn't community property.

"Daddy always said 'Buy stocks in good, solid companies, and don't panic when the market goes down. Companies like Coca-Cola and AT&T will weather anything.' Momma didn't like that plan. It left her short on cash to spend in trendy little boutiques. But it was a good plan, and it worked for Dad, and it worked for me. When Allen left me he cleared out my bank accounts. He got my cash, about fifteen thousand dollars, but he couldn't touch my stocks, or the stocks Daddy left me, or my townhouse.

"I bought this farm outright. Everything here is paid for. I'm not rich. Everything I have here is at risk. I'm counting on selling every one of the foals those mares out there are carrying. I'm working in case something goes wrong and this place can't pay its own expenses."

Drew ran a hand through his hair again. His eyes searched hers, as if looking for a lifeline. "My ex-wife left me for a man who would take her on a thousand dollar shopping spree. The kind of man who would wear three-hundred-dollar suits to work every day and not think twice about it. The kind of man who'd have known the difference between a business suit and whatever other kind of suits there are. The kind of man who liked to call me a poor white trash bastard."

Charlie reached out to take his big, callused hands in her own small, fragile looking ones. "Darby left you for kind of man who killed her," she reminded him. "Don't you see? The money doesn't matter to me. I didn't fall in love with you hoping I could turn you into someone else. I don't need a man for money or social position. I don't give a damn who your parents were or whether they were married."

Drew's voice hissed out low and desperate. "I don't see how I can possibly be enough for you."

"Enough for me?" Charlie allowed a humorless laugh to escape her lips. "Enough for me? You think I want another man who's a national celebrity, maybe? When I married Allen, it seemed like everyone knew him wherever we went. We couldn't walk downtown together without women throwing themselves at him. And then, once he was off the best sellers' lists, once people stopped recognizing him, he quit going much of anywhere. He couldn't stand the lack of attention. I was always trying to make up for things."

Charlie closed her eyes and opened her heart. "I'm scared, too," she admitted. "I keep thinking I'll wake up some morning and you'll be gone. That morning after those boys beat you up, when I woke up and you weren't here, that was so much worse than losing Allen, because you can't lose what you never really had. Whenever you're out of my sight, I'm afraid. Nothing's right until I find you."

Drew's arms encircled her at last. "I'm not going anywhere, Charlie. Where would I run to?"

"Anywhere," Charlie argued. "There are always going to be women throwing themselves at you, Drew. Women who are younger and prettier than I am. Women like that know how to make things happen. By this time next week you could have a new identity. You could be a Chef in a New York restaurant, or the personal trainer to some young rock star out in LA. You're like a cat. You'll always land on your feet."

Drew laughed. "Listen to us, Charlie. We're afraid of the same things. We're both so damn sure that we don't measure up, somehow, that we're looking for a reason to fail."

Charlie stared up at him, her anger fading. "How do we change that?"

Drew wiped her damp face with his shirttail. "I'm not sure. We have to learn to trust each other. Maybe we have to talk more. Tell each other the things we try so hard to keep hidden."

"Like what?" Charlie asked suspiciously.

"Like you, being afraid you'll wake up to find me gone. I'm not going anywhere, Charlie. I don't want to go anywhere. I wouldn't even if I could. But if it'll make you feel better, I'll make sure my face is the first thing you see every morning. I'd have thought that would give you nightmares." His voice held a teasing quality that betrayed his relief.

"I only took the job at Harry's because it was so close and I was lonely," she confided.

"I'll try not to let you get lonely again," Drew promised, nibbling at her jaw.

Charlie closed her eyes and leaned her head back, distracted by the feel of his kisses against the under side of her chin. "I'll try not to spend enough money to intimidate you. I don't, usually. Allen always said I could pinch a penny till it screamed."

"So what was yesterday all about?" His voice was soft, now. A question, not an accusation.

"Freedom, I guess. I knew I could afford it. And I wanted to do something for you. To try to make up for things. I know what it's like, always being the poor kid on the block. The one who doesn't quite fit in. I don't want you to have to feel like that, ever again."

"Charlie, you don't have to spend money on me to make me feel like I belong. You stood beside me, yesterday. You talked to my friends. You invited them into your home. I was scared because I thought the clothes were for you. So I wouldn't embarrass you."

Charlie swept her fingers through his hair, pulling his head down to her height. "No, Drew, no. Never that. You can wear cut off blue jeans to the White House if you want. You'll never embarrass me. You'll probably start a new fashion trend."

"You do know you're crazy, don't you?" His kisses teased the edges of her mouth.

"Maybe you could help me with the book keeping for this place. That way you'd know where we stand."

"We," Drew repeated. "I like that. I'll try to act more like part of a 'we,' and not just a hired hand who's spending the night in the boss's bed."

"We'll buy a new bed, if you want. Together. One that will be ours, instead of mine."

"You don't need to buy a different bed." He looked up questioningly. "That's not the bed you shared with Allen?"

"No, I ruined that mattress," Charlie assured him. "Lead stains badly."

Drew laughed at that. "Okay," he agreed. "We can keep your bed."

"You should have your own money, and your own checking account. The parole people are going to want to see deposit receipts, aren't they?"

"Right now, I don't care what they want." Drew nipped her bottom lip playfully. "You spend a lot of time trying to figure out how to make every one around you happy. What do you want, Charlie? What do you need?"

Her eyes closed as his thumbs skimmed over her breasts, teasing her through the thin fabric of her t-shirt. "I need you. I need the way you make me feel when you touch me – like I'm something special."

"Special?" Wonder tinged his voice as his hands stilled. "Don't you know, woman? You – everything about you – you overwhelm me."

"I don't know anything."

He kissed her again, his lips soft, and incredibly tender. "You are everything to me, Charlie."

Everything. A surge of hope welled up within her. Everything. That was a long way to come for a man who hadn't trusted himself enough to even touch her. It wasn't quite *I love you*, but it would do. Her hands pulled him tightly against her hips, so that she could feel the heat of his cock jumping against her as she offered herself to him. "I need you," she whispered again. "I need to feel your hands one me. I need to feel you inside me. Make me forget that I was ever lonely."

He kissed her gently again, then parted her lips, her breath catching in her throat as his tongue swept over the roof of her mouth, then wrapped around hers in a teasing parody of the mating her body desired. She'd thought she wanted hot and hard and urgent, but he took his time, his hands gliding over her, touching her everywhere, lighting her skin on fire as they skimmed, awakening, promising, worshiping.

It was slow, and languid, and the fires he started threatened to consume her as he kissed his way down from her hungry mouth to her aching breasts. Her t-shirt disappeared, then his hand slipped inside her jeans, stroking, teasing, until she moaned in need. And then his fingers were gone, and she whimpered at the loss, but it was only for a moment, as he helped her out of her jeans.

His old flannel shirt and worn old jeans disappeared faster than she'd have thought possible, and then his arms were back around her, touching, stroking, reassuring, as he dropped to his knees, falling back gracefully onto the barn floor, his body protecting her as they went down.

The loose hay on the floor of the barn felt strangely exotic, heady and fragrant at close range, like a hint of captured spring. His arms around her took away the fear, promising things that he couldn't say with words. His fingers traced over her skin, memorizing ever curve and hollow, working down her back now to lift one leg over his hip, and then skimming up her inner thigh to part the warm, wet folds of her labia, stroking her in rhythm to the lap of his tongue over her breast, until the ache she'd felt when she went looking for him was but a dim memory.

"Your turn." She had to fight for enough coherent thought to get the words out. "Tell me what you want."

"I want you." His words came out muffled as they played over her breast, and then his lips moved back to her mouth, nipping gently, then kissing her deeply. "I want those decades you talked about." He punctuated his sentence with kisses that heated her blood even as his stroking fingers plunged deep inside her. "I want to know that even when we fight, because we will, I'm not going to lose you."

"You're not – going to lose me." She buried her fingers into the hard muscled curve of his butt, clenching even as the first waves of release had her tightening around his fingers. She rode out the wave, then slipped her fingers between them to stroke over his balls, feeling them contract in her hand, massaging gently as he groaned at her touch. She shifted her grip to his cock, so full and ready for her, closing her fist around him, stroking slowly until he responded to her rhythm.

Wet fingers slid out of her, wrapping around her hand, stilling her busy fingers. "I wanted to make this last for you. But I won't last long if you keep doing that."

"You're driving me insane. I want you. Now."

He moved her hand under his to trace over her clitoris with the head of his penis, laughing as she tried to direct him down lower and in. She arched hard against him, her body screaming with need. "Greedy, aren't you."

"Yes!" she nearly screamed.

He just held her, watching her face as he outlined her opening, the traces of his fluid mixing with hers, scorching her with his heat. "I'm greedy, too. I thought – I was afraid it was just sex. I want more. I need more. I need this to mean something."

More? How much more? Was he asking her for some kind of commitment? Her eyes closed as he slipped inside her. She remembered the night she'd first met him, and the look in his eyes. She'd pegged him then. A drifter, headed from nowhere to somewhere else. How could she hold him? How could she trust a man who wouldn't say *I love you* with so much of her soul?

He stroked into her, hard and wanting, the slow languid play gone now as his body demanded her response. Everything. She opened her eyes as she met him thrust for thrust, pulling him against her with her leg wrapped over his hip. Everything. "This means everything to me," she offered. "I love you. You can have those decades. A lifetime if you want it."

His mouth claimed hers again, and she could have sworn he was fighting back tears. She felt his control shatter. He rolled with her until she lay underneath him, pulling her knees to either side of his chest. She could feel the weight of his balls slapping against her exposed perineum, heavy and full, as he plunged into her. She tightened around him, her grip fierce, as she came for him, climaxing so violently she felt she might lose consciousness.

She sucked in her breath in a rush as she realized she'd forgotten to breathe. "Yes!" she laughed, looking up at him. "Come for me."

He grinned down at her, pumping into her furiously. "Now?"

She moved her hands to stroke her own breasts, knowing she was pushing him over the edge as she rolled her nipples between her fingers.

It was like watching a fighter take a knock out punch. He went stiff with the impact, though his hips gave a few last convulsive thrusts as he broke like a wave crashing into the beachhead. She tightened around him again, milking him of his cum as if it were the elixir of life.

"You destroy me," he managed at last. "Every time. Every single time. I'm not sure who I am until you touch me again."

She held him locked within her as she pulled him down close enough to kiss him again. "Mine. Whoever you are, you are mine."

He buried his face in her hair, his words barely audible. "I need you, Charlie. I've never needed anyone like this before. I need to know I have the right to touch you, whenever I want to, no matter who's watching. I want to take you to my high school class reunion and say 'Hey Guys! Look who I'm with!'"

He rolled so that she lay on top of him, her hair spread over them like a covering as she snuggled against his chest. "I want to walk down the street, and know that when people turn to stare, it's because of the beautiful woman I'm with, not because they're whispering 'There goes Andrew Bailey. The murderer.' But most of all, I want to know that, no matter what happens, I won't end up alone again. Even if I don't get invited to my high school class reunion. Even if I did kill Weasel. I want to know it doesn't matter, that I won't lose you."

"You'd play hell trying to get rid of me," Charlie assured him again. "I'm not someone you can lose. I promise. I'll go anywhere you want with you, any time. Whether it's your high school class reunion or the grocery store or the Feed and Supply or even a football game. I like being seen with you. What woman wouldn't be flattered to be seen with a handsome man beside her? As for Weasel, if you did kill him, you probably did society a favor."

Charlie chewed on her lower lip again, searching his eyes for the truth. "Do you want me to quit asking questions about Bob Waite?"

Drew rose to pace the barn floor, pausing to pick up their clothes. "No. No, I can't do that. I need to know what really happened. I was sure, before. I knew I'd killed a man, and I'd learned to live with it. Now I'm not sure, and I don't think I can live with that. I want to know, whatever the truth is. I just need to know that you can live with the answers, no matter what they turn out to be."

Charlie sat in the hay, her knees drawn up to her chest, watching him dress with methodical precision. "I can live with the answers," she promised. "And I can live through the questions. As long as you're part of the package."

Drew paused to search her face again. "What do you see when you look at me, Charlie?"

Charlie smiled up at him. "I see a kind, sensitive, caring man who makes me feel very special."

"Why don't you see an ex-con who's down on his luck and looking for a free ride? That's what anyone else would see."

"Because that's not who you are," Charlie assured him. "It's just where you've been."

Drew took a deep breath and let it out slowly. "What would happen if I asked you to marry me, Charlie?"

Charlie blinked, twice, not sure she'd heard him right. "Did you just propose to me?"

"No. When I get the nerve to do that, I'll do it right. I just need to know if you'd ever even consider the possibility. If I even have the right to ask. I know what position that would put you in. You have family to think about. Your people aren't going to be happy at the idea of you even knowing an ex-con, let alone living with one."

Living together. Was that what they were doing? Charlie hadn't thought about it that way. The old Charlie would never have agreed to live with a man she wasn't married to. Her world had re-aligned itself around a set of circumstances she never could have predicted. "I swore once I would never get married again," she answered slowly. "But I never expected to fall in love again, either. I thought I'd resigned myself to being alone." She met his eyes, finding his soul laid bare before her. "You don't need my permission to propose to me, Drew. But I'm not going to answer you until you ask."

"What about your family?"

"My family will love you. But you may not love all of them. I warn you, Mother was very upset when I ran off to the Justice of the Peace with Allen. She'd insist on a Church wedding, a rather large one. I have a lot of relatives. Mother is the youngest of seven children. All of her brothers and sisters are married and they have children my age and older. My sister has adult children, and most of them have children, too. Mother loves to throw a big party. And then there are the relatives on my father's side."

"Wait a minute!" Drew appealed in confusion. "You said your mother ran off when you were ten!"

"I said she moved out," Charlie corrected. "She went home to her mother's. Grandma's still alive, incidentally. She's ninety-three. All her sisters have made it past one hundred. They're still around, too. All five of them."

"What makes you think a family like that would welcome me? Why would they? They'd probably all disown you as soon as they find out I have a prison record. What then, Charlie?"

"I spent a weekend in jail for shooting at my ex-husband a year ago, remember? You paid your debt, if there ever was one. Anyone who would hold that against you doesn't need to be part of my life. They aren't going to say a thing. At least not where I can hear them. They expect me to do crazy things. All they need to know about you is that you make me happy."

"Do I? Do I make you happy, Charlie?"

"You make me very happy, Drew. Happier, I think, than I've ever been before. Quit worrying about my family. None of them are all that normal, anyway. Grandma got remarried last year to a seventy-six year old retired marine."

Drew shifted his weight, stretching to look out the upper half of the barn doors. "Any other surprises?"

Charlie scrambled to her feet, trying to see what he was looking at, but she was too short. "Like what?" she prompted, trying not to sound too worried.

"Like that car coming up the driveway. A white Cadillac Eldorado convertible. About a fifty-four. Why is a twenty thousand dollar car bumping up a dirt lane, Charlie?"

"Father, Bless me, for I have sinned," she recited hastily as she grabbed for her clothes. "I have not made confession in over fifteen years. I have dredged up the Ghost of Christmas Past. I have opened Pandora's Box."

"Let me guess," Drew commented dryly as he cracked the lower door open to get a better look. "You're all Catholic, too."

"All," Charlie confirmed. "All hundred-and-thirty-eight, at the last family reunion. Irish Catholic, at that. On both sides."

"Then the very tall priest would be your cousin." Drew's voice was stoic. Resigned.

"My brother, Jamie," Charlie corrected.

"Wait a minute! I know you told me your cousin was the priest."

"Was is correct," Charlie explained. "David left the order to marry a nun."

Drew frowned and shook his head like a dog clearing the rain from his coat. "I could have sworn you just said your brother has children!"

"No," Charlie reiterated patiently. "My brother is a Priest. No children. I said I have a sister who has children. My sister Frances. The tall red-headed woman getting out on the other side of the Caddy."

"Oh, Lord," Drew groaned.

"You don't have to convert," Charlie assured him. "Children follow the mother's religion."

"You definitely said we couldn't have children," Drew insisted.

"Well, I wouldn't think so, at my age, but the church always plans on miracles, which is why when Catholic men marry Protestant women, the woman has to convert."

"Oh, good Lord," Drew repeated as loud barks signaled Ghost's belated notice of their visitors. "I've got to get that dog." He kissed Charlie hard on the mouth and pushed her away. "You're a mess. You don't want them to see you like this. Go do something with your hair and come up through the barn yard."

"Tuck your shirt in!" Charlie warned.

Drew shoved his shirt into his Levi's as he ran out the side door.

"Hail Mary, full of Grace, the Lord is with thee," Charlie recited as Ghost shot by the barn doors dripping mud. Drew disappeared, hot on the big dog's trail.

"No! Ghost! NO! DOWN!" she heard Drew's deep voice thunder as she entered the black hole of the barn stairs. "Damn it DOG! Don't you ever listen?"

Chapter Ten

Drew had already managed to curtail the dog, though he still held Ghost firmly by the collar. He was helping Jamie up off the ground. Jamie looked distinctly out of sorts, his professional dignity definitely muddied. Ghost didn't look too happy, either.

Charlie gave a shrill whistle. Ghost lunged toward her, nearly dislocating Drew's shoulder before the man had the good sense to release the dog. "Ghost," Charlie ordered quietly when the dog slid to a stop before her, eyes laughing merrily. "Bring in the horses." One-hundred-and-fifty pounds of fur hurtled down the barnyard steps to streak across the front pasture and out of sight.

Drew's mouth formed a thin, straight line as his gaze shifted from Ghost's retreating mass to Charlie's approach. "How the – How do you do that?"

Charlie thought better of answering.

"I'll go make some coffee." His voice had dropped to a low growl.

She knew that stance so well. Shoulders bowed. Head bent. Big man, trying to fade into the background.

"Drew?"

Charlie spoke his name softly as he turned to slink away.

He pivoted slowly, raising his eyes to meet hers.

"We've got coffee."

Their eyes held for the space of two heartbeats.

Stay here with me. Face them with me. You don't have to go.

Slowly, so slowly, a muscle at a time, his shoulders settled back. He stood straighter, taller, head raising as he extended a hand to her, palm up. With a smile that lit her eyes, Charlie moved toward him. Drew took a step in her direction, slipping an arm around her waist as their fingers met, his touch light, tentative, as if she might pull away. Charlie laced her fingers through his and leaned against him.

Jamie and Frances suddenly came back to life, moving and talking and shutting car doors all at the same time. As if trying to cover the awkwardness of their previous silence. Noisy. Strained.

Frances flashed her most professional smile. "Well, aren't you going to introduce us?"

Charlie gave a good imitation of her sister's plastic facade. "Of course. Jamie, Frances, I'd like you to meet Andrew Bailey."

What should she call him? Employee? Handy man? Boy friend? Lover?

None were quite right, so Charlie left it at that, just Drew's name, and his arm around her waist, and offered no further explanations. No defense. Let them figure it out.

Her siblings exchanged glances again, and the quiet settled back in. Jamie checked to make sure he had his briefcase, fidgeting unnecessarily, avoiding Charlie's eyes. He knew, she thought. Jamie had run those names she'd sent him. He knew who Drew was.

Or at least where Drew had been for the last twelve years.

Charlie repeated the assurances she'd given Drew to herself. Jamie and Frances were going to love Drew. They weren't the kind of people who would judge Drew solely on the basis of his prison record. Charlie took a deep breath and tried to steady her nerves.

Frances, as usual, was the one to take the initiative. She gave her Harris Tweed suit jacket a twitch to straighten the hem, then marched around the Caddy to Charlie's side. Frances started at the bottom, with the broken down boots, and let her eyes travel slowly up Drew's long, lean frame until she had to tilt her head back to meet his eyes. She smiled as she extended her hand. "Pleased to meet you, Mr. Bailey. Jamie's been talking about you for days, but still, you're something of a surprise."

Drew took the offered hand, meeting Frances's gaze levelly. "It's Drew, Ma'am. I hope I'm not too much of a shock."

"I don't know what I expected, really," Frances admitted. "Let's just say that you're absolutely nothing like Charlie's ex."

Drew bent slowly, elaborately, to look down, pulling on the fabric of his jeans at the thigh, then looked back up again, meeting Frances's questioning gaze with a perfectly straight face. "You're right," he observed. "Not one bullet hole."

A little laugh forced it's way from between Frances tightly pressed lips. Then, despite her best efforts, another one made it, then a most unprofessional snort. Charlie tried not to laugh, but once Frances lost her composure, Charlie wasn't far behind. By the time Ghost brought the mares in, both sisters were rolling in the soft, cool grass, trying to catch their breath. Charlie saw Drew look over at Jamie, one eyebrow cocked, and shrug, as if completely mystified, which only made her laugh all the harder.

Drew turned toward Jamie, his expression sedate. "Coffee?"

Jamie agreed with a curt nod, and the two men walked off toward the house together, leaving the women to work things out.

"The place looks great," Jamie observed as they turned away.

"Thanks. I'm nowhere near the gardener my grandmother was."

"I saw you play, years ago..."

The men's voices faded away as the wisteria closed over them like a sheltering canopy.

"My God, he's gorgeous! What a hunk! You could have knocked me over with a feather when he came around the barn."

Charlie smiled, her gaze still focused on the wisteria. "You should see him in a suit."

Frances offered a throaty chuckle. "Mmm. I think I'd rather see him out of a suit."

"I never did learn to share."

Frances continued, seemingly ignoring her younger sister's warning tone, though a smile tickled her lips. "Maybe he has a secret fantasy about sisters."

"You're happily married, remember?"

"I may be married, honey, but I'm not dead." Frances turned her attention back to her sister, no longer even trying to hide her smile. "You never share. You're such a spoiled little brat."

Ghost stood looking down at them, his mouth open and his tongue hanging out one side. It looked like he was laughing at them. Charlie hugged the big dog as she pulled herself up and dusted off. "I think I like being spoiled. Allen didn't invest anywhere near enough energy in spoiling me."

Frances followed her down the barnyard stairs, stopping to scratch a nose here or there as they opened the stall doors to let the mares in. "The mares are looking fat and sassy. You even look like you've managed to gain a little weight, yourself."

"Three pounds," Charlie reported happily.

"You look good. Are you as happy as you look?"

"What do you mean?" Charlie was never sure where a question from Frances was leading.

Frances pushed at her shoulder playfully. "Don't get defensive. It's not a trick question. I just want to know if you're happy. Does Andrew Bailey make you happy?"

"Happy? Most of the time," Charlie acknowledged. "I don't suppose anyone's ever happy all the time. Drew and I have had a few disagreements. Who doesn't? He makes me feel necessary, Franny. He makes me feel loved. He actually needs me. And I need him."

"What about the other times?" Frances insisted. "The times when you argue? Are you safe with him?"

Charlie stopped, turning to face her sister, a red flush creeping up her cheeks. "Safe?"

"The man is more than twice your size, Charlie, and he's got a reputation for violence. I see the results of domestic disagreements every day. I suppose you already know Andrew got out of the West Virginia Penitentiary last May."

Charlie headed for the feed room. "I know about Moundsville. And you know I can take care of myself. If any man ever tried to hurt me I think I'd kill him. But Drew hasn't, and he won't. Not now. Not ever. I've never felt safer with any man. We've had a few fights, like I said, but Drew doesn't even raise his voice to me. Some local boys ambushed him one night last summer, wanted to scare him away, and Drew wouldn't raise a hand to defend himself. He ended up with three cracked ribs and his arm in a cast. I think he's afraid of his own strength. I had trouble convincing Drew I wouldn't break. He's gentle and kind and considerate. He's good for me."

"He sounds too good to be true," Frances teased, as if trying to lighten the mood. "What's the catch?"

"There is no catch," Charlie assured her. "Unless you count the prison record. I think I fell in love with Drew the first time he washed the dishes. And he's a fantastic cook."

"The man washes the dishes and he cooks? And you haven't married him yet?"

"Not yet." Charlie casually measured oats and bran and corn into seven black rubber buckets.

"Not yet?" Frances repeated in alarm. "You've been discussing marriage with a man who just got out of prison?"

Charlie moved to the bale of hay Drew had already opened for her. "I'd marry him in a heartbeat, Franny. I'm old enough to know what I want, and I want Drew Bailey."

Frances stared at Charlie as if she'd never seen her sister before. "Have you lost your mind? The man just got out of prison. Not just any prison, either. The West Virginia Maximum Security Penitentiary at Moundsville. One of the toughest prisons in the country. Right up there with Leavenworth. They only put the really tough ones there, Charlie. Your kind, gentle rose has a few thorns. He killed another man with his bare hands!"

"Maybe." Charlie shifted around Frances, tossing the hay over the old wooden rails with a practiced swing.

"What do you mean, maybe?" Frances demanded angrily. "Andrew Bailey is a murderer! He confessed to killing a man! He pled guilty!"

"You've left out a few details, big sister." Charlie plunged the pitchfork into the hard packed runway. "First of all, Drew was dead drunk. He doesn't know what happened that night. All he remembers is hitting the man. Once. Just once. Except that before Drew hit him, Weasel, the man Drew is supposed to have killed, was bragging about how Bob Waite had hired him to kill Darby Waite, Drew's ex-wife. And get this. Bob Waite is now the County's duly elected sheriff."

"Wait a minute." Frances held out her hand like a traffic cop. "You're telling me Andrew Bailey confessed to a murder he didn't remember committing?"

"That's about the size of it," Charlie conceded. "Except Drew never actually confessed. He just pled guilty. He refused to sign a confession, because he didn't remember what happened."

"Well," Frances commented melodramatically. "That changes everything, doesn't it. The man is not only an ex-con, but he's a moron as well!"

"Drew woke up in jail, wearing a shirt covered with dried blood. A sheriff's deputy told Drew he'd killed a man," Charlie explained with more patience than she felt. "Drew remembered hitting Weasel. The lawyer told Drew that if he didn't accept the prosecutor's offer of second-degree Manslaughter, he'd end up spending the rest of his life in prison. Drew knew his grandfather couldn't afford the attorney's fees for a long, drawn out trial. The attorney told Drew that if his case went to trial, he was going to lose, anyway. So Drew pled guilty."

"Andrew woke up in jail still wearing his own shirt? His shirt had blood all over it and the investigating officers didn't put it into evidence?"

"No one ever tested Drew's shirt," Charlie confirmed. "As far as I know, no one collected any other physical evidence at the crime scene, either. No one even took statements from any of the witnesses or even made a list of who the witnesses were."

Frances turned her back on Charlie and began to pace. Charlie smiled to herself. This was always the best part of an argument with Frances – when Frances had changed sides, and didn't even know it yet. Frances started talking again, her voice distracted. "When Jamie got your e-mail, he brought it to me, and we did some research. I managed to get copies of Drew's case files. It looked bad then. It looks worse now, with you in the middle. A whole lot worse. I thought maybe you needed help, and were thinking of hiring the man. I came here to warn you to stay out of this mess, but I guess it's too late for that."

"Way too late," Charlie agreed. "I'm in love with Drew, Franny. I love him more than I ever thought I could love anyone. And he loves me. I know he does." *Even if he hasn't said so.* "I have to find out what really happened that night. There has to be a way to make Bob Waite pay for what he did to Darby. She wasn't much of a wife to Drew, but she didn't deserve to die like that. Drew still believes Weasel was telling the truth. He believes Bob Waite paid Weasel to kill Darby."

Frances folded her arms across her chest and stared off into space for a few moments before she answered. "There's no statute of limitations on murder," she said finally.

Charlie waited patiently. There was no point in rushing Frances at this stage.

"If we had enough evidence, we could get Waite brought up on charges, even after all this time," Frances offered cautiously. "But that wouldn't clear Andrew, even if Waite was convicted of both murders."

"Of course it would!" Charlie argued, astounded. "Two men can't have committed the same crime!"

"Drew pled guilty," Frances explained. "The only way to get him a new trial would be to prove that there was something wrong in the way the first trial was conducted." Frances was pacing back and forth across the runway again as she talked, thinking out loud, not really even seeing Charlie. "And that wouldn't even work, because there wasn't any trial. You'd have to prove that Drew's lawyer didn't represent him to the best of his ability, or intentionally gave him bad advice, or that the prosecution suppressed evidence. Conflict of Interest would do, too. If, for instance, the prosecutor just happened to be on the real murderer's payroll or something."

Frances stopped momentarily to switch directions, changing from pacing the width of the runway between the stalls to its length, so that she could extend her stride. "It would be easier to get a judge to set aside the guilty plea if Bob Waite would be kind enough to confess to the murders. Then we could have the conviction overturned, or the sentencing set aside, or maybe even convince the Governor to issue Drew a pardon."

Charlie shut the feed bin with a resounding thump. "That's not going to be easy. A lot of people around here think Drew killed Darby."

"Great. That's just great. That's so convenient." Frances changed directions, staring down at Charlie for a moment. "Andrew didn't confess to murdering his ex-wife, too, did he?"

"I told you, Drew didn't confess to anything, and I don't believe he murdered anyone."

"Yeah? Prove it." Frances's tone was a challenge. A call to arms.

"How do you suggest I do that?"

"To start with, we find a witness who saw the fight." Frances's tone was calm now, analytical.

"Drew doesn't remember anything about that night. He has no clue who was there."

Frances stuck a finger in Charlie's chest. "You know who was there. The same people you find in any bar on any given night. The bartender. Probably a bouncer or a doorman. The town drunk. One or two locals, regulars. Have Drew make a list. Names of everyone he can remember who was there any other night of the year. Then find some of his old buddies. His best friend. Anyone who was close enough to have stayed around when things got ugly. Find out who was with Drew that night. Write down whatever Drew can remember, and don't start asking too many questions around town yourself. Stirring up a twelve-year-old murder could get real nasty real quick. This guy Waite sounds dangerous. I'll send Parkman up to handle the investigation."

Frances had that tone in her voice. Efficient. Determined. Bossy. "Who's Parkman?"

"Private Dick," Frances replied offhandedly. Frances was already making notes to herself in the electronic organizer she always kept in her pocket. "He does a lot of work for us."

"I could call one of my old friends from the Agency," Charlie offered reluctantly.

"A bit overkill, don't you think?" Frances observed dryly. "We're not trying to hunt down international terrorists, here. Besides, Parkman does this sort of thing for a living. He's very discrete. I'll give him a good cover. He'll be doing an investigative report on you for some gossip rag or something like that."

"Send me the bill," Charlie offered with a sigh.

Frances stopped her pacing again to turn her full attention to Charlie. "Can you afford that?"

Charlie took a deep breath, preparing for another battle. "I'm going back to work a week from Monday."

"Really." Frances pushed her glasses up on her nose. "For the Agency?"

"Independent," Charlie assured her sister, hoping that explanation would be enough.

"Charlie, do you need money? You know I'll be glad to help out here. No strings attached. Don't do something you don't want to do just because you've overextended yourself trying to feed my favorite gals."

"I want to go back to work, Franny. I need to go back to work, you know? It's time."

"Does Drew know?"

"As much as he needs to know. As much as I can tell him."

"He doesn't know. He's bound to find out. You want him to hear it from Ma? Or will you tell him yourself?"

"I'll tell him," Charlie conceded. "Before he meets Mom."

"Don't put it off," Frances warned. "Ma wants to see you. You know what she's like once she makes up her mind. She very nearly came along today."

"Oh, no. No, Franny. You can't let her do that. That would not be good. Please don't let her do that." Charlie tried to keep the panic out of her voice.

"Then you go see her. Bring Andrew down to meet her. Come for Sunday Dinner. You don't have to stay long. A few hours. Just enough to satisfy her motherly curiosity. Leave after dinner. Tell her it's a long drive home or something."

"No! I can't face that yet," Charlie insisted, her voice sliding up an octave. "I'm not ready yet! I can't put Drew through that."

Frances kept her voice calm. Reasonable. "Every family closet has a few skeletons, Charlie. Drew can handle ours. You might as well let him see what he's getting."

"No!" Charlie insisted.

"Why are you being so stubborn?" Frances demanded. "It's not the Grand Inquisition or anything. We're just talking about Ma. And Grandma. It won't be all that bad."

"Oh, yes it will!" Charlie argued. "You remember what it was like. Mother was always so nasty to Allen. And I'm living with Drew, and we're not married. And I'm divorced. Once she gets done lecturing me on the evils of divorce and how immoral it is and how she and Daddy never got a divorce, she'll start in on living in sin. I can't sit through that. I can't ask Drew to sit through that. I'm just not ready to face Mother yet." Charlie took long, slow breaths, concentrating on her quiet place, pushing back the panic.

"You just have to know how to handle Ma," Frances argued. "Don't tell her you're living with Drew. Tell her he manages your farm. She'll absolutely adore him."

"She didn't 'adore' Allen, and I was married to him for ten years," Charlie reminded Frances.

"Mom despised Allen because she never thought he was good enough for you," Frances pointed out. "Mom thought Allen was a user, from the very beginning. And for that matter, I think she was right. Allen didn't love you. What's more, Allen never looked at you the way Drew does. Like you personally ordered the sun to rise every morning strictly for his benefit."

* * * * *

The sisters heard the voices before they even made it past the kitchen patio. Loud, angry male voices.

"You Moron!" That was Jamie. Who never lost his temper.

"What a goddamn idiot!" That was Drew. Who never raised his voice. Whom Charlie had never, before today, heard swear.

Two very loud groans. Like men in great pain.

Charlie felt the panic rising again as she dashed for the door. Frances looked down at her little sister with pursed lips and shook her head. And uttered the forbidden word. "Football."

Charlie looked at her watch. Sure enough, it was after 1:00 PM on Sunday afternoon. "I thought the season didn't start until next weekend."

"Preseason game," Frances explained. "Last one."

"Oh, God, no," Charlie wailed.

"YES!"

Two voices at once. The whole house shook. Ghost came bounding up to see what all the ruckus was about. Frances looked at Charlie and winked. She opened the door for Ghost. And waited.

The voices were different this time. "No!" Jamie barked.

"It's all right, Ghost. Ghost! Down!" That was Drew.

"Charlie! Come get your damn dog off me!"

Jamie again.

Laughing, the women followed the noise toward the living room, to find Ghost plastered across Jamie's lap, growling, while Drew bounced off the couch at the next incredible stupidity on the TV set.

"I thought you couldn't get cable," Frances observed, unconcerned.

"Satellite," Charlie explained. "It's on the roof of the barn. Evidently Drew's grandfather had it put in some years ago. Picks up everything. Drew hooked it back up...Last week. Damn."

"Just in time for the regular season," Frances observed dryly.

"Drew played football in high school," Charlie explained.

"He played!" Jamie piped in, the first sign of intelligent life from that side of the room. "Drew did a little more than just play! He was MVP three years running, the leading quarterback in the State for yards rushing and pass completions all three years, and recruited by a dozen major colleges, including WVU and Penn State."

"Yeah. All that and a buck'll get you a cup of coffee at Harry's," Drew observed with a snort. "I ran into guys at Moundsville who could out run me, out pass me, and out think me. They just couldn't keep their grades up good enough to make the teams. I remember one guy who made it all the way through his freshman year of college before somebody finally noticed he couldn't read. He got a law degree while he was in prison. And still used me for a dust rag every time we hit the field."

Frances shook her head. "I will never, to my dying day, understand the male provocation for fighting over a silly piece of inflated leather. If you will excuse us, gentlemen, Charlie and I have some dossiers to discuss."

Jamie called back over his shoulder as Frances scooped up his brief case. "Would you take this damn dog with you, please?"

Charlie snapped her fingers, once. Ghost, who seemed to have gotten rather comfortable on the couch once he decided Charlie was in no danger, took his time ambling back to the floor. He padded silently after the women as they moved to the kitchen table.

Bob Waite, Wendell "Weasel" Macey, Darby Anne Bailey Waite, and Andrew Bailey. It seemed a lifetime ago Charlie had sent off those e-mails. Now one folder lay on the table for each name.

"I don't see a folder for Savannah," Charlie pointed out. "Drew's daughter."

"No luck there," Frances reported. "Not easy to find anything on minors. Drew's file is mostly copies of his arrest record and the case notes. You don't want to know how I got that. Macey's is a collection of petty arrests. Breaking and Entering. Vandalism. Burglary. Grand Theft Auto. Anything for a buck. Waite is the one that concerns me. You better be careful with this one, Charlie."

Charlie pulled the folder close and laid the cover open. A Re-election poster stared up at her.

Calm, wide spaced eyes, strong jaw line, long, straight nose, mouth that held a no trace of a smile. He stood tall, broad shouldered, lean but muscular, his stance that of a fighter, feet spread just a little, weight towards the toes. A classic pose, not quite full front, just a little off to the side. Dark hair, tanned skin, wide set eyes that met you head on. A handsome man, in an odd sort of way. Not that his features, individually, were all that remarkable. The photograph, taken in uniform, had managed to capture confidence. Determination. This was a man who would follow through on his promises.

Or his threats, Charlie thought with a feeling of foreboding.

The rest of the file did nothing to settle her nerves. Whatever his reasons, Waite certainly hadn't run for Sheriff because he needed the money. There were newspaper clippings about his father's death, and Waite's subsequent sale of the bank. There was also a copy of the financial disclosure statement he'd used when he ran for office.

This wasn't about money.

Darby's obituary was in the folder, too. Darby Waite. Robert Waite Junior, grieving widower, had donated the money from her insurance policy, half a million dollars, to the Catholic Relief Fund.

Charlie stared down at the article in disbelief. "Why?" she puzzled. "I don't understand why he had her killed. That's the one piece of this puzzle that's missing. No motive."

"You never had to live with her."

Charlie looked up into Drew's stormy gray eyes. "But you loved her."

"I thought I did, at the time. I hated her, later. But not enough to kill her. She wasn't worth going to prison for."

"Was Wendell Macey worth going to prison for?" Frances shot back.

Drew turned to face her squarely. "No, Ma'am. No one is. But at the time it seemed like my only option."

"And now?"

"I'd probably still do the same thing. Not because I killed anyone, but because prison is where they put people who can't afford good lawyers."

"I can't believe I'm doing this." Frances held out a hand toward Drew. "Give me a buck."

Drew's eyes flicked from Frances to Charlie and back again, looking puzzled, but he obediently pulled out his wallet and handed Frances a one-dollar bill.

"Congratulations, Mr. Bailey, you now have an attorney on retainer." Frances extended her hand. Drew took it, still hesitant. "My first bit of professional advice for you, Mr. Bailey, is, never, never answer any questions without your attorney present. Not only will you be likely to incriminate yourself, but you'll piss me off, and you really don't want to do that."

"I assure you, Frances will do a much better job than your last attorney did," Charlie promised Drew.

"That wouldn't take much," Frances observed dryly.

Drew surveyed the small gathering dubiously. "If you don't mind my asking, just what do you ladies have in mind?"

Charlie circled the table to take his hand in hers. "Drew, Frances thinks we should try to have your conviction set aside."

Drew just stared at her for a long moment. "On what grounds?"

It was Frances who answered. "Failure to provide you with an attorney prior to questioning. Failure to adequately inform you of your right to council. Incompetent representation. Failure to provide you with medical attention prior to questioning. Failure to properly secure evidence at the crime scene. Coercion. And that's just off the top of my head. I'm sure I can think of a few others. I'm going to send up one of my best men. A Private Detective named Parkman. If this Wendell Macey told you about killing Darby, he probably shot his mouth off to someone else. Somebody, somewhere, knows what really happened to Macey. If we can prove Waite ordered the murder of both your ex-wife and Macey, the State should be more than happy to set aside your conviction, before the media gets wind of what a bungled job the local authorities did on your case."

Drew's answer was a long time coming. "I would like nothing more than to see Bob Waite behind bars. And I do want to clear my name. But you ladies can't lose sight of the fact that I'm on parole, and Bob Waite is still the county sheriff. I will stand behind anything the two of you want to do. But I promise you this, Ladies. I will put a gun to my head before I let them put me back in Moundsville."

Jamie raised his head and quickly sketched the sign of the cross.

Chapter Eleven

A chill passed through Charlie, like the first blast of winter. She turned away, rubbing her upper arms for warmth. A noise like the ocean rushing in, waves crashing on the beach, echoed through her head. She realized belatedly that it was beginning to get dark out. Funny. She hadn't thought it was that late. It got dark so much earlier now.

Charlie wandered back out of the kitchen, trying to get away from the noise. She stopped, raising her hands to her face, choking back a scream, when she saw him. He was sprawled across the dining room table. Blood. So much blood. She heard a moan, from far away, and realized, almost surrealistically that the voice was her own.

"No," she pleaded. "Please God, No! Not again... Not again..."

* * * * *

"We knew things weren't going well, but we just didn't realize how bad it had gotten. We didn't ask enough questions, any of us. We talked about options, but that one just never occurred to any of us. After all, we're Catholic. It's a mortal sin."

Frances was whispering, her voice almost conspiratorial. "Charlie was the one who found him. I guess she never really got over it."

Charlie listen to snatches of their conversation, feeling almost like an eavesdropper. She wasn't sure how long she'd been unconscious. Strong arms held her, rocking her gently. Warm arms, strong and alive. Work roughened hands stroked her, her hair, her skin, as if he felt the need just to touch her.

Charlie struggled up through the muddied water, fighting her way back to the surface. She needed to let them know she was all right, so they wouldn't worry. So they wouldn't be embarrassed by anything they said that she wasn't supposed to hear. She tried opening her eyes, just a peek through the lashes, but the blood was still there, like an angry red haze, so she squeezed them shut again. A tremor convulsed her frame. She was cold. She was so cold.

"Charlie."

She wanted to tell him to go away. Wanted to tell them all to go away, let her be, but she didn't have the strength.

"Charlie. I know you can hear me. Everything's going to be all right. I'm sorry I frightened you. I'd never do anything to hurt you. Please believe me. Please don't be afraid. It was a stupid, thoughtless thing to say. I won't hurt you like that. I promise I won't. Charlie, Honey, look at me. Open your eyes. Everything's going to be all right, I promise."

His voice was far away, but persistent, like his touch, and it mesmerized her, like a snake charmer's flute. Charlie opened her eyes, slowly, because he asked her to, and because she hated him blaming himself. She should have told him. Should have trusted him with more of her past. Lord knows, he'd trusted her with his.

Green eyes locked onto hers, pushing everything else back.

"Drew?"

"I'm here, Darling," he assured her. "I'm here. It's all right, Charlie."

He looked so frightened. "I'm sorry," Charlie managed. "I guess I must have passed out. I ruined the party."

"You don't have anything to apologize for," Drew assured her. "I'm the one who needs to apologize. I never thought about what the people left behind have to deal with. I am so sorry, Charlie. It must have been terrible for you."

"I should have told you," Charlie managed. "I wanted to. I knew I needed to. It's all just so hard to talk about."

"It's okay, Charlie," Drew assured her. "You don't owe anybody any explanations, least of all me."

"I should have told you," Charlie repeated. She closed her eyes and hid her face against his chest, snuggling closer, breathing in the warm, masculine smell of him. He smelled so...alive. She felt safe there, in his arms, safe and protected.

"I'm so tired," she told the second button on his shirt.

There was a low rumble in his chest, and Charlie realized Drew must be talking to Frances and Jamie, but she didn't try to listen. If she looked up, if she talked to them, they'd ask questions she didn't want to answer. She'd have to think about things she didn't want to think about. She'd have to make excuses. She'd have to face their doubts.

She had enough of her own.

She felt safe, there in Drew's arms – safe and warm and protected. Yet it wasn't going to be that easy. It never was. Charlie knew Frances and Jamie wouldn't leave as long as they were worried about her. They had no reason to trust Drew. Not yet. They hardly even knew him.

"I'm okay, guys." Charlie spoke without leaving the safe haven she'd found against Drew's chest. "Honestly. I'm all right. I'm just a little tired. I just need some sleep. I'm fine, really. There's nothing to worry about. Just let me sleep for half-an-hour and I'll be back to normal."

"You can do whatever you want to do, Charlie," Drew promised. "Nobody's going to try to stop you. Don't you worry about anything."

Charlie closed her eyes. When she woke up again, she was still snuggled securely in Drew's arms, there on the couch, bundled against his chest like a child. Charlie came around slowly, stretching a little, feeling like a contented cat. She wasn't cold anymore. He'd wrapped her in a blanket, but it was his own body heat that had filled her. The TV was playing softly in the background, but there were no other voices. "Who won?" she asked.

"I did," Drew assured her. He pushed the hair back from her face and kissed her forehead. So soft. So gentle. As if she were very fragile.

For now, just this once, it felt good to be fragile. "The game." She didn't want to have to move out of his arms. Ever. "Who won the football game?"

"I turned the TV off in the third quarter. Made me too mad," Drew confessed with a soft laugh.

They'd had company, before..."Jamie and Frances went home?"

"About an hour ago." His hands moved over her back, touching her, stroking her, not like a lover, but like a father with a frightened child.

Charlie sat up, slowly, reluctantly, hating to leave Drew's embrace. It felt good to be held, pampered, maybe even spoiled a little. But she had too many years practice living as an adult to allow Drew to think of her as a child now.

His eyes were worried. His face looked older. "I must have scared you pretty badly," she told him, running a finger over the lines etched on either side of his mouth. "I didn't think that could ever happen to me again. I should have warned you."

"I am so sorry, Charlie. I feel like an idiot. You did tell me, in a dozen little ways, and I just wasn't paying enough attention. That's why you panic when you can't find me. That's why you were so angry, that morning I left, when you knew I was hurt. That's why you hate to wake up alone."

Charlie ran her teeth over her bottom lip. "Jamie and Frances told you what happened?"

"They told me." He kissed her forehead again. "They told me everything. It's all right. It doesn't matter. You're all right now, Charlie."

"It's not all right. I should have been the one to tell you. I should have trusted you to understand. I had a nervous breakdown, Drew. I spent three months in a mental hospital."

"I know," Drew assured her. "People do, Charlie. Even tough people, like you. No daughter should ever have to go through what you went through. Maybe your brain just needed a little vacation."

Charlie chuckled softly at that. "I never thought of it quite that way."

"Jamie said you hadn't taken any time off at all in over 5 years. You were physically exhausted, and maybe a little burnt out."

"I never took vacations back then," Charlie remembered. "Not after I got married. I couldn't afford to."

Charlie took a deep breath. "I never told Jamie and Frances what really happened that night. They had enough to deal with. I didn't think they needed to know." She pulled her knees up in front of her, wrapping her arms around them to hold in the warmth she had captured from Drew's body. "You need to know."

Still, she hesitated before she told her story. Drew waited. "It was a little over three years ago. I was working in DC at that time. I actually had an assignment where I was home every night. I thought it would bring us closer, but Allen didn't like me being home so much after all. I cramped his style. I invaded his personal space. I asked him where the money was going.

"Allen and I had had an awful fight that morning before I went to work, and I wasn't looking forward to going home, so I went over to see Dad when I got off. It was a Wednesday. Dad usually got home earlier than I did, so I was surprised when no one answered the door, but I figured he'd gotten tied up in traffic. I had a key. I let myself in."

Charlie could see it all so clearly. She had to fight to keep the panic out of her voice. "I found him slumped over the kitchen table when I opened the door. I told everyone Daddy was dead when I got there. I didn't want them to know, to think about what it must have been like for him...I couldn't tell them...."

Drew held her close, stroked her back, but didn't try to stop her. Charlie swallowed hard. When she continued, her voice was matter of fact.

"It didn't work right. He didn't do it right. Dad shot himself through the heart. He was still alive when I got there. People think you die if you get shot in the heart. You don't always. It depends on where you're hit. There was so much blood. I called an ambulance, but I knew they'd be too late. I'd taken life saving courses, CPR and emergency first aid, but there was nothing I could do for him. I tried direct pressure, but it was no good. He'd lost too much blood. I held him until the ambulance got there. He was gone by then. He died in my arms. He tried to say something, but he didn't have the strength. He wanted to tell me something so badly, but he died.

"He had been diagnosed with lung cancer two months earlier. A friend of the family had died that way when I was younger. Dad didn't want to go through all that just to die anyway. He didn't want us to have to go through that with him."

She took a deep breath and met Drew's eyes squarely again. "When you die, the last thing you do is to piss yourself. What a rotten way to go."

Drew looked away, over the top of her head, his face a mask of emotions, raw and bitter at the same time. She wondered if he understood what she was trying to say. After a minute or so, he unfolded himself from the couch and held out a hand. Charlie took it, following where he led, asking no questions. His huge hand felt hot where it folded over her smaller one.

Drew led her across the gravel parking area where the Caddy had been parked earlier and around the side of the barn to the main upstairs doors. Inside, he headed for the far edge of the haystack in the narrow aisle way along the outside wall. He released her hand there and dropped to his knees. Charlie remembered wondering why "George" left that aisle down the far side when he stacked the hay all those months ago. As Drew pulled out a hay bale from the ground row, she realized where they were and why. A secret for a secret. Drew had spent May and June living inside her haystack.

He crawled into the opening in the hay, and Charlie had no choice but to follow him. She had to know. Had to see what he'd endured to stay here.

The hay was cleverly stacked so that the bales above them formed a solid looking and feeling roof, but Charlie was sure that one broken baling twine could collapse the whole thing. It gave her the creeps. They were at least six bale lengths into the tunnel through the haystack before Drew stopped again. It was totally dark here. "Wait here a minute," he instructed, his voice little more than a whisper.

There was a creaking noise, and then he disappeared. Charlie couldn't exactly see him vanish. She just felt the absence of his warmth. She stuck out her hand, reaching blindly for him, feeling her way along, and encountered the edge of what appeared to be a hole in the floor. A trap door, she surmised. A light flickered, a match, and then a candle lit up a small room below. The sharp stench of sulfur filled the air.

There was no ladder. Drew stood under the trap door and held up his arms. Charlie wriggled around and lowered herself through the hatch, feet first.

The stalls on the side of the barn nearest the house ended short, butting up against what appeared to be a solid rock wall two-thirds of the way across. Charlie had assumed the builders had run into a massive stone outcropping and just quit there, unwilling to blast the thing apart. They hadn't. They'd turned it into a secret room. A hideout, perhaps, against Indians, as she'd been told the original barn had been built in the mid 1700's.

The room was perhaps ten-foot square, with chiseled fieldstone walls and absolutely no furnishings. Drew had dropped four bales of hay down to use as a bed, covered with an old horse's shipping blanket she didn't remember having lost. There was another hay bale for a table, too, and a plain, round candle sputtered on it now, the kind Charlie kept around for emergencies, an open book of matches beside it. The sulfur smell still lingered in the air.

A Bible lay near the candle.

An old flannel shirt of hers lay on the bed, wadded up like a pillow.

She had allowed this. She had allowed the man to live like this. Because she didn't want to know. Didn't want to take the chance. Because not knowing was convenient. Drew had done everything for her, and all she had to do was stay out of the way.

Drew sat down on the hay-bale bed, and Charlie dropped beside him with a sob, huddling into the protective circle of his arm.

When he spoke, maybe a minute later, his voice was so soft she could barely hear him. "Would you wait for me?" he asked.

Charlie understood what he meant. She wanted to tell him that there was no way he'd ever go back to prison. No way she'd allow such a thing to happen to him. But she knew that didn't really matter. He needed to know. He'd said it before. The worst part of prison was knowing there was nothing to come home to. "I'd wait for you. For a year or twelve years. Whatever it takes. I'd be there. I'd take a job in Moundsville or Wheeling and I'd be there every day that I was allowed, and I'd write to you every day. And I'd never quit fighting for you."

Drew looked down at her again, a brave clown smile painted on. "Seven years of celibacy would kill you."

"I was practically a born again virgin until you came along," Charlie assured him. "Three years."

"What?" The distant look wiped off his face in an instant. "You were married!"

"After Dad died, after I got out of the hospital, Allen quit even pretending to care about me," Charlie explained. "I was an embarrassment to him. He was afraid people would find out that his wife was mentally unstable. And then there was the money thing. Things were tight, money-wise. I was off work for almost four months. I had plenty of sick leave I'd never used, but I'd been making a good deal more with all the overtime.

"We fought about how much money Allen was spending. He asked me to liquidate some of my assets to pay his bills. Sell off Daddy's stocks. I refused. Frances has my Power of Attorney. Allen couldn't do anything while I was in the hospital. He was furious that nothing was in his name. I called Allen a selfish bastard. I told him he ought to go out and get a job himself if he wanted money. I'd never said anything like that to him before.

"Allen refused to make love to me again until I apologized. I tried, I really tried, but I just couldn't do it. One of the last things Daddy ever said to me was that Allen was a self-centered egotistical bastard, and that he'd dump me the moment he didn't need me any more. After Daddy died, I began to think he was right. I just couldn't apologize.

"Allen kept his word. For the last two years we were together, he never touched me. I was planning to change all that the night I got home from California. I wanted to make our marriage work, no matter what it cost me. That was the way I was raised. A simple apology didn't seem like such a high price to pay for a little peace and harmony at home. But I got home a day early, and I didn't call ahead. My mistake."

"That bastard," Drew swore. "You had nothing to apologize for, Charlie," he assured her. "Nothing at all." His hands rose to either side of her face, and he kissed her. A long, slow, lingering kiss that shared his hopes and dreams and fears.

"Father Jamie asked me why I'm here. He wanted to know if I'd marry you just to get my farm back. I don't think I could lie to Jamie, even if he wasn't a priest. His eyes kind of see through you. I told him the truth. I did think about some kind of plan like that, before I met you. I know there are men who do things like that. Go around looking for women with money to support them. Particularly older women. Someone who might be flattered by the attentions of a younger man.

"I couldn't do that, Charlie. Not to you. Not to any woman. I don't think I could make love to a woman I didn't have feelings for. I never knew how to separate sex and love. And I know you're older than I am, but I'm not young enough or handsome enough or self-confident enough to ever pull off a scheme like that, even if I wanted to. And then there's this other problem.

"You see, I fell in love with you the very first time I ever saw you, there in the truck stop. My tired goddess in the waitress's uniform. You had your hair stuffed up on the back of your head, held up with a pen, of all things. It fell out and the whole mess came tumbling down as you walked across the room. Your hair made a halo around your head. You lit up like an angel on fire. You stuffed it all back into a funny twist with that same pen, and walked over to me, and smiled. You smiled at me. There I was, this big, dirty, wet drifter, sitting in your restaurant, and you smiled at me. You laid your hand over mine. You asked if I was hungry. I was so tongue-tied I couldn't answer you.

"The touch of a woman's hand is a powerful thing, Charlie. You do it so automatically. You probably never think what it means to people. But I've watched you. You walk up to some trucker who's having a bad night, and you lay your hand on his. Some of these guys, it's been months since a woman touched them. For me, it was twelve years. My grandmother gave me a hug, there in the courtroom, the day I was sentenced. She died, two years later.

"I haven't got much to offer you, Charlie. I don't own anything. I don't have any money tucked away in a secret bank account. Better than half this town thinks I murdered two people. God only knows why you'd want me. But I love you, Charlie. More than my freedom, if it comes to that. I love you."

Charlie let her eyes slide closed, ignoring the tears that ran down her cheeks. "I never thought I would ever hear those words," she told him, "I would never have married Allen if I'd still believed in love. I thought love had passed me by, somewhere, and I'd missed the opportunity, like the one perfect pair of shoes that sells out of your size just before you get to the shoe sale, and you never find anything to match that outfit again, so you have to settle for something that's almost right, that almost fits, that doesn't look too bad from across the room, but never passes muster up close. I thought I'd grow old alone, somebody's aunt, somebody's daughter, somebody's ex, without ever being part of that thing that makes two people one."

"Maybe we both had to go through what we've lived through to get to where we were meant to be, here, with each other, now. Maybe our hearts are like steel, tempered in life's fire, so that we can be strong enough to love each other."

"I thought if I told you about the breakdown you'd lose faith in me. You wouldn't be able to trust me anymore. People tend to figure if you've had one breakdown, you can have another, almost any minute. They start looking at you, watching you, looking for signs, warnings that it's coming. I even wonder sometimes. Could it happen again? Could I let myself get so out of control? Sometimes it's hard to trust myself. And I still have a real hard time with blood."

"You're a strong woman, Charlie. I already know how you handle a crisis. You were tough out there in that field, with those boys. You and Ghost, you saved my life that night. I'd trust you in any situation. With my life. With my heart."

"I love you, too," Charlie assured him. "More than I thought I could ever love anyone. I love you so much it scares me."

"Don't be scared, Charlie. I promise, I'll be here for you. When this is over, this thing between Bob Waite and me, I'm going to ask you to marry me."

"Why not now?" Charlie appealed.

"Because I want you to know for sure what you're getting. No surprises."

"I think you should ask me now," Charlie insisted.

Drew swallowed hard. "You do."

"I do," Charlie confirmed.

Drew reached over and snuffed out the candle. The damp, musty air closed in around them oppressively without that small flickering pinpoint of light. His voice sounded almost mystical in the sudden darkness. "What if this was all there was, Charlotte. A five by seven stone cell. What if this was my whole world."

"I'd be here with you if I could," Charlie promised. "Better here, with you, than out there, alone."

He was quiet again, his head resting against her hair. "Charlotte Giles, I love you with all my heart. I want to share the rest of my life with you. Would you do me the honor of becoming my wife?"

"I love you, Andrew Bailey. I would be your wife, your lover, your best friend. Anything you want me to be. Everything you want me to be. Here, in this little room. In that house out there. In a mansion somewhere. It doesn't matter. As long as I'm with you, nothing else matters."

He was quiet for the space of two long heartbeats. "I don't even have a ring for you."

"I don't need another ring. All I need is your love."

There in the dark, side-by-side on a horse blanket covering a bale of hay, his mouth sought hers, and her fingers caressed his face, wet with tears.

"I never thought I'd love anyone again," Drew whispered hoarsely. "Never thought anyone would love me. You, Charlotte, you've given me a reason to live. No matter what happens."

She prayed silently that, this time, she would be enough.

* * * * *

"Tell me about Terry Masters."

Charlie was sitting on the attic floor, Drew's yearbook open across her lap. The team picture took up both pages. It was one of the few color photographs in the entire book. Blue and gold uniforms looked freshly laundered. Drew was in the middle of the front row, down on one knee. The big white number 80 stood out in bold relief against his blue jersey. He looked so young, so self-confident.

There was something else about the picture that struck her. These weren't just a bunch of boys crowded together. They were a unit. A team. They were used to counting on each other. They trusted each other.

Drew was in the middle. He belonged there. That was what was different. That was what she'd felt rekindle in the Feed and Supply. The men Drew talked to last Saturday were in this picture, too.

There were thirty-eight young men in uniforms, plus the two team managers, and two coaches. A quick scan of the names printed below showed her that not one of them was Terry Masters.

"Who was Terry Masters?"

"I wondered where you went," Drew commented as he bent over to kiss her upturned mouth. "What'cha got there?"

"I found these when I was getting ready to remodel the house," she explained, smiling up at him. "And I put them up here with the stuff to deal with later. Lucky the roofers didn't damage them. Where's Terry in these pictures?"

Drew pulled up a battered footstool and looked over her shoulder. "Flip a few more pages," he suggested.

She liked the way he didn't reach out and snatch the book from her hands. Instead, she handed it up to him. "You show me."

He flipped slowly past the cheerleaders and the band members, through the baseball team, to the class pictures. There, on the page with all the other upperclassmen, Drew located the face he was looking for. He tapped the picture once with his index finger and handed the book back to her.

Charlie read the inscription penned in so carefully. It was signed simply "Terry."

There was nothing remarkable about the picture. Long, thin face. Straight nose. Solid chin. Dark, curly hair. A mouth that looked just ready to smile. She could have passed him on the street and never remembered him. Might have, at that. "How did you ever fit into his suit?" Charlie demanded.

Drew laughed, his eyes focused somewhere in the past. "Terry borrowed the suit from his older brother, Roger. Half-brother, actually. Roger was a wrestler. The suit fit me pretty good. However, Roger had bought it to wear to the Prom. It was blue. Bright blue."

"I bet you looked as handsome as any blue jay," Charlie decided. "Was it formal, with a white ruffled shirt and a blue cummerbund?"

"No, just a plain white shirt, a very bad case of nerves, and the Judge at the County Courthouse in Winchester, Virginia," Drew recalled. "Did you...Did you find any photo albums?"

"No, afraid not. I guess there was an estate auction. There wasn't much left in the house. Just trash, mostly. All the furniture was gone. I found these yearbooks in the bottom of the built in bookcase in the library. I never saw any photo albums."

"I'm surprised you didn't throw these out." Drew was flipping through the pages randomly, now.

"I was going to take them down to the used book store, along with these books of Allen's, but I never got around to it," Charlie explained.

Drew frowned and closed the yearbook. His gaze sought Charlie's, but her focus was on the box. "Charlie," he interrupted softly. She looked up, her expression slightly guilty. "It must have been more work to haul all these books way up here than it would have been to take them out to the truck."

Charlie didn't answer. After another quick glance at her rather forlorn expression, Drew pulled the box closer. The paperbacks were Allen's, all right. Books he'd written. Drew pulled one out and turned it over to read the back cover. A distinguished looking man who appeared to be in his mid 50's sat on an ornately carved chair. He was wearing a dark blue and green plaid kilt, his legs encased in gartered knee high socks, and a huge sword in a battered scabbard rested across his knees.

Inside the front cover was an inscription. "For Charlotte, May your star always shine, Allen McGregor."

Drew put the book back in the box and unfolded himself from the stool. "Come on," he teased. "I can't carry you and the box."

Charlie followed Drew anxiously down the stairs, trying to think of some explanation. "I'm sorry," she said at last. "I should have gotten rid of them."

Drew ignored her and headed for the living room. He arranged Allen's novels next to his yearbooks, on a shelf in the bookcase where she'd first found them.

"If you'd had the photo albums, with the pictures of my first wedding, would you have wanted me to get rid of them?" Drew asked when he was done.

"Of course not!" Charlie insisted indignantly.

"Are you still in love with Allen?" he asked, one eyebrow raised slightly.

"You know I'm not!" Charlie admonished, her tone a little hurt. "I never loved him in the first place. How could I still be in love with him?"

"Then why should we pretend he never existed?" Drew argued. "I was married before. There are pictures of Darby in these yearbooks. You were married. You loved the man's books. Why try to pretend it never happened?"

Charlie laughed in relief and threw her arms around his neck. "You are the most unexpected man," she assured him. "I don't think there's a mean or jealous bone in your body."

"I don't know about that," Drew replied a bit dubiously. "Let some asshole make a pass at you, and you'll find out I can be pretty jealous. Just not over the past."

Charlie took the yearbook back down from the shelf. "Show me a picture of Darby."

Drew cocked an eyebrow, hesitating a moment before he flipped the pages to the cheerleaders' section.

She was tall. A leggy, curvy blonde in a tight sweater and a short skirt with a look that said she knew what she wanted and she expected to get it. "She was so beautiful," Charlie whispered, a bit daunted.

"Yeah," Drew agreed, his face looking like he'd just smelled sour milk. "And she would never let you forget it, either. It's hard to believe I thought that would be enough. I never even looked to see what was inside that package. All I ever saw was the wrapping paper. Terry tried to warn me, but I wouldn't listen. I was seventeen and in love and I wasn't about to let common sense get in the way." His voice wasn't bitter. Just sad.

Charlie stared at the picture thoughtfully. "What did Terry try to tell you?"

"Terry said Darby was only after the bottom line. She figured I'd go pro. She didn't want me for myself. She wanted the money. The notoriety. She wanted to be a celebrity's wife. Getting pregnant just got in the way. She would have gotten an abortion if she could have. Terry said to let her, but I wouldn't do it. I couldn't help her kill our baby. I wanted the baby. I wanted to get married.

"Once I decided not to go to college, Darby turned bitter. She said I'd never amount to anything. She loved Savannah, she was good to the baby, but she blamed me for keeping her trapped in this backwash of a town, as she called it. I guess she was right."

Charlie touched her fingers to his lips. "Darby was wrong. Who you are comes from inside, not the job that you choose to do. I'm sorry she couldn't see that. She threw away a chance at something real to chase a dream that killed her." Charlie shut the yearbook and shoved it back into the shelf. "Let's go find Terry. He seems like he had some sense."

"How can I find Terry?" Drew protested. "I don't even know where to look."

"Well, let's start with the phone book."

"I checked," Drew admitted. "The second day I was back. While I was at the Mission. I was desperate. I really needed a friend. But he's not listed."

"Did you try the Internet?"

Drew flushed slightly. "I've only ever used your account that one time, Charlie. I really try not to invade your privacy."

Charlie smiled up at him. "Maybe you should. Look how well that turned out." She got just the reaction she'd wanted when he framed her face with both hands and kissed her passionately. "You know what I like best about you?" she purred contentedly.

"My impeccable taste in women?" Drew teased.

"That, too," Charlie replied with a laugh. "I never feel like I'm interrupting your life."

"You are my life," Drew assured her with another kiss.

"I'll probably live to be at least a hundred, like all of Grandma's sisters. I'm less than half way there, but I felt old before I met you," Charlie confessed. "You make the rest of my life seem a great deal more worth living." She gave Drew a quick kiss on the bridge of his nose and headed for her computer. "Let's get to work. Show me what you can do with this thing."

Drew rolled his eyes. "You mean you didn't change your password?"

"Of course I did. But I don't care if you know what it is. Not now. I just didn't want to be in the number one range any more. It's 'Ghost.' In your honor. George Washington Carver was too long. Now, we need to get you your own screen name and password."

Drew blinked slowly, his expression rather dubious. "Isn't that kind of expensive?"

"Time can be a little expensive. It's $2.35 an hour plus the long distance charges. The screen name doesn't cost anything, though. We have up to five screen names on this account. Now get to work." Twenty minutes later, they sat down at the phone with a list of nine "Terry Masters."

The closest one lived in Arlington, Virginia- about an hour-and-a-half away. Coincidentally, this Terry Masters also lived within twenty minutes of Charlie's grandmother. None of which Charlie mentioned out loud as Drew picked up the phone. He listened for about a minute, then hung up. "Wrong number?" Charlie asked, a little surprised at the brevity of the call.

"Answering machine." Drew blew out his breath slowly. "It's him. I'd recognize that voice anywhere. He's married and he has two kids. The kids seem to have run off. His wife's name is Michelle and his kids are Ben and Jerry."

"Like the ice cream?" Charlie commented with a laugh.

"Ice cream?"

"I have so much to teach you," Charlie groaned. She punched re-dial and listened to the answering machine message herself. "Ben and Jerry aren't his kids," she explained. "He was making a joke. He meant that he and Shelly are probably out buying ice cream. Why don't you stuff yourself into one of those suits you hate while I grab a quick shower and find something that doesn't smell like grease or the barn, and we'll go get some really great ice cream."

Drew closed his eyes tightly. When he opened them again, his expression was wary, but resigned. "A suit? To track down Terry Masters? Why do I get the feeling you've got more in mind than ice cream?"

"Me?" Charlie inquired innocently. "I'll be ready in about eighteen minutes."

Drew folded the computer printout so that Terry's address showed and left it on the kitchen table without commenting on her eighteen minutes. Although he did wonder how Charlie could possibly have it all timed out so thoroughly. It amused him to throw her off schedule. "I get the shower first," was all he said as he turned and dashed up the stairs, taking them two at a time.

"Hey!" Charlie protested as she ran after him. "Don't use up all the hot water!" He was already out of sight. It still amazed her that Drew could move so fast. She smiled softly to herself, wondering how much of her plan he'd already figured out. Probably more of it than she had.

"You pick out the suit," Drew called from the bathroom as Charlie opened the closet doors. She laughed and pulled the dark charcoal. It would accent his eyes the best. Charlie put an extra shirt for Drew and a spare pare of jeans in the bottom of her overnight bag, just in case, then added all the other necessities. "And don't forget a change of socks!" his voice bubbled from under the shower spray. "I have a feeling we're going to do a lot of walking. Who's going to feed the ladies?"

How did he know she was packing an overnight bag? "I'm calling Janelle now," she hollered back. "Ghost will let her into the barn."

Janelle actually had the day off. She promised to come over around five to feed the mares. Charlie sighed as she hung up the phone. The girl had no social life at all. It almost seemed as if she'd gone out of her way not to make any real friends here. As far as Charlie could tell, she never dated. Charlie picked out a suit for herself, and turned to lay it on the bed. She stopped in mid-stride, captivated by the sight before her. She hadn't even noticed when the water quit. A slow, appreciative smile spread across her face.

Drew stood in the doorway, naked, like a statue of some Greek god, a towel thrown over his shoulder, water glistening in his ebony hair, the dampness lending a glow to lines of long, hard muscle. She let her eyes devour him, sweeping slowly up and down the polished athlete's body, until her eyes came to rest on his warm green ones. Daddy was right. The eyes were the windows to a man's soul. And Drew's soul was hungry. Devouring her, in turn.

"That was quick," was all she could think of to say. Damn. Words always failed her when she felt like this. So overwhelmed with love and lust and need.

"It was lonely in there," he answered with a cat like smile.

Charlie answered his smile with one of her own, amazed once again at how well their thoughts harmonized. "Did you miss me?" she teased in her most seductive voice, lowering her gaze to watch him respond to the suggestion in her tone. She wasn't disappointed.

Drew looked down, too, and shook his head. "Now see what you've done. How am I supposed to get dressed like this?"

Charlie hung her suit next to his, deliberately turning her back on him as she stripped slowly out of her clothes. He was still there in the doorway when she turned back around. She took the pins out of her hair and shook it loose, watching his eyes follow the glittering beams of sunlight from the open curtain. She walked slowly across the room, stopping only when she could feel the heat radiating off his damp skin. "You were right about me taking this week off," she told him. "I'm feeling much more rested."

Charlie moved with the wiry, muscled grace of an athlete. She was filling out some here and there, in just the right places, now that he was cooking. But she was still hard, lean muscle, with just a few soft curves. Drew closed his eyes for a moment to concentrate on the scent of her. "I could find you blindfolded," he whispered, "Just by the flavor you leave on the air."

"I guess I do need that shower," Charlie chuckled. She tried to duck under his arm, but he brought it down quickly to block her path, curling her against his chest. Charlie caught her breath, jumping just a little.

Not that she wanted to get away. She just never anticipated his next move. One moment she was ducking under his arm. The next she was standing with her back against the wall, his arm around her, his nose buried in her hair. She retaliated by kissing whatever she could reach, which just happened to be his throat. His mouth sought hers, plundering greedily, as both hands moved to tangle in her hair. She shoved her hips against his cock, but she couldn't quite reach. The difference in their heights kept the equation unbalanced. Charlie shot one muscular leg out to wrap around Drew's waist, pulling him towards her. His hand dropped down her back to cup her rump, lifting her up enough to slide slowly into her. She wrapped her other leg around Drew's waist as well, holding on with the grip she'd developed riding bareback, reveling in his strength as he lifted her higher, gasping in pleasure as his hot shaft filled her. "Will this work?" she asked, a little breathless.

"I don't know," Drew laughed. "But I know how to find out."

She was hot and slick and wet and she felt so ready. His body was tensed for action, but he forced himself to move deliberately. His mouth sought hers again, and he backed her against the wall, taking his time, kissing her thoroughly, forcing himself to be content for the moment just to be inside of her. "I had plans," Drew managed when he came up for air. "I was going to seduce you properly. Women are supposed to want foreplay. It says so in all the best books."

Charlie shivered as his teeth nipped her earlobe. "Foreplay is all about being in the mood," she rationalized. "I watch you walk across a room, and I'm in the mood. All I have to do is listen to the sound of your voice, or see you standing there in the doorway, and I want you."

"That's good," Drew assured her, "Because I want you, in every way a man can want a woman. I want to touch you and love you and hold you and never let you go."

"You better take me over to the bed. There are a whole lot of places I want you to touch me that you can't reach right now."

Drew ran his hands around her bottom for support, willing to oblige any request. As he turned them around, she concentrated her kisses on his breastbone. In a demonstration of sheer athletic prowess, he dove backwards onto the bed without letting her get away, pinning her feet underneath of him.

Her hands were tangled in his hair, and now her thumbs massaged his ears. "Oh, God," Drew groaned. "You find places on me I didn't even know were crying out to be touched." He began to move inside her, in rhythm to her hands.

She leaned down to kiss him again. His eyes had drifted shut, but they snapped open wide in surprise as she nipped at his nipple. "Did that hurt?" Charlie asked, pulling back in concern.

"No, it didn't hurt, not really," Drew replied, his voice hesitant. "I just...Men aren't supposed to...Women..."

Charlie laughed her low, seductive laugh. "I used to do exactly what I thought I was supposed to." She ran her tongue slowly around the small brown circle, enjoying the way he shuddered. His body jerked inside her in response. "But somehow sex was always a little disappointing. I thought it was just me. I thought if I felt like there was something missing, it must be my fault."

Her slow pace was driving him crazy. Drew pulled her against him and rolled them both over until he was on top. He got the response he wanted when she gasped in pleasure as he drove into her. "Is there something missing now?" he teased as he kissed her again.

"Oh, no," Charlie gasped. "Not at all."

His hands were braced on either side of her shoulders, like he was doing pushups. "Then it wasn't your fault, was it?"

"Yes," she laughed. "I married the wrong man."

She shrieked with laughter as he licked her ear. "We're going to fix that, aren't we?"

"Yes!" she fairly shouted. The slow dance was over. They moved now to a faster beat. Charlie grimaced as she strove to meet his pounding pace.

"When?" he demanded.

"When what?" Charlie laughed.

"When are you going to marry me?" Drew reiterated.

"Soon," she promised.

"Charlie?" he panted, his teeth grazing over her shoulder.

"What?" she gasped.

"I love you."

She arched against him, her voice a cry of triumph and release as the final shudder ripped through her. "I love you," she promised, her fingers biting into his hips as she pulled him closer. He slammed against her, his hot seed filling her as he found his own release.

And in the soft glow of the aftermath he said a silent prayer that whatever her investigation turned up wouldn't destroy the fragile dream they'd built in the shadow of his past.

Chapter Twelve

Drew finally roused himself enough to look at the clock. "Shouldn't we warn your mother that we're coming?"

Charlie's eyes widened in surprise. "How did you know..."

"Terry's in Arlington. Your mother's in Alexandria. If I'm going to violate parole, we might as well get it all done at once."

"Oh, no!" Charlie froze, her face a mask of panic. "I didn't even think about state lines!"

"Relax. I'll call my parole officer before we leave." Drew laughed. "Any chance we'll get to see that car again? I never did get to take a really good look at it."

"The Caddy?" Charlie asked. "We could go visit Jamie and his car, instead, if you like. I'm sure he'd love to show it off for you."

"We have to go to your mother's," Drew decided. "I wouldn't miss meeting her for the world. I seem to have a new found confidence with women."

"I never noticed you lacking any confidence," Charlie teased.

"It took a while to convince myself that you weren't going to get hysterical if I wanted to try something different," Drew admitted, his voice serious. "I think I still half expect you to yell at me, and slap my hand, like a bad little boy caught with his hand in the cookie jar."

"I love it when you're bad," Charlie laughed. "Nothing with Allen was ever spontaneous. He had a schedule. Every Sunday morning before Church."

"Every other Saturday night, missionary position only," Drew remembered. "I felt big, and awkward, and clumsy. She made me feel guilty about even suggesting sex. She said I hurt her. After a while, we quit even trying. I told Terry once that sex wasn't all that great. He said he felt sorry for me. Now I understand why."

"I felt like I never measured up to Allen's expectations," Charlie agreed. "His heroines were always better lovers than I could ever picture myself being. I can't believe I wasted all those years with a man who didn't make me feel like this. I've been a nomad, out there alone roaming the desert. You're my oasis."

"I feel like I wasted a lot of years, too," Drew acknowledged. "You don't know what it took for me to stand there in that doorway, naked. I argued with myself all the time I was in the shower. Darby never wanted to see me without my clothes on. It frightened her. I never walked around the house naked. Not even in our bedroom. I didn't know it could feel so erotic just to have a woman look at me."

"You have a gorgeous body," Charlie purred. "I can't think of a more enticing picture."

"I look like somebody used me for a pin cushion," Drew responded with a snort. "Pretty big pins, at that."

Charlie ran her fingers over the largest of the scars, an angry red line that ripped across his chest, extending from his collarbone on the right side nearly to his solar plexus. There were two other, smaller knife wounds below his breast bone, and two more on his back, one near the spine and one nearer his right shoulder blade. "I don't mind the scars," she told him. "At first they made me angry, because someone tried to hurt you. Now I think of them as reminders. You're a survivor, Drew. You just keep coming back, against all the odds. I love to look at you. Scars and all. And I love making love to you."

"I had no idea that there was a woman waiting for me who might want to make love to me in the middle of the morning, on a weekday," Drew marveled, his fingers tangled in her hair again. "Who might change her plans just to make love to me."

"I hate to disappoint you, but I didn't change any plans," Charlie assured him. "You were supposed to end up here beside me all along."

"So you think this little scuffle was your idea?" he demanded incredulously.

"Of course."

Drew laughed, recovered enough to roll to his side. "Don't you know you can't lie to me?" He pulled her to him, kissing her slowly, thoroughly, until she was gasping for breath.

"Can too."

He kissed her again, plundering the inside of her mouth with his hot, rough tongue, wanting everything at once. His hands were everywhere, touching, teasing, stroking. "You know I'm right. Admit it," he demanded as he shifted his teeth to one small, firm breast. He nipped at the hard little bud of a nipple as his hand slid down across her belly.

She bucked against his probing fingers, languor giving way to need again as she roused to his touch. "Drew," she managed, his name a plea for mercy.

"Tell me," he demanded again. He kissed his way across her belly and down as his fingers parted her soft fur to slide deep into her wet heat. Clever fingers spread her wide as he ran his tongue slowly across her wet flesh, teasing, licking everywhere but where she wanted him most. She arched hard off the bed, clutching at his shoulder, as his tongue skirted her throbbing clit.

"Drew…"

"Tell me." He breathed the words against her sensitized skin.

"I – I was the second gunman." Her breath caught in a sharp cry as his tongue stroked deep inside her. "I admit it all. I killed Kennedy."

Laughter vibrated across her trembling thighs as she clenched her fists into the bed sheets. "More…"

"God yes…" She cried out again as he licked once over her clit before sucking her into his mouth. His hands locked on her hips, as if preventing her escape. "I shot Nixon, too."

He loosed his hold on her hips to drive two fingers deep into her as he licked over her clit until she writhed against him. "Drew!" Somehow his laughter vibrating over her clit made her twist violently against him.

"Nixon isn't dead."

One finger traced her anus, probing gently. "Oh, God!" she shrieked as she shuddered against him.

"Too much?"

"No…" Her hands searched for something, anything, to grab on to as the finger slipped inside her. "Drew!" she shrieked as she shattered against him, climaxing so violently that the room grew dim for a moment.

He laughed again as he waited for her to catch her breath. Slowly the room came back into focus. "We lied. We used a body double."

"Right." His tongue replaced his fingers inside her, stroking her back to fierce need faster than she'd have thought possible.

She tangled her fingers in his hair. "The chimp – Regan's chimp. We used him. The body double."

He was laughing so hard that his legs started to slide off the bed. "I could almost believe that one."

"We did. We…" Charlie let out a long, low moan, no longer able to form a coherent sentence. "Please," she whimpered.

His fingers thrust deeper as tongue circled around and around her clit, ever closer to the throbbing ache of relief. "Admit it," he coaxed, his own breathing ragged now.

She broke like Waterford crystal on a New York sidewalk. "I love you," she moaned. "I love you, Drew Bailey."

"And?" he demanded.

She twisted and squirmed against him, shattering again as he drove her relentlessly. "I want — more."

"Yeah?"

She half rose up, bending from the waist to grip his head as she climaxed against him. "Inside me. Now."

"That's better."

"Fuck me," she moaned.

He laughed, glorying in his power over her. "Tell me."

"Drew," she sobbed.

She wanted to scream as his breath sent shivers of pure electricity shooting through her. "Tell me. Admit it."

"This one was all your idea."

He found his feet and pulled her hips toward him, her knees over his forearms as he slid inside her. "This what you want?"

"No."

"Liar."

Her heels locked against his hips as she arched up hard against him. "Kennedy isn't dead."

"Yeah?" He slammed into her, hot and full and burning with every stroke, still shaking with laughter. She clenched around him, trying to keep from screaming as she fought for breath. "Where is he?"

His body went rigid as she convulsed around him again, losing the room once again to a sea of darkness and stars. She heard his voice as if from a long way away. "I love you, Charlie." She felt the hot gush of his semen flow into her abraded flesh, scalding even as it soothed her.

"Bethesda," she managed at last. "Naval Hospital. Fish tank in the basement."

He collapsed next to her on the bed, laughter wheezing out between breaths. "You are insane, woman."

"Yeah. I'm crazy for you."

* * * * *

"Why don't you drive?"

He hadn't ever asked. But then, she hadn't offered. She'd learned by now that Drew took nothing for granted.

"No, thanks!"

His refusal caught Charlie completely off guard. "You do have a driver's license?"

"Yeah. I have a driver's license." Drew looked off across the fields, his gaze focused beyond her line of sight. "I know better than to go anywhere without a valid State ID. I had to take the driver's test over again. One of the guys who works at the Mission took me down. Let me use his car. My driver's license and my parole papers are always in my wallet."

"So why don't you want to drive?" Charlie queried, mystified.

Drew shrugged, still focused light years away. "It's not my truck." As if that were such an obvious answer.

Charlie pushed back her quick surge of temper and decided on another approach. She tossed him the keys. "Okay. Now it's your truck. We'll add you to the insurance policy and change the title over tomorrow morning at the D.M.V. in Martinsburg."

Drew caught the keys reflexively, then stood staring at them for a long moment. He looked up, his expression puzzled, confused. "Charlie, you can't just give me your truck."

"Why not? We're having the feed delivered now, so I don't have to haul grain in this damn thing every Monday. The hay and straw make it into the barn on their own. If we need other supplies, you can go get them just as easily as I can. Easier, actually, since I'll be working days starting next week. Why do I need a truck? Besides, it's mine, free and clear. I can do whatever I want with it."

Drew's mouth opened and shut twice, but no sound came out. "You need your truck," he finally managed. "You're supposed to start your new job Monday. What will you drive to work?"

"I thought I'd pick up my car. It's been in storage since I moved out here."

"Your car," Drew repeated. "You own two vehicles."

"I own a car," Charlie corrected. "You own a truck." She skirted around to the passenger's side, pushing none too gently when he just stood there, staring at her.

"I can't afford to own anything, Charlie." Drew stood his ground, immobile as a tree stump. "There's insurance and taxes and repairs. How am I supposed to deal with that? I can't even afford to buy you an engagement ring. I can't be spending money on myself."

"Please don't buy me an engagement ring," Charlie begged. "I hate jewelry. I never wear any! A plain little band will do nicely. And you can't even go looking for a wedding ring without a vehicle to drive. We better open that checking account for you before we go to the D.M.V. tomorrow. There's title charges, too, and you'll need a new plate. We can negotiate a salary while you drive."

"Why are you doing this?" Drew demanded, his voice somewhere between puzzled and irritated.

"Because I want my car, and if you won't drive, I can't bring it home. I can't drive two vehicles at the same time." There were other reasons, but tomorrow was soon enough.

"It must be some car," Drew speculated, finally allowing himself to be pushed away from the passenger's door.

"Oh, I think you'll like it." Sibling rivalry made Charlie want to brag, but she decided not to spoil the impact. "Daddy got it for me, when I graduated from College. Maybe, if you're a very good boy, I might let you drive it. Occasionally. Every once in a while. When I'm in a very good mood."

"Oh, yeah?" Drew responded, sliding slowly behind the wheel. "What is it, a 72 Volkswagen Beetle?"

"I am not about to tell you," Charlie decided smugly. "It's going to be a surprise. You'll just have to wait and see for yourself."

Drew snapped his head around, eyes bright, as if an idea had just hit him. "You kids don't all have matching cars or something, do you?"

"No," Charlie laughed. "It is definitely not a '54 Eldorado. I wouldn't own a boat like that. It's not a Chevy, anyway."

"A Cadillac is not a Chevy," Drew argued as he experimented with the clutch pedal.

"A Cadillac is made by GM," Charlie countered. "That makes it a Chevy."

Drew wiped his palms on his slacks, pushed the clutch in, cranked the key, and eased into reverse, looking as if he was saying a silent prayer. "Corvettes are made by GM, too, but..." He stopped in mid sentence, missing first gear. "It's not a Corvette!"

"I told you, it's not a GM product at all," Charlie insisted with a yawn.

"You're going to regret forcing me to do this," Drew advised as he finally found first gear and convinced the Jeep to buck its way down the long, twisting farm lane. "I'm about twelve years out of practice." He seemed to relax just a little once they reached the paved road. He glanced over at Charlie, discovering she wasn't holding on for dear life. "A Dodge Viper."

Charlie raised one eyebrow, then snuggled down for a nap.

"A Ford, then," he guessed, unwilling to wait patiently.

"It's a car," she commented noncommittally. She sang softly "Over the river and through the woods to Grandmother's house we go."

"You're going to torture me with this, aren't you. I've noticed, you really like torturing me."

"It's only an hour and a half to Grandma's house," Charlie consoled him. "You can wait that long to find out. We'll go get my car first, then drive it over to Terry's. It'll be much more impressive than showing up in this old pickup."

"Impressive," Drew repeated speculatively. "What kind of car would you think is impressive? Let me see. A '76 Lincoln Continental. Black."

"NO!" Charlie shrieked, chortling jubilantly. "I wouldn't drive one of those if you gave it to me! And I am not going to tell you!"

"A Fairlane," Drew insisted. "A Falcon. A Maverick. A T-bird. That's it. It's a T-bird, isn't it?"

"The T-bird belongs to Frances," Charlie relented, willing to drop at least a few hints. If he was guessing, he wasn't busy being nervous about driving.

Drew groaned, too concerned with her mystery car to notice how easily he'd fallen back into the habit of reading the road. "My attorney drives a T-bird? What year is it?"

"It's a '57," Charlie obliged. "A blue convertible."

"Lightning Blue? With the portholes?"

"Soft Top," she told him. "No, wait. I think she does have the hard top for it, too. I don't know if it has portholes. She usually keeps it wrapped up in a cocoon in her garage. It's hard to remember. I haven't seen it very often."

"If you've ever seen it with the hard top on, you would remember the portholes," Drew assured her. "There's no other car in the world that looks anything like a '57 T-bird with the hardtop and the portholes."

Classic cars and football, Charlie thought with a little laugh. Her invisible hero had turned into a flesh and blood man, with all the fears and insecurities and quirks that went with everyday life. So unlike one of Allen's heroes. Yet she found she didn't mind. She could spend a lot of years with this man and never get tired of him. "It has the portholes," she relented.

"You knew that all along," he accused, catching on to her game.

"Maybe," Charlie replied, snickering at Drew as he missed fourth gear again. He'd turned east leaving the farm, instead of heading for the interstate, which meant 45 miles of twisting, turning back roads before they hit Highway 7 in Virginia. And hundreds of gearshifts.

"Don't you laugh at me," Drew warned. "You railroaded me into this. I told you I didn't want to drive."

"You never want to do things until you've tried them," Charlie pointed out. "You didn't want to trust me. You didn't even want to touch me. You didn't want to leave the farm. You didn't want to look up any of your old friends. You didn't want to let me buy you suits. But you made it through everything, and you're doing just fine." She closed her eyes again. "By the time we make it to Virginia, you'll feel like you've been driving this truck for years."

"If we make it to Virginia at all, I will have been driving this truck for years," Drew argued defensively.

"It's like riding a bicycle. You never forget."

"Yeah. I never was much good at that, either."

"All right, then. It's like making love. You were just as out of practice at that, and you've managed to pick it up again quite nicely."

Drew's frown of concentration softened as he glanced at Charlie. "That's turned out a lot better than I ever could have hoped it would. But you're wrong about one thing. You said I didn't trust you. I wanted to touch you so much that I couldn't trust myself. I've always trusted you. From the first moment I saw you."

Charlie laughed and shook her head. "I love you," she professed, "And I trust you with all my heart and even with my – your – pickup, and even the checking accounts, if it comes to that, but this isn't a matter of trust. I still like surprises, and I am not going to tell you any more about my car."

"Damn!" Drew laughed. "I thought I had you that time. Is it American made? It's not a Porsche, or something, is it?"

"It's not a Porsche or an MG Midget or a BMW," she confirmed, "And even if you name it, I'm not going to tell you. You're right. I do like torturing you."

"I've noticed." His voice dropped a little lower, sliding into the range that made all Charlie's nerves begin to tingle. "Like that thing you have with buttons. Is that a personal vendetta? Did you have a traumatic childhood experience involving buttons or something?"

Charlie blushed a bright crimson. "No, it isn't anything like that. Just curiosity, really."

"Curiosity?" Drew repeated, mystified. "You want to explain that one?"

"Allen used to let me proof read his books. In *After Sunset* he wrote a scene where the woman undressed the man who was guarding her using her teeth, because her hands were tied behind her back. I said it couldn't be done. Allen said if I were a little more adventurous I'd know there were lots of things that could be done with my teeth. I made the mistake of asking him how he knew so much about it, and we got into a huge fight, and I never had a chance to see if it would really work."

Whatever Drew was about to say got lost as he rounded the bend and took his first look in twelve years at the Shenandoah River.

"Holy Shit!" he exploded.

"What's wrong?" Charlie demanded anxiously.

"They moved the fucking bridge!"

"What are you talking about?" The bridge was right there in front of them.

"The road used to be over there," he nearly shouted, pointing up river. "When you came around the bend the road jogged to the right and there was this old blue bridge. It was a tall, narrow, boxy thing made out of steel beams with no place to walk on the sides. See how the bridge crosses the river at an angle? Well, the old bridge crossed the river dead on, so the road had to twist on each side to meet the bridge abutments. From there it was almost straight up hill on the other side. The old pilings aren't even out there in the river anymore. The whole side of the mountain is gone."

Charlie stared at the wide modern bridge before them and the gentle slop on the other side and tried to picture what it must have looked like, but it didn't work very well. There were no steep cut away sides to show where the natural grade had been. It was long enough gone that nature had reclaimed the restructured land, making it all one again.

"A lot can change in twelve years," she replied at last.

"Yeah," Drew agreed. "People grow up, they grow old, sometimes they die. You hadn't even met Allen yet when I went to prison. Now he's history. Except for his books."

"I'm sorry. I shouldn't have brought him up." Charlie flushed brightly. She seemed to have developed a fascination with her hands, which were folded in her lap. She shrunk back towards her side of the truck. Her tone was contrite, non-confrontational. "I shouldn't have..."

A complete stranger sat beside him. Drew stared at her in amazement. "Charlie?" Drew interrupted. "Please don't go on auto-pilot on me."

Her head snapped up and she stared at him, open-mouthed for a moment. "Auto-pilot?" she queried. "What do you mean?"

"You apologize like a pro," he explained. "Like you don't even know what you're apologizing for, and it doesn't really matter. Like someone who'd say anything, do anything to avoid a fight. Like someone who's used to being wrong." He laid his hand over her two small ones. "I know. I've been there. I know how it feels. Lost and hopeless inside. I don't want you to ever have to feel like that because of me. I don't want to ever feel like that again, either."

Charlie's eyes opened wide. "You feel as if you just threw the Earth out of it's proper orbit, and you would say or do anything to put it back where it belongs, but you can't. You just can't. No matter how hard you try, you just can't." She barely noticed that he'd pulled over, stopped the Jeep on the side of the hill that wasn't there anymore. Drew's arms around her finally penetrated the chill that had overwhelmed her.

"Disagree with me. Argue with me. Punch me again if you if you have to. But please, don't ever let me think you're disappointed in me," Drew implored. "I don't think my heart could stand that again. And I'd rather carve my heart out and hand it to you than to put you back there."

Charlie snuggled closer. "I think we both have to learn not to expect each other to be disappointed."

"That will get easier with time," Drew promised. "I do trust you, Charlie. And I'm learning to trust myself. Knowing you love me makes it easier."

"About the books..." she began again.

Drew's low, throaty chuckle made her spine tingle. "You were there. Do you think I could ever regret anything about that morning? Is there something you regret about that particular morning?"

"No." Charlie repeated it again with more determination. "No. No, I don't. I enjoyed that morning. I enjoyed that whole day. I don't think it should matter where I got the idea about the buttons. And I may well try it again."

"I may just read a few of Allen's books, myself, if there are scenes like that in them," Drew teased. "I may find a few new ways to torture you."

"You might. I remember a scene in a car, where this man . . "

Drew kissed her and retracted his arms. "You are not going to distract me. We are going to your mother's, and I am going to find out about this fantastic car." He managed to get his foot from the brakes to the gas without stalling the truck out. "It's a Mustang. Three children. Three classic cars. Three convertibles. A '54 Eldorado, a '57 T-bird, and a Mustang. Frances is 9 years older than you are, so that would make yours a '66. Maybe a '67. Jamie's is white, Frances's is blue. That would make yours red. Red, White, and Blue. Your father must have planned this for years. Were they surprises, or did you get to pick them out?"

"Dad had a list of possibilities he'd found, and we went to look at them all. He gave us his assessment of each car mechanically," Charlie explained. "We all made the final decision together. And they didn't have to be any specific year, or any particular color. Just something we thought would become a classic."

"We need a tractor."

"A tractor! Where the hell did that come from? Why do we need a tractor?"

"Mustang's don't have great ground clearance. I need to take the humps and low spots out of the lane or you'll rip the exhaust system off."

"I never said it was a Mustang. That was your idea."

Drew glanced at her out of the corner of his eye, keeping his attention on the switch back curves before them. "You can't lie for shit and you're not saying it isn't, either, so it's a Mustang. And we still need a tractor."

"We have a tractor. Your grandfather's tractor. It sort of came with the place. It's been sitting in at the Feed and Supply for six months now, waiting for parts. Carburetor. The bushhog is there, too. It needs three new disks. Or maybe it needs blades and the cultivator needs the new disks. And there's some sort of a scraper blade thing. Since I don't know how to drive a tractor, I haven't been pushing them about it. I guess I will, now."

"I'll take care of it. Ray's probably still trying to make some old junkyard carb work. For an extra hundred-and-fifty dollars you can put a new carb on it, and it'll run for the next 25 years. Something tells me you won't mind parting with the extra hundred-and-fifty dollars."

His smile was affectionate, not antagonistic. He was getting over his hang up about money, Charlie decided. And he'd volunteered to deal with a situation that would put him in contact with people outside of the farm, probably more than once. Small steps, but steps, just the same. She smiled softly. "It's more maroon than red."

Forty-five minutes later, Drew opened the garage door, too impatient to wait for Charlie as he pulled the car cover loose at the corner. "Maroon my ass. That's red. Red, white and blue. The All-American Giles kids. You guys are a regular three ring car show." He circled the Mustang slowly, examining it in critical detail. "It's all original. This wasn't a restoration job. This is the original paint. Even the interior is original."

"It's always been garage kept," Charlie confirmed. "It was my graduation present from my father. It was only ten years old when I got it, but they were already becoming collectable. It's been in storage for the last ten years. Allen wanted me to sell it. Said it was impractical. I just might have, too, if Franny hadn't suggested I put it on loan with a classic car museum. They kept it maintained for me for the last ten years. They start them and keep the oil changed and stuff. So it didn't cost me anything to keep it all these years."

"Charlie?"

Drew spoke so softly, she almost didn't hear him. "You shouldn't have to be practical all the time. You weren't responsible for the way your marriage turned out, Charlie. You've got to believe that, and stop feeling guilty. Guilt's the weapon people like Allen and Darby use against us to control us."

Charlie moved into the circle of his arms and laid her head against his chest. "I love you."

"And I love you. You and your car."

Charlie laughed at that. "It is a little impractical. I got it back last fall, but I couldn't take it to the farm when I moved this spring. I thought it would be okay, now. I figured to put it in the empty shed behind the barn. The shed's not in great shape, but it'll keep the weather away."

"That'll do for now," Drew agreed. "But she deserves a garage. It's not that much work. We can get it done before winter if we get the concrete poured before Thanksgiving. Much after that and they have to add antifreeze to make it set up slowly. How 'bout where the chicken coupe used to set?"

"Young man, are you interested in my daughter, or just her car?"

Her voice had the slightest hint of the old south. Quality. Breeding. Sophisticated charm. Drew raised his gaze to find a statuesque beauty standing in the doorway to the interior of the house. Her carriage was straight and proud, despite her seventy or so years. Her hair was pure fine-spun silver, waving softly back from her face into a loosely wrapped knot high up on her head. Her eyes were the same warm coffee that laughed at him from Charlie's face. There could have been no doubt as to her identity, even without her introduction.

Charlie felt her heart wrench with panic at the sound of her mother's voice. She should have gone to the front door first. She should have listened to Drew and let Mother know they were coming. She should have warned Drew about Mother's nasty temper. A hundred should-haves beat like waves against the shoreline of her conscience. Her mouth went dry as she tried to think of something to say, a way to smooth over the introductions.

There was no need. Drew flashed a brilliant smile and crossed the garage to Mother's side. "Ma'am," he replied, his drawl thicker than usual, "My heart belongs to Charlotte, but that does not interfere with my appreciation of classic beauty." He took the hand she offered and raised it to his lips like a southern gentleman. "Please allow me to introduce myself. I'm Andrew Bailey."

"I know who you are," Mother answered, a devious smile flitting across her face. "You are the ex-convict who plans to marry my daughter."

Drew didn't miss a beat. "I am," he agreed. "I apologize for not asking your permission first."

Charlie found her feet, if not her voice, and moved once more to Drew's side. He didn't take his eyes off her mother, but he knew she was there, and his arm slipped around her automatically.

"Would it have mattered?" Mother demanded. "If I had said no, what would you have done?"

Drew shifted his gaze to Charlie for a moment. "I'd have done my best to change your mind, Ma'am," he decided. "I wouldn't want to come between the two of you, but I don't think I could let her go." He studied the silver haired beauty before him. "Would you have given it? Your permission?"

Mother brought her eyes to Charlie, as well, then focused on Drew again. "You'll never know, now, will you?"

Charlie felt Drew's arm tighten around her waist. "Mrs. Giles," he intoned, "I should like very much to have your permission to marry your daughter Charlotte. I love Charlie and I want to spend the rest of my life with her. I haven't got a lot to offer, but I promise to be the best husband I know how to be. I hope that will be enough."

Mother stepped down into the garage to stand looking down into Charlie's eyes. "Is this what you want?" she asked, her voice softening just a little. "Are you happy?"

Charlie looked up at Drew and found his eyes searching for hers. It was like finding the land beneath her feet when she swam in the ocean. "This is what I want," she stated firmly. "Drew is what I want, Momma. More than anything. And yes, I am happy. Happier than I've been in years. Maybe ever."

"Young man," Mother addressed Drew, "I never liked the other one. He never asked anyone anything. Just told everyone what he was going to do, whether they wanted to know or not. I believe I rather like you. I think you'll do just fine. As for permission, Charlie does whatever she wants to, she always has, never really listened to anyone except her father. But thank you for humoring me. If my permission is worth anything, you have it. Take good care of my girl. The good Lord knows she won't help you much there. She's her own worst enemy most of the time."

Drew bent to kiss the older woman on the cheek. "Thank you, Ma'am. I'll do my best."

"You may call me Sylvia," Mother informed Drew. "Now, what are you really here for?"

Drew and Charlie exchanged glances. "The car," they both answered at once, laughing.

Charlie threw her arms around her mother impulsively. "I love you, Momma," she professed, dangerously close to crying again.

"Good," Sylvia answered matter-of-factly. "Stay for dinner."

"Well, actually," Charlie began.

"That will work out fine," Drew finished. "We're planning to look up an old friend of mine later, but we can do that after dinner. That would probably be more convenient, anyway, if it isn't too much trouble for you."

Sylvia smiled warmly. "Andrew, this house can always manage to hold a few more people for dinner."

"What can I do to help?" Drew offered.

Sylvia raised an eyebrow quizzically. "You know your way around a kitchen?"

"I'm actually marrying him for his cooking," Charlie pronounced with as serious a face as she could muster.

"I should have known. I do believe you've gained weight, child. At least five pounds."

"I'm learning to enjoy sitting down to dinner," Charlie agreed. "A handsome man across the table and good food on the plate, even intelligent conversation served up for dessert. What more could I ask for?"

"Grandchildren," Sylvia replied promptly.

Charlie felt her spirits sink again, but Drew came to the rescue quickly. "I have a daughter who just turned twenty-one,

Ma'am. Maybe she'll take care of that for all of us in a few years."

Chapter Thirteen

It was after eight when they wound their way toward Arlington. Even with Charlie's knowledge of the area, it still took some time to find the place. When they did, it turned out to be a typical Arlington townhouse. Brick exterior. Narrow front lawn. Not much different from the one Charlie had once owned in Alexandria. The parking spaces in front were head in, numbered, apparently two per house. There was one empty space available, which could have belonged to either Terry or his neighbor.

Either way, one of the cars out front was likely to be Terry's. Or his wife's.

Charlie pulled the Mustang into the open space between a Lexus and a BMW and turned off the ignition. Drew made no move to get out, and she didn't rush him. Instead, she reached across and took his hand. His fingers closed around hers automatically. After a moment, he looked over and smiled. "The worst he can do is slam the door in my face. Lets do it."

Charlie pocketed her keys and grabbed up the bag of Cherry Garcia. She would have lagged a little behind, let Drew get to the door first, had he not wrapped his arm around her possessively. Drew buried his nose in her hair for a moment before he reached out to ring the doorbell.

It took a full minute for the door to open. When it did, there was a woman standing there. She stopped, her hand on the storm door, staring at Drew for a moment, then turned away abruptly. "Terry!" they heard her holler as she disappeared. "Terry! Get your ass down here!"

Moments later a male head appeared to make the same inspection. The man was tall, wiry, almost gaunt. His hair, what there was of it, was dark brown and curly, much like it had been in the yearbook picture. His worried frown quickly turned to a look of pure amazement. As he threw the door open and lurched out onto the concrete stoop, Charlie realized he had a noticeable limp.

"Drew? Andrew Bailey?" The voice fit the man. Higher pitched than Drew's, but warm and friendly, though a shade incredulous.

Drew offered a hesitant smile in return and glanced at the bag in Charlie's hand. "Ben and Jerry followed me over here."

Terry jumped off the little porch to throw his arms around Drew in a back pounding bear hug. It took only half a heartbeat for Drew to raise his arms in return. When he did, Charlie worried he'd crush the smaller man. The door opened behind Terry, and the woman reappeared.

When they broke apart, Terry introduced his wife. "You remember Mickey? She was Michelle Everett?"

Drew frowned for a moment, then recognition flooded his face. "Tom Everett's little sister? We had to get you out of the tree at the Junior Prom?"

"You did not need to bring that up," Mickey pointed out, but she also offered Drew a warm hug.

Drew pulled Charlie against his side again, bolstering her confidence. "I'd like you two to meet Charlotte Giles. My...Fiancée."

Charlie was expecting the same introduction she'd gotten last weekend with his friends at the feed store. A lifetime passed for her in the pause as Drew weighed his options.

Fiancée worked just fine, Charlie decided.

Terry grinned wickedly as he took the hand Charlie offered, raising it to his lips rather than shaking hands. He cocked one caterpillar of an eyebrow. "My friend, your taste in women has improved dramatically."

Remembering Terry's dislike of the blonde bombshell from the yearbook, Charlie laughed delightedly. "Not that I'm arguing with you, but that's quite a judgment call to make in less than thirty seconds."

Instead of releasing her hand, Terry held it up for inspection. "You're not blonde, you don't look like a cheerleader, and you're wearing an MIT class ring," he pointed out, "Which means you have a brain that's useful for something besides your wardrobe, and I'm guessing that little baby is yours." He pointed to the Mustang. "The class ring looks garage kept, like the car, so I assume this is a special occasion."

"We just left my almost mother-in-law's," Drew explained. "Charlie picked up some things she'd left there. Like the car. And a jewelry box full of girlie things she doesn't like to wear," he teased.

Charlie fingered the sapphire stud posts she'd reluctantly stuck through her ears. "Would you like the car tour?" she offered by way of a distraction.

Terry addressed his answer to Drew. "The lady's good at changing the subject, too, but it is a tempting offer."

Drew turned and waved his hand like an usher. "After you."

"We'll put the ice cream in the freezer," Mickey called after the men. They didn't seem to notice.

The town house had that comfortable, lived in feeling. Neat and tidy, but not too spotless. Just enough clutter here and there to be a home, and not just on display. Mickey watched the men through the living room window. "Thank you for coming," she said without taking her eyes off Terry. "He needed this."

Charlie wasn't sure which "he" Mickey meant, but either way, she agreed. "I'm surprised they didn't keep in touch," she offered.

Mickey studied Charlie with a shrewd eye. "You don't get through MIT on good looks and charm," she observed. "My guess is Drew knows better than to try to keep anything from you. Just how much do you know?"

"I know it's easier to explain the design of a circuit board than to figure out what goes on in a man's head," Charlie replied. "I know about Moundsville, if that's what you mean. As for the rest, it's hard putting the pieces together so long after the fact. I know Drew and Terry were best friends in high school. That's about it as far as they're concerned. I know about Drew's divorce, and Darby's accusations in court. I know Drew was so drunk he could barely stand the night of the murder. There are some things he just doesn't remember."

"It sounds to me like there's a lot I could fill you in on," Mickey offered thoughtfully. "I don't think I'd be violating anyone's sacred trust here." She poured them each a cup of coffee. "I was two years younger than Drew and Terry. Terry and I didn't get together until we were both in college. Back in high school, Drew and Terry did everything together, before Darby came along. Terry practically worshiped Drew.

"Kids picked on Terry because of his clubfoot when he was in grade school. Then one day Drew got tired of seeing this little kid get beat up all the time. He took Terry aside and taught him how to fight. After that, they were always together. They were even planning to go to college together. Drew had a football scholarship and Terry had an academic scholarship.

"Then along came Darby, and next thing you know she's pregnant. Darby wanted to have an abortion, you know. She and Drew fought like crazy over it. Drew refused to pay for it or even help her get it. He wanted to get married. Terry told him he was crazy. That he was throwing away his life. But Drew wouldn't listen. Terry says Drew never would listen to anyone, once he made up his mind to do something. He and Terry drifted apart after Drew got married. Darby didn't like Terry much, and she didn't try to hide it.

"Drew was a bear after Darby divorced him. He got a bad reputation around town. A fight looking for a place to happen. He acted like the world owed him something. Terry wasn't around much then. He was busy with college. But they got together whenever Terry was in town. Then they usually ended up in a fight. Either with six other guys, or with each other, if there was no one else handy.

"Drew absolutely fell apart when Darby was murdered. He got drunk every night for over a week. Terry went with him every night, too, until the night of the fight with Weasel. Drew asked Terry to go down to the Red Shed in Shepherdstown with him that night, too, but Terry refused. I'd come down pretty hard on Terry about his drinking, and the Red Shed had quite a reputation. There had been several stabbings down there. The cops eventually shut the place down.

"Terry sobered up enough to tell Drew he wasn't going back again. They got into a shouting match that turned pretty ugly. Terry even slugged Drew a couple of times. I think he busted Drew's nose. But Drew wouldn't hit Terry. He never would. He just walked away. Terry's always felt that if he'd gone down to the Shed with Drew that night, Weasel never would have been killed."

Charlie shook her head slowly as if willing the pieces to fit together. "If Drew had already been in a fight before he got to that bar, then that explains where the blood came from," she mused.

Charlie looked from Drew to Terry as they came in the door and sighed. "When's the last time you two talked? Really talked to each other?"

Drew shrugged, looking uncomfortable. Terry was the one who answered. "That camping trip. About a month before graduation. You had just found out Darby was pregnant."

Drew frowned, and then nodded in agreement.

"I thought you were supposed to be best friends?" Charlie demanded in frustration.

"We were!" Drew spit defensively.

"We are!" Terry asserted.

"I don't believe this! You're a pair of pig-headed jerks!" Michelle decided. "For twelve years I've been listening to this sob story about how it was all your fault that Drew ended up in prison, and you never even apologized to him?"

"How was it your fault?" Drew demanded in amazement. "And what on earth did you have to apologize for?"

"I tried to apologize!" Terry protested. "I went down to the jail four times. You wouldn't even see me!" he insisted, his voice bitter.

"What the hell are you talking about?" Drew exploded. "No one came to visit me when I was in jail. Absolutely no one! All you guys dumped me like a piece of old trash."

"No," Terry insisted, "No, it wasn't like that at all. I went down there four times. They told me you didn't want to talk to me. I thought you were still pissed because I hit you."

"You hit me," Drew repeated incredulously. "Like hell you did! When the hell did you hit me?"

"You don't remember? I've been feeling like an ass for twelve years and you don't even remember?"

"What the hell are you talking about?" Drew demanded again. "I never refused to see anybody and I sure as hell never had a fist fight with you. I'd have beat my own skull in before I hit you, no matter how drunk I was!"

"You didn't hit me, you asshole! I begged you to, but you wouldn't! You tried to drag me back down to that damn bar. I told you to go to hell. You were already wasted. I was so pissed I hauled off and hit you, but you wouldn't fight with me. You never would. You just stood there. I landed five, maybe six good punches before you picked me up and tossed me into Mom's pool. Before I could get back out you were gone."

Terry crossed the room to a small liquor cabinet, his limp even more pronounced than it had been earlier. "I never saw you again. I went down to the jail as soon as I heard on Sunday, but visiting hours were over. I came back Monday and Tuesday, and then again on Friday, before I went back to college. I was working on my Masters Degree. I had a teaching fellowship, or I'd have blown off the start of the semester. I kept trying to see you before I left, but they told me you said to go to hell."

"Son-of-a-bitch." Drew looked like he wanted to punch something. "You gave me those busted ribs, then."

"Yeah, I sure as hell did. For all the good it did me." Terry downed two fingers of Scotch and refilled his glass. "Broke your nose, too. You bled like a stuck pig." He looked over his shoulder and raised the bottle questioningly toward Drew, who just shook his head.

"Haven't had a drink since that night," Drew revealed.

"You never were much of a drinker," Terry commented morosely. "Figured that was my fault, too. First thing I did when you came over to my place the day after Darby was killed was to put a drink in your hands." He downed the refill, as well. "I thought we'd go down to the Shed, get drunk, sleep it off, and that would be the end of it. But it never ends, does it?"

Drew crossed the room and took the bottle of Cutty Sark from his friend's fingers. He put the cap back on it and closed the liquor cabinet. "I got drunk because I wanted to, Terry. You didn't pour it down my throat. You didn't even buy it for me. You tried for a solid week to get me to quit drinking. That much I remember. You say you even punched me, for God's sake. Christ, man. If I'd hit you back I might have killed you! You risked your neck trying to save me. If I didn't want to listen, it sure as hell wasn't your fault."

Terry looked up at Drew, staring at him for a dozen heartbeats. "Then why the hell wouldn't you see me?"

"Because nobody ever told me you were there," Drew insisted. "I never would have refused to see you. You should know that. You're the closest thing to family I ever had. As far as I know, I never had one single visitor except my grandfather and that son-of-a-bitch of a lawyer."

Terry just stared at Drew for a while, trying to rearrange his concept of the past. "Didn't you get my letter?"

"Son-of-a-bitch," Drew repeated his new favorite phrase. "There was a letter, too?"

"Shit, yes! Did you think I'd just disappear and not even try to contact you? You were my best friend, for Christ's sake."

"I expected to hear from you. I expected to hear from all of you. I even asked Granddad. He said no one had been by the house. No one came to visit me. Yeah, I know, you tried, but I didn't know that. After a while I quit expecting. I figured no one wanted anything to do with a murderer."

"Yeah," Terry agreed, his voice equally bitter. "Yeah, I can see that. I'd dump my best friend just because you beat the crap out of some asshole who had it coming anyway."

"Hell, I'd have come and had it out with you if I could have," Drew insisted. "But I was just a little indisposed."

"Why would the cops have lied to me?" Terry questioned.

Drew hesitated before he replied. "Because I didn't kill Weasel." For the first time, Charlie heard certainty in his voice.

"What? What do you mean you didn't kill him? What the hell are you talking about?" Terry echoed.

"I blacked out that night," Drew explained. "I don't remember much of anything. Except hitting Weasel. I think I only hit him once. He walked right up to me. Told me Waite had paid him to murder Darby." Drew's voice broke and he focused on the ceiling for a long moment. "He wanted me to know what a nice piece of ass she was." Drew fingered the liquor cabinet door, and Charlie held her breath while he decided whether or not to open it. Finally, he turned to face Terry again, the cabinet's contents safe.

"I wanted to kill him, Terry. I wanted him dead so damn bad. I remember hitting Weasel. My hand felt like it exploded when it connected with his jaw. Next thing I knew I was in jail and Weasel was dead. I felt like I'd been in a fight, I had cracked ribs and broken knuckles, and I was covered in blood. The cops told me I'd killed Weasel. By the time the trial got there, I didn't give a damn. Granddad had already spent $24,000 on that damn lawyer. I was afraid he'd lose the farm. The lawyer said if I pled guilty, the Prosecutor would reduce the charges to second-degree manslaughter, and I'd do twenty-five years instead of life. So I pled guilty. Figured I might get out in time to enjoy my grandchildren."

"Shit," Terry concluded. "I bet you busted your damn knuckles on the concrete block wall next to the pool. You got so mad at me you took a swing at the wall instead." He slumped onto the couch. "I never thought about getting a message to you through your grandfather. If I had, you'd never have gone to prison."

"You don't know that," Drew argued. "I might have fought the whole thing, cost Granddad the farm, and still ended up with a life stretch. If I'd just listened to you, I wouldn't have even been there. I walked right into Waite's trap. Charlie thinks Waite sent Weasel down there to start a fight with me on purpose. Get rid of me and Weasel in one move, and there's no evidence to tie Waite to Darby's murder. I was supposed to kill Weasel, but if my hand was already busted, I doubt I did all that much damage. Somebody else had to finish the job for me."

"It would have taken a lot more than one punch to kill Weasel anyway," Mickey observed. "Weasel was tough. Not all that big, but wiry. A real scrapper. A couple of years older than you, too, and mean as a...well, as a weasel. A nasty, horrible man."

Terry stared at Drew, like he was seeing him for the first time. "If you only hit Weasel once, then..."

"Who actually killed Weasel?" Mickey finished.

Charlie looked around the room quickly until she spotted what she wanted. "May I use your phone?" she asked. "It's a local call."

"Of course," Michelle answered.

"Call Germany if you want to, if you think it'll do any good," Terry put in.

Frances answered on the third ring, sounding sleepy. "Have Parkman find out who brought Weasel in to the emergency room the night he was killed," Charlie ordered abruptly, not stopping to bother with an introduction. "I want to know how Weasel got there, and I'm betting it wasn't an ambulance."

"Charlie?" Frances queried. "I fell asleep watching the news. What's going on?"

"There wasn't any fight in the bar that night, Franny. Not that Drew was involved in. Drew's bruises didn't come from Weasel. That happened about an hour earlier. Whoever took Weasel to the hospital either killed him or knows what really happened. Or at least more about it than we do."

"I'll call Parkman now," Frances confirmed, all the sleep gone from her voice. She hung up abruptly.

"I have another question to put before you." Terry had a thoughtful, grim look about him. All eyes focused on him attentively as he rested his eyes on Charlie. "Who got the money?"

"What money?" Charlie responded, baffled.

"When we went out to look at your car, Charlie, Drew told me you bought his Granddad's farm," Terry elaborated. "Where did the money go? Who was at closing to accept the check? Even at a five hundred dollars an acre, you would have paid a hundred twenty five thousand for that place, and last I heard land was going for closer to three times that up there. Drew was the only family the old man had. Everything should have gone to Drew, and after him to Savannah. Who was at closing? Who got the money?"

Charlie frowned and shook her head blankly. "The farm was sold by the Estate's Executor. The lawyer and the real estate agent and I were the only ones at closing. The Estate Executor had already signed the documents before closing. I don't have any idea where the money went. I never even thought about it."

"A hundred and twenty five thousand?" Drew repeated, sitting down abruptly. "You paid a hundred and twenty five thousand dollars for Granddad's farm?"

"No, I certainly did not," Charlie answered stiffly. Drew's relief was short lived. "I didn't steal it from anybody. The farm had already been on the market for six months with an asking price of fifteen-hundred dollars per acre. No one had come anywhere close to that. I topped the highest offer by twenty percent and offered a cash settlement at closing. I paid nine-hundred-twenty-five dollars per acre for two-hundred-thirty-seven acres."

"So we're talking about a quarter of a million dollars," Drew stated calmly. "Assuming Granddad left the farm to me, I stand to inherit a quarter of a million dollars."

"Actually, the farm would have sold for $219,225," Terry calculated automatically, "Out of which about $13,153 went for brokers' fees, and about forty-five will go to estate taxes and Attorney's fees. So you're looking for about a hundred sixty thousand, give or take a few dollars. You can afford a few cups of coffee. Invest it right, and you may be able to avoid paying half of it out in income taxes."

"Let me guess," Charlie speculated. "When you're not out hunting Ben and Jerry's, you're an investment counselor."

"CPA," Terry and Mickey answered in unison.

"A hundred sixty thousand," Drew repeated.

"Drew?" Charlie queried apprehensively.

"You paid cash for a quarter-million dollar farm," he managed in amazement.

"Well, cash isn't really cash," Charlie explained. "It was a cashier's check. It just means the sellers didn't have to deal with banks and financing holdups."

Drew's voice betrayed minor annoyance. "I didn't think you showed up with a suitcase full of small unmarked bills," he snorted. "Don't you think this makes the whole suit argument look a little petty?"

"I won't argue with that," Charlie agreed a little too smugly.

Drew just stared at her.

"If that money is actually sitting waiting for you some where," Charlie pointed out, "You have a better bank balance than I do at the moment by far. Should I be worried?"

"You know better than that!" Drew objected.

"Are you two actually arguing about money?" Mickey asked in amazement.

"Drew tends to be a little intimidated by large sums of money," Charlie replied with a shrug.

"That's pretty stupid," Mickey observed. "If you'd gone pro, you'd have been earning at least four times that every season. Hell, by now, if you were still playing, you could be earning that much per game."

"And spending thousands of it having me find ways not to give it to the IRS," Terry added with a laugh.

Drew studied Terry thoughtfully for a long moment. "You really know how to put things in perspective," he said at last.

"And you never did," Terry agreed jovially.

Drew held out a hand to Charlie with a soft smile. When she put hers in his, he pulled her gently into his lap. "I don't know why you put up with me," he sighed as he nuzzled her hair.

"That's easy," Charlie replied smugly. "You're a great cook. Everyone knows the way to a woman's heart is through dessert."

"Speaking of which," Michelle interjected, "Let's attack Ben and Jerry."

"Just what the hell is Cherry Garcia, anyway?" Drew demanded.

The other three exchanged glances and began to laugh. "You have a lot of catching up to do," Michelle informed him affectionately.

* * * * *

It was a long trip home, following the taillights of the Mustang through the dark. Too much time alone. Too much time to think. Drew felt as if he had merely been an observer, rather than a participant in his own life. How many times had he walked right into Waite's traps? More to the point, how many times would he do it again?

"Why?" seemed but a marginally important question any more. How and where the next attack would come were of much higher significance. And who would get hurt this time.

They could see the lights glowing red and blue well before they made it down the rutted farm lane. Ambulance lights. Squad Car lights. Sirens echoed through the night. Ghost was barking furiously. All his instincts said to run, to just keep driving, but Drew pulled up next to the barn and ran to Charlie's side as she jumped out of the Mustang.

Charlie was screaming Janelle's name, searching frantically for her among the police officers and EMT's.

"What's going on here?" Drew demanded.

"And you are?" the Trooper responded, his voice a little harried.

"Andrew Bailey. Farm manager," Drew answered, handing out the title Charlie had offered him with ease.

Another Trooper intervened. This one seemed to be in charge. "I'm Sergeant Keefe," the broad shouldered giant introduced himself. "We could sure use some help down here. Call off this damn dog before we have to shoot him."

Drew followed the Trooper quickly down the steps to the tack room, where Ghost stood in the doorway, barring the EMT's access to a shredded looking body. Drew turned away from the scene to survey the chaos everywhere. "Charlie!" he bellowed. In moments she reappeared, fighting her way through the crowd to him. "You need to help these officers," he explained when she got to him. He stood blocking the door to the tack room. "You need to call Ghost. Don't go in there. Don't even look. Just call the dog, and take him down to the feed room. I think you better put a leash on him when you get there. I'll meet you in a minute or two."

"Is it Janelle?" Charlie asked, her face pale.

"No," Drew assured her. "Ghost's got a man down in there. He won't let the EMT's do their job. You've got to get the dog out of here. Janelle's probably already gone home, but if she's here, I'll find her," he promised.

"Thank you," Charlie responded in obvious relief. "Ghost!" she commanded. "Come here!"

The barking stopped at once, leaving relative silence except for the wail of the ambulance's siren. Ghost bounded happily to Charlie's feet, a playful hundred-and-fifty pound puppy again. Except for the blood coating his muzzle. Drew caught the big dog's head in a firm grasp and scrubbed his face with a handkerchief, quickly palming it out of Charlie's sight.

"I'm all right," Charlie assured him. "It's no worse than the groundhogs. I'm not going to pass out on you," she promised.

Still, Drew watched with obvious concern as she led the dog away. She was all right until she raised a hand to the feed room door and found it covered with blood from Ghost's fur that Drew had somehow missed. Sure enough, Charlie did a graceful swan dive into the dirt. Drew sprinted toward her, but he wasn't fast enough to catch her before she hit the ground. With a sigh of frustration, he scooped her up and deposited her in the hay next to the feed bins.

"Ghost!" he ordered angrily. "Go take a bath!" To his surprise, the dog happily ran off toward the stream. It was the first time Drew could ever remember the dog doing what he told him to.

By the time Drew got back to the tack room, the EMT's had the intruder bundled onto a stretcher and on his way up the barn yard stairs. "Have you seen Janelle?" Drew demanded, as soon as he found Sergeant Keefe again.

"Janelle?" Keefe repeated, obviously confused. "Who's Janelle?"

"Tall kid, slim, brown hair, green eyes. Just out of college."

The officer shook his head.

"Who called you here then? "

Sergeant Keefe pointed up the stairs. "Your would-be burglar had a cellular phone. He called it in himself. Can you beat that? Said he was breaking into the tack room and the dog had him cornered. He'll probably try to sue you for keeping a vicious dog. Has the dog had all his shots?"

"Absolutely," Drew assured him, though, in fact, he'd no idea, other than the fact that Ghost belonged to Charlie, and Drew knew she was thorough about such things.

"Well, then, just keep an eye on the dog for a few days," Keefe decided. "I won't order him quarantined. Kind a looks to me like you need him."

"Thanks," Drew offered as the ambulance pulled off, taking its sirens with it. The night seemed suddenly very quiet. As if knowing there were people talking about him, Ghost reappeared, dripping with stream water. "NO!" Drew hollered, but it was too late. The big dog stood there, laughing at them, as he gave his thick coat a mighty shake, spraying them both with icy drops of mud.

"Ghost," Charlie called softly from the bottom of the stairs, trying not to laugh. "Go get the horses." With another sideways dog laugh, Ghost bound off into the night, disappearing as easily as his namesake.

Drew glared down at her, trying to decide whether to be glad she had regained consciousness or angry that she was laughing at him. "This," he said with a flourish toward the mud-covered charcoal that he knew to be her favorite, "Is why I do not wear three-hundred dollar suits."

"It's just a little mud," Charlie observed, unconcerned. "We can drop it off at the dry cleaners on the way to the D.M.V. in the morning. I'm going to go call Janelle and make sure she made it home all right."

Charlie was laughing openly as she disappeared down the sidewalk. "It was worth the dry-cleaning bill just to see the expression on your face," she assured him.

"I take it she can't handle blood," Keefe commented dryly.

"Sometimes," Drew speculated. "I'm not sure what it is, really. Charlie stood off a bunch of young hoodlums with a shotgun one night. They were trying to convince me to leave the State. There was plenty of my blood around that night, and she never even flinched. Then tonight she passes out at a little blood in Ghost's fur. I haven't quite figured her out."

Keefe closed his little book. "I know you don't remember me, but I was a fan of yours years ago. I was Junior Varsity when you were Senior. Some of the guys have been talking around the barracks. They figure we need to keep a pretty close eye on you, being fresh out of Moundsville and all. Me, I always believe in giving a man the benefit of the doubt. You won't have any trouble from me over this."

"Thanks," Drew offered. "I remember you, now. You were pretty good. I'm surprised you didn't go on to play college ball."

"I did," Keefe explained. "But I wasn't that good. I played at Shepherd College for two seasons. But college just wasn't what I wanted to do back then. So I joined the Marines. Came home when I got out. I figured, some of us have to come back home. Most of the guys I went to school with are working in Texas or D.C. or somewhere." He turned away, only to stop at the patrol car's door and look back over his shoulder at Charlie. "My buddies and I, we stop in the truck stop at night sometimes, just to check up on the girls. I've seen you in there. Recognized you right away. You're kind of hard to forget. Never knew the lady was a computer programmer till just recently. I'm glad you got her out of Harry's," he mused. "That's some woman you got there."

"Yeah. Isn't she though," Drew agreed.

Chapter Fourteen

Drew was, Charlie decided as she snuggled even closer against him, the perfect man to wake up next to. The thing she liked most was the way his smile reached all the way to his eyes when she finally peered reluctantly between her lashes. "I love you," was the best she could do at voicing any of those thoughts this early in the morning.

Drew turned her gently in his arms and kissed her thoroughly. Charlie had never really been much of a morning person. She dealt with mornings because she had to, but she'd never liked them. Waking up with Drew's body folded around hers made mornings more tolerable. A slow, lazy smile played across her lips. This morning, Drew had been studying her face as if trying to memorize it. His expression seemed so serious. This shouldn't have been a serious day. "What were you thinking?" Charlie asked, her voice still the sleepy rumble of a lazy cat.

"How beautiful you are when you wake up," Drew replied, kissing the end of her nose.

"Before that," Charlie reminded him. "You looked so solemn. You're not still mad about the suit."

"I was never mad about the suit," Drew admonished with a laugh. "Frustrated, maybe, but not mad."

"You didn't look happy," Charlie pointed out.

Drew's smile dimmed. "It wasn't anything important."

"Everything about you is important to me."

"I was just remembering where I was this time last year," Drew confessed. If he closed his eyes, he knew he'd hear it again. Every day started the same. The whir of the big motors. The sharp, metallic clang of three hundred and forty sets of steel doors ramming home like mortar fire. There were no special days in the pen. A birthday was just another reminder. Another year gone. Another year ahead. "Sometimes I get a little scared when I think about it too much. It didn't seem to matter all that much, before. But I've got so much to lose now."

"You're not going to lose me. I'm not about to let you get away from me." She kissed him again, trying to distract him from his train of thought, but it didn't seem to work. "You don't talk about Moundsville much," she offered.

Drew's voice was hesitant. "Didn't really think you'd want to hear about it."

"Sometimes I watch you staring out the window. You get that look in your eyes. I feel like I've lost you, at least for that moment. I know you're back there."

"Prison is boring," Drew told her with an ironic little smile. "Mostly it's just boring. Everything's routine. Same thing at the same time every day. You can tell what day it is by the smells from the mess hall. The most exciting thing that happens is the annual softball game with the local Church team. Sometimes we'd lose. We figured if we won every year they might give up and not come back the next year.

"Everybody has jobs. I worked in the kitchen. Ever make mashed potatoes for 750 men? Try boiling 200 pounds of potatoes. Try skinning 200 pounds of potatoes. Boring. Sometimes one inmate makes a knife called a shiv out of a piece of his bunk frame, just so he can stab another inmate, but even that doesn't generate all that much excitement, unless you're the one getting stabbed. Then you end up in the infirmary for a few days. If you live.

"For everybody else it means a lock down and a shake up. That means everybody has to spend several days in their cells while the guards go through and search every cell from top to bottom. The guards usually take that opportunity to destroy anything you have if they don't like you. Pictures. Letters. Whatever. You aren't really allowed to have much. A TV. A radio. Not more than three newspapers. That's because sometimes guys use the old newspapers to start fires. They try to get the guards to come in where they can attack them.

"There's a 'dead-line' in front of the cells, two-and-a-half feet out. Guys from another cellblock can come down to visit and use the showers, but they can't cross the 'dead line.' That's to keep everything out in the open where the guards can see what's going on. There are four guards to three-hundred-and-fifty men. The guards can see you, but if you get attacked, you're pretty well on your own. They can't get to you fast enough to save you from another inmate with a knife. They sit behind wire cages in a tower, sort of like an open elevator shaft.

"The guards are just there. Most prisons are pretty much run by the gangs. I've heard the gangs are racial in other prisons. Moundsville's almost all white. The gangs there are motorcycle gangs. If you belong to one of their gangs you wear their colors. A tattoo on your upper arm. If you don't belong, you stay out of the way. Try your best not to attract attention.

"After a while, everything inside you sort of dies. You quit feeling. You don't want to see anyone from the outside, because they wake you up again. They remind you that there's a real world out there. They make you think. You don't want to think. You don't want to care. You just wait. You just do your time."

And you try not to think about birthdays, or your kid growing up without you. You try not to remember…

Drew closed his eyes, and Charlie pictured him as she'd seen him that first day. Cold. Wet. Shut down. Closed off. She brushed her hand across his cheek, smoothing the hair away from his face. "They're shutting Moundsville down, you know," Charlie reassured him.

"We always heard that. Every new man would bring the stories. Lawsuits. Court orders. Some judge said it had to be phased out by the end of 1992. But a year-and-a-half later, I was still there." He ran his hand over her skin, absorbing her warmth, breathing in the soft scent of her, but he couldn't quite shake the damp, musty smell, or the chill that came over him when he drifted back there in his mind. "Have you ever seen the place?"

Charlie shook her head. "Just a few pictures on TV. There were riots, I think."

"There were riots," Drew confirmed, his voice grim as he remembered. "The prison was built just after the Civil War. They modeled it after Joliet in Illinois. God knows why they picked that place. Joliet was old then. Moundsville is a Gothic hell. It's built like a stone fortress. The weird thing is, it's right there in town. A residential district grew up all around it. People's houses back right up to these massive stone walls, like a medieval castle.

"In the middle of the front is the old Administration building. The walls are hand-quarried stone, five-foot thick at the bottom. It was all built by prisoners. There are two main cellblocks, sort of like wings off the administration building. North Hall and South Hall. Guys call North Hall "The Alamo," because if you screw up badly enough to get stuck in there, it's your last stand. Guys in the Alamo spend twenty-two hours a day in their cells. They even eat in their cells. The guards take them outside individually for exercise in these little cages like they use for the lions at the circus.

"All the cells are stone and concrete, five foot by seven foot. There's no heat in the cells. It's supposed to come in through the bars on the front of the cells, where the doors are, from the radiators in the aisle ways around the cellblocks, but once you get cold in the fall you know you'll stay cold until next summer. It's always damp and musty in the winter. It's drafty, but you never seem to catch a real breeze." The smell was there. It was always with him. He buried his face in her hair, trying to block it out.

"There's barely enough room for the sink and the toilet next to the bunks," he continued. "The plumbing's shot. The toilets won't flush half the time and the faucets never quit dripping. The ceilings are only 7 foot high, so there isn't really even room to stretch. Each cellblock is four stories tall. Your ceiling is the next guy's floor. You're so close you can hear each other breathe."

He ran a hand over his shoulder, remembering. "The worst riot was on New Years Day in '86. I got my collarbone broken. We got a new kitchen and dining hall after that. They started transferring guys to the new prison, Mt. Olive down in Fayette County. But I knew I wasn't going anywhere. I used to have this dream, like a premonition, that I'd die there, almost like those old stone walls were trying to suffocate me." He closed his eyes, remembering the dream. "I keep thinking I'm going to wake up," Drew confided. "I'm afraid this isn't really happening to me, and I'm going to wake up back in prison, with another thirteen years ahead of me and nothing to come home to after that. You can live a lifetime in a dream that's only a few minutes long. Maybe I've been cut again, and I'm in the infirmary, and they've given me morphine, or something. Maybe..."

Charlie wrapped her arms around him and pulled his head down into a fiercely passionate kiss, determined to drive away his demons. He felt cold. His arms closed back around her at last, cold skin slowly growing warm again. "I'm real, Drew," she insisted. "I'm real. You can't lose me. No matter what, you can't lose me." She thought about the hidden room in the barn. It was more than twice the size of the cells he'd described. "I promise, no matter what happens, I'll never let them take you back there," she vowed.

She felt him shudder. "Don't make promises you can't keep," he warned with a sardonic smile.

"Let's go to Mexico," she blurted impulsively. "Just pack a couple of bags and hop in the Mustang. I can be ready in a hour."

"Mexico?" Drew repeated, laughing now. "Mexico? You can't just walk away from all of this, Charlie. You can't abandon Ghost and Allegro and all your Ladies. I wouldn't ask you to. I don't want you to. Besides, I don't want to run away from this. I don't want it hanging over my head the rest of my life. I want to grow old here, on this farm, with you. Maybe one day I'll fall asleep on the front porch like Granddad and never wake up. I don't want to live the rest of my life on the run. We've got to see this thing through, Charlie."

Charlie sighed, knowing he was right. "Then I guess it's time to go talk to that real estate agent," she decided. "Let's find out where the money went."

"It's a start," Drew agreed. "At least it's something we can do ourselves. I can't stand the waiting. If we'd been here yesterday..."

"If we'd been here yesterday, we'd have kept Ghost from half killing that man, and we'd have found out who sent him before the cops hauled him away," Charlie stated firmly. "I'll check the e-mail for Parkman's report before we leave, too," Charlie added as she rolled out of bed. "Maybe he's found something."

Charlie was still sitting at the computer, looking distressed, when Drew appeared, showered and shaved and dressed for town.

"What's wrong?" he asked as soon as he saw her face.

Charlie handed him the printed copy of Parkman's latest report. Drew skimmed it quickly. Most of it was routine. Dead ends. False lead. Nothing on last night's attack. According to Parkman, the bouncer had been outside checking licenses at the time of the fight. The bartender had mysteriously been absent from his post as well. The town drunk hadn't arrived yet, and the cocktail waitress was serving a different table and hadn't seen what happened. "Isn't that convenient," Drew mused.

"Keep reading," Charlie commanded.

Drew raised an eyebrow, but followed orders. "Who is this one from?" he queried, holding out the second page. "There's no name. Just a number."

"An old friend I asked for help," Charlie responded enigmatically.

Drew raised an eyebrow, but kept reading. "Son-of-a-bitch!" he exploded half way down the page, beyond a garbled mass of headings. There it was, exactly as Charlie had predicted. Waite had taken out two half-million-dollar term life policies on his new bride. The policies were only worth the amount of the premiums for the first two years, however. "So what he gave to charity was only one of the two policies," Charlie pointed out.

Drew shook his head. "Less than that. Half of one policy. Insurance policies almost always pay double for murder."

"Keep going," Charlie suggested, more gently this time. "It gets even more interesting."

Drew glanced at her, then turned to page three. It was from Parkman again. It included a copy of the admitting form for Wendell Macey. He'd been brought in by someone named Kit Flannery. "I don't know this Kit Flannery," Drew revealed, disappointed.

"Do you remember lunch at Peccadillo's?" Charlie reminded him.

"Of course," Drew asserted.

"Did you look at that deputy's name tag?"

"No," Drew replied slowly, beginning to get her drift. "I suppose you did."

"Kit Flannery," Charlie confirmed.

Drew ran a hand through his hair, trying to absorb it all. It hit him, then. She was too quiet. "What else?" he asked suspiciously.

"That's all of Parkman's report," Charlie insisted.

"What else was in your e-mail?" he persisted.

"Just a letter from Jamie," Charlie muttered, as if she were trying to slide it under the rug.

"And?" Drew pried.

Charlie felt her lip quiver and bit it angrily. "He won't marry us."

Drew's jaws clenched in an angry bulge. "Because I'm an ex-con?"

"That has nothing to do with it," Charlie assured him.

"Then what is it? He just doesn't like me? Is it the age thing? Or is it because we've both been married before?" Drew queried, still not understanding.

"No. Jamie adores you." Charlie insisted, near tears. "You know that. That has nothing to do with it. And he's more interested in football than our ages. The church didn't recognize my first marriage because we went to a Justice of the Peace, and your first wife is dead. It's because you're not Catholic. Jamie says we have to join the local parish and go through the classes, and attend mass on a regular basis, and you don't have to, but he would like you to convert."

A slow smile spread across Drew's face. "Charlie," he suggested, "Think about the names around here. Have you noticed anything?"

"Like what?" Charlie demanded, not following his drift.

"Kit Flannery, Wendell Macey, James Keefe, Moss Sullivan, Duane MacNeally, Drew Bailey?"

Charlie frowned up at him, still not getting the picture. "There are a lot of Irish families around here. So what?"

Drew laughed and bent down to kiss her quickly on the forehead. "There are a lot of Irish names, my dear, because this little town was settled primarily by Irish immigrants. Former railroad workers who moved their families out of Martinsburg to form their own community. An Irish community. A parish, to be specific."

"A Parish? A Church Parish? Andrew Bailey!" Charlie barked angrily. "Are you trying to tell me you're Catholic?"

"My grandfather was Catholic," Drew confirmed. "His grandfather was Catholic. His grandfather came over here during the potato famine, and he was Catholic. I was raised in the Catholic Church. I went through confirmation, and all that stuff. I haven't been to mass in fifteen years. Since I was divorced. I suppose I'll have to spend a few hundred hours in penance. But at least I don't have a murder to confess to."

Charlie aimed and fired a fierce look at Drew. "I thought you were Native American, your skin is so dark."

Drew's grin was wicked. "I'm a lot of things. Catholic is one of 'em."

"Why didn't you tell me?"

"You never asked."

Charlie frowned up at him suspiciously. "How many other things don't I know just because I haven't thought to ask?"

Drew cocked his head to one side and treated her to that infuriatingly sexy grin again. "Let me see. You don't know how I got your Social Security number. You don't know when my birthday is. And I know you don't know when I first fell in love with you."

Charlie tried on her most seductive smile. "Okay. How did you get my Social Security number?"

"You left your purse in the barn one morning, and I put fifty dollars in your wallet, because I was afraid you were going to catch on to the tips at Harry's," Drew confessed. "I also looked at your Driver's License."

"You saw my Driver's License once, and you remembered my Social Security number weeks later?" Charlie repeated in amazement.

"I saw it again the day I tried to run away. I almost took it, just to have a picture of you. And I'm good with numbers."

"My birth date's printed on my driver's license," Charlie observed.

"It sure is," Drew agreed, the grin growing wider.

She stared up at him, remembering her anxiety over their age difference. "You knew how old I was all along," she accused.

"I knew how old you were," Drew confirmed. "It didn't occur to me that it was any big deal. Younger women get involved with older men all the time. Nobody freaks out. Except maybe their mothers. And your mother had a good point about that. Why should a woman spend the last third of her life alone?"

Charlie abandoned the computer to wrap her arms around Drew, ready and willing to be kissed. "And when did you fall in love with me?" she asked, deciding she liked this game after all.

"That first night. At the truck stop." Drew obliged her with a quick brush of soft, warm lips over her upturned smile. "The very first time I ever saw you."

Charlie felt her heart miss a beat. "I thought that only happened in romance novels," she whispered.

"When did you fall in love with me?" Drew asked in a low, husky tone.

"When you were still my invisible hero," she revealed. "It was sort of a gradual thing. It might have been when you started washing dishes. But the rose did it for sure. It just took me a while to figure it out, that's all. I was so afraid to let myself fall in love with you."

"You fell in love with me because I washed the dishes?" Drew laughed incredulously.

"The first morning I came down to the barn and you'd washed the dishes, I almost cried. I felt like somebody was actually taking care of me for a change," Charlie explained. "I always took care of everybody. After Mom left, Frances and Jamie were away at college and seminary. I pretty well took care of the house and Daddy. Then, once I was on my own, I still tried to look after him. I lived alone for years before I married Allen. I had a boyfriend, but we didn't live together, and he sure as hell never took care of me. And Allen, well, you know about Allen. I never felt like anyone ever knew me well enough to try to figure out what I needed, until you came along. It seemed like sometimes you knew what I needed even before I did. How could I not fall in love with you?"

"I should have stayed invisible," Drew whispered sadly. "Lately I've been too busy trying to stay out of prison to pay attention to what you want or need."

"That's not true! You always make time for me. Whatever you do, you always let me know you're thinking about me. You're every married woman's fantasy. You should write a book. Teach other men how to make women happy. Title it *"What Every Woman Secretly Wants: A Wife."* You'd be a best seller in weeks."

"Will you type it for me?" Drew asked with a mischievous grin. "I'm not sure I can remember how to turn on the computer," he added, trying to look helpless.

Charlie whacked him with her hat and chased him out to the car. They ran circles around the Mustang twice before he abruptly changed directions and let her run smack into his chest. Still laughing, he gathered her up into a hungry kiss that was anything but helpless. "Wear your hair down for me today," he whispered. "I love the way the sun lights it up and catches it on fire. Like a red halo around your face. You're my own personal angel. It's always been lucky for me when you wear it down."

"What's so special about today?" Charlie teased as she obligingly freed her braid from its fabric-covered rubber band. She did her best to purr as he ran his fingers through the braid, shaking it loose.

Drew shrugged. "Who knows. I may be about to inherit a quarter-of-a-million dollars."

Charlie shook her head, swishing the jumbled mass into a curtain of fire. When Drew caught his breath, like a child watching a magician perform some impossible trick, she did it again, just to see his mesmerized smile. "A-quarter of-a-million dollars would make for a pretty good day, I guess," she agreed, tossing him the keys.

"Oh, no," he protested, although he caught them reflexively. "I'm not driving your car."

"You can't hurt it just by driving it," Charlie argued as she jumped into the passenger's seat. "Besides, if you can drive that dammed old truck, you can drive anything."

"Be careful what you say about my truck," he warned, sliding reluctantly behind the wheel. "You'll hurt her feelings."

"Speaking of which, we have to stop by the bank, the insurance agency and the D.M.V. I'll navigate."

Drew worked to keep his spirits up, determined not to ruin the day for Charlie by wallowing in his own depression. He'd have been happier just to spend the day with Charlie, losing himself in her arms until he forgot what day it was, where he'd been, and all that he'd lost over the years. He hated the paperwork, even if it did mean that he owned something, even the tired old Jeep. The insurance agent stared at his drivers license for a moment, then looked up as if to say something, but he shook his head at her. He didn't want any happy birthdays. Certainly not from a stranger. And he didn't want to have to explain to Charlie why he hadn't told her, hadn't trusted her with this one small thing, knowing she'd try to make it better for him.

Some things even Charlie couldn't make better.

The insurance agent frowned slightly, then shrugged as she finished off the temporary insurance card and handed it over. "Here you go, Mr. Bailey," was all she said.

They were well away from the D.M.V. before Drew glanced at the temporary registration the clerk had handed him along with his new License Plate. "Hey, they got the year wrong on this," he commented. "It says 1948 Jeep. It's old, but it's not that old. It's a '77, isn't it?"

"It must be a typo," Charlie agreed with an unconcerned shrug. "I told you that woman was having a rough morning. We need to get to the Real Estate Agent's before they close for lunch. We can call D.M.V. tomorrow and get them to fix it before they mail out the title."

"Well, I certainly hope I don't get pulled over in the meantime," Drew observed petulantly.

"You probably will. For driving too slow," Charlie teased. Drew just growled at her and stuck the registration back in its envelope.

The office manager at the Real Estate Agency claimed to have already archived the records from Charlie's sale, and the agent she'd worked with was no longer there, so the manager directed them to the deed book at the County Court House.

Voicing his dislike of courthouses, Drew elected to wait in the car while Charlie checked the deed. She was back sooner than he'd expected. "The trustee is listed as a lawyer in New York City," Charlie revealed. "Let's run up there. It's only about a five hour drive."

Drew sighed and shrugged. "At least it's closer than Mexico."

"We still have to stop by the bank," Charlie reminded him. "Then we'll need to run by the house and throw some stuff in an overnight bag. I guess you better check in with your parole officer, too."

"Oh, yeah," Drew responded glumly.

He'd lost some of that earlier fizz. Charlie decided it was time to cheer him up. "Want to put the top down?" she suggested.

His eyes widened in surprise. "What about your hair?"

"You'll just have to help me untangle it later," she invited, grabbing a quick kiss before he recovered his balance. "I know the perfect place. A hotel room in Mid-town Manhattan tonight, a hot shower, a little conditioner, and everything should work itself out just fine. There's nothing quite like a New York pizza."

Drew laughed and grabbed her back up for another, longer, kiss, that promised he'd do more than untangle her hair in that hotel room.

The bank took a little longer than Charlie had expected, making up for the quick work at the Land Office. It was almost exactly one o'clock when they got back to the farm. Drew hopped out and headed straight for the house. "Wait!" Charlie called after him. He stopped and turned toward her quizzically. "Don't you want to...shouldn't you put the new tag on the truck now? Before the little stickers and things get lost?"

"I never lose anything," Drew reminded her.

"I really wish you'd put it on now," Charlie insisted. "It makes me nervous having stuff like that lying around while we're gone."

Drew raised an eyebrow, started to argue, and then thought better of it. With a shake of his head and an indulgent smile he came back and got the plate from her, then headed for the rickety old garage behind the barn.

"I'll go pack," Charlie volunteered, heading off toward the house.

Drew stopped dead in his tracks, the old wooden door before him halfway open. There was a Jeep inside, all right. A cherry red 1948 Willy's Jeep Pickup with a huge red bow on the spare tire.

She knew. Charlie had known what day it was all along, and hadn't said a word. Must have known for weeks now to pull off something like this.

Drew ran the screws into the license plate bracket and tried the keys in the ignition. They were on a little plastic key chain with a picture of an eagle on it. He hadn't really looked at it before. He turned it over now and read the back. On the other side, it said, "If you love something, set it free." He started the old Jeep and backed it out of the garage. It sent gravel flying when he hit the gas and spun it around.

Drew just knew Charlie would be standing at the door, watching, waiting. He floored the old Willy's and headed across the gravel parking area toward the lane. At just the last moment, he turned the wheel and drove across the lawn to the back door, parking the truck on the patio under the wisteria.

"You nut!" Charlie cried as she ran out the door to meet him. Drew vaulted to the ground. The sunlight caught her tangled mane and set it on fire. He scooped her up and spun her around in his arms, laughing like a mad man.

"I love you, Charlie."

"Yeah, I know."

"I love you enough to stick around, no matter what. I'm not here because I don't have anywhere else to go, Charlie. If I walk out of that attorney's office with a hundred grand in small bills, I'll still come back here with you. Because I love you."

Charlie closed her eyes and pressed her face against his shirt, the way she did when she didn't want him to see how frightened she had been. "I love you too. Enough to let you go if that's what you needed."

"I know, Charlie. And that just makes me all the more determined to stay." He lifted her face up to kiss her, then picked her up off of the ground to toss her in the air as if she were a small child. "So. Is this thing in good enough shape to make it to New York and back?"

"Of course," Charlie assured him. "It had a complete frame-off restoration about five years ago, and my mechanic went over every inch of it before I bought it. And then it had to pass the State inspection here."

"Do you have any idea how much I love you?" Drew asked as he nipped at her ear.

"As much as I love you," Charlie whispered. "Happy Birthday."

Chapter Fifteen

It never occurred to Drew to ask the obvious questions. The ones most people would ask. Like why the Trustee for his grandfather's estate was located in New York City. Why his grandfather even had a trustee. Those questions would occur to him later, while he sat waiting in the attorney's office. Although they showed up promptly at ten, despite the morning traffic, the receptionist merely took down their information and left them to wait for over an hour. Drew was ready to walk out after twenty minutes, but Charlie smiled and told him to be patient. "You'll never forgive yourself if you don't see this thing through," she reminded him. "This could be our best chance to track down Savannah."

Drew paced the room until he had a path matted in the thick plush carpeting before the clerk reappeared. "Mr. Everett will see you now," a young law clerk informed them, frowning pointedly at the carpet. Drew abandoned his customary slouch long enough to stretch to his full height – nearly 6'9" in the boots – and stand square shouldered, just a little too close, glaring down at the smaller man before he deigned to follow him anywhere.

Everett was an older man with thinning hair in a slightly rumpled looking navy blue pinstripe suit. Somewhere along the line he'd traded distinguished looking for comfortably worn-in. Charlie liked him at once. He waved them toward worn leather chairs, but Drew continued to pace.

"So you're Rabbit's grandson," Everett offered as a greeting. "You've the look of him about you." The man didn't stand up or extend a hand. He just pulled his glasses down far enough to look over them and survey Drew carefully.

"Rabbit?" Drew stopped in his tracks. "You called Granddad Rabbit? *My* grandfather?"

"Sure did," Everett agreed with a sigh of reminiscence. "I still miss the old buzzard. He went in his sleep, though. That's the way to go if you're gonna go. Peaceful and quiet like. Sure beats the hell out of getting shot."

"Why would anyone have shot Granddad?"

Everett looked up over his glasses again as if it was Drew who wasn't making any sense. "Well, Son, there was a war going on, you know. People tend to get shot. Plenty of guys we knew died out there."

"I'm sorry," Drew responded, sounding anything but sorry. "Are you sure you're talking about the right case, here?"

"Son, there wasn't but one Rabbit Bailey, and there wasn't anyone else's estate I would have handled. I don't do estates. I work with book publishers, putting together contracts for writers. Things like that. Rabbit and I, we were two of the four guys left from my unit after D-day. All he could talk about was getting home to that farm in West Virginia and his wife and baby girl. You look enough like him to bring back some old memories."

"My grandfather was nicknamed *Rabbit* and was in the Army during W.W.II," Drew summarized, dropping heavily into the worn leather high-backed chair.

"Of course not." Everett sounded mildly incensed. "We were in the Marines. We met in boot camp. I went on to OTC, that's Officers Training School to you civilians, from there. We met up again later. Rabbit was in my platoon. I made him my Sergeant. After the war, I used my GI Bill to go to Law School, and he went back to his farm in West Virginia. But we kept in touch, and I did little things for him. Helped him with the custody paperwork for you after your momma died. Wrote up his will. Handled his estate. I assume that's why you're here."

"My mother," Drew repeated, completely dazed by now. "She died? When? How?"

"Air Force. She was a nurse. Died in Viet Nam in '69. About broke Rabbit's heart."

"I never knew her," Drew whispered.

"Seems to me there's a lot you aren't too up on," Everett surmised, his accent sounding more New England Yankee than New York.

"That," Drew agreed, "Is putting it mildly."

"Jan had already been accepted into the Air Force Academy when she found out she was pregnant. Rabbit wanted her to stay home. He never spoke to her after she left. He was a stubborn man, and there was no changing his mind once he made it up. He'd say, 'Andrew, you're a good friend, but you're not my Commanding Officer any more, and if you were, you'd have to court-martial me, because I'm going to do this my own way.' Which is exactly why I'm still alive today. He refused a direct order and saved both of our lives. He told me the same thing that day. 'You can court-martial me later,' he said. 'I'm not going to let you get us all killed.' Sure enough, he was right. Though we lost a lot of men, four of us made it through that day, and that's four more than would have without him."

"Your name is Andrew?" Charlie asked. "Was Drew named after you?"

"You're quick," Everett told her with a wink. "Jan called me Uncle Andy. Promised she would name her first son after me. Did it, too. Always liked that girl. Shame, the way that man treated her."

"My grandfather?" Drew surmised hesitantly.

"Rabbit was hard on her, but he never treated her bad. I meant your father. He should have married her. Given you a proper family. Taken responsibility for his actions."

"Did you know him, too? My father?" Drew asked at last, his voice barely above a whisper.

Everett wrinkled his nose in distaste. "Didn't know him. Knew of him. Jan explained it all to me, how he had to protect his place in the community, or it would effect the bank. Coward is what he was. Bastard wouldn't even let her put his name on your birth certificate."

"Bank? What bank?" Drew demanded. "Not Rosemont. You don't mean to tell me…"

"Of course it was Rosemont," Everett confirmed. "Jan had the misfortune to fall in love with her employer, the president of Rosemont bank, Robert Waite."

Charlie opened and shut her mouth a few times before the words would stumble out. "You mean that Robert Waite Junior…"

"Is my half-brother," Drew confirmed. "Which explains a lot."

"Like why he only had you framed, instead of killed," Charlie agreed.

"Framed? For Macey's death? What did Waite have to do with that?"

"Charlie and I think Waite had Darby murdered. Macey told me someone had paid him to kill Dee. The next day Macey was dead and I was in jail. I thought I'd killed Macey. Now I think Waite had him killed and framed me for the murder. That way he had his revenge, without having my blood on his hands."

"I thought you were just here for the money, but that's not it at all, is it?" Everett demanded.

"We're trying to find Drew's daughter, Savannah," Charlie explained. "We thought we might be able to track her down through the estate."

It was Everett's turn to look startled. "Savannah didn't send you here?"

"No. We're looking for her."

"She isn't with you? How did you find me, if Savannah didn't send you?"

"We tracked you down through the Land Office," Charlie explained.

"Where is Savannah? What do you know about her?" Drew demanded, pacing the room now.

"Savannah went back to West Virginia when she graduated from Julliard last spring. Darby's parents had gone back to Up State New York after Darby's death, and neither Rabbit nor I had any contact with her until it was time to settle Rabbit's estate. She took off for West Virginia as soon as she graduated."

Drew ran his fingers through his hair, pushing it out of his face. "What's she doing in West Virginia?"

"Savannah's grandparents told her you died in prison. When she came to see me about the estate, I told her different. She kind of freaked out. Started pacing the room and muttering about Waite wanting to find you," Everett explained. "She didn't tell me much about it, but I believe she thought you were in some kind of trouble." He reached in his desk drawer and pulled out a handful of letters. "She wrote to me with instructions about the estate. She got a job in some truck stop, working as a cook."

"Janelle!" Drew and Charlie exploded together.

"Janelle?"

"Savannah," Drew explained. "Savannah is Janelle. Or Janelle is Savannah. I can't believe I didn't recognize my own daughter."

"If she'd opened the door at the farm, you wouldn't have had any trouble recognizing her," Charlie comforted him. "You weren't looking for her as a cook in a truck stop. Why would you? You didn't expect her to be there, so you didn't see Savannah in her. But what's my excuse? I worked with her for months, and never noticed the resemblance, though now that it's been pointed out to me, it's plain as day. But what does she know about Robert Waite?"

"She was there," Drew reasoned. "She must have been there, the night Darby was killed. She must know something. That something could get her in trouble if Waite finds out." He turned toward the door, worry etching lines in his face.

"Hang on just a minute," Everett interrupted. "Don't you want your money?"

"What money?"

"From the estate. Your grandfather left everything to be divided evenly between you and Savannah. Didn't have specific instructions as to what to do with your share, so I invested it. Some of it's in a money market account, but I put most of it into stocks. You now own a nice little chunk of Coca-Cola."

Charlie tried hard to maintain a straight face, but she failed miserably. Still, it was Drew who started laughing first. He scooped up Charlie and hugged her tightly. "I am an idiot," he assured her. "Forgive me?"

"Yeah," she agreed. "Take me home. Let's go find your daughter. Robert Waite is a dangerous man. I'm a little worried about what he'll do next. We've pushed him pretty hard. He's got to make some sort of a move here soon."

"You be careful," Everett warned. "If Waite had Darby killed all those years ago, and he's kept it covered up this long, the man is damn good, and damn dangerous. You watch your backs."

* * * * *

It was dark by the time they turned onto the rutted old farm lane. Charlie pulled the Willy's into the shed, and they headed straight for the barn. Ghost didn't pounce on them when they climbed out of the truck. Charlie bellowed his name as she jogged toward the upper barn doors, thinking he'd gotten distracted by some groundhog out in the back pasture somewhere. The big dog's deep, rumbling reply stopped her in her tracks. He was already in the barn. Downstairs. Somewhere downstairs. And he wasn't happy.

"Something's wrong," Drew hissed as he slid to a stop beside her.

"That's the way he sounded that night when he broke up the fight in the back pasture," Charlie whispered in return, trying to keep the fear out of her voice.

"He's not moving," Drew observed. "Either he's got something cornered, or something's got him cornered. Either way, I don't like it."

"It could be a snake," Charlie suggested uneasily.

"Yeah," Drew agreed. "With two legs." He glanced around for a weapon as they slid cautiously into the barn's upper floor. The dog's booming base hadn't quieted in the least. It was as if the big dog was trying to carry on a dialog with them, keeping them apprised of the situation. "I don't suppose you'd go hide in the hay stack, where I'd know you were safe and I wouldn't have to worry about you," Drew suggested doubtfully.

"Not on your life."

Drew handed her the pitchfork he kept upstairs for dealing with broken bales of hay. "Take this. Please, stay out of sight. If there's somebody down there, I'd rather they thought I was alone. You're my emergency back-up plan, okay?"

Charlie didn't bother to argue that she was probably better trained to handle a situation like this than he was. Now was not the time. She simply nodded her head in agreement.

"I'm going go down through the trapdoor we use for the hay. Whoever's down there already knows we're here. They would have heard us pull up, even if you hadn't called the dog. With any luck they'll be watching the barnyard stairs. I'll drop down behind whatever's going on, where nobody'll be expecting me. Don't start down the stairs until at least thirty seconds after I'm out of sight. You'll know when I've got their attention," he added with a note of wry humor.

"I don't like this plan," Charlie objected. "We should stay together."

"Like Picket's charge?" Drew offered sarcastically. "I'm really not into frontal assaults. I've noticed the casualty rate's a little on the high side. Let's go."

Before Charlie could offer a counter plan, Drew was gone, out of sight in the blackness of the unlit barn. For just a moment, Charlie considered crossing back to the main switch panel and flipping on every light in the whole barn, but that could blind Drew as effectively as it would whoever might be down there. She counted thirty and headed for the stairs, pitchfork gripped firmly in both hands.

Charlie was barely half way down the steep wooden steps when she heard a distinctive thud, followed by an abbreviated cry, like a man being strangled. She scrambled down the rest of the way, caution forgotten, as she raced toward the noises.

It took only seconds to assess the situation. Ghost was barking frantically now from the stud box, where he'd evidently been trapped by one of the two men who was currently climbing back to his feet. The second man was already up, looking like a dim shadow as he circled, trying to get behind Drew.

She'd never really seen Drew in action before, Charlie realized. He was big, but quick on his feet. This was nothing like the fight in the back pasture. All he'd done there was block blows. Now he was the aggressor. While the first man up danced around him like a boxer, Drew laid him out again with a flying tackle. Both men went down, but Drew was back up first, rolling easily back to his feet, already turning his attentions to contestant number two. This man lunged at him like a wrestler. Drew rammed him head first, then caught him with an amazing display of raw physical strength and spun, throwing the man feet first into contestant number one. Number one went back down, tangled limbs interlocked with number two. As Charlie moved toward the end of the runway, however, both men climbed back up to work in unison.

Wary now, they split up, each man circling until they were almost opposite one another. They still hadn't seen Charlie. The crisscrossed beams of the hayracks kept her out of sight. She slipped quietly out the feed room door, unlatching it as stealthily as she could. From the barnyard, it wasn't hard to find the run-in stall's wide-open doorway. And from there, she could almost reach the door to the stud's stall. She moved carefully, quietly, hoping Ghost wouldn't change his song and give her away.

Drew must have seen her, for he finally spoke, confronting his opponents and keeping their attention on him as she opened the door. "You want me?" Drew challenged as the two men circled him warily. "Come and get me, you morons. Tougher men than you two have ever dreamed of being have tried to kill me. Some of 'em even lived through the experience. You know what Moundsville's like, boys? Sure you do. Your mommas used to scare you with it when you were just babies. It's the worst in the country. Tougher than Leavenworth. I learned to eat punks like you for breakfast."

"You just stay right there, Ma'am," a voice behind Charlie warned quietly. "There's no sense in you getting hurt. I'll handle this."

Charlie didn't think. She reacted. Years of training took over. She reversed her hold on the pitchfork and jammed backwards with the handle as hard as she could. Sure enough, it connected with a bone-jarring thud. Hands grabbed at it, trying to knock it out of her grasp, but Charlie kicked back with her right heel, hard, connecting solidly with flesh. She jerked free before her attacker recovered, sprinting for the stallion's door. Her fingers fumbled on the double action latch. Ghost's bark turned to a fierce warning growl as he lunged at the steel webbed door.

"I'm trying to help you, damn it!" the voice behind her groaned. A strong hand jerked at Charlie's shoulder. She rolled out of the hold, her attention focused on the latch. She tumbled across the dirt floor as the stall door burst open. Ghost sailed by, his fangs glistening in the pale moonlight. He wasn't barking any more.

Charlie regained her footing in time to see both of Drew's attackers leave the ground, one massive fist closed around each throat. They slammed into each other, heads meeting with a resounding crack. With an incoherent roar, Drew flung them into the solid oak pillar that supported the center ridge beam of the barn. He spun to face the third man, but Ghost had him down, both huge front paws planted on the man's chest as the massive jaws closed over the hand that had grabbed his mistress.

Charlie rose, brushed the dirt off her suit, and crossed the barn floor almost casually. With a flick of her wrist, she shot four hundred watts of light onto the situation. With another snap, she flooded the outer barnyard with massive spotlights. "Anybody else?" she shouted. "Anybody else want to get their goddamn head beat in tonight?"

No one answered. She turned and crossed the room slowly to Drew, ignoring the bodies sprawled around her. His stance was slightly crouched, his weight on the balls of his feet, arms bent, fists open, eyes wild. His breath came in ragged gasps, but he appeared unhurt. Except, of course, for his knuckles.

"Drew." Charlie pitched her voice low, almost seductive. "Drew. It's over. Come back to me, Drew."

Slowly, very slowly, Drew shifted his focus to the woman who stood before him, who faced him fearlessly and called him back. He dropped his eyes to meet hers, and his stance relaxing just a little. "Are you all right?" he managed. "If that son-of-a-bitch hurt you I'll rip his heart out."

"I'm all right, Drew," Charlie promised, forcing more calm into her voice than her hammering heart felt. "I'm all right. Why don't you check your bodies over there and see if they're both still breathing while I look to see what Ghost's having for dinner."

Drew nodded and turned away slowly, still breathing like a horse just back from a stretch around the track. "Both still alive," he reported with disinterest as Charlie came to stand looking down at the third member of the ambush team.

"Good. Ghost," Charlie ordered. "Go get the horses."

Ghost gleefully released the bloody wrist from his mouth and bounded out the door and across the field.

"This one's wearing a uniform," Charlie reported. "A sheriff's department uniform. How about yours?"

"No uniforms here. Just a couple of scum bags."

"Funny," Charlie mentioned, as if she were talking to herself. "I never saw a sheriff's department car out front. Never saw any car, for that matter. Never heard any kind of verbal warning or identification, either. Not from any of these men. Nobody's shown me a badge. I wonder, should we call an ambulance or the newspaper?"

"Let's just finish 'em off and throw them in a hole," Drew replied. "No hassle. No trial. No lawyers."

"There's that sink hole out in the back pasture," Charlie agreed. She took a better look at the man on the ground, who was now sitting up, binding his wrist with a pocket-handkerchief. She didn't see any point in telling Drew his name. They didn't need any actual dead bodies to deal with. "Deputy, I suggest you collect up your men and leave the same way you got here," Charlie offered. "Or would you prefer to stick around while I call some real police officers?"

The deputy got slowly to his feet, staying well away from Charlie and her pitchfork. "I don't really expect you to believe me," he pronounced with a sigh. "But I don't know who these men are. I am not here with them. I had nothing to do with them. I'm here in an official capacity." He inspected himself and put his uniform back to rights. "As for my patrol car, it's outside under the light in the gravel parking area. When I pulled up I heard a commotion, so I came to investigate. In the process, I was attacked by your dog. I assume the dog has had all its shots? It would be a shame to have to have the animal destroyed."

"Ghost has had his shots," Charlie assured the injured deputy. "I'm sorry I missed mine. I should have killed you while I had the chance. Get out of here before I change my mind."

"I'm afraid I can't do that," Deputy Flannery advised, regaining his well-trained official polish, despite the bleeding wrist. "I'm here to serve a warrant." He raised his eyes across the room and fixed his gaze on Drew as he produced a folded paper from his shirt pocket. "Andrew Bailey, this is a warrant for your arrest." He crossed the barn floor as he spoke. "You are under arrest for the murder of Mrs. Darby Waite. Anything you say can and will be used against you in a court of law. You have the right to an attorney. If you so desire and cannot afford one, an attorney will be appointed for you by the court." Handcuffs appeared as he headed for Drew, and a pistol in his right hand. "Do you understand these rights as I have explained them to you?"

"What happens now, Flannery?" Charlie hissed angrily. "Does Drew resist arrest while handcuffed in the back of your patrol car? Do you have to pull over and beat him to death like you did Wendell Macey? You shouldn't wait till you get to the jail, you know. Too many witnesses there." Charlie pressed her pitchfork hard against the small of Flannery's back. "You shouldn't have turned your back on me, Flannery. You haven't done your homework well enough. I'm crazy, you know. Crazy and dangerous. Just ask my ex-husband. I think I'll just kill you now. So much less hassle in the long run."

"I don't expect you to trust me," Flannery admitted. "I know you requested copies of Macey's hospital admittance form. Or your PI did. But I swear to you, I did not kill the man. I am not your problem. This whole damn thing stinks. Has from the very beginning. But I'm under orders. I can't just back off of this. I will call a State Patrol Unit for transport. While I'm at it I'll tell dispatch to send an ambulance for these two. But I'm taking Andrew in. It's my job."

"You'll turn and walk away from here, and we'll show up at the District Attorney's office voluntarily tomorrow morning with Counsel," Charlie corrected.

"I can't do that!" Flannery objected angrily. "I have a warrant!"

"You'd best tell whoever asks that you couldn't find us," Charlie reasoned. "And that your two friends here, the ones you don't know, fell down the stairs and bumped their heads. Because I swear I will end your miserable excuse for a life before I let you lay your hands on the man I love. I'm a desperate woman, Flannery," Charlie cautioned. "I warned you I was crazy, remember? There's no telling what I might do. The voices, you know. The voices in my head tell me to kill you now. The sinkhole is hungry. So why don't you collect up your goons and get the hell out of here. You can serve your warrant tomorrow. In the DA's office. Otherwise, the three of you can feed the hole tonight. Patrol car and all. It's a big sinkhole. We never saw you. And who would really miss you? Bob Waite? I don't think so. You're just an inconvenience he's had to keep on the payroll all these years. I doubt he'll even look for you. If he does, there won't be anything to find."

The service revolver slid slowly back into its holster. "I probably deserve most of what you think of me," Flannery acknowledged. "If not for what I did, then for what I didn't do. But I swear to you, I did not kill Wendell Macey. I am not on Waite's personal payroll. Never was, never will be. I didn't lay a hand on Macey, other than to take him to the hospital that night. And I didn't bring these two idiots out here tonight. Though I'm not too surprised to see them. I'm pretty sure I know who they work for, and so do you. It was probably just bad timing that we arrived here at the same time. I got this handed down to me earlier than was intended, I imagine." Flannery moved slowly, sticking his handcuffs back over his belt at the small of his back. "What the hell did you ever do to make Waite hate you so much?"

"A simple accident of birth," Drew explained dryly, enjoying the shock value of it. "Waite is my brother."

Flannery just stood there, staring at Drew, for the space of several long heartbeats. "I don't believe for a minute that either of you are stupid enough to kill an officer of the law. But I don't expect you to trust me, either." He met Drew's gaze levelly. "Do I have your word you'll show up at the District Attorney's office tomorrow?"

Charlie held her breath while Drew made up his mind.

"You have my word."

"All right. You do what you have to do. Call your attorney. Turn yourself in. Just don't make me come looking for you."

Flannery dragged the fallen men to their feet, persuading them none too gently to accompany him out to the patrol car.

Drew and Charlie climbed the stairs together as the horses thundered into the barn, watching the patrol car pull away. "I guess I better go call Frances. This one's going to need some explaining."

Drew's arm tightened around her waist, needing to keep her close for just a moment longer. "You were great back there."

"You weren't too bad yourself. Pretty amazing, actually."

Charlie spoke softly, without taking her eyes off the retreating taillights. "Tell me you have an alibi for the night Darby was murdered. Lie to me if you have to. I don't want to believe this is really happening."

"Do you still want to go to Mexico?" Drew offered instead.

Chapter Sixteen

The Magistrate perched his glasses on the end of his nose, looking over them at Drew, his lips pursed like a dried up prune. "And just exactly how did you find out that there was a warrant out for your arrest, Mr. Bailey?" he demanded.

"Your Honor, someone from the sheriff's department called to verify my address this morning," Drew lied. He was wearing the charcoal suit today, freshly cleaned, and looking especially handsome. Charlie fingered the rosary beads she'd dug out of her childhood jewelry box.

"Let me get this straight. You're here to turn yourself in on a warrant. The same warrant the sheriff's department claims to have been unable to serve." The Magistrate adjusted his glasses back up his nose as he read the paperwork before him. "And of course you know nothing about Deputy Flannery's mishap in your barn."

"Mishap, Sir?"

"Deputy Flannery can not be here today, I'm told, because he spent half the night in the emergency room. He was attacked by your dog."

"Ghost is very protective," Charlie offered. "It's his job to keep snakes and rodents out of the barn."

The magistrate shifted his consideration to Charlie, assessing her shrewdly for a few moments before he went back to studying the paperwork before him.

"Mr. Bailey, according to this paperwork, you are being charged with the murder of your ex-wife, Mrs. Darby Waite. These are very serious charges. In view of the fact that you are already on parole for another murder, I hardly think it wise to set you loose on the streets again. I am inclined to support the District Attorney's opposition to bail."

"Your Honor," Frances interjected, "I'd like to remind you that my client turned himself in to the District Attorney voluntarily, with the express intent of putting an end to these ridiculous allegations. It is our intent to appeal my client's earlier conviction. Furthermore, the DA has presented absolutely no physical evidence to warrant presenting this case to the Grand Jury.

"The victim was, according to the coroners report, raped. My client has volunteered to undergo DNA testing to offer conclusive proof of his innocence. Although the murder took place before DNA testing was available, there wasn't even a simple blood test conducted on the bloodstains on her clothing or at the crime scene. We can't obtain any semen samples from the rape to test now. The DA cannot provide even this highly critical evidence to verify their case because they've misplaced the evidence. How convenient. Their case is based entirely on circumstantial evidence, and there isn't even much of that."

"The Prosecution's case doesn't look all that bad from where I sit," the magistrate observed. "Your client had motive, and means, and he has no alibi. The prosecution has an eyewitness. Motion denied.

"Mr. Bailey, you are hereby remanded to the Eastern Regional Jail, pending an investigation by the Grand Jury." The Magistrate's gavel came down hard, echoing through the courthouse like the clang of a Moundsville cell door.

Insistent hands separated Charlie from Drew. She heard an eerie keening, and realized belatedly that it was her own wail of grief.

* * * * *

"Bailey!" the guard barked. "You have a visitor."

Drew closed his eyes for a moment, tempted to tell the guard he didn't want to see anyone, but he couldn't hurt Charlie like that. He knew he had to maintain the illusion of hope for her, right up until the bitter end. He wouldn't let her know how quickly he'd given up himself. He couldn't let her know. He pulled on his bravest smile and followed the guard to the visitation room.

But it wasn't Charlie who waited for him in the visitor's room. He recognized her even from the back. Long, elegant neck bowed slightly as she stared down at her hands. Black hair swept up into a French Twist. Wide, square shoulders set with determination.

It was Janelle.

Savannah.

Drew kept moving, because there was a guard beside him, and twelve years of experience had taught him it would have been very foolish not to, but he'd have run if he could have. Have done anything rather than have her see him here. Like this.

He'd have done anything rather than face the questions she was bound to ask. Because her condemnation would be so much worse than any sentence a judge could ever hand down.

Savannah heard them coming and turned on her chair, her face a cunning mixture of his own and Darby's, yet uniquely individual. A face he knew, but had never really seen before. She was, as Charlie had once called her, drop dead gorgeous. As a man, he hadn't really seen it, because his attention had been focused elsewhere. As a father, he noticed.

Savannah didn't seem startled by his appearance. But then, she'd known who he was all along, Drew reminded himself. She met his eyes, saying nothing, waiting. He sat down across from her, not knowing what to say. "I'm sorry," seemed like a good place to start. "I've pictured meeting you a hundred ways through the years, but it was never quite like this."

"Funny. I've pictured meeting you a hundred times over the last twelve years, and it was always pretty much like this. Orange is not your color." Savannah's voice had an angry edge to it. "Nanna says I'm lousy at hiding anything. My face gives it all away. I can see I get it from you. You've given up already, haven't you? Just like you did before. Charlie's out there working her butt off to get you out of here, and you've already given up on her. Why is it so easy for you to just give up? Isn't what you've got with Charlie worth fighting for? Wasn't I worth fighting for?"

The accusation stunned Drew to the bone. His mouth opened and closed a few times, but nothing came out. "You're right," he admitted at last. "I did give up back then. I didn't even think about what was best for you. I wasn't thinking about Charlie now. Or you. I was thinking about me. In my heart, I lost you the day that first judge took you away from me. Part of me died that day. Nothing after that has ever seemed to matter very much. Because when I lost you, the light went out of my world. I didn't think I had anything left to fight for. I just gave up. Without you and Charlie, I'd do the same thing now."

Savannah's eyes opened wide. "That's why you never came to see me, after Momma left the farm? You didn't have visitation rights?"

Drew frowned suspiciously. "What did your mother tell you?"

"Mom said you didn't love us any more. But I never believed her. You made me a promise. You said you would love me forever. Baileys' never break their promise."

Drew remembered that promise. Savannah had been barely three. He and Darby had had another fight. "I never quit loving you," he assured her. "Not for a moment." He placed his hands flat against the barrier, and she spread hers over them. Their warmth penetrated the barrier, a symbolic joining. "I never will," he promised again. "And I'll try to remember that I have something waiting for me that's worth fighting for. My two girls. My family."

Savannah shook her head, as if struggling to make sense of it all. "Why would the judge have ordered you not to see me?" she demanded. "Why would he do that?"

Drew chose his words carefully. "All of this started before your mother and I separated. Your mother and I had a fight. She fell down the stairs. She told the judge I pushed her. Maybe she even believed it. But I swear to you, I never tried to hurt your mother, Savannah. Not then, not three years later. I never hurt her. I was angry with her. But I never pushed her. And I didn't kill her."

"I know that," Savannah assured him calmly. "You don't have to convince me. I was there."

Alarms went off in Drew's head. His body jerked like he'd been hit with a cattle prod. "Don't say another word, just nod your head," he whispered as softly as he could. "Are you telling me you saw what happened?"

Savannah nodded, her eyes big as she caught the fear in his voice.

"On the stairs? The night your mother fell down the stairs at the farm?" *The night she lost the baby?* he almost added.

Savannah shook her head.

"The night your mother was killed? You saw your mother murdered?" Savannah nodded. Once.

"And you never told anyone? No one else knows you know what happened?"

Savannah shook her head.

"Does Charlie know you're here now?"

Savannah shook her head again.

"Listen to me, Savannah," Drew ordered. "Don't trust anyone, especially not the cops. Don't talk to anyone but Charlie about this. I want you to stand up, yell at me, say something angry, anything, and get out of here as fast as you can. Go straight to Charlie. Charlie will take you to her sister Frances. Tell Charlie and Frances what you know. No one else."

Savannah stared into his eyes for a long moment. When she spoke, her voice sounded strangely childish. "I never told anyone else. He made me promise not to tell anyone, ever. He said he would hurt you if I ever told anyone."

"Savannah, listen to me!" Drew hissed between his teeth. "I can take care of myself. There's not statute of limitations on murder. This man knows you can still identify him. I can't keep you safe while I'm in here. Tell Charlie to send Frances in to see me. But the two of you stay away from here. Tell her I said to be very, very careful."

"But if I tell the cops what really happened, they'll have to let you go, won't they?" She sounded normal again. A rational adult. As if he'd only imagined the other thing.

"You'll have to testify in court. Then they will have to let me go. But don't tell anyone else. Go straight to Charlie. Now, honey. Do it just like I told you, okay?"

"Okay. One innocent, affronted daughter, coming up." Savannah took a deep breath, holding her hands against the barrier just a moment longer. She rolled her shoulders twice, head down, like a boxer preparing for a fight. Finally she pulled her hands away with a jerk. Her expression flashed with rage. "How could you do this to me?" she screamed, and spun away, running toward the door. She beat on it with her fists. "Let me the hell out of here!"

"I love you!" Drew shouted after her, fifteen years of grief that was all too real escaping in his voice. "I love you!"

Savannah continued beating on the door as if she hadn't heard him, but he knew better, and even as rough hands pulled him back towards his cell, he called after her again. "I love you, Savannah!" he shouted as the steel doors clanged shut behind him.

* * * * *

"You're out late tonight."

Flannery froze in his tracks. "I hope you're not still lugging around that pitchfork," he managed with a heavy sigh.

"No pitchfork," Charlie assured him. "No shotgun. Not even a .25 semi-automatic. The dog's not even with me."

"I've never been held up with a pitchfork before. It's a little embarrassing." Flannery shut the car door softly. "I decided to do a little checking up on you. Got a copy of your resume from a friend in personnel over at City Hospital. She says you're supposed to be one of the best computer programmers in the country. Funny thing is, none of your references for the last twenty years check out at all. They all lead to dead-ends. Places that have gone out of business and people who have died. All of them. Every single one. I found that absolutely amazing."

"The kind of people I worked for don't appreciate being listed as references. Resumes are for people who have a past. The question is, are you going to have a future?"

"That's about what I figured," Flannery decided, ignoring her question. "CIA? Military Intelligence? National Security Agency? Secret Service? What?"

"You seem like a decent sort, Flannery. Even if you do ask too damn many questions. I'd really like to believe you didn't kill Macey. But somebody killed him. I want to know who, how, and why. Otherwise, I will play alphabet soup with you. I'll take what I know to my friends. They'll call in the FBI, the DEA, and the ATF. Those guys all get real hot when it comes to the subject of bad cops. I'll rip this can of worms open so wide the whole State will be under investigation for the next thirty years."

"I don't know anything at all about Darby's murder," Flannery argued. "I'd tell you if I knew. I'd have probably gone straight to the prosecutor myself, but I don't know a thing."

"You know what happened to Wendell Macey."

"What the hell good is that going to do now?" Flannery spun around to face the disembodied voice at last. But he still couldn't really see the woman. She was somewhere in the shadows, probably only a few feet from him, by the sound of her voice. He should have noticed when he drove up. The security light had burned out again. He wondered if maybe it hadn't had a little help.

"Waite's crossed the line with this one, Flannery, and you know it. He's got no evidence against Drew. I don't believe he's got a real eyewitness for one minute, and neither do you. Waite's banking on public sentiment to pull Drew down. West Virginia old school good-ol'-boy politics. Waite figures Drew's reputation will be enough to convict him before the trial even starts. Waite's had this all planned out for years. But he miscalculated. He didn't count on me. And he did count on you.

"Waite's convinced he's got you in his pocket, Flannery. Prove him wrong. Let me help you find a way out of this mess you've got yourself into. It's the only way you're going to come out of this looking like anything but a crooked cop."

"Waite will kill me if I help you," Flannery pointed out. "And then he'll kill you."

"Let him try," Charlie offered with a cynical laugh. "I'm not all that easy to kill. Why don't you let me worry about Waite. We're talking about you right now."

"So I tell you what you want to know. Then what? If Waite goes down, I go down with him. He'll bury me in the debris when he pulls the whole sheriff's department down around him. I'm too young to retire. All I ever wanted was to be a cop. I don't want to spend the last ten years of my career as a guard at the race track."

"What kind of a cop helps send an innocent man to prison, Flannery? Was that the kind of cop you wanted to be? As I see it, Waite's going down. You can either go down with him as a co-conspirator, or you can come over to my side and salvage something of your reputation. I can't promise you anything as far as your job goes. But you have a better shot at keeping your career intact by doing what's right than you do by staying on Waite's side."

"I was never on Waite's side," Flannery assured her bitterly. "I've done some things I'm not proud of. But I was never on Waite's side."

"There are only two sides to this now. My side, and the wrong side. I assure you, I will not let go of Drew without a fight. The kind of fight a man like Bob Waite will never win."

"Are you sure you know what you're getting into?" Flannery asked after a long silence.

"Waite doesn't know what he's gotten himself into," Charlie argued ominously.

Flannery closed his eyes and let his shoulders slump. "What do you want to know?"

"Start at the beginning," Charlie advised. "How did you ever get messed up with a rat like Waite in the first place?"

"You might as well get comfortable," Flannery advised. "This is going to be a pretty long story." There was a soft metallic click as Charlie turned on a micro cassette recorder.

* * * * *

"How'd you get in here?" Waite demanded, stopping in his tracks as a shadow detached itself from the wall.

"It wasn't all that hard. Your security could use some work, Waite." Charlie kept her voice pitched low, so that Waite had to concentrate to catch every word. "There's no place you can ever go that I won't be able to find you, Bob. You pick up things, working the places I've worked."

"At Harry's truck stop?" Waite snickered.

"Right." Charlie perched on the edge of Waite's massive old desk. "You should have done your homework, Bob, before you decided to mess with me."

"What homework?" Waite demanded, sounding irritated, but not really frightened yet.

"You got away with it, Bob," Charlie pointed out, pointedly ignoring his question. "You killed two people, you ruined Drew's life, and you got away with it all. And made quite a stash in the process. You had everything you wanted. Drew was conveniently out of the way. You should have been set for life. Why wasn't that enough for you? Why are you still here? Shouldn't you be in the Caribbean somewhere, soaking up the sun on a nude beach?"

"What stash? You mean the insurance policy? If your sources are so good, you should have known I didn't get that money," Waite argued with a sneer. "Those insurance policies were a wedding present we gave each other. I was heartbroken over Darby's death. I gave the money all away to Charity. There was a big article in the paper about it. Local Banker donates half a million dollars to the Catholic Relief fund. But I forgot. You're not from around here. You wouldn't know what went on locally. I can't imagine the affairs of an old country banker would hold much interest for a city girl like you."

"The affairs of one old country banker in particular interest me quite a bit. Half a million dollars would have caught my attention, too," Charlie assured him. "Especially when there's three times that much in an off shore account earning 8% interest."

Waite's face turned shrewd. "I told you I donated that money to charity."

"But there were two policies. And each policy offered double indemnity for murder after the first two years," Charlie pointed out. "You figured it was worth giving the face value of the first one away just to keep your reputation as the grieving widower intact. You're quite a philanthropist, really."

"Somehow I don't think you came here just to discuss my charitable donations," Waite surmised.

"I want the charges against Drew dropped," Charlie stated bluntly.

"I couldn't do that even if I want to!" Waite assured her with a grim laugh. "I don't have the county prosecutor under my thumb. He's an ambitious young punk, but he's an honest man. He did this on his own. He'd never have pushed this if he didn't believe Bailey killed Darby."

"You wanted Drew dead. If you couldn't have him dead, you wanted him back in prison. You planted the idea in that ambitious young punk's head that Drew killed Darby in the first place. You produced the mystery witness after all these years. That young punk owes you, and he knows it. So you persuaded him to drag Drew back through the mud.

"But you didn't do your homework well enough, did you, Waite? You didn't figure on me. I'm going to make your life a living hell, Waite. My friends from the Justice Department are already on the job. Every case you ever had anything to do with as a sheriff will be under investigation. They're the kind of friends who get real put out when anyone messes with me.

"I have friends in the IRS, too. They've already pulled all your 1040's for the last seven years. Then there's the question of inheritance. You know, of course, that your brother was entitled to half your father's estate. Still is, for that matter. There's Macey's death, too. There's no statute of limitations on murder, as you well know."

"Who the hell are you, anyway?"

"I'm just a computer programmer," Charlie insisted, a vicious smile tickling her lips. "With a few connections. I know people who know things. Like the account in the Caiman Islands. If you want all that money to stay there, I suggest you find a way to have the charges against Drew dropped."

"I don't give a damn about the money. And I don't really care about you or what you know about me. There isn't anything I can do about Bailey. I didn't bring the charges against him, and I can't have them dropped. Wouldn't even if I could. That son-of-a-whore killed my first wife. There isn't anything left that I care enough about for you to use it against me, little lady. I don't give a damn about my reputation anymore. My mother's dead. Died of a broken heart. My second wife died last year. She was the only good thing that's ever happened to me. Destroying Andrew Bailey is just about the only goal I've hung on to. Sorry. I'm not about to let go of that for you. Nice try, though."

"If that's the case, you won't mind if my boys move that money around a little," Charlie speculated. She drew a heel up and hooked it over the edge of the desk as if bored.

"Give it all to Savannah," Waite suggested. "She was a good kid. She didn't deserve to get caught in the middle of all this."

"Do you care about staying alive?" Charlie challenged. "I wouldn't have to do it myself, you know. One of the boys would do it for me if I asked. If they get wind of what's up here, they may, anyway. But I want it to be me. I'm good, you know. I was on the U.S. Target shooting team while I was in college. I was headed for the Olympics. I could knock you out from half a mile away with a weapon the boys'll loan me that can never be traced.

"I'll be everywhere you go, Waite, for the rest of your very short life. You see, I don't have anything to lose, either. Nothing but Drew. And he's gone. You've already taken him away from me. You'd better figure out how to give him back. Or I swear I'll take you down. I won't just kill you. I'll pull your whole world apart, piece-by-piece, until one day you'll turn around, and there I'll be. And you'll be dead."

"You don't scare me," Waite snickered. "You're just a woman. A flesh and blood woman. I could kill you with my bare hands right now and you wouldn't last long enough to give me the satisfaction of a good scream."

"Try me," Charlie invited. She used that hard muscled leg she'd drawn up to catapult herself into the air, landing with an elbow into Waite's throat. He was down, gasping for breath and writhing on the floor, before he could bring up a hand to defend himself. Charlie placed her foot hard against his crotch. "On second thought, don't bother. I don't think you're up to it, Bob. I should kill you now and get it over with. But I want to see your face the day Drew gets cut loose, free and clear. I want to see you behind bars, Waite. I'd like to come visit you in Moundsville. Just to see how you like being some biker's girlfriend."

She ground her heel a little harder before she moved out of his field of vision. He never heard the door latch behind her. When he could move, Waite surveyed the office thoroughly. When he opened his personal filing cabinet, a Jack-in-the-box jumped out at him. He sat down heavily in his chair, cursing, only to end up on the floor again. It was a simple thing, really. She'd taken the screws out of the seat. He threw the parts across the room in frustration. It was then that he noticed the breeze against his face. The window was open. As he slammed it shut, a shadow detached itself from the wall across the street and saluted him smartly before it disappeared again into the unlit alley. Waite cursed softly as he rubbed at his bruised larynx.

* * * * *

"You shouldn't be here," Drew hissed, concern evident on the lines that seemed to have etched themselves permanently into his face. He looked different. Older. Smaller, somehow. His shoulders had taken on that old hunched look again.

"I told you I'd come. Every day that they'll let me. Frances says to tell you that things are looking good. She says 'Hang in there.'"

His eyes were the color of weathered driftwood. "I don't have much choice about that, now do I?"

Charlie frowned in disapproval. "Don't go all maudlin on me. I wish they'd let me bring you some decent food. You're losing weight again."

"How the hell does Frances figure things are looking good? The magistrate didn't pay any attention to what Frances had to say at all. The Grand Jury didn't seem too impressed with her arguments, either. If there was enough evidence to convince the Grande Jury to indict me, I'm back where I was twelve years ago. On my way to Moundsville."

"I thought you knew what to expect. You've been through this all before."

"I didn't go through any of this last time. I pled guilty, remember?"

Charlie pressed her fingers to the glass, "Well, this isn't going to be quite that simple. I know the waiting is difficult for you, but try to think positive, okay? Frances knows what she's doing."

Drew sighed and ran a hand through his hair. "I guess I thought once Savannah told you two what really happened, that would be the end of all of this. Instead, I've been indicted."

"The Grand Jury doesn't hear witnesses. Savannah won't testify until the actual trial. All that indictment means is that there's enough evidence on both sides to warrant a trial. Next week is the pre-trial hearing. Frances will try to get the prosecution's witness excluded. She says not to expect too much. It's only a formality at this point. They have to have a pre-trial hearing and she has to make some sort of a motion to suppress something, or someone might get the idea we're actually looking forward to the trial. Frances won't do anything to push the trial date back. She wants you out of here as much as I do. I know this is hard for you, but Frances knows what she's doing."

Drew tried to smile, for Charlie's benefit. "It's hard not to get depressed in here, but I promise I'll do my best. I'm not much on television. The radio's been a godsend. Thank Savannah for me again. How's she doing?"

"Savannah's fine," Charlie assured him. "She quit Harry's. She's working at Peccadillo's. She's taken over a lot of your chores at the farm. I don't know what I'd do without her. You know I can't cook worth a damn."

"She seemed...odd. When she came to see me. She did this thing with her voice. Sounded like she was about five years old. Scared the shit out of me."

Charlie frowned, then shook her head. "I'll ask her about it. Are you sure she wasn't just horsing around or something?"

"I'm sure. And don't say anything to her about it, either. Just keep a good eye on her, would you, please? She's been through so much all ready, and now this..."

"I will. I'll take good care of her, I promise. Try not to worry."

Like he had anything else to do in here. "Charlie, I know you've been through a lot, too. Thank you. Thank you for standing by me. Please, take care of yourself, too." She'd lost weight, too much weight, but Drew decided not to mention it. Knowing Charlie, she'd already be self-conscious about that. "Please be careful," he warned instead. "I saw the article in the paper about Waite being under investigation by the IRS. I don't know how you did it, but I'm worried. I don't think you understand just how dangerous Waite really is."

"The whole sheriff's department is under investigation. Seems Waite may have been helping himself to a little of the taxpayers money. I think Bob Waite is just beginning to understand how dangerous I am."

She glanced up as a prisoner sat down at the next visitation booth. The man gave Drew a curt nod. "Who's your new friend?"

"Guy named David Walker," Drew informed her. "In for assault."

"David, is it? That's a new one." Charlie nodded at the man, then looked away. "I didn't know he was coming. He's a good man. You can trust him."

Drew glanced around at the man, startled, then pulled the mask back over his face again. "You're just full of surprises," he observed dryly. "One of these days we're going to have to talk about the places that aren't listed on your resume."

"There are a lot of things I can't talk about. Let's just say I know a lot of guys like David, and leave it at that, okay? I hadn't planned to ask for their help, but apparently I don't have to ask. I'll sleep a little better knowing David's watching your back."

"I think maybe I'll just have to get to know 'David' a little better. In the mean time, you watch your back. And remember, no matter what happens, I love you. I'm gonna make it through this, Charlie. I just have to keep reminding myself, I'm not back where I was twelve years ago, because I have you. And you're worth fighting for, even if the only fighting I do is in my own head."

"I love you," Charlie assured him. "More than life itself."

He'd said those same words to her, less than a week ago. It seemed such a long time, now. Drew wondered uncomfortably just exactly what she meant by those words. He wondered, too, if he'd ever know all there was to know about Charlotte Giles.

Chapter Seventeen

"All rise."

The courtroom was packed. Drew stood in front of the defendant's chair, next to Frances, surveying the room carefully, without seeming to. He recognized many of the people in the courtroom. Men and women he'd gone to school with. People from his own community. People from his own church.

Savannah stood beside Charlie—Charlie as he'd never seen her before. A cool, suave, sophisticated Charlie. A woman who owned Coca-Cola stocks and raised $20,000 foals. She wore a knee-length blue velvet dress that clung to her gaunt frame. She'd piled that gorgeous mane artfully atop her head in a French twist. Diamond stud earrings accenting her delicate face. She'd lost too much weight, he thought again. She looked pale, almost wraith-like.

He ached to touch her, to hold her, to loose that twist from her hair and let it cascade over him, like a curtain that could hide his soul from the world.

Brown eyes met his, bringing him back from his private hell, where Charlie was just out of reach. Jamie stood to Charlie's right, with Silvia beside him. They were all there to support her. And, in a way, to support him.

There were men in the courtroom Drew didn't know, as well. A handful of men, strategically placed around Charlie and her entourage. Men who didn't look directly at Charlie or each other, yet who seemed, to Drew's practiced eye, to be a team. He wondered absently if they were all named 'David Walker.'

There was a brief flurry of movement as the judge entered.

"This session of the Circuit Court of Berkeley County, West Virginia is now in session, Judge Judith Brinkman presiding. You may be seated," the bailiff announced.

Shelby Morgen

Drew caught himself clenching his jaws, and remembered Frances had warned him not to do that. She said it made him look fierce. Dangerous. And that was definitely not the impression they wanted to give the members of the Jury.

Frances wanted the football hero. The All-American Boy.

Drew searched hard for that hero, but he kept running up against a wall of fear. He glanced again at Charlie, and then at Savannah. A man sat next to Savannah. A very large, solid looking man. A former linebacker, Drew guessed. Not one of Charlie's friends. This man wasn't trying to be inconspicuous. Far from it. He must be Parkman, the private detective and now body guard. Savannah ignored the man beside her. The girl seemed all right now. Drew would have sworn she was bolstering Charlie's spirits, and not the other way around. If it hadn't been for that other voice back there in the visitation room, he'd have thought her extraordinary, surely enough, but certainly not unstable. Yet now he had to wonder. What if this hearing, and the trial to follow, was too much for her? Could hearing this, seeing this, put her over the edge? Was she really up to testifying about what she'd seen all those years ago?

Frances was speaking again. Drew tuned back into the courtroom. "...prosecution has no actual evidence. In light of which, we request that all charges against my client be dismissed."

"Mrs. Dixon, I am not inclined to dismiss this case without hearing any evidence. You may begin your opening arguments."

Dixon. Frances had a last name. He'd never thought to ask. A great many things struck Drew as odd today.

Frances was just getting warmed up. Drew decided she could have been an actress, had she not gone into the legal profession. But then, perhaps they weren't so different, after all. "Thank you, Your Honor."

"Your Honor, members of the jury," she announced, "As you know, nearly thirteen years ago a terrible crime was committed. A beautiful young woman, the mother of a small

284

child, was viciously raped and murdered in her own home by an unknown attacker or attackers. The prosecution would have you believe that this attack was an act of passion. A sweep of vengeance carried out by Darby Waite's jealous ex-husband. But there was another crime committed that night. A crime that we need to address here today.

"Darby Anne Bailey Waite was not alone in her house that night. The single eyewitness to Darby's murder was never questioned. The investigating officers never gathered any evidence from the crime scene. Even though a rape had been committed, no physical evidence was ever collected from Darby's body. Had the investigative work been carried out with even the barest of attention to proper police procedure, we could now present you with DNA test results that would absolve my client of any guilt in this case. Instead, no investigation was ever carried out. The house was cleaned. The body was cremated.

"You have to ask yourselves why. Why was so blatant a cover-up conceived? The answer is simple. Someone thought that the people of this county are ignorant enough to believe whatever they are told. Someone thought that, by pulling Andrew Bailey's reputation down around him, you, the jury, could be convinced that my client should be convicted, by reputation alone, without a single shred of evidence.

"I don't think any of you are that gullible.

"All of you live here. You grew up here. You know Andrew Bailey, or you know of him. Some of you went to school with him. Your sons played football with him. There is a good-sized crowd in this courtroom today. These men and women are your neighbors, your friends, your children's schoolteachers. They are all prepared to testify as character witnesses for my client. You know what they'll say. A solid, responsible, hard working young man who always met his problems head on.

"Twelve years ago, Andrew Bailey pled guilty to another murder. You know that, too. I am prepared to prove to you today that these are not separate, unrelated crimes, and that, in fact, Wendell "Weasel" Macey's death was directly related to

Darby Anne Bailey Waite's death. Furthermore, I am prepared to prove to you that my client had nothing to do with either murder." A collective gasp filled the courtroom, followed by a round of murmured speculation. The judge rapped her gavel loudly three times. Gradually the courtroom subsided to silence.

Next, it was the prosecutor's turn. "Ladies and Gentleman, you are here today to decide not Andrew Bailey's guilt or innocence in a crime he already pled guilty to. You are here because twelve years ago, in a fit of jealous rage, Andrew Bailey made good on a threat. You don't need a high priced Washington lawyer to tell you what happened here twelve years ago.

"We do not have DNA test results to show you here, because twelve years ago DNA testing did not exist. What we do have is Darby Anne Bailey's own testimony, in court, under oath, that Andrew Bailey threatened her life, should she ever try to leave him. We have her testimony stating that the defendant, Andrew Bailey, attacked her and pushed her down the stairs of his grandfather's house, causing her to suffer the miscarriage of their second child.

"Mrs. Dixon will try to convince you that this crime and the murder of Wendell Macey, the murder to which Andrew Macey has already confessed, are related. We will show you that these two crimes are, indeed, related, and that Andrew Bailey is guilty of both murders.

"Why, you ask? Because Wendell Macey was Andrew Bailey's accomplice the night of Darby Waite's murder. Andrew Bailey, ladies and gentleman, is, indeed, a man of his word. He promised to kill Darby if she tried to leave him, and he did. And then he killed the man who helped him commit the murder. Nice and neat. Except for a few details, which have brought Andrew Bailey here before you today. Details like an eyewitness who was at the scene of the crime twelve years ago. An eyewitness who saw Andrew Bailey brutally murder his former wife. I think you will indeed find that the State has more than enough evidence to warrant convicting Andrew Bailey of murder in the first degree."

Whispers and titters circulated like a swarm of small insects. The judge rapped her gavel again. "You may call your first witness," the judge told the prosecutor.

For the next three hours, the jury listened to transcripts of Darby's testimony about Drew's violence towards her during their divorce, and the investigating officer's descriptions of the crime scene. Frances intervened only twice, both times to establish that no physical evidence had been secured from the crime scene other than photographs.

The court recessed for lunch. When the judge reconvened, it was time for the prosecutor's star witness.

"The state calls Larry Washburn to the stand."

Drew stared at the man, trying to remember where he'd seen him before. Then it hit him. He scribbled a note to Frances. *Played for Martinsburg. We kicked their butts.*

Frances merely smiled.

The prosecutor stood up from his desk, but his eyes stayed buried in his paperwork. "Mr. Washburn, can you tell the court please just how you happen to know the defendant?"

"Yeah, I sure can. Drew and me pulled some small jobs with Weasel some years back."

The prosecutor moved a little closer. "By small jobs, you mean exactly what?"

"B & E's, mostly. Burglaries. Rich people go away for the weekend, we heist their stereos. That kind of stuff."

"You, Wendell Macey and Andrew Bailey broke into peoples houses and stole their TV sets and their stereos. Not just once. Several times. Is that correct?"

"Yeah. That's it."

"And on the night of November 27th, 1981, where were you?"

"We did a job up on the Heights. I remember it, cause it was my kid's birthday, and I wanted to get home before the old lady put him to bed. This banker guy was supposed to be out of town. It was supposed to be an easy job. Lots of high powered stuff."

"And was the house empty?"

"No. We were in there maybe five minutes, and this lady comes out of the bedroom upstairs and starts threatening us with a golf club."

"What happened next?"

"She starts yelling at Drew. Calls him all kinds of names. He takes the golf club from her and lays her out with it."

"By lays her out, you mean he killed her."

"Nah, not at first. He didn't hit her so hard, you know? He just knocked her down and had a little fun with her. Then, afterwards, he killed her."

"Had a little fun with her? Could you please explain that, Mr. Washburn?"

"He raped her."

"No further questions, your Honor."

"Your witness, Mrs. Dixon."

Frances walked slowly toward the witness stand, allowing her spiky little heels to beat a low staccato. She leaned casually against the witness' booth. "Larry, how old are you?"

The witness met her smile with one of his own. "Thirty-seven, Ma'am."

"The same age as Andrew Bailey."

"If you say so, Ma'am, I guess it must be true." That brought a little laughter from the crowd.

"You two were the same grade in high school."

"Yeah, I reckon we were, Ma'am."

"You were a pretty good football player, weren't you, Larry? A quarterback, I believe."

"I was okay."

"Come on, don't be shy. You were damn good."

"Okay. I was good."

"Good enough to play for WVU?"

"I don't know. They didn't ask me to. They must not have thought so."

"How many games did the Bulldogs lose to the Eagles that year?"

"Two."

"How many games were you away from a playoff position in the state finals?"

Larry hesitated at that. "Two."

"If your team had gone to the state finals, where would you be today?"

Larry snorted bitterly. "Probably retired from the NFL."

Frances nodded slowly. "You hated the Eagles."

"Yeah."

"You still do."

"It ain't been that long, Lady."

"Mmm." Frances turned and walked slowly back to her chair, giving Larry ample time to admire her departing backside. He didn't even have the good grace to look guilty when she stopped and turned suddenly back to face him. "Larry?"

"Yes, Ma'am?"

"How much money do you think Drew Bailey and the Eagles stole from you?"

Larry Washburn colored slightly, his anger near the surface now, ready to break loose. "Ten million or so."

"Ten million dollars. That's a lot of money." Frances tapped a pencil lightly on her notepad. "You were arrested recently, weren't you, Mr. Washburn?"

"Yeah."

"You mind telling me how that went down?"

"I got a bum tip. The house wasn't empty. Turned out the guy who lives there's a trooper."

Frances nodded her head slowly. "What kind of a deal did the prosecutor offer you to testify in this case?"

Larry looked from the prosecutor to Frances and back again. "I walk."

"You testify in this case, and you get full immunity on the other case. The burglary on the state trooper's house."

"Yeah."

"The burglary you were set up to take the fall for."

Larry narrowed his eyes at that one, and they flicked off across the courtroom for the briefest of moments. "Yeah. It was a set-up, all right."

"Back in '81, when you and Weasel worked together, what was your job?"

"I was the driver. Driver and lookout."

"So you stayed outside while the robbery was going on."

"Usually, yes ma'am."

"Why were you in the house when Darby Anne Bailey Waite was murdered?"

Larry hesitated, blinking slowly. "I heard a car. Down the road a ways."

"I see." Frances took a long pause to search though her notes. "So let me get this straight, Mr. Washburn. On November 27th, 1981, just five years after you graduated from high school, you were teamed up with Wendell 'Weasel' Macey and the star quarterback from the team that kept you out of the NFL, to commit a robbery. A robbery that went bad because you were given a bad tip and there was someone in the house. You left your post as a lookout long enough to go in the house and watch the victim get raped and murdered, because there was a car coming. Then, last month, you were conducting another robbery where you were again given a bad tip, and now you want this court to believe you waited twelve years to get your revenge on Drew Bailey?"

"Objection."

"I withdraw the question, your honor. No further questions."

The noise level in the courtroom rose from a buzz to a small wave of protest. The judge banged her gavel down resolutely. "Court will reconvene at nine o'clock tomorrow morning. At that time, we will begin hearing witnesses for the defense."

Charlie smiled bravely at Drew as he was led, handcuffed, from the courtroom.

* * * * *

It was Frances's turn.

"I would like to call Berkeley County Sheriff's Department Deputy Kit Flannery to the stand," Frances announced.

Flannery? Drew felt his face turn hot with anger. What the hell was Frances doing? She was supposed to call Savannah. Surly she was going to call Savannah. Flannery was on the other side!

Frances pressed Drew's hand without even looking at him and walked toward the witness. When she did glance back at Drew, her look said "trust me." Drew took a deep breath, trying to maintain his All-American Hero look. He was pretty sure it wasn't working.

Flannery raised his hand over the Bible and Frances went to work.

She looked like a librarian, studying her notes almost absently, pausing now and then to look over the top of her half-glasses, which had slipped down on her nose. "Deputy Flannery, where were you employed during November and December of 1981?"

"I have been a deputy with the Berkley County Sheriff's Department since 1972, ma'am." Flannery looked calm, complacent, almost bored.

Frances shuffled her papers again. "I understand that, Deputy Flannery. But is it not also true that you were working a second, off duty job during November and December of 1981? 'moonlighting,' I believe it's called?" Frances made it sound like a joke, but Drew knew it wasn't.

Flannery frowned rather fiercely. "I was working a second job, ma'am, but it was not moonlighting. Moonlighting refers to an illegal or unsanctioned activity. I was picking up some extra hours as a security guard for Rosemont Bank, with the full knowledge and consent of the sheriff's department."

"I beg your pardon, Deputy Flannery. I didn't mean to imply that you were doing anything illegal or illicit." Frances smiled beguilingly. "You wouldn't like that, would you. Doing something illegal or illicit."

Flannery flushed slightly. "No, ma'am."

Frances changed tactics abruptly. Gone was the flustered librarian. In her place was the sharp, exacting counselor. "Deputy Flannery, when you worked your extra hours at Rosemont bank, who was your immediate supervisor?"

Flannery shifted slightly in his seat. "Robert Waite, the bank President."

Frances looked over the top of her glasses again, the schoolteacher questioning an evasive answer this time. "Was Robert Waite the only person who gave you orders?"

Now Flannery looked decidedly uneasy. "No, ma'am."

Frances smiled softly, but her smile didn't quite reach her eyes. A look that, Drew decided, would make him nervous should she ever turn it on him. "In fact, most of your orders came from Waite's son, Robert Waite Junior, didn't they, Deputy Flannery?" She gave the 'Deputy' just a little extra emphasis.

"Junior occasionally gave me instructions, yes, ma'am," Flannery agreed.

"On the night of December 7th, 1981, you personally admitted Wendell 'Weasel' Macey to the Emergency Room at Kings Daughters Hospital, correct?"

Flannery looked decidedly uncomfortable at that. "I'm not sure, Ma'am. That was a very long time ago."

Frances produced a single document from the evidence folder. "Is this your signature, Deputy Flannery?"

Flannery glanced at the paper in Frances' hand. His jaws clenched into tight knots. "Yes, ma'am, that is my signature."

"Would you please explain to the jury what this form is?"

Flannery looked away from Frances, away from the paper, apparently studying the back wall of the courtroom. "A King's Daughter's Hospital admission record for Wendell Macey dated December 7th, 1981, and signed by myself."

"According to the sheriff's department records, you weren't on duty December 7th, 1981, Deputy Flannery. Yet the admitting nurse will testify that you were in uniform. Were you functioning in your capacity as a sheriff's deputy or a security guard at that time, Deputy Flannery?"

Flannery stared off into space, his tone noncommittal. "As I mentioned, it was a long time ago, Ma'am. It's hard to say."

Frances had lost her soft, pretty look and taken on a hard edge. Her tone sneered at Flannery's vagary. "A man died that night, Deputy Flannery. That's hard to forget, isn't it?"

Flannery worked his jaws again, but didn't reply.

"Objection," the Prosecutor threw in at last. "We are not here investigating the death of Wendell Macey. This witness was called by the defense, your honor. Is there really any point in badgering the witness over a case that was closed thirteen years ago?"

Frances ignored the prosecutor, a harried looking, tired little man, and turned her smile on the judge. "I would ask for your indulgence, Your Honor. The prosecution's most significant evidence against my client seems to be that Mr. Bailey has a reputation for violence. I intend to show the relevance of this line of questioning shortly."

"You may proceed," the Judge decided. "However, as the prosecutor has pointed out, Mrs. Dixon, Deputy Flannery is your witness, and you have not declared him a hostile witness. Do you wish to do so at this time?"

"I don't believe that will be necessary, your Honor," Frances assured the judge with a great deal more confidence than Drew felt was warranted.

"Proceed," the judge ordered.

Frances refocused her attention on the unfortunate deputy. "Deputy Flannery, do you remember the night of Wendell Macey's death?"

"I guess so, yes, Ma'am," Flannery admitted grudgingly.

Frances kept her tone sweet, almost demure. "Who were you working for when you rushed Weasel Macey to the emergency room, Deputy Flannery?"

Flannery ground his jaws again. "Rosemont Bank, ma'am."

Frances laid her paperwork down and approached Flannery, resting her elbows on the rail in front of him as she had with Larry Washburn. "And just where did you acquire Mr. Macey's battered body, Deputy?"

Flannery hesitated for the space of three whole heartbeats. "Rosemont Bank, Ma'am." A murmur ran through the crowded courtroom.

"Rosemont Bank," Frances repeated, facing the jury this time as she spoke. "You're sure. Absolutely sure you found Wendell 'Weasel' Macey, beaten so badly that he would never recover, at Rosemont bank on December 7th, 1981."

Flannery spoke with thirteen years of anger in his voice. "Yes, ma'am."

"And where did you find this broken, beaten body, Deputy Flannery?"

A grim smile settled over Flannery's face. "In Robert Waite Junior's office, ma'am."

There was another collective gasp from the audience in the courtroom.

Frances returned her attention to Flannery, her tone almost conversational, curious, as she spoke this time. "What was the condition of Robert Waite Junior's office when you found Wendell Macey's body, Deputy Flannery?"

Flannery was matter of fact, now, an officer reporting his observations. "The furniture was in disarray, several sculptures had been knocked over and broken, and there were pictures knocked off the walls and papers scattered everywhere."

Frances picked up her paperwork again and jotted several notes. She looked up again, as if she'd just remembered something mildly important. "Was anyone else in the office? Anyone at all besides Wendell Macey?"

"No, ma'am." Flannery was curt, but not evasive any more.

"Was anyone else in the Bank?" Frances queried.

"Yes, ma'am."

"Who?"

"The janitor, ma'am," Flannery revealed. After a very slight pause, he continued. "And Robert Waite Junior."

Frances appeared to give this some consideration. "Did you notice anything unusual about either of those two people, Deputy Flannery?"

"Yes, Ma'am," Flannery reported. "The janitor was doing his best not to make eye contact with me. And Robert Waite Junior was wearing a ripped shirt with what appeared to be blood on it, and his knuckles were bleeding. He'd cut his tie in half and wrapped it around his hands."

"Did he say anything to you?" Frances asked speculatively. "Robert Waite Junior, that is?"

"Yes, ma'am. Waite said, 'Take care of this mess, Flannery. Get him to the hospital. You don't need to file a report on this. I'm not going to press charges.'"

Frances tapped her pencil on the clipboard thoughtfully. "What did you understand Robert Waite Junior to mean, Deputy Flannery?"

"My understanding was that Macey had attacked Waite in his office, ma'am," Flannery reported.

Frances changed personalities abruptly. Now she was the cold observer again. "Were you surprised when Andrew Bailey was charged with Macey's murder?"

"Yes, Ma'am," Flannery admitted, sitting back in his chair, hands clasped loosely together.

"Did you tell anyone what really happened that night?"

"I was off duty. I filled out my log for Rosemont Security Office exactly as I observed the events that night."

"You didn't answer the question, Deputy Flannery," Frances pointed out. "Did you report to anyone what really happened that night?"

Flannery sighed and flexed his hands, as though he'd been sitting too long. "This is what they call a Good Old Boys State, Ms. Dixon. Rosemont Bank held the mortgage on my house. I have four kids."

"So what you're saying, Deputy Flannery, is that if you had come forward with what you saw on December 7th, 1981, you would have lost your house," Frances reiterated.

"No, ma'am," Flannery argued. "I'm saying that I filled out a detailed incident report for Rosemont Bank's Security office, and I made a report at the hospital. No one else ever asked me any questions."

"No one ever asked you any questions at all about how Wendell "Weasel" Macey actually died," Frances repeated.

"No, ma'am," Flannery confirmed.

Frances braced her hands on the edge of the witness box. "Were you surprised to find Wendell Macey in Robert Waite Junior's office that night, Deputy Flannery?"

"No, ma'am," Flannery replied without hesitation.

"Why not?" Frances demanded.

"I had seen him there two weeks earlier. The day before Thanksgiving."

"You're sure about the date?"

"Yes, ma'am," Flannery said with a hint of a smile. "I worked that night and Thanksgiving Day. The missus didn't like it much, but Waite paid double time for holidays. With four kids, you do things like that."

Frances peered over the top of her glasses, looking mildly surprised. "What was Wendell Macey doing in the bank the Wednesday before Thanksgiving, Deputy Flannery?"

"I believe he was applying for a loan, ma'am," Flannery speculated. "Apparently Waite turned him down, and they had quite a row."

"Did you see Macey again before he died?"

"Yes, Ma'am," Flannery reported. "I saw him leaving the bank just at closing time on Friday, November 27th, the day after Thanksgiving."

"And did Macey and Robert Waite Junior argue again on that day?"

"No, ma'am," Flannery assured her. "In fact, Macey was whistling when he left the bank."

"Whistling," Frances repeated. "Thank you, Deputy Flannery. No further questions, your Honor."

"Does the prosecution wish to cross examine the witness?" the judge asked.

"Yes, your Honor," the Prosecutor assured her rather vehemently.

"Your witness."

"Deputy Flannery, I remind you, you are still under oath."

The prosecutor was short, and to the point. "Deputy Flannery, did Robert Waite Junior ever tell you that he was responsible for Wendell Macey's death?"

"No, sir," Flannery assured the little man.

"Did you have any reason to believe that Macey was anything more to Waite that a customer who'd been turned down for a loan?"

"No, sir," Flannery repeated.

"No further questions, Your Honor."

"Next witness."

"Your Honor, I wish to call Savannah Bailey to the stand," Frances announced.

Another hushed murmur buzzed through the courtroom. Savannah came forward and was sworn in. Frances smiled at her kindly, and spoke to her as if she were still a child. She knew, Drew thought. She knew how fragile Savannah was. God, please don't let this hurt my baby, Drew prayed silently.

"Savannah, when did you move back to West Virginia?" Frances asked.

"The end of May, right after I graduated from Julliard," Savannah replied promptly.

"You've been using another name, haven't you?" Frances coaxed.

Savannah blushed guiltily. "Yes, ma'am."

"Why did you change your name, Savannah?"

"I was afraid," Savannah revealed.

Frances kept her tone warm and friendly. "Were you afraid of your father, Savannah?"

Savannah straightened at that, her cheeks flaming red. "No, ma'am! Of course not!"

"Of course not?" Frances repeated, her tone still soft and reasonable. "Most people think your father murdered your mother, Savannah. That would be a good reason to be afraid of your father, wouldn't it?"

"That's not true!" Savannah insisted.

"How do you know it isn't true, Savannah?" Frances coaxed.

"Because I was there." Savannah insisted. "I saw him."

"Where were you, Savannah? What did you see? Who did you see?"

"I was at the house on the hill, with my mother. A man came. He pushed the door open. Momma told me to go run and hide, but I didn't. I didn't," she repeated, sobbing.

"It's all right," Frances soothed. "It's all right. Just tell the judge what you saw."

"The man hurt Momma. He pushed her down and did things to her. She screamed. He kept hitting her. I ran down the steps and hit him and told him to get off my momma, but he shoved me away and hit Momma again, and then she was quiet. He chased me, and I ran, but he caught me. He told me if I ever told anyone what I saw, he'd come back and do the same thing to me he did to my mother. He made me promise not to tell anyone."

"What happened next, Savannah?" Frances continued gently.

"My stepfather came home," Savannah remembered. "Then the police came."

"Did the police talk to you?"

"No." Savannah sobbed.

"Did anyone ever ask you if you saw what happened that night?"

"Yes," Savannah revealed.

"Who?" Frances asked softly. "Who wanted to know what really happened, Savannah?"

"My stepfather."

Shelby Morgen

"And what did you tell your stepfather?"

"I said I didn't know."

"Why did you lie to your stepfather, Savannah?"

The little girl was back, her voice broken as she told her story. "I promised the other man I wouldn't tell anyone. Besides, I didn't like my stepfather. He didn't like me and I didn't like him. He used to yell at my mother, and tell her she was stupid. He hit her once. He made her cry. He scared me."

Frances crouched down a little, trying to get Savannah to meet her eyes. "Savannah, this question is really important. Do you know who the man was who killed your mother?"

Tears ran down Savannah's face. "Yes. He'd been to the house before. My stepfather called him a Weasel."

A ripple went through the crowded courtroom. Frances returned to her notes, and withdrew a photograph. She showed it to Savannah. "Is this the man who killed your mother, Savannah?"

Savannah looked at the picture and nodded her head, sobbing audibly now. "That's him. That's the man who killed Momma!"

"Your Honor, please let the records indicate that the witness has positively identified Wendell "Weasel" Macey as Darby Anne Bailey Waite's killer."

The uproar that filled the courtroom would not be quieted by the judge's gavel. Drew stood up, ignoring the bailiff who moved quickly to block his path, knocking the man aside with one powerful blow from a massive forearm. In three quick strides he was beside his daughter, gathering her into his arms. Drew glared up at the Judge. "That's enough!" he ordered, all of Frances's warnings forgotten. "She's had enough!"

Frances smiled quietly to herself. The father fiercely protecting his daughter. Had he tried, Drew couldn't have looked more like the All-American Hero. Several courtroom reporters worked quickly to sketch the rugged rescuer, arms clasped tightly around the sobbing young woman. The caption below the pictures in tomorrow's paper would read "Home Town Hero Exonerated!"

"Your Honor!" the prosecutor announced as the noise began to subside. "The prosecution moves to dismiss all charges against Andrew Bailey!"

The judge wisely decided to abandon her gavel and sit this one out.

* * * * *

"Welcome home."

Drew turned away from the door where he'd been watching Savannah's car disappear down the lane. He seemed surprised, as if he'd forgotten Charlie was in the room, and then he looked even more surprised, as he realized she hadn't been in the room, but was just coming down the stairs.

She was wearing a very tiny scrap of black lace that left absolutely nothing to the imagination.

Whatever he'd been about to say disappeared as he stared at her.

"You don't like it. I told them it was too—"

"Good Lord, woman. Like it? It's perfect, if what you had in mind is for me to rip it off of you."

"You don't have to," Charlie explained, blushing furiously. "You just—"

"Come here and let me figure it out for myself."

But she paused on the next to the last step, too embarrassed to cross the room to him. "The girls—"

He crossed the room in two long strides, his eyes fixed on her like a predatory cat. "The girls thought it was time to go home for a very good reason, I see. All that bullshit about it being a long day was because they took you shopping."

"Yeah."

He stopped, close enough to touch, without raising a hand. "What's wrong, Charlie? Are you still angry with me? Afraid of me? What?"

"No! I just feel foolish. I never—I'm not—I don't know how to wear stuff like this. I've never been much of a—a *female* sort of person. I know horses and cars and computers. I'm not—I'm not *sexy*."

He laughed at that, really laughed. His arms closed around her and he pulled her down to sit on the step with him as buried his face in her hair, the laughter fading gradually into soft chuckles as he just held her, rubbing his cheek across the top of her head affectionately. "Charlie, if you were any sexier you just might be the death of me."

She punched him none-too-gently in the arm. "Now you're making fun of me. Let me up you idiot."

Drew captured her hand in his and raised it gently to his lips, all trace of humor gone from his eyes, though he continued to smile. "Don't you know, sweetheart, that I love every incredibly sexy bone in your body? You have the sexiest hands I've ever seen. Small, and yet big enough to hold my heart captive. And those hands are attached to the most amazing arms, strong enough to wrap themselves around me and not let go, even when I didn't have sense enough to hold on." He kissed his way up to her shoulders, his lips caressing until the anger melted out of her and she surrendered to his touch.

"What about my neck?" she whispered.

"Long and slender and succulent," he pronounced, nibbling his way along the pulse at her throat. "And then there are your ears." He sucked the lobe of her ear as if it were some new confection he'd suddenly grown addicted to. His hand moved to cover her breast, then pinch gently at the nipple through the sheer fabric of the negligee. "God, I missed this, Charlie."

"I missed you," she agreed as her hands stroked through the length of his long sable curls. She took her time unbuttoning his shirt, enjoying the way his hands stilled as she touched him, knowing he was watching every flick of her fingers as she worked her way down the front to where the tails were tucked into his suit pants. She brought her hands back up to push the collar open, pausing to study the contrast as she laid her hands against his bronzed skin. "I love the look of you. I love the way your skin feels under my hands. So warm and alive and so incredibly sexy. I want to spend hours looking at you, touching you."

Drew scooped her up, laughing once again. "Your wish is my command, fair lady." He took the stairs two at a time, only to pause at their bedroom door. "You opened this for me, the very first time. I wasn't sure you would."

She reached out to open it now. "I told you to put me down before you screwed up your back, too."

He stepped through the doorway and did just that, letting her slip down his chest, then holding her tightly so the she could feel the heat of his penis trapped between them. She moved her hips in inviting circles against his thick, rigid cock, her breasts straining for release as his hands reached to massage her suddenly aching nipples.

"You are," he breathed into her hair, "The sexiest woman God ever created."

She started to argue with him, wanted to, then changed her mind as his clever fingers moved to the bow between her breasts. With one tug the trailing ends of the ribbon the flimsy garment separated. He nuzzled it back off her shoulders until it slipped to the floor, then continued to nuzzle his way down her chest until he captured one aching nipple between her lips.

"You make me feel sexy," she assured him as her nails raked across his scalp. "You make me feel sexy in a way no negligee ever could."

"You make me feel horny."

She laughed at that, reaching between them to free the clasp at the waist of those suit pants. "What are you going to do about that, big guy?"

"I'm going to fuck you until you can't see straight."

"Not if I fuck you first."

"Yeah?"

She shoved him back toward the bed. "Yeah."

"Is that a declaration of war?"

Laughing, she climbed onto the bed, straddling his knees as she wrapped her fingers around his throbbing shaft. "Yeah." She lowered her head, her hair cascading over him as she sucked him slowly into her mouth. His hips rose up off the bed at the first touch of her tongue, his breath holding, then releasing in one long shuddering moan. "Dear God, woman."

She released her hands to pull the whole length of him slowly into her mouth, her tongue massaging the pulsing vein that stood out on the underneath side. Her fingers dropped to stroke over his balls as they contracted, drawing up rigid and tight in her hands.

With a growl he rolled them to their sides, pulling loose from her long enough to change positions, until her hips were in his hands and her soft patch of truly red hair lay exposed before him, the tiny little black panties whisked away. He parted her fur to run his tongue over her in one hard, demanding swipe. Her breath caught as he came back again, sucking her clit into his mouth as if he meant to devour her. "Drew!"

"Yes my love?" His breath blew over her sensitive flesh as he released her long enough to answer, his voice thick with laughter.

He captured her again, his tongue swirled around and over the tight little bud caught between his lips, even as his fingers slipped inside her. She cried out wordlessly as the first orgasm ripped through her needy, neglected body. Her hands clawed at his shoulders, pulling, demanding. "I want you. I need you. Inside me."

Strong hands rolled her until he could pull her hips back against his throbbing cock. Charlie gasped in surprise as he slid into her, fast and hard and demanding. This wasn't what she had wanted, was it? It was primitive and almost painful, granting him full access while she could reach nothing at all. His hands reached around to cup her breasts, kneading the painfully distended nipples between his thumbs and forefingers. It was primitive, primal, rough and demanding. She came again, convulsing around him almost violently as the orgasm ripped through her. He could touch her in places he hadn't reached before, his thick, hard cock filling her until she thought she might break from the sensations that threatened to overwhelm her.

More. She wanted more. She dropped her shoulders, pushing her ass against him harder with every thrust, opening even more of herself to him. She felt his breathing change, felt the increased desperation in his thrusts as the pace increased, and she folded one arm under her shoulders to support herself while the other hand reached back to touch, stroking over his balls as they slapped against her.

"Charlie!" She felt his balls tighten and contract under her touch, felt the last of his control break as he slammed against her, his seed flooding her as she rode out the final wave, tightening around him to milk him of all he had to give.

Exhausted, he dropped to his side, her body still clasped tightly against him as he slowly subsided within her. "You destroy me," he whispered against her ear, his breath coming in hot, desperate pants. His nose muzzled into the hair at the nape of her neck, and his teeth nipped gently. "I wanted to do this right for you, slow and perfect."

Charlie laughed at that, her breathing equally ragged. "Well, it wasn't slow, but it was perfect. We can try slow next time."

"Okay," he agreed in a sleepy mumble.

"Drew?"

"Not just yet, my love. Give me a minute or two."

She laughed again. "Welcome home."

* * * * *

It was entirely possible, Charlie reflected, that she'd never really had a weight problem. She'd simply never been properly fed before. She came to this conclusion while packing away six pair of jeans that no longer fit. She was, she decided with a little pirouette in front of the mirror, probably the only forty-four year old woman in the world so pleased to have gained ten pounds.

They set the date for the wedding tentatively for December 11th, as Terry insisted that it had to be before the end of the year. Between the stocks Charlie had cashed out and the interest and earnings on Drew's inheritance, Terry seemed unduly concerned about their tax returns. Charlie, of course, just wanted to get married. Mother, on the other hand, seemed to think two months was nowhere near enough time to plan a wedding.

Only Savannah seemed to truly understand Mother's concern over the wedding details. She quickly picked up Charlie's slack in following through with the phone calls, reservations, and guest lists. Savannah insisted on catering the affair herself, though with Drew's help, of course. He refused to be left out of any food preparations.

Drew had missed the beginning of the football season while he was in jail. However, the Sunday Afternoon Football parties were a tremendous success once they got started. It was past the half-way-point in the season, and there were twelve men crammed into the back room, greedily munching on Drew and Savannah's wedding food practice dishes.

The Robinson Boys' mother stopped by during the game to deliver a housewarming pie and an apology. Charlie decided she wasn't ready to forget, but she could be big enough to forgive.

Together, she and Drew bid goodbye to all the guests, just as the sun was setting over the back pasture. They stood together, arm in arm, watching the last crop of hay turn blazing red with nature's paintbrush. There had been few enough moments like this for them. Quiet, peaceful, serene endings to perfect days. They linked arms and headed for the barn, capping the day off with a quiet hour spent feeding the mares. All the ladies were well along in their pregnancies by now, and moving more slowly as they took on the swinging barrel girths of their ninth months.

Charlie was lost in thought, or she might have noticed something out of place as she entered the barn. Drew caught it, that undeniable feeling of wrongness, but before he could pinpoint its source, it was too late. All he could do was grab Charlie and shove her behind him as the figure appeared out of the shadows of the tack room. Drew swore softly under his breath.

"Welcome home, Little Brother," the apparition spat.

"You sorry ass son-of-a-bitch," Drew responded. "What the hell are you doing here now? What did you do? Think up some new murder charge to try to pin on me?"

"Yeah," Waite responded with a sneer. "Mine." He stepped out farther into the light. He was out of uniform. He carried no weapon. "Come and get me, little brother."

The man was big. As tall as Drew. Maybe an inch taller. And definitely heavier. Not that he was fat. Far from it. He was, instead, densely muscled, with the build and stance of a wrestler. His every movement radiated raw physical power. A dangerous kind of power. A lion barely leashed.

"What the hell did I ever do to you, anyway?" Drew demanded as he approached the bigger man cautiously. "I didn't even know who you were until two months ago. What makes me so important to you, to try so hard to destroy me?"

"You don't even know, do you, you little Bastard." Waite circled slowly, keeping Drew moving without letting him know what to expect. "You killed my mother. That little whore who bore you could have gone away quietly, like any decent woman would have, but no. She had to parade around town with her belly showing, letting everybody see my father's mistake, until finally, my mother couldn't take the ridicule any more. One morning about two years after you were born my mother put a gun to her head and pulled the trigger.

"I was twelve years old. Do you know what Mother said in the letter she left for my father? She told him to find the woman he loved. To give you a father. He'd have done it, too. He'd have brought you into my home if he could have. Into the home my mother created. He'd have shared the bed he bought for my mother with another woman. I couldn't let that happen."

"So you destroyed your mother's letter," Charlie surmised.

"I had to," Waite confirmed.

"You destroyed your father's life, and then mine," Drew concluded. "And denied your mother her dying wish."

"It was your fault!" Waite practically screamed. "If you hadn't had his eyes, she'd never have done it!"

"If your father hadn't seduced a young girl the school board entrusted to his care as an employer, I wouldn't have had his eyes!" Drew countered bitterly. "You may have lost a mother, but so did I. And I never had a father. The bastard never even gave me his name."

With a cry of rage, Waite attacked. He dove in head first, like a line-back going for a tackle. Drew sidestepped and let the bigger man's momentum carry him straight into a left to the solar plexus. Waite came up short, gasping for breath, but recovered all too quickly. He countered with an overhand right to the head. Except that Drew's head wasn't there when the punch should have landed. Drew ducked under the blow to land a short right jab against the side of Waite's ribcage. The impact was solid, but not heavy enough to do any real damage. Waite came back with a left uppercut that rattled Drew's brain.

Drew danced back, shaking his head, trying to clear the fog that threatened for just a moment. A good solid right came out of nowhere and knocked him off his feet. Waite seemed to be content to allow Drew the time to get back up. Drew borrowed a move from Waite's own playbook, and dove in for a tackle before he'd fully straightened up. He caught Waite off guard, and, therefore, off balance. The two men went down together, fists still flying and fabric ripping. Drew was the first to roll away and regain his footing. He wiped a hand across his bloodied mouth.

"Done already, old man?" he taunted. "Come on. Get up. Isn't this what you've been wanting all along? You've wasted most of your life waiting for this chance to get even with me. Now's your chance."

With a roar like an angry bull, Waite charged in, fists swinging hard and fast. Drew met him toe-to-toe, giving as good as he got. Charlie winced as a solid right connected with Drew's left eye, swelling it shut almost instantly. She remembered a time when she'd actually enjoyed watching two men slug it out in the ring. Now she longed for the bell.

Drew landed a left-right-left combination to Waite's midsection that slowed the bigger man down, but failed to drop him. Charlie found herself wanting to coach from the sidelines. She wanted to shout at Drew to change to headshots, but decided to bite her lip and keep her mouth shut. But when he landed two more body shots that failed to bring the big man down, she couldn't help herself. "Go for his head!" she shouted.

That was all it took. In the split second when Drew turned, just a little, to focus on Charlie, register what she'd said, a huge right hand connected solidly with his chin, sending him staggering back several steps before he went down hard on his back. When they talked about it later, Drew would insist that it was his swollen left eye that had prevented him from seeing the blow coming, but Charlie knew better. She'd distracted him, and everything that happened after might have been prevented had she kept her mouth shut.

But then, perhaps not.

She hadn't seen Savannah enter the barn. Hadn't heard her. It wasn't until the shot rang out that Charlie even looked toward the door. Charlie felt like she was reacting in slow motion. She turned toward the muzzle flash, recognized Savannah, and heard her own voice screaming "No!" but it was already too late. A second shot went off before she could reach the girl.

Savannah walked calmly to her victim, ignoring Charlie. "I never broke my promise to you," she told the fallen man. "I never told anyone you were there."

Waite looked up at her, his breath coming in short, ragged gasps that painted his lips with bubbling blood. "You talked," he rasped. "I told you I'd kill him if you talked."

"But I've killed you, instead," Savannah argued calmly.

"What do you think it will do to him to see his only daughter go to prison?" Waite managed, his face settling into a hideous grin.

"Oh, no," Savannah argued. "That won't happen. For you see, I'm quite insane." She slowly raised the barrel of the .25. Charlie screamed again, knowing all ready that she would be too late, and sprinted across the tack room, even as Savannah pulled the trigger, the barrel pointed directly at Waite's head.

The hammer clicked home on an empty chamber, but the girl just stood there, pulling the trigger over and over again, until Charlie reached her and gently pried it from her fingers.

She heard sirens in the background. Savannah looked up at her and smiled calmly. "I called 911," she revealed. "I told them there was a man in the barn, attacking my daddy." Her voice was the young child's again. "He made me promise. He said if I ever told anyone, he'd kill my daddy. He was in the courtroom. Staring at me. And then I knew. He was here tonight to kill my daddy." She looked up as Drew came to take her in his arms. "I couldn't let him hurt you again," she explained as Drew's arms closed around her. "He killed Mommy. He'd have killed you, too. He told me he would if I ever told what happened. The other man was there, too, but he killed my mommy."

Deputy Flannery was the first man through the door. Perhaps, Charlie reflected, because he knew the place better than the rest of them did. "Where's the little girl?" he demanded, surveying the room. "County dispatch said a little girl called in. Said a man was trying to kill her father."

"I couldn't let him do it," Savannah replied. "He said if I ever told anyone, he'd kill my daddy. I couldn't let him kill my daddy."

Horror dawned in Flannery's eyes. He looked beyond Savannah to Drew. "I killed him. If he's even dead," Drew responded. "I shot him."

Flannery shook his head. "We're not quite the bumbling idiots we were twelve years ago," he reasoned. "There will be paraffin tests. Fingerprints. A whole batter of psychological tests." Other officers were piling in behind him now, filling up the doorway. State police. Other deputies. "I'm going to have to take her in. But I promise you, Bailey, she'll never do time for this. Not in prison. At the worst they might send her to the state mental hospital for a little while. But after what she's been through, maybe that's not such a bad thing, you know?"

Drew hugged her more tightly, reluctant to let her go. "Aren't you going to at least check on Waite?" he demanded.

Flannery sighed and went to examine the body with obvious reluctance. "Son-of-a-bitch!" he exploded when he knelt beside the body. "Johnson, get that ambulance crew down here! This bastard's still alive! Call for a medivac! With any luck, this asshole may live long enough to go to prison yet!"

Charlie felt lost in the flurry of activity that followed. It seemed as if an army had invaded her tack room. Every light in the barn came on, plus a few lights from the emergency rescue trucks. By the time the ambulance crew had Waite strapped to a board and attached to a dozen wires and tubes, the medivac was there to take him away. One of the state troopers had driven off with Savannah. Someone had taken Charlie's .25 caliber pistol.

Flannery was the last to leave. "Where's that damn big dog of yours, anyway?" he asked cautiously as he headed for the door.

Charlie looked around helplessly, consumed with guilt that she hadn't thought to ask the question first. "I don't know what Waite did with him!" she exclaimed. She ran to the door. "Ghost!" she screamed with a voice that should have awakened the dead. "Where are you, Ghost!" There was no answering bark to be heard on the now quiet night. Charlie started to shake. "If that son-of-a-bitch hurt my dog I'll kill him myself!" she professed.

"I really wish you wouldn't say things like that in front of me," Flannery replied in a weary tone. "It just makes my life more complicated. Where did you first see Waite tonight?"

"At the back of the tack room," Drew replied. Following Flannery's line of thinking, he bolted for the stairs. "Check all the stalls!" he called as he disappeared.

It was something concrete she could actually accomplish. Charlie flew out of the tack room and started examining the stalls one by one. Flannery followed, but with slightly less enthusiasm. His look was decidedly uneasy as he investigated the feed room. "Ghost won't hurt you as long as you're not trying to hurt us!" Charlie assured him. Flannery didn't look like he found her explanation all that credible.

Nevertheless, when Drew returned empty handed, Flannery produced a huge flashlight from his patrol car. "Turn on all the outside lights," he instructed Charlie. She proceeded to light the outside of the barn up like a Christmas tree.

Still, although the three of them searched for half an hour, there was no sign of Ghost.

"How did Waite get here?" Flannery asked when they met back at the barn stairs.

Drew shrugged noncommittally.

"There were a lot of cars here earlier," Charlie put in. "We had a football party. Maybe he stowed away with someone."

"More likely he hid his vehicle somewhere. Let's see if we can't find it." Flannery opened the doors on the patrol car.

"I've never ridden in one of these things voluntarily," Drew reported, hesitating for just a moment.

"It's got big spotlights," Flannery countered.

They found Waite's car at the edge of the old dump, just inside the grove of trees in the back pasture. Charlie spotted Ghost first. A large mat of fur stretched out alongside the driver's door. She shrieked the dog's name and bolted out of the patrol car even before it came to a full stop.

Not far behind her, Flannery lifted the dog's bloody head from Charlie's arms. "He's still got a pulse," he reported. "Bailey. Help me get him onto the back seat."

Together, the two men half dragged, half carried the unconscious dog into the cruiser. Charlie climbed into the back seat, cradling the big dog's bloody head in her lap while Drew rode up front.

"Can't honestly say I've ever been in the front seat of a patrol car, either," Drew commented dryly.

Flannery glanced at him sideways as he turned on the lights and headed out of the trees. "Buckle up," was the only comment he made.

Once they were turned around and back on the dirt lane, Flannery reached for his microphone. "Flannery to dispatch."

"Dispatch," a woman's voice answered.

"Karen," Flannery called back. "Call Doc Keeler for me and tell him I'm on the way in with an emergency."

"Keeler!" Karen responded. "Keeler's a vet!"

"I know he's a vet, Karen," Flannery replied, his patience obviously a bit thin. "Would you please make sure he's there before I drive fifteen miles out of my way for nothing?"

"Ten-four," Karen replied, still sounding a bit dubious. She was back just as they reached the interstate. "Keeler's waiting," Karen confirmed. "He wants to know what to expect."

"A dog," Flannery replied. "A very large dog. Tell him Drew Bailey's dog Ghost was hit over the head hard by an intruder out at Spring Meadows Farm tonight."

"The dog that ripped open your arm?" Karen returned in disbelief.

"That's the one," Flannery replied.

Karen was gone again. When she returned, her voice was serious, professional, again. "Flannery," she instructed. "Keeler says to come to the back door. He'll have a gurney waiting."

"Ten-four," Flannery replied. He hung up the mike and gave Drew another sideways glance. "This is a first for me, too," he offered with a hint of a smile. "I've never made an emergency run on a dog before."

"Maybe you better avoid the station tomorrow," Drew replied with a snort.

"Won't do any good," Flannery observed. "Too many scanners out there. I'll be surprised if there aren't at least three reporters at Keeler's place by the time we get there. That's why I used your name. You're news. Handle the reporters right, and Savannah will never come to trial. They won't prosecute the girl who saved a local celebrity's life. Not in this county."

Drew studied the man thoughtfully. "This is the second time you've stuck you neck out for me," he observed. "Thanks."

"The third time," Flannery corrected. "I filed a report on the whole Wendell Macey incident with the sheriff's department twelve years ago, in addition to the one I filed with Rosemont Security. I was younger then. I still believed in the system."

"We're all a little older now, Flannery," Drew commented. "I guess we've all learned a lot in the last twelve years."

"You can call me Kit," Flannery offered as he turned into the Animal Hospital. "Hey, I underestimated. Four reporters. Two photographers. I bet Keeler's in a great mood. Hang on to your hats, kids. The ride is just beginning."

Chapter Eighteen

"Drew! Come look at this!" Charlie called.

Drew stabbed the pitchfork into an unopened bale of hay and slammed the feed room door shut. "What's wrong!" he called back as he took the barnyard steps two at a time.

"Nothing a week home with you wouldn't cure," Charlie assured him as she searched for a place to put her arms that wouldn't hit a bruise. "You look worse than you did this morning. I think we should have a doctor look at that eye."

"You took a year off my life to tell me I have a black eye?" Drew complained.

"No, silly. I finished up early and came home to show you this newspaper story. But now that I see you I'm pretty sure you won't be able to read it."

"Keeler called. Ghost finally came around this afternoon. He's still a little disoriented, but Keeler thinks he should be all right by tonight. We can go visit him if you want to."

Charlie's face lit up with relief and gratitude for a moment before her brows pulled together again in a worried frown. "Have you heard anything about Savannah?"

"I haven't heard anything from anybody. Including Frances." Drew ran a hand through his hair, the way he did when he was worried or nervous.

"Well, take a look at this article. Flannery was right about the reporters." Charlie started to unfold the newspaper there in the driveway, but the cold October wind snatched at it. Drew put an arm around her shoulders and led her across the gravel parking area and into the kitchen. There was, as always, a pot of coffee waiting. Drew filled her favorite cup, added two creams and two sugars, and sat down beside her at the little round table.

The paper was a little hard to focus on with one eye swollen half shut, but Drew wasn't about to admit it. Or the fact that at least two of his ribs were probably cracked. Again. He could make out the picture of Charlie and himself and Doc Keeler crowded around Ghost on a gurney with the sheriff's department Cruiser in the background, lights still blazing. And the headline wasn't too hard to read. "K-9 Hero critically injured by Off Duty Sheriff."

Charlie snuggled closer and read him the rest. "Lights flashing and siren blasting, Deputy Kit Flannery of the Berkeley County Sheriff's Department rushed a critically wounded patient to the hospital last night – The North Side Animal Hospital, that is. The drama began about 6:00 PM when off duty Sheriff Robert Waite Junior attempted to enter the barn on the Spring Meadows Farm, North of Martinsburg on old Route 11." Charlie snorted. "We're not on Rt. 11!"

"We're closer to Rt. 11 than anything else," Drew pointed out.

Charlie gave him one of those I-don't-agree-with-you looks and went back to the article. "Waite encountered the farm's watch dog, a hundred-and-fifty pound. St. Bernard named Ghost, as soon as he got out of his vehicle. The dog was seriously injured when Waite smashed a police baton over the dog's skull, but not before Waite received bites requiring fifty-one stitches to his forearm and left calf.

"After leaving the dog unconscious, Waite proceeded to wait in ambush for farm manager Drew Bailey, whom he attacked and apparently intended to kill. Waite himself was critically injured when Bailey's daughter, Savannah fired 2 shots from a .25 caliber semi-automatic pistol into his chest and shoulder. Waite is expected to recover, and according to the county prosecutor, will stand trial for the murder of his first wife, Darby Anne Bailey Waite, as well as attempted murder in the attack on Andrew Bailey. According to Deputy Flannery, it is unlikely that any charges will be brought against Savannah Bailey, who undoubtedly saved her father's life."

Charlie folded up the paper. "The article's continued on another page, but it really doesn't say much of anything else. I know it was dark down there, but you'd have thought I'd have noticed that Waite was all chewed up."

"He didn't punch like he was messed up much," Drew agreed, shifting slightly to ease his ribs. "On the other hand, you know Ghost didn't just walk up and stick out his head for Waite to clobber him either."

Drew craned his neck to look out the window over the kitchen sink. "Damn. We better get that dog back here soon. Somebody just pulled up. I think it's Frances."

"She said she'd be up today," Charlie remembered. "I just didn't expect it to be this late." She met her sister at the door. "You look awfully pleased with yourself," Charlie observed by way of a greeting.

"I am," Frances confirmed. She moved aside, and Savannah followed her in the door. "I've had a busy day."

With another one of those lightning quick moves that still took Charlie by surprise, Drew crossed the room and scooped up Savannah in his arms. Laughing, he spun her around the way he had when she was three. "Are you all right honey?" he asked. "What happened? They told me I couldn't even see you until tomorrow!"

"Aunt Frances happened," Savannah answered. "I think she threatened the Prosecutor."

Drew set Savannah down again and picked up Frances, spinning her around next, then kissed her on the cheek as he set her back down. "What's happening, *Aunt Frances*?" he teased. "Can I keep her?"

"You can keep her," Frances laughed. "The prosecutor's agreed not to press charges. She has a series of interviews with the psychiatrist for competency testing with regards to testifying against Waite. But, other than that, everything's fine."

"Are you all right?" Drew asked Savannah again.

Savannah smiled, understanding what he was really asking. "I'm not really nuts," she answered with a laugh. "The little girl was a character from a play I was in. I do community theater."

"That was an act?" Drew exclaimed incredulously. "You sure had me fooled!"

"That was the idea," Savannah replied. "If you'd been called on to testify against me, what would you have said?"

"Totally whacko," Charlie confirmed.

Drew grew suddenly very serious. He took Savannah by the shoulders and stared hard at her. "Tell me the truth, now. Honestly. Did you come here to kill Bob Waite?"

Savannah hesitated a moment too long before she answered. "No," she replied at last. "No, I didn't. But I knew there was going to be trouble. And I hated Bob Waite. I could have killed him, easily enough. I spent seven years in therapy after I moved in with Grandma. It took a while to learn not to be afraid of him. The counselor taught me to understand what had happened. I taught myself to hate him instead of being afraid of him. I knew he'd go after you as soon as you came home. And I knew he had to be stopped. But I didn't plan to kill him. If I was going to do that, I don't think I'd have waited this long. I didn't really have a plan. I just knew I had to come here and face him, and I had to tell someone what really happened."

"You're a very brave young woman," Drew told her, "And I'm very proud of you. But I'm beginning to get a little paranoid about being around women with a history of violent shootings. Let's end this here, okay, girls?"

"Okay," Charlie agreed, laughing.

"Me, too," Savannah agreed, "Once was enough."

"I haven't even had a turn, yet," Frances complained.

"It might cost you your license," Drew pointed out.

The phone rang before Frances could think of a glib retort. Charlie grabbed it. Those around her listened anxiously, but heard nothing more than "Are you sure?" and "I see. Please schedule that as soon as possible." Then "Thank you."

Drew crossed the room to steady her as she hung up the phone. She'd turned pale and looked like she'd finally seen that ghost. "What's wrong?" he demanded.

Charlie looked up at him with an expression of shocked disbelief. "When I had my physical for the Hospital they did a blood work up on me. The results came back today. My cholesterol is high. And I'm pregnant."

Drew shouted and grabbed her up in a bear hug, kissing her soundly. It took him a minute to realize that no one else was as excited as he was. "Am I missing something?" he asked, setting Charlie back down gently. He studied her face carefully, trying to read her state of mind. "Charlie? Do you want to have a baby?"

Charlie snapped her head up like she'd been struck. "Yes! Oh, yes!" she exclaimed. "I tried for years to get pregnant with Allen. I wanted a baby so badly! I want this baby! I want to have your baby! It's just that I'm a little scared, is all."

"What is there to be scared of?" Drew demanded. "You're only forty-four. That's not so unusual. This is a Catholic community, remember? Big families. I grew up around kids whose moms were in their forties when they were born."

"Yes, but this is Charlie's first," Frances explained. "There can be problems when a woman has her first baby when she's over forty. An increased risk of birth defects."

"They want to do an ultra-sound, to make sure it's in the right place, and amniocentesis, to check for genetic defects," Charlie told them. "I asked Brenda to schedule the tests as soon as possible. If everything's okay, then it should be a fairly normal pregnancy, she says, but they'll keep a close eye on me, anyway."

Drew searched her eyes. "And if it's not normal?"

Charlie searched her soul. "I don't think I could give up this baby, even if it wasn't perfect, as long as I had a choice." She tried to read Drew's soul in his eyes. "I know how difficult it could be, and you have a say in this, too, but I want this baby. No matter what."

"As long as your life isn't in danger, I'll support any decision you make," Drew assured her. "We can handle anything, if we do it together."

Savannah was rummaging through the drawers in the kitchen counter frantically. "What on earth are you doing?" Charlie demanded with a laugh.

"Looking for a God-blessed calendar!" Savannah hissed in exasperation.

"Why?" three voices asked in unison.

"I want to make sure I'm going to be here when my baby sister is born!"

"What? Where are you going?"

"*Le Cordon Bleu Paris.* I put it off a year to come here."

"That's fantastic!" Drew nearly shouted. "Baby, I'm so thrilled for you!"

"When do you start?" Charlie asked.

"August."

Charlie let go of Drew and walked across the room to still the agitated hands. She picked up the long, slender fingers and folded them down one at a time. "November, December, January, February, March, April, May, June. I'm not a horse. I won't take 11 months."

Savannah stared down at her fingers, then began to laugh. She flung her arms around Charlie and gave her a bear hug that rivaled her father's. "Thanks, Mom!" she teased.

The phone rang again, and this time Drew dove for it. He said no more than "Thanks," before he hung up. "Ghost wants to come home," he told an anxious audience.

"Did he tell you that himself?" Charlie laughed.

"As a matter of fact, he did," Drew acknowledged with a grin. "He was barking so loud all I heard was 'Come get this damn dog!'"

Charlie glanced around the room. "I think I'm going to have to trade the Mustang in on a Mini-van!" she threatened.

"I'll drive," Frances offered. "Ghost deserves a ride in the T-Bird."

* * * * *

"Where are you taking me?" Charlie demanded with a laugh as the old Willy's jounced her over what felt like yet another set of railroad tracks.

"It's a surprise," Drew reiterated. He glanced over to make sure the blindfold was still in place. "I told you I wanted to do this once. But instead we did it your way. Now it's my turn," he added cryptically.

"I have no idea what you're talking about," Charlie admitted. "And I've never really liked surprises, but I'm trying to be patient."

"You're trying to get me to change my mind," Drew informed her perceptively. "But it won't work. You will like this, I promise." At least I really hope you will, he added to himself. Despite everything, he was a little nervous. It didn't make any sense, really. He didn't have any reason to be nervous. Charlie'd already said yes. But that seemed like half a lifetime ago.

Drew turned right into Harpers Ferry and proceeded down the hill to the Historic District. At the top of High Street, he turned right onto a narrow alley, just barely wide enough to accommodate the Willy's. Nothing had changed. Not really. The alley banked up steeply, then suddenly fell off before them, plummeting abruptly down toward the church. Drew pulled into the tiny parking lot overlooking the cliffs and parked. "Stay right there," he ordered. "I'll come around to get you."

Charlie shivered with excitement as Drew's door slammed shut. She'd known since that first four-leafed clover that he had a romantic streak. But a twenty-mile drive blindfolded in the Jeep had to be something a little out of the ordinary in any woman's life. Even a life as exciting as hers had been of late.

The door opened and Drew was there, offering her his hand and helping her out of the truck. He led her a few steps and then positioned her, like a mannequin, before he reached up and pulled off the blindfold.

It was spectacular. Nothing short of spectacular. She was standing at the edge of an ancient stone retaining wall, several hundred feet above the joining of the two rivers, looking down on an ancient town. Across the rivers, the mountain ranges seemed to come to an abrupt end, with a jagged gap just wide enough to let the joined waters pass. The craggy rock slopes gave way to gorgeous fall colors as she looked up river from the juncture. And then as she turned her head, she saw it. An old stone church, perched high up on the edge of a cliff overlooking it all. The most beautiful church she'd ever seen. "Oh, Drew," she gasped softly. "It's perfect."

Drew led her down the steep path from the parking lot to the small rocky courtyard in front of the church itself. There was a stone bench there in front of the church. Charlie accepted Drew's offer to sit down thankfully, overwhelmed by the spectacular view. She didn't realize for a moment that he wasn't sitting beside her. Instead he dropped to one knee before her.

Charlie gasped in surprise, and a hand flew to her mouth instinctively. Of all the things she'd thought of on the ride over, this hadn't even been a possibility.

"I told you once I wanted to do this right," Drew began with a little smile. He withdrew a small box from his suit coat pocket, and opened it before her to reveal an emerald, cut like a solitaire, surrounded by tiny diamonds. "Charlotte Giles, I love you. I have loved you since the first moment I ever saw you. I will love you until the day I leave this earth, and beyond, until the end of time, if that's possible. There will never be another woman for me. You have my heart, my soul, and my life in your hands. Will you take my name, as well? Will you marry me, here, at Saint Peter's Church, on December 11th of this year?"

"Oh, my," Charlie gasped again. "Yes! Oh, yes!" She flung her arms around his neck and kissed him passionately, laughing and crying all at once. "I love you!" she managed at last.

Drew scooped her up and spun her around, returning her kiss as he did so. "I love you, Charlie," he repeated as he took her hand and slid the ring onto her finger. "I know you said you didn't want a ring, but..."

"It's gorgeous," Charlie interrupted. "It's the color of your eyes."

The wind picked up over the cliffs, catching Charlie's hair, which had somehow come loose, and spreading it out behind her like a fan. The sunlight caught it and painted it the color of summer's most glorious sunset. "I love you, Charlie," he whispered again. "More than life itself."

* * * * *

It was a small wedding, there on the hillside above Harpers Ferry, a small traditional Catholic wedding. Everyone said the church had never looked better, decked out in garlands of red roses. Charlie wore her grandmother's wedding gown, a fragile silk and lace creation with a heavy brocade underskirt and an endless train. Frances stood beside her, along with Savannah, while Terry stood as best man. The late morning sun caught the old stained-glass windows and painted the little church like a festival of lights.

Charlie wore her hair down, at Drew's request, except for a little braid at the temples that secured her headdress, a simple veil of antique lace handmade by her grandmother's grandmother. A hush fell over the church as she entered, and Drew nearly forgot his well-choreographed moves. He recovered in time, though, and offered Charlie his arm with a smile that rivaled the brilliance of the sun on that chilly

December morning. With all the solemnity the occasion demanded, he led her down the aisle to stand before Father James Giles.

Jamie treated them both to a special smile before he began his incantations. "We gather here today in the Presence of God Almighty to join these two..."

Charlie barely listened to the words as she stared up at Drew, her heart in her eyes. He'd bought a new suit for the occasion, a formal affair, dark charcoal, just for her, with a cummerbund and a formal, pleated front shirt. He looked as handsome as any Greek god. His hand over hers felt warm, almost damp. He towered over her, his head bent to look down into her eyes, a look of wonder on his face. As Jamie's voice continued, it occurred to Charlie that even Allen had never written a scene so perfect.

It was a long wedding, in the Catholic tradition, followed by a longer reception. It was early evening before the newlyweds escaped, driving off in the Mustang.

Drew draped a car robe over Charlie's wedding dress as he helped her out of the Mustang and led her around to the front of the house, up the seldom used front steps to the porch swing where they'd sat so many months ago, talking about their pasts.

A fine, powdery snow fell from the late December sky. The Christmas lights twinkled merrily on the front porch columns and along the roofline. Charlie and Drew snuggled tightly under the heavy wool car blanket.

"If someone had said to me a year ago that I'd be here tonight, a free man, sitting beside the woman I love, a baby on the way, I'd have asked them what drugs they were on," Drew whispered as he buried his nose in her hair.

"If someone had told me a year ago that I'd be sitting here tonight beside the man I love, wearing his ring and carrying his child, I'd have cried and told them it was a cruel lie," Charlie mused.

"We've been through trial by fire," Drew philosophized. "We've earned this."

"No regrets?" Charlie teased.

"Only one," Drew answered, kissing her hair. "Not being able to make love to you for the next six months. But I've waited a lot longer than that for you. And it was well worth the wait."

"Where did you ever get such a crazy notion?" Charlie demanded.

"That you were worth waiting for?" Drew queried.

"That a pregnant woman can't make love, you big goof!" Charlie chided him.

"You mean you can?" Drew demanded in surprise. "Are you sure? Did you talk to your Doctor?"

"Of course. We have to be careful, especially toward the end, and I probably won't be in much of a mood for the last month or so, but I'm certainly not going to wait another six months to make love to you!" she assured him with a laugh.

"Well, I'll be damned," Drew chortled in amazement. "Then what the hell are we doing out here when we could be upstairs in bed?"

"We'll make it upstairs and into bed eventually," Charlie promised. "I'm not about to let this marriage go unconsummated." She wrapped her arms around his neck and pulled him down for a long, delicious kiss that tasted like spiced apple cider. "What other myths can I dispel for you?" she whispered when at last their lips parted.

"Oh, there's the one that says pregnant women don't like to have their breasts touched," Drew revealed.

Charlie let her eyes drift shut as she guided his hand to the delicate lace bodice.

His fingers worked their magic and she heard herself moan softly as he lifted the heavy brocade skirt. "And I know you don't want me to touch you here," he told her as his fingers brushed along smooth, sensitive skin of her inner thigh. "Or here."

A long, low bay echoed back to them from across the fields as Ghost ran some creature foolish enough to show its face in winter into its hole.

"Drew?" Charlie managed with a gasp. "I love you."

"And I love you too, Mrs. Bailey," he told her as he scooped her up, blanket and all, and proceeded to carry her across the threshold and up the stairs to their bedroom.

Epilogue

"Mommy, Mommy, Daddy's home!"

She hadn't even heard the truck come up the gravel drive. Charlie ran down the stairs, her heart in her mouth.

He stood in the kitchen, their little girl cradled in the crook of his arm, his eyes smiling at her as she ran to him. He swept her up easily with his free arm, pulling her into a tight embrace as he whirled around with both of them. Sara laughed as her head bent back, her bright red hair streaming out behind her.

He smelled like soap, and aftershave, and something else, something indefinable that was uniquely his own. Charlie breathed in deeply, capturing the essence of him and holding it tightly. She laughed as she slid slowly back to the floor, still holding him close enough to feel how much he'd missed her. "Welcome home," she whispered against his lips. "We missed you. How was Ottawa?"

He grinned down at her. "Ottawa is for short people. I barely fit in the kitchens. Bet I'm the tallest person to ever graduate from La Cordon Bleu Ottawa."

Charlie laughed and hugged him again, running her hands over his curved backside in a way that let him know just how much she'd missed him. "Congratulations! So, Paris next?"

Green eyes glittered as they met hers. "No. Not for a while. Maybe not ever. I think I'll be perfectly content to stay home with my two darlings for a good, long while. You two, this place, its all perfect. Like a piece out of a dream I used to have, only the reality is so much better than the dream ever could be."

"Drew?"

"What darling?"

"I love you."

"I love you, too." He kissed her, then kissed the baby again. "Come on, little darling. I think its time for your nap. Mommy looks like she could use one too."

Sara draped her arms around his neck, too sleepy to protest. "Welcome home, Daddy," she whispered instead.

Author's Note

The West Virginia Penitentiary at Moundsville was originally modeled after The Northern Illinois Penitentiary at Joliet. Construction was approved in 1867, following the end of the Civil War, after West Virginia was officially declared a separate state from Virginia. The prison was to be located in the Northern counties as many of the Southern counties had expressed Southern sympathies during the war and it was feared that insurrection might once again rear its ugly head.

The Penitentiary at Moundsville was designed in the Gothic Architectural style, complete with battlements and turrets like a medieval castle. The prison yard of a little over 240,000 square feet was enclosed by a massive stone wall, two-and-a-half stories tall, five foot thick at the base and tapering to a thickness of two-and-a-half feet at the top, and extending five foot below ground level. The prison, which was originally designed to house 882 convicts, was so overcrowded that by the 1930's three men were housed in each five-by-seven-foot cell.

Although Moundsville was the State Maximum Security Penitentiary, 60% of the prisoners housed there were serving one to ten year sentences for crimes ranging from Breaking and Entering to Grand Larceny.

Plagued by poor conditions and overcrowding throughout its term of service, The Penitentiary at Moundsville was the scene of repeated escape attempts and riots. During the decade of the seventies alone there were more than 230 escapes from Moundsville. One of the most notable riots occurred on New Years Day of 1986, when 16 guards were taken hostage and three inmates were killed.

In 1982, thirty-six lawsuits against the State of West Virginia regarding conditions at the prison were combined into one case. Judge Arthur Recht ruled that conditions at

Moundsville violated a prisoner's Eighth Amendment right prohibiting "Cruel and Unusual punishment." In 1986, the state lost its final appeal, and the facility was ordered closed by July of 1993.

After 128 years, the old prison was finally closed by yet another Court Order due to conditions which were deemed inhumane beyond any hope of repair. In March of 1995, the last prisoners were transferred from The West Virginia State Penitentiary at Moundsville to the new Mt. Olive Maximum Security Prison in Fayette County, West Virginia.

The Moundsville Economic Development Council now offers tours of The West Virginia Penitentiary at Moundsville throughout much of the year.

About the author:

Shelby knew from an early age that she wanted to write. Growing up with Tolkien's **Lord of The Rings** and TV's "**Star Trek**," Fantasy Literature seemed the natural choice. The only problem--her favorite genre didn't have a place for Romance! Shelby pursued a degree in Communications, graduating from Shepherd College in 1981. Since then she worked as a Radio On-Air personality until she and her husband started their own business. When Shelby found Ellora's Cave, she finally felt her writing had found a home!

Ellora's Cave has provided Shelby with yet one more valid reason for avoiding 'housework' of the common type. Residing in West Virginia with Bill, her husband of 21 years, Shelby enjoys building computers and online role-playing games. When she's not on-line, Shelby can be found in the garage tinkering with her motorcycle--or anywhere but the kitchen!

Shelby Morgen welcomes mail from readers. You can write to them c/o Ellora's Cave Publishing at P.O. Box 787, Hudson, Ohio 44236-0787.

Shelby Morgen welcomes mail from readers. You can write to her c/o Ellora's Cave Publishing at P.O. Box 787, Hudson, Ohio 44236-0787.

Also by SHELBY MORGEN:

- Way of the Wolf: The Northlanders
- Too Hot To Handle
- Song of the Bear I: A Mercenary's Prize
- Song of the Bear II: A Prisoner's Desire
- Song of the Bear III: A Sentinel's Secret
- All I Want For Christmas
- Plain Brown Wrapper
- The Marker
- Threshold Volume 2 anthology with Stephanie Burke

Why an electronic book?

We live in the Information Age—an exciting time in the history of human civilization in which technology rules supreme and continues to progress in leaps and bounds every minute of every hour of every day. For a multitude of reasons, more and more avid literary fans are opting to purchase e-books instead of paperbacks. The question to those not yet initiated to the world of electronic reading is simply: *why?*

1. *Price.* An electronic title at Ellora's Cave Publishing runs anywhere from 40-75% less than the cover price of the <u>exact same title</u> in paperback format. Why? Cold mathematics. It is less expensive to publish an e-book than it is to publish a paperback, so the savings are passed along to the consumer.

2. *Space.* Running out of room to house your paperback books? That is one worry you will never have with electronic novels. For a low one-time cost, you can purchase a handheld computer designed specifically for e-reading purposes. Many e-readers are larger than the average handheld, giving you plenty of screen room. Better yet, hundreds of titles can be stored within your new library—a single microchip. (Please note that Ellora's Cave does not endorse any specific brands. You can check our website at www.ellorascave.com for customer recommendations we make available to new consumers.)

3. *Mobility.* Because your new library now consists of only a microchip, your entire cache of books can be taken with you wherever you go.

4. *Personal preferences are accounted for.* Are the words you are currently reading too small? Too large? Too...**ANNOYING**? Paperback books cannot be modified according to personal preferences, but e-books can.

5. *Innovation.* The way you read a book is not the only advancement the Information Age has gifted the literary community with. There is also the factor of what you can read. Ellora's Cave Publishing will be introducing a new line of interactive titles that are available in e-book format only.

6. *Instant gratification.* Is it the middle of the night and all the bookstores are closed? Are you tired of waiting days — sometimes weeks — for online and offline bookstores to ship the novels you bought? Ellora's Cave Publishing sells instantaneous downloads 24 hours a day, 7 days a week, 365 days a year. Our e-book delivery system is 100% automated, meaning your order is filled as soon as you pay for it.

Those are a few of the top reasons why electronic novels are displacing paperbacks for many an avid reader. As always, Ellora's Cave Publishing welcomes your questions and comments. We invite you to email us at service@ellorascave.com or write to us directly at: P.O. Box 787, Hudson, Ohio 44236-0787.

Printed in the United States
21874LVS00001B/60